Mira's Story

Nikki Ali

Published by Cinnamon Press,
Office 49019, PO Box 15113, Birmingham, B2 2NJ
www.cinnamonpress.com

Designed and typeset in Adobe Garamond Pro by Cinnamon Press.
Cover design by Adam Craig © Adam Craig.
Cinnamon Press is represented by Inpress

Mira's Story

Paloma invites me over to her place for a pre-Valentine's Day weekend. As I pack my stuff, Andre says, "I sure miss you when you go over there for the weekend."

I drop the T-shirt I've been folding. "Do you not want me to go?"

"I don't not want you to go," he says.

"Andre, if you're not okay with all of this, with Paloma and me, then I won't do it anymore."

"I am still okay with it," he says. "It's just. I like the idea of you having a girlfriend. I really like you being happy, Mira. It's just. The reality of you having a girlfriend is something I'm still adjusting to."

I abandon my packing to sit with my husband on the bed. "It is a lot, isn't it?" I ask.

He nods. He's wearing a pair of basketball shorts, sitting cross-legged on our bed. There's a gash on his knee—he and Dashiell collided while playing ball the other day and they both went down, skinned elbows and knees—that makes my heart hurt with tenderness. I remember him as the sad, lonely twelve-year-old boy who gave me my first kiss.

"It is a lot," he says.

"I will stop if you want me to," I say.

He shakes his head. "I don't want you to. I want you to keep being with her. If you're happy."

I nod. He takes my hand, gazes down at my palm. He traces the lines on my hand.

"Want to come stay with me at her place this weekend?" I ask. His head pops up at this. "She always tells me that you're welcome to come and stay too. Participate, watch, have a sleepover, eat dinner, hang out. We can all sleep in her bed or on the floor like a slumber party or you can sleep in the other bedroom. Whatever you want. Paloma is really into… communal relationships. You know?"

"Mira," Andre says. "I know Paloma is your girlfriend. But she is still, for me, a professional colleague. We used to dance and perform together. We used to teach and demonstrate in partnering class together." He shakes his head. "I wouldn't feel comfortable sleeping in the same bed with her. Let alone doing anything, like… sexual with her. You know?"

"Yes. I know. I'm sorry."

"Nothing to be sorry about." He laces our fingers together, palm to palm. "But maybe I will come stay."

My heart thrills so hard it jumps into my throat, startling me. I had no idea how much I wanted him there with me. "You will?"

He caresses my face with his other hand. "If it makes you look like that, then yes, I'm definitely coming to stay."

"I love you, *papi*," I say.

"I love you too, hummingbird. *Pero oye,* okay? I'm not comfortable doing anything with Paloma. I wouldn't even feel comfortable watching you two. I can hang with you, eat dinner together or whatever, but when you take it into the bedroom, I'm out. I'll sleep in the other room."

"Okay." I pause. "But what about, like… hearing us? Like, we wouldn't be tryna be all loud on purpose, but…"

He thinks for a moment. He doesn't share any of his thoughts, but I see a little light come on in his eyes. Finally, he nods. "If I were to hear something," he says, "that would be just fine with me."

I laugh out loud.

He checks his Fitbit. "My break is over. I'd better log back on to work. What time are you gonna be at P's?"

I reach for my phone on the bedside table. "Oh, shit. I'd better finish packing and get dressed for work. We're closing early today 'cause they have to repair some shit in the back room. So I'll probably be there four forty-five-ish?"

"How about I get there a little later?" he says. "Like eight or something? We could eat a late dinner together?"

"*Lo que quieras, papi,*" I say.

"It's just," he says. He fidgets a little. "I don't know if you two. Like. Do stuff as soon as you get there? Or…"

"Ah," I say. "Honestly, yeah, we probably will do some stuff as soon as I get there. Last time I spent the weekend, yes, Paloma was all over me the moment I got in the door."

He strokes my hair. "Of course she is," he says. "I bet she dreams about you every minute you're not there." He leans forward, kisses me. "Because you're you."

I am melting, let me tell y'all.

On the train to work, I text Paloma and tell her that Andre will be coming with me. She's excited, starts planning what we'll eat and drink and do. I tell her what he said he'd be comfortable and not comfortable with doing, and she's cool with it. I spend my short shift at Anthro in a haze, my emotional and sexual body already on the Upper West Side. The store is selling a frothy profusion of romantic dresses for V-Day. They're saying that the city is gonna reopen indoor dining soon, within the next few days, for Valentine's and the Lunar New Year. Paloma just got her first dose of the vaccine. There's still a cloud of danger and sadness hanging over our city, but maybe also a hint that there may, someday, be a life on the other side of all of this.

When I get to Paloma's in the late afternoon, she opens the door for me wearing nothing but an emerald necklace.

"Oh, my God, wow, okay," I say, blinking straight ahead at her enormous bare breasts, with their already hard nipples. I am not sure when my sad, ratched little life transformed into a softcore porn movie, but I am here for it.

"Come here," she says.

I step into her embrace, closing the door behind us with my foot. Bags—my overnight bag, my guitar case, my crossbody work bag, a bag of gifts for her—knock around us. But I have no fucks left to give for any of that. All of this girl's fucks are currently occupied, consumed with the overflow of naked woman in my arms—her miles of soft, warm skin, her breath on my shoulder, the jiggle of her ass when I cup it in both hands.

"Mira," she says.

"I don't wanna bring you no germs, *mami*," I say. "I better wash my hands."

"Hurry up," she says. "I'm dying for you."

Paloma takes all of my bags and brings them to the bedroom. It's quite the sight, watching her do that naked. While I'm washing my hands at the kitchen sink, she wraps her arms around me from behind. I feel her breasts, her belly, the warmth at the center of her. She nuzzles my neck. Her hands go to the button of my jeans.

"Can I?" she whispers.

"Please, *mi nena*."

Paloma unbuttons and unzips my jeans, pulls them and my lacy thong down my legs and to my feet as I'm washing my hands. "Step," she says, from the floor, and I step out of my pants and underwear. I swiftly lose my sweater and bra on the way to her bedroom, and then I'm as naked as she is, in only the necklace she gave me and a little pair of gold hoop earrings and my wedding ring.

"I need you so much, Mira," she says, gasping, in a fit as I play with her nipples on the bed.

"I'm right here," I say.

We decide to try sixty-nine. I love how adventurous we get in bed. Paloma is giggly and ever-ready, always open to trying something new. I like it better than I would have thought: me on top of her, my feet finding purchase in the pillows as she buries her head between my legs, her pussy open to me as a flower for me to lick her, and lick her, and lick her. She whines and squeals for me. She comes so hard that she farts right in my face, multiple times. We scream with laughter at this. I roll off of her body, laughing. I'm still laughing when she makes me come too, the way I like best, her index finger pressing my clit.

"Mira," she says. She puts her fingers in her mouth, sucks them. She kisses me; I taste myself. "*Estoy loca por ti.* I miss you. I dream about you. I feel like a teenager. I like the coolest girl in school." She squeezes my bun. "With her big beautiful hair and her badass guitar-playing self."

"Paloma. *Ya.* Come on. I ain't nowhere near that cool, baby."

"You come on," she says. She nudges me. "I love you, Mira. I can't get enough of you."

"I love you too," I say.

By the time Andre joins us, around eight, I feel pummeled and molded into submission, in a puddle of heavy-limbed, heavy-lidded, delicious exhaustion. Paloma and I have had a lot of sex. She seems soft too, but energetic, flowing around the room in a floor-length green nightgown with long sleeves. The neck is cut a little low; her emerald necklace nestles between her breasts. I sit at the table in an old T-shirt of Andre's and my leggings, drinking hot tea.

"I ordered steaks on Uber Eats," Paloma tells Andre when he comes.

"You did?" he says. He hugs her, kisses me on the lips.

"I did," she says. "It's a great night. We're celebrating."

"Oh, yeah? What are we celebrating?" he asks.

She shrugs extravagantly. "I don't know! Being here! Being alive!"

Andre smiles. "I'll drink to that," he says.

He says he's brought her a little gift, which turns out to be those shiny-foil-wrapped chocolate-covered Oreos you find in stores around Valentine's Day. "Aww, Andre!" she says, opening the clear plastic tube, shaking out a cookie, and peeling it open. "I love these! How did you know that?"

"I remember some guy you were seeing once brought you some after class, around Valentine's Day one year. You were so excited."

She laughs. "Yeah! I love these!"

I take one of the cookies, unwrap it, and bite into the soft chocolate shell, the crunch of the Oreo inside, and the innermost layer, the cream.

"I wanted to say thank you for what you sent for my birthday," he says. For Andre's birthday, Paloma had tacos and nonalcoholic craft beer—so I could have some too—sent to our place. "You did not have to do that."

"I wanted to," she says. "You're my metamour."

He smiles. "I'm guessing that's some kind of poly thing?"

"Yes." She smiles back. "You're also my friend."

"Well," he says, "thank you." He takes an Oreo too.

"You know, Andre," she says, "when I first met your mom, she was pregnant with you."

Andre sits back. "She was?"

"Yup. Auntie Lisette was the first pregnant person I ever knew. I remember when she had you, dude. She brought you to the ballet studio when you were probably just, like, a week old. You were a tiny, tiny baby. So adorable. She and my mom sat me down and helped me hold you. They were all like, 'You gotta be gentle, Paloma; he was just born.' I was a little kid myself. It was the first time I ever held a baby."

"Wow," Andre says. "You've known me literally my entire life. That is wild."

"That," I say, "is the cutest fucking thing I have ever heard."

The food arrives. We eat tender steak and hot, creamy mashed potatoes. This may be the first real time I have ever eaten steak, and for sure steak like this, all melty and rich and medium well. I take little savoring bites. Paloma puts on music, classical music.

"Swan Lake," Andre says, because of course he knows. (He plays piano, and damn well; most ballet dancers are taught at least some piano, but for him it stuck, because he's a bastion of black excellence and all of that.)

She smiles. "Thought it would be appropriate for the season," she says. They talk about performing some parts of Swan Lake in a community performance for Valentine's Day in 2016, when Andre had just turned eighteen. I remember that one well.

Paloma puts the last chocolate-covered Oreo into her cookie jar, which is pink and in the shape of a dove. "That's really cute," Andre says. "Your cookie jar."

"It's a dove," she says. "For my name."

"Huh?" he says.

"My name," she says. "Paloma. It means *dove*."

"It does?" he says. "Huh. Can you believe, all this time, I never knew that?"

"More trivia," she says. "Guess what song I was named after?"

"No," he says. "Paloma, no."

"Yes, Andre, yes. I was named after 'When Doves Cry,' by the immortal Prince. May God rest his soul in rock and roll heaven."

"Wait," I say. "Wait, wait, wait. How can you just lay all this amazing shit on us like you're not blowing our minds? You were named after 'When Doves Cry'? One of the greatest songs ever written?"

"Mira," Andre says.

"Oh, come on. Prince is the total goat. Everyone knows that."

"More trivia?" Paloma asks.

"Yes, girl, please. I am so here for this."

"My parents claim I was conceived the night of a Prince concert. They are both completely obsessed with him. They went to a show together and it was the best night of their lives. So they came home and, like, made a baby."

"Eww," Andre says.

"A dove baby," I say.

"No," Andre says.

"You're just like your mother," I say. "You're never satisfied."

"No," he says. "Please stop."

"Stop making me laugh, Miranda," she says. "I have one more piece of trivia for y'all. Okay? Guess my middle name."

"No, Paloma," he says. "Please don't tell me your parents did that to you."

"*Espera*," I say. "Your middle name is Prince? How did I never know this, *nena*? How did you never tell me this before?"

"It takes me some time to trust anyone with my middle name," she says, fluttering those lashes at me. "I mean, I'm not ashamed of it, baby. Prince is the goat. Like you said. But. You know my last name is Charles. And that makes it sound like my parents named me after an unfortunate member of the British royal family."

"No," Andre says. "You are killing me over here. This is too much."

"Okay, y'all." I get up from the table. "Do you know what it's time for now?"

"Nope," Andre says.

also implicated myself, acknowledging my own part in holding onto a belief that hurt me and hurt others.

I also wrote in the article that, when I finally began exploring some of my sapphic desires for myself, I realized the true depth of sex and sexuality. I realized that there are whole dimensions of sex. I realized that sex is something you have in the present tense. I admitted that I wish I could have learned this truth through sheer maturity and enlightenment. But I didn't; I learned it through my own experience. Life ain't a lesson in a textbook, though, right? Sometimes you just gotta jump in there and get yourself dirty.

"Thank you," I tell her. "That means a lot, Paloma. This was the hardest piece I've ever shared."

"I know," she says, wiping her eyes again. "You said that in the article."

I smirk. "Honestly, *nena,* everything I wanted to say is right in there. I left it all out on the field." This is, I believe, a baseball metaphor. My brother would be proud.

"You sure did, Miranda Marcela. Thank you for writing this. It's beautiful. I love what you said about sapphic love affairs also having urgency and a kind of erotic violence." She tears up again, looking down at my words. "You're so wise. I feel like your words are making love to me."

I open my mouth to say something but nothing comes out. I know it's not a whole published book like some people have. (I won't name any names, not yet, anyway; let me have my moment, all right?) But isn't what we want, when we release our words out into the world, for a voice to come back saying that we have touched them? Denying the importance of what Paloma's telling me, refusing the gift she's giving me, is a whole lot like saying that what we did last night wasn't sex. And I ain't gonna do that.

"And this," I tell her, "feels like a dream come true. I always wanted to feel like I was touching somebody with my writing."

"Well," she says. "You're sure touching me."

Paloma offers me several choices for breakfast. I say I'll just have some tea and toast. "Your man is out for a run," she tells me. "He left shortly before you got up."

"Oh," I say. "Cool."

"Now he's never gonna stop calling me Prince."

I burst out laughing. "I can't, *mami*. It's the coolest name ever. I also will literally never get over it. Ever."

She rolls her eyes, but she's smiling. "Maybe I never should've told y'all."

"Uh-uh, baby. No takebacks."

I hum "When Doves Cry" while taking my morning medications. Paloma chides me, but you can tell by her sparkly eyes and smile that she's eating it up, my cheeky girl who loves attention. Andre comes back while I'm having some toast and tea. He kisses me and says, "Good morning, Mira. Paloma Prince."

"Yeah, yeah, we get it," she says. "My parents named me after the artist formerly known as Prince."

"Bless them," Andre says, and we all laugh.

He goes to take a shower, then comes back and has coffee and toast and a banana. Paloma says how much she loves my hummingbird tattoo, holding my wrist tenderly, drawing her thumb gently over my art. My skin and my breath respond to her touch. Andre watches us closely. He looks at my face and smiles.

"We got tattoos together," he says. "It was Mira's idea."

"I know, she told me," Paloma says.

"I got a panther," he says.

"That's badass," she says.

"Wanna see it?" he asks. "It's on my chest."

"Sure," she says.

Sitting there at her kitchen table, Andre pulls his T-shirt over his head. He shows Paloma the panther tattoo on his pec. He shows her the ink on the back of his shoulder too; it's the continent of Africa, inside of a heart. On the inside of his left forearm, he has a violet, which he got shortly after we got married; we gave away violet plants as wedding favors at our reception.

"Beautiful ink, Andre," she says.

"Thank you," he says. "You have any tattoos, P?"

She shakes her head. "I'm scared. I don't like pain," she says.

"You don't have to get any tattoos if you don't want them," I say.

She nods.

Andre puts his T-shirt back on. "I just want you to know," he says, "that's all I really feel comfortable, like, showing. I think Mira told you. But I would not feel comfortable doing anything sexual. The three of us together." He looks at me. "But I'm so glad my wife is happy."

"I am happy," I whisper. It can be hard to admit that sometimes, ain't it; even harder, maybe, than admitting that you're in pain. But I've said it. And it is out in the world.

Paloma and I get ready to go out together. She tells Andre, "Mira and I are gonna have a little shopping date. You're welcome to join us. Also to stay here and hang out."

"I could just head home too," he says. "I don't wanna be imposing in your space when you're not even here."

"Not at all." She shakes her head firmly. "Stay here. Watch my collection of vintage Mets documentaries. Order Uber Eats on my account. Whatever you want."

He thinks he should say no; you can see it in his furrowed brow. But what he ends up saying is: "Vintage Mets documentaries?"

"Yeah, dude. Wanna watch the 1986 World Series?"

"Uh, yeah," he says.

Paloma pulls the DVD off of a special shelf that seems to house her collection of Mets crap and hands it to him. "Here you go, friend. All seven games. Maybe save game six for me, though? I'd love to watch it together when we get back. If you're up for it."

"Oh, P, you're on. Poor Bill Buckner." He shakes his head.

Paloma shrugs. "That's the curse of the Bambino for ya."

Andre nods seriously.

"Wow," I say. "I have no clue what is being said right now. At all."

Paloma smiles. "Look at us, forming a real-life polycule. Kitchen-table polyamory for the win."

"I'm gonna have to educate myself on the language," Andre says. I love being married to a total nerd.

"Don't worry," Paloma says. "We can understand and define things as we go along. For now I'm just saying I'm really proud of us."

We both nod.

Paloma hands Andre her iPad. "If you want anything, just go on my Uber Eats and order it."

"That's totally not necessary," he says.

"If you wanna do an exchange," she says, "I'd love a partner in the studio sometime this week. I really miss dancing with other humans in real life."

"You got it," he says. "Text me the time and place."

Paloma and I put on our coats and leave the apartment. She gets us an Uber downtown, to the Strand bookstore in Union Square. It's been ages since I've been to the Strand and I'm hungry for it. It's a wonderland of narrow shelves, creaky wooden floors, huge mysterious fans blowing gusts of air like the breath of giants, a mix of crisp, trendy new books and pre-owned yellowing old books. The basement is what Araceli, years ago, dubbed the "Platonic ideal of basements": musty and hot, the floor uneven and concrete, the air smelling of damp. Being down there always gave me a headache, but I loved it, so I roughed it out.

"Damn, I ain't been here in a minute," I tell Paloma. There are enormous bottles of hand sanitizer set up by all of the elevators. That's new.

"How long has it been?" she asks me.

"I dunno. Before the pandemic, for sure."

"Me too," she says.

"Thank you for taking me."

"My pleasure, baby," she says.

When Celi was at NYU, we used to come here all the time. She'd look at the philosophy books in the basement. I'd look through the advance reader's copies of just-released novels, several shelves tucked in the back, a secret known only by the initiated. (Don't tell nobody, you hear?) We'd take the elevator upstairs (those stairs were way too much for pre-lung-surgery me, that's for sure) to the second floor to page through erotic photography books, to the third to look at the rare books, some of which cost tens of thousands of dollars. Signs say that that floor is closed to the public now. I wonder if Paloma used to shop there, buying first editions and antiquarian volumes. Araceli used to bring dates here, or pick up people: queer NYU students, dance and theater kids, once an old Greek guy in his 60s that she'd met through OnlyFans, who used to give her his credit card and tell her to buy all the philosophy books that her heart desired.

I tell Paloma about that guy. "That's quite a kink," she says. "An unlimited book budget."

"Celi loved it," I say. "Such a nerd."

"I don't have a credit card, just Apple Pay," Paloma says, "but you can get anything you want, Miranda."

I laugh loudly. It echoes off the shelves. A couple people turn and look, the bottoms of their faces swathed in masks. "Our new rap song," I say.

"Lesbian ballers at the bookstore?"

I crack up, leaning against the nearest shelf. "Exactly."

Paloma leans against the shelf next to me. "I really want to kiss you right now, Miranda," she says.

"I want to kiss you too," I say. "Fucking masks."

We did come to the bookstore for something in particular, so we go grab that first. Hassan has a new book out. It's a collaboration with a graphic novelist—she's really cool; I've been following her on Instagram for years—on an illustrated version of one of his novels. *Vestal* takes place in ancient Rome, and it's about Cornelia, a girl who likes other girls and doesn't want to marry or follow the singular, narrow path society has laid out for her. So she becomes a vestal virgin, one of the priestesses of the goddess Vesta who lived in her temple, kept her sacred hearth fire burning, and served her community. Then Cornelia begins having dreams. In the dreams, she meets and eventually falls in love with Aphrodite, goddess of love and sex. The novel version was hazy and atmospheric and sweet, a little intellectual and heady, like Hassan's books tend to be. I liked it— loved it, even; devoured it in one long night—but my achy little sapphic heart, never having even kissed another girl back then, did crave a deeper, more explicit exploration of girl-on-girl intimacy.

We find the graphic novel of *Vestal*, which is sitting on the store's special LGBTQ+ book table. We both squeal a little, looking at it—it's so cool, ain't it, seeing something made by somebody you know, out there in the big bad world? Paloma picks up the top copy and I sidle as close to her as I can get, so we can both look at it as she pages through. I squeal again. I can't help it. It's beautiful. It's all in a rosy-pink color palette and the art is in the graphic novelist's signature style, all lush and femme, with a hint of that cute anime girl vibe. She goes by Nikki Q and I just love her, I'm so excited she's starting to get noticed.

Paloma picks up the entire stack of the Strand's copies of *Vestal*—six of them—and buys them. "I want to give them to some friends," she says. "And one for you and one for me to keep."

"Thank you," I say.

The person behind the register says, "Oh, this has been selling really well."

Behind her mask, Paloma beams. "It was written by a friend of mine."

"You know the author? I follow him on Instagram and I've just started watching his cooking show on YouTube. He seems so cool. I'm so excited to read this book."

Paloma nudges me. "He's her brother-in-law."

I'm low-key annoyed; I do not love being put on the spot unexpectedly. I know it's silly, but my stomach bottoms out, I feel hot and then cold, and I already know I'm going to either stammer or say something totally bizarre, or both.

"Um," I say, glancing up. "Yeah?"

The cashier laughs. "That's rad! Is his husband your brother? Marco something? He sometimes posts about him or has him on the cooking show!"

"Uh," I say. "Yeah."

"Wow! That's really cool. Hey, would you like a bag?" Paloma finishes paying, shakes her head, takes the books, and slips them into her tote bag. "Enjoy the rest of your day."

"You too," says Paloma.

We resume wandering the store. It takes my heart a while to come back down. Your girl Mira may be just a little bit afraid of talking to strangers; please don't judge. Finally I manage to say, "Can you believe they knew Marco?"

"I know," Paloma says. "That's wild."

"My brother's famous." I feel a momentary sense of wonder, then roll my eyes. "I always knew my brother would be famous."

Paloma stops, wraps her arms around me and squeezes me. "To me, you're a rock star, Mira," she says, gazing down at me. "I worship you."

"Paloma," I say. "Come on."

"Later," she says, "if you're up for it." She slides her lips down to my ear. "Put on that big strap-on. Put me on my hands and knees. Show me who owns me."

"Girl." I give her a squeeze. "Come on."

We look at the writing books. I point out all the ones I've checked out from the library and read. She offers to buy me a new one I haven't seen before, about finding your voice as a writer. I say yes, thank you. We look at the poetry. Once, in this part of the store, I saw a guy using an oxygen tank. He was all short and skinny, your typical CF patient body type. I asked Araceli to go over and ask him if he had CF. He said yeah; she pointed me out; he and I waved and avoided coming within six feet of each other while we were both in the store. He sent me his number through Celi and he became part of my CF-acquaintance group chat (different from my close-CF-friends group chat, of course). Last year, around the time of the lung surgery, I texted him, just to say hi and see how he was doing. His mother, who had his phone, replied that he had passed away a couple weeks before, age twenty.

This story, I do not tell Paloma. I keep it to myself.

We look at the ancient history books. Paloma chooses a book about the Minoans. I ask who they are; she says they were a people who lived on the island of Crete before the arrival of the ancient Greeks. She says she took a great class as an undergrad on Minoan and Cycladic art, and the final paper she wrote for that course has evolved into a chapter in her dissertation, on the famous "goddess" statues found in Cycladic tombs.

I don't understand all of this. But I say, my voice shaky, "Paloma. I've applied to go back to school."

She stops abruptly, takes my arm. "Mira. You have?"

I nod. "I have."

"Mira, that's amazing," she says. "Where?"

"City College." I swallow. My throat's so dry. "It's near my apartment. And they have an English BA with a concentration in creative writing."

"Mira." She hugs me, incredibly hard. My heart can barely take this, y'all, how happy this girl is for me. She gets it. She sees me. We are not perfect together, I get that, but this is why we're here; we see each other. "My college girl. I am so proud of you."

We pull back. "I haven't gotten in yet, *mami*." I grip her biceps.

"You will," she says.

We resume looking at books. I say, "Paloma, can I ask you something?"

"You can ask me anything," she says.

"Who's the oldest person you've ever been with?"

She thinks for a while, then says, "The admin assistant for the art department at Columbia. I was twenty-one, a junior. She was fifty-five. We used to stand in the hallway in the art department and talk for, like, hours. She was an artist herself. I heard she taught one of those drunk-painting classes for extra money. So I went. I stayed till everyone else was gone. We finished a bottle of wine together and had sex in the bathroom. She was married. It was not my finest hour, I'll admit. It only lasted a couple months. But it was intense. I was obsessed with her. That all-consuming attraction and love that you can have for an older woman when you're really young."

"That's hot," I say.

She nods. "It was."

"What happened?"

"Her wife found out. She didn't know who I was. But she knew there was a much younger girl. Then her mom got sick, out in Arizona. They left to take care of her and work on their marriage."

"Did they stay together, do you know?"

Paloma shakes her head, soft dark hair brushing her face mask. "No. They broke up. But she started working on sculptures made of wire and found materials and now she has three hundred thousand followers on Instagram."

"Oh," I say. "Wow."

We take the elevator down to the basement and look at the advance reader's copies, but nothing jumps out at us. Back on the main floor, Paloma stops in front of the display of enamel pins. "I love these," she says. "Pick one for me? Which one seems like me to you?"

I pretend to study her with intense scrutiny; she laughs. I turn to the wall of pins. I select a sunflower pin whose delicate petals are all the colors of the rainbow. I hand it to her. "You're colorful and playful," I tell her. "You're also so tall and strong—you seen those huge sunflowers that grow towards the sun?" She nods. I do too. "You're like that."

"Mira," she whispers.

"And you make me happy," I tell her. "Like, really, really."

"*Igualmente*," she says. Her voice is a little thick with tears.

I nudge her. "Pick one for me?"

She looks at me, then at the wall. With a laugh, she plucks a pin of a cassette tape, in pastel pink and blue. "Because you're cool and vintage. I mean, you have an old soul. In the coolest way. You're the realest person I know, Mira. And you're quirky and talented. Everybody wants you; you're in high demand, but you're limited edition."

I laugh my ass off at this. Paloma forces me to choose a tote bag; she says I need one, to pin my cassette tape to. I choose the one with images of the zodiac, which, apparently, also glows in the dark. Paloma and I leave the store with new books in our tote bags and our pins fastened to the thick canvas.

We walk to a Starbucks and sip our drinks on a bench outside, though it's February and really too cold for that. Paloma has a hot chai latte, I have a white chocolate mocha. She calls Hassan on her phone, puts him on speaker and lays the phone in the couple of inches of space between us on the bench.

"Hey, tiger," she says. "I have Mira here with me. And we have just bought copies of your brand-new book."

"Oh, my," he says. This makes us both laugh. "Do you like it?"

"Hassan, baby, it's beautiful," I tell him. "It's delicious."

"It is, it's gorgeous, honey," Paloma says. "I love Nikki Q's aesthetic. It matches your narrative style so perfectly."

An ambulance wails by.

"Are you two outside?" Hassan asks.

"Yes," Paloma says.

"Have you gone mad?" he says. "Why are you both calling me from outside? It's cold! Paloma, are you not taking proper care of our Miranda? Take her inside! It's cold."

"Okay, okay!" We both laugh. "I will take her inside. Warm her up." She winks at me. Of course, winking on her looks sexy and cool; on me, it looks awkward as fuck. My face flushes. She's warming me up already.

"Good," Hassan says. "Thank you for buying the book. Thank you for supporting us. Now go. Get inside."

"Say hi to Marco for me," I say, leaning down towards the phone.

"I will," he says.

We finish our drinks, laughing. Paloma says she can't come down to Union Square without visiting the spiritual bookstore; would I like to go? I certainly never say no to a good witchy store, so I say of course.

We walk the few blocks to the spiritual store. It's hot and close inside, the air fragrant and warm with incense. Books on divination and vodou and candle magic and angels and dragons and mystical poetry and pendulums and lunar phases rise nearly to the ceiling in high shelves. You have to hold your bags close to your body to avoid bumping into tables of incense sticks and burners and little glass spheres for scrying and crystal-ball reading and figurines of animals—lions, dragons, sacred ancient Egyptian cats—in glass and jade and carved wood. There must be a hundred different kinds of tarot and oracle decks. There's erotic tarot and feminist icon oracle cards and flower oracle cards and a special deck for healing from trauma. Paloma says we have to buy the erotic tarot; we can't not.

My favorite part of the store is the crystals. There are raw crystals: clear quartz and amethyst emerging from dark rock, rough and grainy to the touch, the facets of the crystals like glass in contrast. There are the cheaper, tumbled crystals that I sometimes buy, smooth as marbles. There are crystals you can wear on keychains and jewelry: aquamarine for clarity, carnelian for joy, fire agate for courage, black tourmaline to dispel negative energies. My eye keeps being drawn to a necklace on a long chain, a raw piece of amethyst wrapped in wire.

"Can I buy that for you?" I ask Paloma.

"I would love that," she says, and I love that she doesn't argue, she lets me do it.

I buy her the necklace, which is twenty-five dollars, a lot for me, though nothing to her, I'd imagine. She puts it on immediately; it nestles against the other necklace she's wearing, a silver chain with a dove pendant obviously made out of diamonds. I asked her about it once; she said her dad's best friend's family owns all the major jewelry stores in Grenada, where her dad is from. The son of the family, around her age, gave her the dove necklace for her sweet sixteen. Their parents hoped for more, she said, but she and Victor were only friends.

"He died in a motorcycle accident a year later," she told me. "I wear the necklace sometimes and remember him. It was the first time I lost someone. He was sweet."

I like that Paloma and I exist in this web of erotic and romantic and bittersweet memories; that the ghosts of all the people we knew still trail like silvery comets among us. I wonder if, after I am gone, she will tell someone else the story of me; how on a cold February Saturday in New York I bought her this amethyst necklace. I want to ask her to wear it, after I am gone. But as much as our hearts are starting to open to one another, I am just not there yet. I only think it instead.

In the back of the store, a tarot diviner gives readings behind a white curtain. "Would you like to have a reading?" Paloma asks me, as we read her price list, on a laminated card pinned to the wall.

"Sure," I say, "if you'd like to."

"I never say no to a tarot reading," she says.

We get a group text then, from Andre, saying that he's going to order pizza, and do we want some, and what toppings? We reply to that, then decide to each just get a one-card reading, so we can head back home soon. "Want to go first?" Paloma asks me, and I say sure, and slip behind the white curtain.

The tarot reader isn't leaning into the witchy vibes at all, dressed in jeans and a T-shirt and a Yankees ball cap. Her face mask is a disposable black one. She stands from her chair behind the table to greet me, waves instead of the handshake she probably used to give clients, before the pandemic.

"Hello," she says.

"Hi," I say.

"Would you like a reading today?" she asks.

"Sure," I say. "The one-card reading."

"Please," she says. "Sit down."

I gather my Strand tote bag into my lap and sit down on the other side of the table. There's a little plexiglass divider between us, which one hundred percent was not there prior to March 2020. On the table there's a red cloth and her tarot deck.

"What's your name, sweetheart?" she asks.

"Miranda," I say, playing with the frayed edge of my hoodie sleeve.

"That's a beautiful name," she says.

"Thanks," I say.

"I'm Sammy." I tell her it's nice to meet her. She picks up her deck. As she shuffles, she says, "I used to have clients do this, but…" She trails off with an articulate shrug.

"Totally," I say, nodding.

"Have you ever had a reading before, Miranda?" she asks.

"Not from a professional, no," I answer. "My friends and I read for each other sometimes. And I read for myself all the time."

"Ah," she says. "You do look like an experienced tarot reader."

I just look back at her. I wonder what about me makes me look like an experienced tarot reader, or if Sammy says that to all the girls.

"Well." She sets the shuffled deck on the table. "Do you have a question for the cards today, Miranda?"

I nod and swallow, hooking one leg around the leg of the chair and slouching myself a little smaller. I feel shy. It seems ridiculously intimate, asking a question of the cards through this stranger, revealing even a tiny piece of my heart to her. Half of me wants to run away. Half of me yearns forward.

"Yeah," I say. "Am I spending my time doing the right thing? Like, with my life?" I start to blink rapidly. I will not cry in this tarot reader's chair. "Life… life is short, I guess. I'd like to ask if I'm spending it wisely."

Sammy gives me a long, long look. It almost scares me. I think she's going to ask more, but then she flips over my card. It's the Lovers.

"The Lovers," Sammy says. "One of the main meanings of this card is relationships and partnerships of all kinds, though of course it holds other meanings as well." She looks up at me. "Are you in a romantic relationship, Miranda?"

My face warms. "I am in multiple romantic relationships," I say. "We've been exploring polyamory."

She nods. "Are one or more of these relationships very new?"

"Yes," I say. "Well, one of them's my husband. We've been together forever. Since we were kids. But the other one… yes, it's very new."

"The element for the Lovers card is air," Sammy says. "The air element suggests the need for open and honest communication. The only way to make relationships flourish. Especially when you are at the center of multiple relationships at once."

I nod.

"The Lovers is about harmony, balance, union, a coming together of different things," she continues. "How have you been feeling, Miranda?"

"I don't know," I whisper. How do I even begin answering that question? I feel choked up, at the kindness in her voice, her close look at me, the warmth of the room behind her white curtain. "I've been feeling good. Happy. But also… kind of overwhelmed. The truth is, my health hasn't been great." I glance up from my hands twisted in my lap and at her. "I have a chronic illness. A genetic disorder I was born with. I had a lung transplant last year and I'm doing… better. But it's been a huge adjustment. Just, like… life."

"That's a lot, Miranda," Sammy says. "Have you been taking care of yourself? The Lovers card is also about our relationship with ourself. Ensuring that you are listening to yourself, to the desires of your own heart; allowing those desires to form and following them despite what the external world might say."

"I could probably do better," I say slowly, "taking care of myself."

"You're doing wonderfully, Miranda," she says. "You are taking on so much."

I nod.

"I'm seeing a conflict of desire at the core of your path right now," she says.

"A conflict of desire?"

"Yes. Wanting things that seem mutually exclusive. Conflicting."

"Oh," I say faintly. "That makes some sense."

"There is a way," she says. "For all your desires to come together. That's the meaning of Lovers. There can be balance in wanting different things. You are allowed to have big and varied desires, Miranda."

"Okay," I say. "Thanks."

We both gaze down at the card. Two naked bodies stand in front of a mountain. Trees flank them; around one tree trunk a snake is wrapped. In the clouds above them there is a deity, arms and wings spread in blessings. The being's hair is the color of fire.

"The zodiac sign of the Lovers is Gemini," she says, "which suggests intellectual pursuits. Are you studying something, Miranda?"

I ball my hands into fists inside my sweatshirt sleeves. "No," I say. "But I want to be."

She nods. "The cards say go for it, sweetheart," she says. "Your intellectual pursuits are going to be very successful."

Sammy tells me she will think of me and send me all the good energy. She says she'd love to have me come see her here anytime. I thank her. When I stand up, Paloma comes behind the curtain with us to pay for my reading. She hands Sammy thirty dollars cash. "For hers and mine," she says. I squeeze Paloma's shoulder and return to the main part of the store. I wonder what card Sammy is going to pull for her.

I wander the store while I wait for Paloma to finish with Sammy. I'm tired and overstimulated and I want to go home. I look at a book about sex magic. Sometime when I have more energy, I'd like to look at that book more. I look at pretty cloth notebooks with handmade paper inside. My eyes fade out of focus. Mentioning the lung surgery has brought me back to those days. I'd spent a hell of a lot of time in hospitals and clinics and doctors' offices by that time, but the transplant was the first time I had ever had surgery. My body, sick and malnourished and exhausted from its daily management, was only just barely strong enough to withstand the trauma that major surgery entails. The pain was intense—like nothing I'd ever experienced, bone deep and carving, which I guess is what surgery literally is—and the recovery long.

Not long after I woke up from the surgery, feeling so disoriented and nauseous and in such pain that I asked them if they could put me back under, I learned that Andre had lost a lot of blood from some complication in his surgery and needed a blood transfusion. He got the transfusion and recovered well and was fine. But this is me telling the story from the vantage point of now, the future. At the time, I had no idea. All I could see, when I tried to imagine a future without him, was a path that had gone black, where there was nowhere to take even one more step further.

Before we all went under, the three of us, Andre and Marco and me, I closed my eyes and cast the strongest spell I have ever cast. I prayed that, if the underworld spirits wanted a soul that day, they take mine. I am sure that Andre and Marco also promised the same: that they would die in my place, were it required. All of the power of those conflicting desires must have canceled each other out. We all lived. We all live.

Paloma emerges from Sammy's corner to find me looking halfheartedly at a table of divination tools. Her eyes are tender, red and wet. "You okay, *mami*?"

"Can I have a hug?" she asks.

"Course you can."

I gather her up. Maybe I should, but I do not want to let her go.

I hold her till she pulls back. I brush strands of hair away from her face. "Did something happen?"

"My reading was just a lot," she says. "I got the Devil. I hate that card. It brings back bad memories."

I touch her temple, one of the only parts of her face I can get to, with the mask. I feel her strong pulse under the thin skin. "Anything you want to share? I'm here, baby, if you do."

She nods. "Just people in my family judging me. For my lifestyle. For the way that I love."

I shake my head. "The way that you love, it's beautiful."

"Thank you, Mira," she says.

The guy from behind the counter approaches us, asks if we're okay. "We are okay," Paloma says, in her crisp, authoritative, rich-lady voice. "Thank you." She selects a couple of items from the table we're standing near—a mini crystal ball, a black obsidian crystal pyramid—takes them up to the counter and buys them. Her total is over one hundred dollars. Just hearing that makes my head spin. What would it feel like to be able to just throw that kinda money around, from one second to the next?

We take an Uber back to her apartment. We hold hands in the car but don't talk. I want her, powerfully. I couldn't explain it in words if I had to, but wanting her like this, I know what the tarot reader meant, about conflicting desires.

The apartment smells like pizza: melted cheese and warm crust and sweet tomato sauce, ricotta cheese and the green scent of slightly burned spinach (these are my pizza toppings of choice; I love white pizza with spinach, a preference that Marco, a pizza purist who believes in pepperoni or nothing, teases me about to no end), spicy pepperoni and hot sausage. I give Andre a hug in the dining room, where he has the pizza boxes spread out on the table.

"I'm sorry, I don't think I can eat right now," I tell them both. "I need to get some rest first."

I look at Paloma. It's not the long, detailed conversation we probably need to have about my health if this is gonna get any more serious, but it's something: a moment of honesty.

"Go rest, baby," Andre says. "Do you need anything?"

"Can I bring you some water?" Paloma asks. "Or anything else?"

I nod. "I should probably drink some water."

I go to the bathroom and strip down to my T-shirt and underwear. In Paloma's bedroom, I get onto the bed, and Andre leans over and hugs me again. Paloma puts a cold water bottle on the bedside table next to me.

"Do you need anything else, *mi sirena*?" Paloma asks.

I shake my head. "You two please go eat." I slide myself under the unmade covers. "Please eat pizza and watch game seven or whatever it is."

"Game six," they say at the exact same time.

I laugh. My lids already feel heavy. "Exactly."

My two lovers fuss over me a little bit more, then leave the room. I was feeling drowsy when they were here, but once they're gone, I find it hard to fall asleep. My thoughts are racing.

I'm thinking about Paloma. How much of myself should I open to her? How close should I let us be getting? My intuition has been telling me, in felt senses if not in words or concrete evidence, that there is something soft and vulnerable about my girl. But am I patronizing her, disrespecting her, by trying to protect her? How do I be a feminist who upholds other women's power but also takes care of this heart that she's trusting me with? I feel volatile, dangerous; too much to handle. But who the fuck am I to say what she can and cannot handle? She told me today that she has lost someone before. Is it the same to lose a friend at sixteen to an accident as it would be for her to lose me someday, as a grown woman and my lover? It feels wrong to instate a hierarchy of pain. But I don't know. I don't have any answers.

And how do I build anything with her when I am also married? Andre and I have a shared life and plans and dreams. Paloma and I are not there yet. But we could be. What does that look like? How did I move from the girl I was when I started this thing to the girl that I am now?

I see that Paloma has also left for me on the bedside table the crystal ball and the pyramid. The smooth triangle of stone is such a deep black, absorbing all light, and also reflecting light from its polished exterior. The crystal ball is on a small silver stand, clear with the faintest purple tinge. I wonder, if I were to ask it my questions, what answers it would give me.

I listen to them eating pizza and watching the game, a faint drone of the crowd cheering and the scuffing of dirt on the diamond and the thwack of struck baseballs. Slowly I let the distant sounds lull me to sleep.

I wake up from a dream: Paloma had lost her diamond dove necklace. I was helping her look for it, combing through the apartment. Eventually we found it under rugs on the floor, but it was broken into a thousand pieces. Diamonds skittered all over the floor, glittering like an earth-bound sky. It was both beautiful and terrifying.

I sit up in bed. I drink some water and retie my hair. I hear Paloma and Andre in the other room, talking. What are they talking about? I lean my head against the wall behind me and let my body relax. I should go back out there. I shouldn't leave my husband and my girlfriend forced to hang out without me. I know they're friends and ballet colleagues, I know they knew each other before they knew me, but still—things are different now. I should get back out there and be a person.

But I just can't, not yet. Instead I crawl over to my overnight bag on the floor and find inside the novel I've been reading, the latest lesbian romance by Alyssa Cole. I get back onto the bed, cuddle under the blankets, and allow myself to read the next delicious chapter in the story. More than that, I allow myself to sink in, to let go of the carousel ride—exhilarating but dizzying—of my own life, my own thoughts, for a while, and remember my heart in a world of romance and adventure. This is why I've always wanted to be a writer—how good would it feel to know that I am doing this for somebody else?

Reading about these two lovers makes me feel like I can go back out there. So I go to the bathroom and pee and wash my face and put my pants back on. I find Paloma and Andre in the living room, chatting while more baseball plays on the TV, on very low volume. They both welcome me back excitedly, like I've been gone a long while and not a few hours, like my return is a whole-ass event. That does not feel bad, let me tell ya.

I heat up and manage to eat two slices of pizza. This feels like a big win as well. I get my guitar and take some song requests—Paloma wants to hear Lizzo's "Good As Hell," Andre asks for a special treat that I only agree to once in a while, which is "Savage," by Megan Thee Stallion. It has an amazing beat and sounds surprisingly good on guitar. Your girl Miranda Marcela Castillo also may not be that bad at rapping, okay, you know. After I do this song, Andre looks smug—yeah, his girl is just that good—and Paloma is wild, off the hook with praise and accolades and sheer shock.

"You blow my mind every time I see you, Miranda," she says, shaking her head at me. "I had no literal clue you could do that."

"There's a lot of stuff she can do that you don't know about, P," Andre says.

"Ooh, boy," she says.

I laugh. "He's probably right," I say.

When Paloma goes to the bathroom, Andre takes my guitar gently, sets it carefully on the floor propped up against the couch, and sidles next to me. He puts his arms around me and says, "Mira, I am gonna go home now if that's okay with you."

"You can go home anytime you want, baby."

He kisses me softly. "Are you okay here?"

I touch my nose to his. "I am very okay."

"If you need me," he says, "for anything, at any time, just text me, okay? I'll come running."

I want to say something big—about how lucky I am, about what a miracle it is that I get this kind of love, about what an unbelievable man he is. But what actually comes out is: "Baby, you make me feel lit like a match." Yeah, I'm quoting Megan Thee Stallion to my man, 'cause I'm just romantic like that and shit.

He laughs and kisses me on the forehead. "I love you, little bird," he says.

"I love you too."

Andre leaves soon after that, holding and kissing me at the door, hugging Paloma and saying, "Good night, Paloma Prince Charles."

"Shut up," she says, and hugs him back.

We sit on the couch and Paloma says, "Can I play with your hair?" I say sure, so she unties my Afro puffs and plays with my hair, massaging my scalp and working out little tangles in my kinky curls with her fingers. As her arms move her breasts jiggle, and so do her two necklaces, the diamond dove that I dreamed she had lost, and the raw piece of amethyst that I have just given her. It takes me a long time to get up the courage to say what I wanna say next.

"Paloma, I have a gift I wanted to give you."

"You're spoiling me," she says.

I take her into the bedroom. She sits down on the bed, and with shaking hands I take her gift bag out of my overnight bag and hand it to her. I sit down next to her tentatively as she pulls her gift out of the bag.

"This is the journal I gave you," she says, giving me a quizzical look.

I nod. My stomach jumps. "I finished all the pages. I used it as a dream journal. And I've been, uh…" I reach up to squeeze my hair, forgetting that it's loose, tousled by her fingers. "I've been dreaming about you a lot, *mami*. I recorded them all in this journal."

Her eyes have gotten wet. She's quick to cry, this girl, and I love it. "And you want me to read it?" she says.

"Yes." I tuck a lock of her perfect silky dark hair behind her ear. "It's yours. I want you to keep it."

"You do?"

"Yeah, honey." My voice shakes a little. "No one's ever read my journal before. Not Marco, not Celi, not even Andre." I hold her eyes. "Only you."

"Can I read it when you're not here?" she asks. "Sometime when I'm missing you."

I cup her head in both hands, running my fingers through all that hair. "It's yours, *mami chula*. You can read it anytime you want."

I lay her down and pull off her soft little shorts and open her legs with my shoulders. She whimpers for me. I pick up her left leg, kiss the tender, fleshy skin of her inner thigh, then drape her leg over my shoulder.

"Oh, my God, Mira," she says.

"*Así de así, mi nena.*"

For the next very long while, till my girl begs me to stop, I lick her flowery pink puffy juicy dripping wet fruit of a pussy. She must not have gotten waxed for a while, because her mound has a soft, delicious stubble, tickling my lips. She is fucking perfect.

It's night by now. We take a bath together. I'm the big spoon this time, my first time holding her like this under the warm water. I kiss her ear, suck on her hair. The anxious part of my brain, which I am never fully able to shut off, finds something to worry about even here: the bubble of sex in which we have embedded ourselves, ensconced in weekends of dreams and luxury. What happens when it pops? Is there a space for us, for our relationship, in the mundanity of real, regular life?

"Can I ask you something?" I say.

"Anything," she says.

"I think I'd like to know a little more about your… your polycule."

Paloma twists back to look at me, briefly. "Sure," she says. "I'm happy to tell you more, honey. I mean, there are some things my other lovers tell me, or that we do together, that are private, between me and them. Just like with us. But anything that affects you, your sexual or emotional health, I'm happy to share with you, Mira."

"Okay." I stroke her slick hair back. "Well, who are the people in your polycule?"

"You," she whispers. "Laura, the woman I was telling you about before, the art historian. This trans guy Luc who I met in the sex pod I was in before. I still talk to my friend Dante, and we have phone or video sex sometimes, but he's back in France with his family, so I haven't been with him in person since before the pandemic. That's really it, right now. Before the pandemic, I had a lot of casual lovers. I was on two poly apps. I'd hook up with couples as a unicorn sometimes. I'd go to sex clubs at least every couple of weeks and play with different people. I'd host sex or cuddle parties at my place here or upstate. But I haven't done any of that since the pandemic. My circle's a lot smaller."

"How do you feel about that?"

She shrugs, the smooth ball of her shoulder rising against me. "It's good," she says. "I'm rolling with it. My circle is smaller, but it also means that my relationships are deeper. We have more time. Everything feels more special. That's felt delicious."

I nod. I wonder if she can feel it, my heart, thumping against her back. "Do your other lovers have partners?"

"Laura has a partner. They call themselves romantic roommates. I've only met her once before. She's not poly, but she's comfortable that Laura is. Luc is solo-poly. Like me."

"Solo-poly?"

"Yes. It means… well, for me it means that I have no interest in living long-term with any partner. In having children with a partner—or by myself, for that matter—or shared finances or linking our plans together."

"What… what do you mean by that?"

I feel her shoulders tense. But she responds calmly. "Example. I was talking to Hassan at the beginning of the pandemic. Just checking on all my friends, you know. Asking how you and Marco were after the surgery. Anyway, he shared with me some of his anxieties. Marco is applying to med school. How is Hassan going to stay here in the US with him? How are they going to find a place to be together?" She shakes her head. "Poly relationships have their questions and uncertainties as well. Of course. But I have always known that those questions, the ones of traditional monogamous relationships, are not for me. Those considerations are worth it, I understand, for people who choose monogamy. I have no interest in figuring out how to fit my life around a partner's. I am happy, and most able to be present for others, when I am able to go where I want to go and be where I want to be."

"That's beautiful," I tell her, 'cause it is. "Can I ask what happens, though? If one of your partners, like, moves away for some reason?"

"Sure," she says. "Sometimes, honestly, we end our relationship. And there's some sadness there. For sure. But like I said, long-term, this is how I'm happiest and healthiest. Living primarily on my own. Sometimes we do poly long-distance, which is basically a lot of phone and video sex, trips to see each other occasionally when we can manage it. But there is a degree to which I let them go. I like to be most present to the people in my circle when I can."

"Okay," I say. "I understand. Also, can I ask… are you, like, girlfriends with your other lovers?"

She laughs softly. "Laura and I are friends and lovers. We have a lot in common, professionally and otherwise. There's definitely a lot of romance between us, a lot of long late dinners and cuddling. Things are maybe a little bit more… emotional with Luc. He's an intense person. We talk a lot, write each other long epic text messages every day. The sex is super hot but more infrequent. Luc's also still figuring himself out sexually. We're giving him the space to do that. But with you…"

She twists her head back again, to catch my lips in a kiss. "You're a baby poly girl, Mira. And, from what I know of you, you really value a lot of the elements of traditional monogamy. Your and Andre's marriage, this love story you've had since you were children, it's so beautiful to witness, honey.

He loves you with that old-school kinda love, you know? He just wants you to be happy. He's a good friend of mine too. So I am very, very mindful of y'all's marriage. Makes sense?"

I nod.

"So being your girlfriend felt like the right thing, between us," she says. "For what we feel for each other. How long we've known each other. And for where you are on the poly spectrum."

She laughs. I feel myself holding her tighter. It hurts a little, stings, some of the things she's said. But maybe it's like my romantic appropriate edge, to use my therapist Maya's term. It's a good, clean hurt, one that feels good, one that makes me feel like maybe I am growing, experiencing something new. I am new to all this. I am a girl from an old-fashioned love story. I like her acknowledging this; it makes me feel deliciously delicate. I like thinking that, while I am protecting her, finessing her heart, she in turn is protecting me, smoothing my way through some of the thorns of this experience.

"I'd love to show you more about how I feel about you," I whisper in her ear.

She giggles, catching my meaning, swerving with me. "With your big, hard cock?"

"Yes. Exactly. With my big, hard cock." I punctuate the space between each word with a little kiss to her ear, her temple, the side of her face. Her shoulders lower. She softens for me.

Both of us still hot and damp, on her bed, Paloma helps me into my strap-on. Putting this thing on is still awkward, and not sexy, for me. This makes me want to both laugh and cry, because there's a part of me that really wants to be good at this, the kind of badass butch woman who can fuck her girlfriends whenever they need it. The stark act of being naked and being helped into this strap-on penis forces me to confront the gap between my desire and my reality.

I gotta say, though, that it does feel better with Paloma, someone I know and love, than it did with Colleen during only our second time together. Best of all is that, once I'm in it, already sweaty and tired, Paloma lays me down on my back, smears my whole brown cock with a lavish amount of lube, and climbs on top.

"Oh, girl, yes, please," I pant. "Please ride me."

"God, Mira," she says. "My pleasure. Fuck." She groans as she lines her body up with my silicone cock and slides onto me, deep. She takes me down to the base almost immediately, tossing her head back and closing her eyes as she feels me hit her, as my balls make contact with her intimate skin.

"Fuck, Mira." She's so breathless she can barely speak. "You feel so good."

All my inner walls squeeze at this. I reach up for handfuls of her sleek, curvy thighs, squeezing them, a wordless plea and encouragement to keep going, to ride me harder.

I might've been scared that I wouldn't feel nothing, that my girl riding my skinless, nerveless cock would leave me cold. But I can tell y'all, from the very heart of this experience, that that shit is not the case. I know that now to be yet another false dispatch from a world that dearly wants us to believe that the only true, deep, and meaningful sex is when a cis dude puts his dick in a cis woman's vagina. If they were trying to keep us jealously from this pleasure, then I get it. This shit is hot, one of the hottest sexual experiences of my life—so far. I feel every inch of Paloma's warmth, the intimate heat of her body. A jolt shoots through me every time I hear the squelch of her cunt as she moves on me. Her breasts tremble and jump and sometimes she twists her nipple between her fingers, which is so obscene my eyes squeeze closed. Sometimes she rocks forward and gives me a sucking kiss as her hair envelops us in a curtain.

Paloma starts to get close. She pulls back so she can play with her clit as she rides me shallowly. I almost burst into tears of longing and sensation when I see her big swollen black-cherry clit skidding smoothly against the surface of my dick.

"Oh, my God, Paloma," I say, unable to hold it in anymore. "I am almost there. I need to come really bad. Please touch me."

She gasps down at me and tweaks her clit harder, the tip of her finger frantic on the erect bundle of tissue and nerves, and she comes, screaming, squeezing me so hard I swear I can feel her waves tightening my ovaries. Before she's even descended all the way, still visibly riding the aftershocks, she reaches under herself to touch me. It feels so good, I want it so bad, I close my eyes and twist my face away so I can feel nothing but the gushing, pulsing relief of my clit being touched. The tension in me tightens and spirals and compresses itself to a painful little point, and then I explode. I feel myself rippling like waves in a pond, bands contracting and releasing all over my body. I'm a tuning fork, vibrating; I'm a strobe light, pulsating in rhythmic thrums of color.

Paloma eases herself gently off of my penis. We're both still coming down, breath ragged, bodies wet, dripping lube, cheeks salty with tears. She cuddles herself in my arms and I hold her, breasts to breasts, my cock nudging her body gently. I feel the hitches in her breathing, little whimpers of almost-tears. Suddenly I remember my dream. I thought it was about her necklace, which now is gone, as far away as the cold disappearing crescent moon, nestled safely in a clasped velvet box while we have consigned our soft underbodies to painful desire. But, actually, it was about us, the two of us. In each other's arms, curled and curved together, we are two girls gathering the golden strands of our selves back together again.

Well, then something happens.

I don't know if y'all are mistaken about my story or something, but it ain't hospital porn. It ain't no illness fetish. If any of y'all are looking for that, then I suggest you look elsewhere.

My story is shooting stars and laughter at midnight and rainbow-dyed hair flapping in the wind, and fairy lights and harp poetry and licking up sex like a dripping ice-cream cone. That is my story.

But something happens, in mid-February 2021, shortly after Valentine's Day, when Paloma sends to our apartment two dozen orchids with purple-speckled petals, quirky and expressive as faces, and a seafood dinner, and a whole raspberry cheesecake, and Andre and I eat in bed and make love all night with an unbearable sweetness.

Not two days later, the orchids still crisp and sweet-smelling and fresh, I am in the hospital again. This time, though, it's different. I wake up in the middle of the night. My lower stomach is in such pain that I basically crawl into the bathroom and onto the toilet. You know when you're not sure if something is wrong with you, or if maybe it's all just in your head? Well, y'all, this ain't it. I have fine-tuned intuition, but I don't need it this night. Every sense in my body is blaring a red screaming alarm. Something is wrong.

I start to bleed—a lot. I have three thoughts. The first one is that I'll be making my grand return to the hospital, at a time when I started to think that the worst of my hospital visits were behind me, at least for a while. Everything in me crumples, shrinking away. I'm six years old again, confused and hurting and desperately angry. I do not want to go to the hospital. I do not want to be sick. I don't wanna go.

My second thought is that I'm going to miss the orchids—my beautiful orchids. By the time I'm out of the hospital, after whatever the fuck's going to happen to my body has happened, they'll be gone. They'll be dead. They're mine, they were for me, and I am going to miss them. They will never come back, not these, not these particular, unrepeatable orchids.

My third thought is: I'm pregnant. If this is true, then it's a disaster, and for multiple reasons.

I hesitate for a moment, frozen. I know that, when I open my mouth, something gets set into motion, something that I cannot call back.

I start to scream. Within seconds, Andre is by my side, holding me up 'cause I'm about to collapse, looking with me down at the blood down my thighs, mixing in the water in the toilet, drip-dripping down its white porcelain sides.

"Mira," he says. "Mira!"

Then everything moves fast, and slow too, time meaningless, time freezing, time squishing together, time pulling pink and wet and endless like taffy. I'm rushed to the hospital, a trip that also somehow seems to take an eternity. I'm high-risk: I have cystic fibrosis, I had a double lung transplant, I'm experiencing severe bleeding. My body begins to undergo tests.

I let go of my body to a large extent when I go to the hospital and it is time for our tests, like Paloma does when her lovers move away. God, that feels like an age and another planet away, learning that. Yes, they tell me, there is a pregnancy. It's ectopic.

"What the fuck does that mean?" a tearstained and angry and shrunken version of me asks.

They tell me that in an ectopic pregnancy the fertilized egg—the what? I had no clue I had a fertilized egg, the fuck?—implants somewhere other than the uterus, in my case the fallopian tube. There's a lot of bleeding. It's ruptured. I'm going to need emergency surgery to remove the ectopic pregnancy and the ruptured tube.

Things do move fast after that. I learn a lot of what happens later, once I'm awake and somewhat stabilized. I'm alone for a lot of it, because of the restrictions due to the virus. They give me the surgery to remove the ectopic tissue and my ruptured fallopian tube.

Maybe because of the stress of the surgery, shortly after it's successfully completed, my body spirals into a rejection episode with my transplanted lungs. I'm given medications to lower my immune response, to try to keep my body from rejecting the lungs. With my defenses down, I develop an infection. Infection is one of the scariest words, the scariest things, in the world to me. Suddenly it's like the last year—becoming a runner, growing a tiny pair of biceps from lifting my one-pound weights, being able to climb the stairs in Fort Tryon Park, waking up every morning and taking a deep breath—never happened, and it's 2019 again. It's 2019, it's 2015, it's 2007, and I am a scared, sick little girl again, oxygen tube over my mouth as I fight for breath.

My pancreas is failing. I've gained a little weight over the past year, since the surgery, it's true, but I am severely malnourished. My body isn't taking in the nutrition that it needs. Every night, I'm put into a twilight sleep with a light sedative and liquid nutrition moves through my brand-new gastrostomy tube, inserted directly into my stomach, to feed me. It hurts a little, it leaks, it gives me another infection. I have reentered the ring of a fight that I'd thought might be over by now.

My body recovers, slowly. Andre is eventually allowed to visit me, once per day. The nurse shows him how to care for my G-tube; my care team wants to send it home with me, for an amount of time yet to be determined, to supplement my (insufficient) eating by mouth. My immune system and I gather our depleted resources to at once fight off the infections and keep our hard-won new lungs. But we get there. My abdominal region heals most slowly of all, it feels like, from the trauma of everything that's been surgically removed from it. For a while, a long while, I am reduced again: I am a spark of a spirit inside of a fighting body, putting every ounce of energy I get each day into staying alive.

It's March, springtime, by the time I am released from the hospital and sent home loaded down with new medications and instructions and tools and worries and concerns. I do not leave the hospital the same girl I was when I went in, two days after Valentine's Day.

Before I'm discharged, the hospital counselor wants to have a session with me. My care team has been heavily encouraging it: I've been through a lot, they say, I've been through so much, they say, it might be good for me to talk about it, to process some of my feelings, before I am cleared to go home and back into the flow of my regular life, or some semblance thereof.

I don't want to. Having feelings these past few weeks has felt like, as Celi would say, "white-people shit"—in other words, a luxury that I could not afford. Machines were literally attached to this body, helping me do essential things like fucking breathe and eat, medicines were pumped into me to keep my cells from attacking the lungs I hijacked from other people; there was no space left inside me for feelings.

Now, all of y'all who've been sick know that that is a lie. I had feelings. I have feelings. Of course I do. I'm just not ready to unpack them and wipe the crust of infection off them and examine them. I don't have that kinda energy, not yet. But I don't feel like I have a choice. Mira is a good little sick girl, an obedient patient, ever since I was five years old and I asked my mother if I really had to take all these medicines every single day for my whole life, and she said yes, they were going to keep me healthy. So I put on my softest sweatpants and me and my G-tube go to the counseling session.

"I will talk about the ectopic pregnancy if you want me to," I say, basically as soon as I get to her office, "but I have one rule."

"What is the rule?" she asks me from behind her face mask.

"That we don't call it a baby," I say. "Because it was not a baby. It was an ectopic growth in my fallopian tube. Okay? It was not viable. There was no way it could have survived. If we hadn't removed it, I could have died. I had a rejection episode and a lung infection and I almost did die. But I didn't die and now I'm here. With a feeding tube in my belly."

It wasn't a baby. That feels simple enough. But I wish something in my life could be that clean. The ectopic pregnancy apparently had a heartbeat. It wasn't a baby, but it wasn't its fault. It was trying to grow. But it got the shittiest deal in the whole world. And that sucks.

Out of all the things, I find myself spending almost my entire session talking about the orchids that my girlfriend gave me for Valentine's Day, just before I came here. (Is Paloma even still my girl? Do girls who have to get fed through a tube in their tummies even get to do something badass and edgy like polyamory?) "They're dead now, they're gone," I tell the counselor. "They were for me, especially for me because orchids were, like, one of our things. Orchids are expensive and luxurious and hard to get. I had never had orchids before. But they died while I was stuck in here alone and now they're gone. They were for me and I didn't get to enjoy them."

"How does that make you feel, Mira?" she asks me gently.

My eyes fill with tears, so hot and dangerous they feel like lava, two little volcanoes right on my face. "Well, it makes me feel jealous and sad and so, so fucking angry. It makes me feel stupid and ungrateful. You know? Because I'm here and I know I'm supposed to be fucking grateful. For the fucking miracle of just being alive." I take off my face mask. It's soaked with my tears anyway and can't be all that effective. "But I don't want to just fucking be alive. I was happy. I was happy and I want to go back to that. I don't want to grieve or lie around recovering or be sick. I had orchids and I had a girlfriend and I was having all this incredible sex and I had a list. Of amazing things I was doing. So I want to skip past all of this dumb shit and get back to my joy."

I cry for the rest of the session. Crying hurts and it exhausts me. At the end of the session, the counselor calls the nurse and he takes me back to my room in a wheelchair and puts me in bed. I hug myself and cry myself raw. The pain feels almost delicious. Maybe I am not the girl I was before. I have a feeding tube, I had a major rejection episode, I had a second heartbeat where one was not supposed to be. I remember what the tarot reader said, about conflicting desires. Maybe I should be more sad about those things. But I am still a girl who can get all in her feelings about her dead flowers. And that feels fucking good.

Plenty of things happen while I am in the hospital. It's weird, when you're hospitalized for an extended period of time. You think maybe life won't happen without you, like you're in outer space on a whole other timeline, or like your world freezes without you there. But it don't, 'kay? Your world keeps on turning, whether you are there or not. Maybe it's a living glimpse of what it's like to be dead. Your people think about you and remember you, maybe they worry about where you are and if you're all right there, and they grieve that you're not with them, but slowly, they begin to let you go. And life goes on without you. There's a tiny spark of breath in each of us. But there's also a larger fire, called life, and it blazes on, even if our little individual candles get snuffed out.

When I'm admitted to the hospital, Andre takes my phone. This is one of many jobs that he did not knowingly sign up for when he kissed me at age twelve, but that he has found himself taking on over the years. This dance is so seamless between us by now, we don't even have to say anything, Andre just takes my phone when I am hospitalized or too sick to engage with the world, and he informs everyone.

He texts my mother and Marco. He knows enough Spanish—he took it all through school—to text my *abuela,* though he can't give her all the finer details. He texts Araceli. He calls my manager at Anthro and tells her I'm really ill, no one's sure when I will be better and up to working again; when I'm well enough to speak on the phone, I call her and tell her she can give my job away to someone who needs it because I don't know when I will be able to return to the store.

She says, "I can hold your job for you, Mira." My eyes tear up. She's always been great.

"For how long?" I say. "Please. Please don't feel obligated."

"For as long as it takes," she says.

Andre texts Paloma. She's new, of course, to our list of people who need to be informed about my health emergencies. I ask him not to tell her about the ectopic pregnancy, though he included it in the texts to everyone else. It seems too tender, too painful, for someone who's been making love to me to hear about that via text and through somebody else. I resolve to tell her myself, whenever I get out of here and see Paloma again. But just as the last time we saw each other seems a billion years ago, right now I can't even see to a time when we will meet again. And so she and I float in the unmoored middle of a separation, an infinite distance on either side of us, past and future.

When I have my phone, I keep it on do not disturb. I am not well enough right now to be part of the digital world. When Andre is able to visit me, after the lung infection has cleared but I am not yet strong enough to go home, he takes my phone, turns off do not disturb, and looks through my many, many notifications. I either dictate replies to him or reply myself, as much as I can manage. Mom and Marco want to come see me. Paloma does too. (Celi doesn't ask; she's the only one who gets how I feel about that.) I am not up to that. And—pandemic silver lining—the hospital is un-thrilled enough with Andre visiting me, there's no way they will allow anyone else. So I tell them no. I tell them I will see them as soon as I am able.

Andre reads a text to me from Marco one morning, in our family group chat: *Got into med school,* it says. *Will give you all the details later. All that matters right now is Mira getting well.*

Of course he did.

On social media, the news of Hassan's book *Fifteen* being made into a Netflix miniseries is announced. This comes on the heels of *Vestal: A*

Graphic Novel breaking into the *New York Times* bestseller list, graphic novels and manga section. It's number fifteen, the last on the list, but who the fuck cares? It's the literal *New York Times.* It's the first of Hassan's books to ever become an NYT bestseller. The following week, his cookbook, *Nostalgia,* pops up on the bestseller list too. I am not there to celebrate this huge career milestone with my brother-in-law. I take my phone and write him a congratulatory text.

One afternoon, checking my email, Andre freezes suddenly.

"Mira," he says.

"What's wrong, *papi*?"

"No," he says. "Baby, nothing's wrong." He turns the phone around to face me, shakes its bright screen at me. "Mira. You got in."

My head is fuzzy with, like, a dozen medications. "I got in to what?" I ask.

"City College. The creative writing program." He looks at the phone again, reading the message in more detail. "And it looks like they're giving you a lot of financial aid too."

"Oh," I say. "Wow."

I don't say anything else. Is there still a little flare of awe, of joy, buried somewhere behind my overstressed heart? Of course there is. It's a real college degree. It's writing. It's my dream. But right now I am so high on pain meds that I can't even read my phone. There is a feeding tube in my stomach. At any moment my body could turn on my new lungs. I know that school doesn't start till September, and it's March, but I can't even imagine sitting in a classroom, giving a presentation, doing my homework. And all the financial aid in the world from City College won't be able to erase the hospital bill we are going to be slammed with whenever I get outta here. My care team tells me that I am at higher risk than ever for cystic fibrosis-related diabetes. Insulin is fucking expensive. And I'd have to take it every single day.

"Mira," Andre says. There are tears in his eyes. "I am so proud of you."

"Andre," I say. He stands up, puts my phone in his back pocket, and comes over to hug me, G-tube and IV line and all. I hug my man back as hard as I can.

No, in the middle of all of this shit, it does not escape me that my husband is acting as my personal secretary, spending hours with me at the hospital while arguing with the hospital staff about his visits, learning how to feed me through the gastrostomy tube, and still working remotely (reduced hours, because he told his team leader I'm sick, *pero ya*). It's his premium health insurance through work, his money, that helps me get through my life. He isn't sleeping or eating well and I know the worry is a constant, nonstop, twenty-four-hour thing.

He must be having all kinds of feelings, about all of this dismal fucking shit. And I do not feel ready to explore any of them. On top of everything else, I'm a horrible wife too.

I'd love to not know it, but I'm also very aware that he might be grieving our lost pregnancy. After all, that was his fertilized egg with a heartbeat too.

I'm released from the hospital in March and still it's slow, slow, slow. There has finally, for the first time in my entire life, been a real improvement in my nutrition. And all I ever needed was a tube in my stomach and nighttime feedings directly into my body; who knew? The gastrostomy tube is a whole life adjustment that I really cannot even touch yet. I just take it a day at a time.

My new lungs and I have returned to a shaky, tentative equilibrium. I take my anti-rejection meds as always. I'm under strict orders to severely limit contact with just about everyone to keep my risk of infection low, especially with this virus still on the loose. I have no plans to even set foot outside of this apartment door for the foreseeable future.

My care team adjusted my dosage of pancreatic enzymes. I'll be screened often for CFRD. If I am diagnosed with diabetes, that will be a whole new layer of daily illness management. All I can do is hope for the best.

I'm still feeling pain and soreness from the surgery to terminate the pregnancy and remove one of my fallopian tubes. I'm not recovering from that as fast as patients sometimes do, but malnutrition and all the general trauma to my body have slowed my body's recovery, my care team says. I do little but lie in bed, resting and feeding myself a few times a day through my tube. I listen to Andre working in the other room, typing on his laptop or going to Zoom meetings. I try to sleep. I've had terrible insomnia lately, a combination of pain and worry and depression. Lack of sleep is probably slowing my recovery too. But I don't tell my care team. I can't take another pill. I can't even take another tool or technique or management strategy. I will have to do the best I can on my own.

My brother begs to come see me. I say, "Not yet, okay, *nene*? I still feel like my immune system's too weak to see anyone. Let me recover a little bit more first."

"Can I just come stand outside your apartment and talk to you through the door?" he says. "I won't come in. I just want to hear your voice and be near you."

"MP."

"Please," he says.

"All right, fine," I say.

So my brother comes. As promised, he stays on the other side of the closed apartment door. I sit down on the floor on my side of the door; he sits down in the hallway just outside of the door. We talk for ten minutes. I feel bad for making him come all the way up to Inwood to talk for ten minutes, but it's all I can manage for today.

"Put your hand on the door," he says.

I press my palm to the door.

"I'm putting my hand on the door too," he says, and I close my eyes and imagine his palm pressing into the door from the other side.

"I love you, Mira," he says.

"I love you too, Marco Polo," I say.

"I'm leaving you a bunch of groceries and some food Hassan cooked and some other stuff," he says. "Just outside the door." I hear the rustle of plastic bags. "Tell Andre I said hi."

"Hi, Marco," Andre calls. "Thanks for bringing us some stuff."

"No problem," Marco says.

After Marco leaves, we wait thirty minutes, just in case there are any germs on the surfaces, then open the door and bring the bags inside. The mac and cheese Hassan made for me looks and smells so good that I actually eat a little of it, by mouth. I barely managed any of the disgusting hospital food, especially when I knew I had the certainty of the feeding tube. So this is the first real food I have eaten in weeks. I send him a long text saying thank you and all the other nice things I can think of.

Araceli sends me a love letter written on the back of a photo she took of the two of us at Christmas, two dozen pink roses, and a fuzzy rainbow-colored stuffed caterpillar. The caterpillar is enormous, probably about half my size, and so thick with fluffy stuffing that I can use him like a body pillow. This is a tradition, in case y'all are wondering: whenever I get home from a hospital stay, Araceli sends me flowers because she knows I'm a flower child, and the funniest stuffed animal she can find. I lie in bed with my new rainbow caterpillar, curled around him. It makes me feel better than anything else has in a long time.

It never gets easier, knowing my girl Mira is sick. When she's in the hospital, or after, when she's recovering, part of my self is always with her. My phone don't leave my side. My hand is on its smooth surface legit twenty-four-seven, waiting for news from her. I sleep only lightly, my lids open a crack in case I have to awaken in the middle of the night.

This time, I wait and I wait till Mira says she feels well enough to see me. She ain't all the way recovered, she says, not even close. But isolation and sadness are making her recover slower. My girl needs her best friend. And when my girl needs me, I am there.

But because she has been so sick, with a rejection episode and lung infection and all that shit, it's a long-ass conversation, us figuring out the logistics of me coming over for a visit. Mira wants me to spend the night. She doesn't want me to wear a mask, and she wants cuddles and hugs. We decide together, in a three-way group text, that her needs outweigh the potential risks here. No one can get better without human connection. Andre Venmo's me money to take an Uber to their place, so at least I won't be bringing fresh germs from the subway, the world's least sanitary place, directly to her.

He texts me privately in the middle of our three-way convo. I am not sure, honestly, if Mira knows that her man and I sometimes talk about her like this. But if she don't, I bet my girl would get it. She's always the first one to say that cystic fibrosis is a complex disease, no one manages it on their own.

Long as she's ok with it I'm gonna do my best not to be there for your night, he says. *I think she needs best friend time.*

I got u bby, I write back.

Araceli I'm worried about her.

Now, Andre don't text me stuff like this too often. I was editing boudoir photos while talking to them, but I save the photo I was working on now, sit back in my chair and focus on my phone.

What's up, bro?

She won't talk to me, he replies. *She's been through so much and I just think she needs her BFF. See if she will talk to you?*

This ain't like Mira. I chew my thumbnail.

The text bubbles dance. *She's also not eating much,* he continues. *She has the tube but she doesn't like using it. And I haven't seen her eating by mouth at all in the past two days.*

Oh, Mira, I think. My stomach sinks.

That's what it's called, ok? he says. *I read this blog here by a CF-er who's been using a feeding tube for years.* He sends the link. *From what I understand, this girl is saying that normalizing the feeding tube as just another form of eating makes her and other users feel better about using it.* I start to reply, but then I see the text bubbles, for quite a while, so I rest my thumbs and wait. *So last night my mom called and wanted to talk to Mira. We got on speaker. Mom was asking like all these questions. Mira started to get fatigued. Eventually Mom said, so you can't do regular eating at all anymore? Why not? Mira just looked at me & got up & left the room. I tried to talk to Mom. But u know her. So I hung up and I found Mira crying in bed. She was crying for hours.*

Fuck, I reply, in between that text and his next.

So I don't think we should call it "regular eating," yeah? he suggests. *The terminology for that seems to be "eating by mouth." The tube is eating. Eating by mouth isn't the standard. There is no standard. If she uses the tube it doesn't make her irregular or abnormal.*

Of course, bby, I say.

Sorry, he says. *That's what I said to my mom. How she was acting really upset us both.*

Don't u b sorry, I reply. *SMH @ your mama, Dre. Seriously.*

He sends back the eye-rolling emoji. *Try to encourage her to eat with the tube if you can,* he continues. *I tried to talk to her about what happened with Mom but she said she doesn't have the energy to talk about it. So I haven't asked her how she feels about the language yet. But the important thing is that she's eating. If you can get her to eat by mouth, that's great too. We have all the usual high-calorie CF stuff. For the tube, we have a liquid nutrition blend from the hospital. She doesn't like eating it, which sucks, because apparently it has exactly the right nutrients and whatnot that she needs. But I ordered like the world's most powerful blender from this specialty cooking website. I asked Hassan for a recommendation. Anyway so we can blend just about any food and put it in the tube. Her care team said that's ok. Just get her to take in calories if you can, ok Celi?*

Whatever our girl needs, I write back. *So does the tube need like care or management or cleaning or anything?*

Yes, it needs to be flushed out with water before and after she uses it, he replies. *Even if she doesn't use it, that needs to be done every day. And we're checking her stoma, that's the spot on her stomach where the tube goes in, every day for signs of infection, like redness, swelling, etc. She hates doing all that. Probably one of the reasons she's resisting using the tube. But she does it. She doesn't wanna get infected.*

Is it something she can do by herself? I ask.

Yes, she can, he says. *She asks me for help with it sometimes though. She's tired and still healing from the 2 surgeries. The feeding tube and the other tube. We check her stomach together. She doesn't like looking at it.* There's a long pause, in which the dancing dots disappear and reappear a couple of times. Finally he writes, *Honestly I'm nervous about this, Celi. What if she's not feeling up to it and she doesn't wanna ask you for help? I know you are close but do you think she will feel comfortable having you do something like that?*

IDK either, I write back. *She takes her meds in front of me but I've only ever even seen her do the old morning lung routine a couple times. I have never physically helped her with anything before.*

Would you feel comfortable helping her with the tube if she asked?

Course I would, I answer. *But is it like hard? Do I need training from a doctor or some shit? I don't wanna hurt her, Dre.*

You don't need training from a doctor, no, he says. *Mira can show you. I wouldn't say it's hard but it is, I don't know, like delicate? Your hands have to be super clean. And honestly it does feel scary. It feels like medical and I am not a doctor. I feel like I don't know what I'm doing. And like you said, I don't wanna hurt her.* There's a pause. I wait. *But of course Mira reminded me she's not as delicate as she looks. She's all like I'm ok, just fucking do it Andre.*

LOL, I write. Now it's me who has to pause. I feel sick to my stomach, thinking about this next one. *Does it hurt, though? The tube?*

Yeah she says it hurts a little, he responds. *It's uncomfortable she says. She likes to sleep on her stomach normally but now she's trying not to cause of the tube. So she's trying to adjust her sleeping position and like…* The dots dance. My eyes fill with tears. *If I could take all this from her I would,* he says.

I send back the broken heart emoji.

I'm gonna do my best for our girl, I respond. *Anything else I should know bby?*

I mean yeah, he writes back, and I laugh out loud through my tears, loving his honesty. *Some of it I'm gonna have to let Mira tell you if that's ok. This is a lot Celi. This is A LOT.* No hesitation, in his next text bubble he writes, *I need help.*

I GOT U, I write back. And I do. Some of y'all probably be thinking I'm some flighty, tacky-ass ghetto bitch. And, well, at least some of that is true, and there ain't no shame in it. But Andre, this dude who literally could not be more different from me, and I both fell in love with Mira when we were kids. I saw within weeks of meeting her that she, like me, did not have an adult in her life that she could count on. (I mean, Gloria did her thing, but she also did a lot of drugs and a lot of abusive, fucked-up shit, so.) We weren't adults, Andre and me (he sure is now, though, hot damn), but we promised long ago that we would be there for Mira in any way that we could. Marco, I know, thinks that he can save his sister. That is his own fucked-up shit. I know that I can't save my best friend. I know that I can't take her CF from her. Shit don't work that way. Someday, my girl, the love of my life, may die. But while we're here, anything I can do for her, I do.

The moment I walk through the door on Friday afternoon, I know that my girl Mira is different. Probably not like this, but I have seen her low before. I've held her and felt like I was the anchor keeping her connected to the world. I've held my phone to my ear in bed all night long, talking to her and listening to her cry because she felt sick and her mom and Marco wouldn't stop yelling and she wasn't sure if she could take it anymore. We've also laughed so hard we literally peed our pants like so, so many times.

So I have seen Mira at some extremes. She's low today. Her aura is gray and colorless. Her hair, which she normally takes care of lovingly, even when it took all her extra energy, styling it proudly into her two perfect, adorable puffs, is loose and unbrushed. Her face is angry with acne breakouts; they flare when she is stressed. Her sweatpants and tee hang off of her. Her eyes are shadowed with lack of sleep.

I've also legit never seen anything more beautiful than my best friend, my whole heart, after I've not seen her for a month when all I did was worry about her.

I put down all the bags I'm carrying and hug her. I feel her down to her bones. I hold her gingerly, thinking about the tube. I watched YouTube videos on my breaks at work, so I would already know what a gastrostomy tube looks like, in case she needs or wants to show it to me.

She grunts in my arms. "Tighter," she says. "You ain't gonna break me, Araceli."

So I hug her tighter. She sighs in my arms. I feel her breathing, those new lungs. I called Marco and Andre after, each of them, thanked them for doing this thing for our girl, my best friend. I rest my chin in the soft cloud of her hair. Miranda is one of the only girls in the world who is shorter than me. I love her, my perfect girl. Who knows how many days we will get? But every day, I think. We'll enjoy each other every single day that we do get.

Mira pulls back. She holds her arms looped around my waist. She presses forward slightly, so I can feel her tits on mine. I draw in a deep, sudden breath. Wow, okay, girl, I think. Mira gazes up at me with an intentionality, an intensity. Fuck if I know what it means. She's different. She told me by text the other night that she feels so down now, it's like the past year since the transplant and all her work on getting stronger never even happened. But I know it happened, I can see it in her now. There's a new fire in her now, my girl.

"I should wash my hands," I say finally. "I'm also gonna take a shower and change my clothes. Like we talked about."

I wash my hands and shower and put on clean leggings and an oversized tee from Barbee, the punk band I toured Australia with as their photographer and social media manager. I go into the kitchen and find Mira putting the food I brought her into the fridge.

"*Bebecita, no hagas nada,*" I say. "You don't do no work right now. Let me."

She sucks her teeth at me. "Celi. *Ya.* I ain't no invalid."

"*Déjame cuidarte.*" I take the bag she's holding from her. She lets me. "Go sit down," I say.

She sits down. Her forearms rest heavily on the tabletop, shoulders rounding. "Shit, girl," she says. "What all did you bring me?"

"These paper plates in foil have slices of pizza. This is bacon mac and cheese from the mac and cheese place. This is a cheeseburger and fries. This is fried chicken. And this—*mira esto*, Miranda. This is peach cobbler. Skye made it. It was her mom's recipe." Look at your girl Celi now; I got me a woman who bakes literal peach cobblers from scratch, can y'all even believe that?

"Celi. That is way too much." She shakes her head.

"Just wanted to make sure you had all the junk food you needed." I sit down at the table with her. "Do you want to eat something?"

She widens her eyes. "Wow. No. Can we not talk about eating right now? Or the damn feeding tube? Please?"

"*Bien de bien,* Mira," I say. "*Lo que quieras.*"

"If I never have to talk about the G-tube ever again, that would be too soon."

I laugh loudly. "You funny, *chica.*"

"I know." She flutters her lashes.

"How are you feeling, baby?" I ask her.

Her pretty mouth turns down. "Yeah. No. Don't wanna talk about that either, Celi."

"Fine, *mi reina.* So what do you wanna talk about?"

"I don't wanna talk about nothing, Araceli," she says. She gives me a deep, meaningful look.

I swallow. "What you wanna do, then, honey?"

"I need you to cuddle me," she says. "Please."

Mira takes my hand and leads me to the couch. We sit down. Within seconds I have my girl in my arms, her body curled into my lap and melting into me sweetly in every pore. Mira turns all my senses on. I nuzzle my face in her hair. Mira's hair is amazing, all kinky and soft and light-dark with shots of burned gold. She smells like coconut and eucalyptus and sweet almond oil. I squeeze her tighter and feel her heart beating inside.

"I was so lonely in there, Celi," she says. I feel her breath against my neck. "In the hospital."

I let one hand slip under Mira's shirt. I feel the damp, hot small of her back, the rounding of her spine as she curves into me, the hard little knobs under her silky skin. I need to feel her. I missed her, I longed for her, I thought of her and sent her energy every second.

"You're here now," I say. "*Conmigo.*"

"I know," she says. She burrows into me deeper. "I'm so happy."

"Me too, Mira."

"I love you, Celi," she says. "I missed you, I longed for you." She inhales deeply. "I needed you. I'm hungry for you."

"I'm right here, Mira."

Mira pulls back. She shifts around on my lap. I hold her tighter, supporting her. Then she holds my face tenderly and leans closer and kisses me. She lets her lips linger close to mine, breathing my breath, in case I wanna push her away, I guess. But I am not pushing her away. I let her kiss me, tasting my lips.

Mira and I have kissed before, a light, gentle press of our lips together. I've cherished all those kisses. And I think she has too. And I think we always knew we kissed as just a little bit more than friends. And it was cool. But this is different. This shit ain't cool, okay.

It's our first real kiss. And it's hot in a second. I have so much pent up for her; I have wanted her since I was old enough to know what it was to want somebody. I tangle my fingers in her hair and slant my mouth to hers, taking her tongue and sucking it, pulling back to nibble her lips with a gentle heat.

"Celi." She sighs her eyes closed. "That feels so good."

"You feel so good. *Mi nena. Mi dulce. Mi luna.*"

She brings her lips down to mine again. The way I know it's different is because of the aggression in her, the purpose. I let Mira kiss me ragged. I guess I always thought we might kiss someday, but I had no idea it would be here, now, like this. She takes control. I melt for her, submit to her. When I taste the inside of her mouth, a thing I've craved with every hormone, I'm just as wet as our mouths together between my legs. There's a sudden lagoon between my lips and the fabric of my leggings.

Mira pulls back again. She peels her shirt off over her head. Underneath she's in a soft ribbed flesh-colored bra that makes me ache to squeeze her. There's the G-tube, way less scary on my beloved girl's perfect body than it was in the videos. Her lower belly is scarred from the surgery, a small diagonal stripe on the left side.

She sees me looking. Mira takes my hand, trails my fingertips over the scar. She sucks in a breath; her skin reacts in goosebumps. I feel a little dizzy, knowing I can do that to her.

"From the surgery to remove the pregnancy and my fallopian tube," she says.

I cup her head under her hair. "How is my sweet girl feeling?"

Her eyes water. "I could have died, I almost died," she says. "That ain't a baby."

"No," I agree. "That ain't a baby. There is only you, *mi nena.*" Her shift between tenderness and grief, this new thing blossoming between us after so long dormant, and then her pain, it makes my head throb. I do the best

I can to stay in the moment with her. Just before Mira went to the hospital, I called her one night and cried for hours about my photography stuff. Getting an agent was not a magic solution to all of my problems. I cried and cried, saying I was tired, I don't want to work shit jobs anymore, I want to be a real artist, I want to break through. I don't cry much, y'all, so when I do, it's, like, epic. Mira listened and told me my work is so good, it's so good, I am a real artist, I am the realest artist ever. She said my work would find its place. She said good things take time.

"It sucked so bad," Mira says. "It wasn't a baby. But it had a heartbeat. Araceli." She chokes on a sob. "Ain't that fucked?"

"Shit," I say. "Mira, honey." I'm scared I'm gripping her too hard. I ease up. "That is so, so fucked."

She shakes her head. "I don't wanna talk about that anymore," she says.

"You don't have to," I say.

"I'm scared that's all people wanna hear about," Mira says. "But what about me?"

"Miranda," I say. "All I wanna hear about is you. Talk to me."

"Can we eat?" she says. "I have to try Skye's peach cobbler."

I can't wait to tell Skye that her food is making my girl want to eat again.

I spoon large portions of Skye's cobbler onto plates and microwave them for forty seconds, just like she told me. "You got ice cream, baby?" I open her freezer.

"Yeah," she says. "Andre got some the other day. In case I wanted to have a milkshake. Or put a milkshake into my stupid, stupid feeding tube." She screws up her face. "Why would I wanna do that?" She sighs, looks down at the tabletop. "I'm sorry. I shouldn't be *tan grosera*. I should be grateful. And Andre. All he does is take care of me…" Her eyes get wet.

The microwave beeps. I pull the pint of vanilla ice cream out of the freezer. "*No te preocupes*, Mira," I say. "You know you can say anything with me. *Esto es muy duro.* Like you get to say that it fucking sucks. You do not have to fucking express gratitude for every single thing all the time. That is some fake woke, white people yoga shit right there. *No tienes que hacer nada de esto conmigo.*"

She rubs tears from her eyes with the knobby back of her wrist. "Thank you, Araceli," she says.

I put spoonfuls of ice cream onto our peach cobbler and slide one plate in front of her, sit down with the other one in front of me. Even though I certainly didn't make this food myself (making food is, like… not one of my talents, aight?) and I hate that my girl is not feeling one hundred percent, I gotta say it feels good to be the one serving her, taking care of her. It's uncountable, the number of meals I've eaten cooked by Mira or her mother or her grandmother. When Marco and I were together, this boy had no money as well, and worked two and three jobs while going to school, but he would buy me food, take me out to eat, bring me leftovers. The whole Castillo family has taken care of my raggedy little ass, for most of my life. Now I watch Mira bring a bite of peach cobbler and ice cream to her mouth, suck it off her fork, and close her eyes in pleasure. It's the best, and most at peace, I've felt in the past month.

I take a bite myself. The pale cool cream of the vanilla has melted into the thick sweet peach chunks and the soft, tender cobbler crust. It's sublime.

"*¿Me puedes contar sobre el…* feeding tube?" I ask her gently.

She sighs. She takes another bite. "*Tal vez un poquito,*" she says, almost in a whisper. "It's weird. When you use it, and food goes into you, you feel, like… un-hungry. Un-thirsty. Like if you're hungry you feel satisfied. If you're thirsty you feel refreshed. That's weird. 'Cause you ain't putting anything into your mouth. Like it's going directly into your belly."

She shudders. I don't want to push her. I also want her to keep talking to me. Mira and I have always been big on sharing our secrets, processing our shit together, being open and intimate with each other. We have no blind spots, no boundaries. I don't want to lose that.

"Does it… does it feel… okay?"

Mira sighs again. She puts down her fork. "Deal," she says. "We eat this beautiful fucking peach cobbler and you tell me about your woman and your new place and the photos you're working on. Please distract me for just a few minutes from *toda esta mierda* that's been taking over my life. Then I will talk about the G-tube. If you want me to."

"Mira. We've always…"

"I know," she says. "We have. I always feel better after talking to you. I need you, Celi. You know that. And I will tell you everything. Just please. Distract me. Tell me something good. For just a little while."

And so I do. And, it turns out, there is a lot of good in my life right now. Skye and I have a place together. I mean, it's New York City, and she's an artist who works at McDonald's for extra cash and I'm an artist who works at a sex store for extra cash, so we don't have our own place. But we have a room and our own bathroom and a shared kitchen in a three-bedroom apartment on the Upper West Side with four other roommates (Gigi and Preeti, another couple, sleep in one bedroom; Lara, Gigi's sister and a student at Columbia, sleeps in the other; and Paige, who works night shifts for the MTA, sleeps on our couch during the day while everyone else is out about half the time and stays at her boyfriend's the other half of the time). The rent is ridiculous but between the six of us we make it work, and the apartment is beautiful. It has hardwood floors and enormous windows and a fucking balcony off the kitchen and even a tiny washing machine and dryer stacked in a corner. It's the nicest place I have ever lived in, by a long shot, and Skye too. There are a shit ton of us living there and sometimes there are arguments or minor drama, but no one is a drug dealer, no one's pimp comes around threatening people, and it's not an abandoned building with no heat or running water, so.

"Some evenings when we have the place to ourselves for a couple minutes, Skye and I take a glass of two-dollar wine out to the balcony and watch the sun set," I tell Mira. "That erases pretty much all of the shit. That shit makes me feel like a literal queen, *mi nena*."

"You are a literal queen, *mami chulo*," says my girl.

"Thank you, honey. I am, ain't I?"

Mira eats the last bite of her cobbler. I want to text Andre, brag about how I got our girl to eat probably one thousand calories right now. She should marry me instead.

"This is everything I wanted for you, baby," she says. Her eyes shimmer. "Everything I prayed for. Every spell I cast for you."

"Thank you, Mira. You believing in me all these years helped me get here."

She looks at me closely. "You really love her, don't you, Celi?"

"So much," I say. "It's frightening." I wake up in the middle of the night sometimes, and wonder if this could be my real life, making real money off my photography and making time to shoot the stuff that makes me happy too (my latest series is construction sites around the city, all grunge and ugly), living someplace quiet and warm and safe and even pretty, waking up next to this fucking badass woman who makes me scream and laugh and give it all up to her. It probably all did come from a spell from my best friend, 'cause I can't see how I could deserve this much good stuff all on my own. My name might mean "altar of the sky" (it's from Latin, y'all), but I ain't no angel.

"Ain't it cool," I ask Mira, "how my name means 'altar of the sky' and her name is actual Skye?"

She smiles slowly. "That's magic," she says. "And you are so fucking gone for her, Celi, and I am so here for that." She gazes at me for a long-ass time, so long and deep I start to see the flickering pieces of gold in her dark coffee eyes.

"Araceli," she says. "You are gonna have a baby with Skye someday. Ain't you?"

"*Eres tanta bruja*," I tell her. "I got no clue how you know these things, Miranda, but yes. I will have this woman's baby someday. I don't know when; I am not anywhere near ready for that. And Skye and I need way more time together. But yes. We've already talked about it; that's how sure we are about this. About us. Skye doesn't want to carry. She got pregnant once, years ago, when she was married to a guy for a little while. She had an abortion. Being pregnant is not for her. But I, like… there's part of me that's always wanted to carry a baby. To be a mom." I shake my head. "I know. Me. A mother. But I love her. I want to have a baby with her. I want to have a family. I always have."

Mira nods. "I know you have," she says. Course she does; this girl sees me.

Now, I know what I said: about constant and unexamined gratitude being woke white people shit. And I stand by what I said. But I also take a moment to be fucking grateful, in the most spiritually aware way that I can be. If chicks like Mira and Skye and me had been born just one hundred years earlier than we were, we would never be here today. Skye would be trapped in a marriage she didn't want, raising a child in poverty. I never would've gotten to know her, to taste her, to love her. That ectopic pregnancy would have killed my black moonbeam of a girl, one heartbeat to the next. Cystic fibrosis would have colonized her lungs as a child. And without her love, I'd have been lying dead someplace long ago. Now that, my friends, is something to be grateful for.

"So yeah," I say. "We will. Someday. Have a baby together."

"Celi," Mira says. She shakes her head, slowly. "I have to live to see that. Like, I have to. I don't care what I have to do. I'll do anything the doctors tell me. I will fucking cryogenically freeze my brain. I will breathe and eat and shit and do whatever else I have to do by a machine. But I will be here long enough to be an auntie to your baby. I swear to God I will."

"Oh, Mira," I say.

"I'm serious," she says, the fiercest girl in the world.

I nod. "I know you are."

She shakes her head again. "I am so, so fucking sad that I won't get to see how your story ends, Araceli. When I leave here, I am going to miss you so much. You are going to be one of the hardest for me to leave behind."

"Baby," I say.

She smiles, wiping away tears again with the backs of her wrists. "Thanks for not saying that I'm going to live to be a hundred," she says.

"Or that healthy people die young all the time. Or that I could get hit by a bus tomorrow."

She laughs. She hates when people minimize and diminish the difficulty of her illness by saying these things.

"Thank you," she says again.

"I would never tell you that your vision of your path is wrong," I tell her. "*Eres bruja.*"

"And my life is not a tragedy," she says, another thing she says often when we do this kinda philosophizing together. "It's my life. And it doesn't have to be some arbitrary length decided by somebody else to be good enough. It's my life, it's fucking full of joy, and it's going to be the exact perfect length for me."

Mira grabs a napkin, wipes tears from my face.

"It ain't gonna be, like, tomorrow, though, okay, Celi?"

I know I shouldn't, but I ain't actually that strong, okay, y'all. "Promise?" I ask her, my voice watery and shaky.

She cups my face, wipes my cheek with her thumb.

"Promise," Mira says, strongly. "I'm a wet tiger, remember? Still plenty of fight left in me. This shit ain't nowhere near enough to take this girl out. But I've gotta say, *mi nena.*" She closes her eyes, and when she opens them, I can see the sheer exhaustion in them. "*Esto es duro.* I know I'll get better from this. But I honestly don't know when. Or how. This one definitely took at least a couple of my nine lives."

"I am right here," I tell her. "Anything I can do. Anything you need."

"I know," she says. "Thank you. The goddesses gave me you. I'm so fucking lucky."

I lean close and kiss her. I've decided we're kissing tonight, and worrying about the wisdom of deciding to kiss tomorrow.

"Like, it wasn't a baby," she says, suddenly, when we pull back, "but I am still, like, super sad."

"*Mi nena dulce.* I know you are. I am too."

"I still really want a baby," she says. "It was hard. And super not fun." She rubs her hands through her loose hair. "But I sat down with my care team and had a real conversation about the viability of me ever trying to carry a baby myself. We've touched on it here and there, they've known for years I want a baby someday, but we never all sat down and weighed the decision with that kind of intention. And the answer was no." She shakes her head. "With the transplanted lungs. With my pancreatic insufficiency and my nutrition problems. The ectopic pregnancy, which makes you more likely to have another one in the future. The possibility of CF diabetes. It wouldn't be safe for me to try to carry."

"How do you feel about that, *nena*?"

She shrugs. "Sad. Resigned. I kinda already knew it, but now it feels more final. Like, in my body. I cried a little, during our talk. They reminded me that, if I want a child, there is more than one way to have a baby. There's adoption, though I'm not sure how adoption agencies would feel about a young, sick brown girl trying to adopt a kid. There's surrogacy."

I nod. "How do you feel about those options?"

"I'd like to explore them," she says. "Like, sometime in the not-too-distant future." She shrugs again. "But I'm not sure how Andre feels. I couldn't do this without him. When we've talked about it before, he said he wasn't ready. That he wants us to have more time together first. That he wants me to go back to school first. But..." She spreads her palms: it's an open question, for now.

Shortly before she had to go to the hospital, Mira told me that she'd applied to go back to school for her BA in creative writing. Maybe because I'm sitting so close to her, under the glowing umbrella of her aura, I receive a flash of intuition.

"You got in, didn't you?" I ask. "To the creative writing program at City College."

Her cheeks flush, almost like she's feeling guilty. Tentatively, she nods. "I did."

"Course you did."

"And with a whole bunch of financial aid," she says.

"And you're gonna let Marco's sugar daddy pay for the rest of it."

"Celi!"

"C'mon, girl. Money is the colonizer's construct. Men have been making it for millennia on the backs of women and other folks to follow their dreams. Now Hassan is trying to offer it to you to follow your dreams. This is a man actually tryna use money not for himself, like the capitalists want, but for his community. That's the revolution. So do it, Mira."

My wise girl nods, taking this in. Then she says, "Right now, I would really love to cuddle on the couch with you and kiss you more. What you think, Araceli baby?"

I burst out laughing, though I feel my cheeks get all hot and my pussy lips get all slick. I am on my knees for this girl. "The only answer I can give to that is yes," I say.

So Mira takes my hand and we return to the couch. She sits in my lap again, settled on my left thigh. She's so small that she fits on me perfectly, feeling like something delicate for me to cherish, well, except for the way she kisses me like a tigress: biting my tongue, gripping me with strong urgency. I feel awakened, by the revelation that, with every move she makes, she must have wanted me all this time the way that I wanted her.

I kiss the corners of her mouth, wetly. I kiss her cheeks, her forehead. When I kiss down her chin, her jaw, her neck, she starts to moan. It's a siren song for me, that sound: drawing me somewhere deeper that I want to be but know that I shouldn't. I wrench myself away from her lips, an action that feels almost painful. We breathe big, gasping breaths, like having escaped from the ocean. We're so close I feel the wet of her breath on my lips. I loosen my grip on her body. I let my hands whisper up the curves of her sides. I skim the edges of her breasts. Her hardened nipples stand in stark relief, outlined by the soft fabric molded to them. I want to squeeze her breasts as bad as I've ever wanted anything in my life. Some of y'all probably be thinking that Araceli has no self-control, that she's a hedonist in the ancient sense of the word, that she does whatever feels good. But not touching her right now is taking a superhuman amount of self-restraint, y'all, okay?

"Araceli," she says. She tangles her fingers in my short curls. She presses herself to me in a sudden, swift, hard hug.

Then she jerks away sharply, and with a whimper of pain.

My hands fly to her shoulders, holding her, feeling her, as though checking her for anything broken. "Mira, honey? Baby, what's wrong? You okay?"

She winces. "Just when I forget I'm wearing a stupid fucking G-tube, then I remember." She looks down at it. So do I. "It felt really tender when I pressed it against you like that." Her shoulders slump. "I'm sorry."

I kiss her mouth gently. "Why the fuck would you be sorry?"

"Dunno," she says. "Because I'm…"

"You're a goddess," I tell her.

She rolls her eyes. She's smiling though. "Celi?" Her lower lip starts to tremble. She bites it, hard. "Could you? Help me? Every day we're supposed to check my stoma—that's the hole where the tube goes in—to make sure it's not getting infected. Looking at it still really upsets me." The tears she's been holding back spill down, trail down her cheeks. "Could you help me?"

I kiss the wet from her cheeks. "I sure can," I say.

We go into the bedroom and lie down on her bed. When I changed after my shower, I plugged my phone into the charger on her bedside table. I turn on the screen, take the quickest of looks at my notifications. There's Jojo, one of my coworkers, asking if we can swap shifts for next weekend. There's Skye saying hi, asking if Mira and I are all right. There's a text from Andre, in the group chat to Mira and me, which says, *Hope u two are doing ok. If u need me at literally any time, just text me & I'll come home,* plus three heart emojis. I feel a brief pang as I turn off the phone screen. I know Mira and Andre are exploring polyamory right now, that Paloma is her girlfriend. But they also discussed it ad nauseam before so much as touching each other, that style of super aware, super process-y ethical nonmonogamy that real adults with their shit together tend to practice.

Instead of all that, I kissed Mira tonight in my own special signature style, which is hot mess with a steaming side of "ask forgiveness, not permission." Mira is not a one-night stand. She's not an any-night stand; she's my best friend. What will our kisses mean beyond tonight? How will Andre feel, knowing I kissed his wife? Are we gonna tell him?

For right now, though, I gotta help my girl check her feeding tube site for signs of infection.

Mira lies on her back. She sighs, cheek falling against her pillow. "You stay here, *nena,*" I say. "I'm gonna go wash my hands real good."

I go to the bathroom and wash my hands about as thoroughly as I've ever washed them before, with tons of soap and water as hot as I can stand it, under all ten fingernails, all the way up my forearms. When I get back to the bedroom, Mira is dozing lightly. But she wakes up when I join her on the bed.

"Can I check your stomach?" I ask her.

"Please," she says.

So I lean over her and, in the light of the bedside lamp, examine her stoma, where the tube enters her body. I'm not sure what I'm looking for—that I ain't never done nothing like this before is an understatement, okay—but it looks fine to me, the skin soft and golden-brown. Fuck, she's perfect.

"It looks okay to me, baby girl," I tell her. "What should I be looking for?"

"Like redness, swelling, irritation, *así de así*," she says. She looks up at me with a kind of tender-eyed trust that guts me. Oh, fuck, I love her so much.

I shake my head. "*Nada de eso*. Does it need anything else? I don't know, cleaning or something?"

She nods, hair rustling against the pillow. "We can clean and dry the area and put on some of the antibacterial cream."

"Would you like me to help you with that?" My voice shakes, even though I try to get it to stop. I am not, by the way, normally at all shaky or shy.

"I would like you to do it for me," she says clearly. "I mean. If you don't mind."

"I don't mind," I whisper.

Mira points to the skin wipes, washcloths, and tube of cream on the bedside table. As gently and carefully as I've ever done anything, I wipe the skin around her G-tube, pat it dry, and smooth on a small amount of the cream. She whines as I rub it into her skin.

I pull my hand away. "Does it hurt?"

She grunts. "I mean. It don't not hurt, you know what I mean? But it's okay. Keep going, baby." I nod, re-approach her body slowly with my hand and finish rubbing in the cream.

"All done," I tell her.

"Thank you," she says. I lie down next to her, feeling drunk on her sweetness, and the nearness of her warm body, and getting to touch her, and care for her.

"Yeah, it does hurt a little bit." Her voice is so soft I have to slide my head closer to hers to hear it. "Like it feels tender and uncomfortable. I mean. It's a literal tube that's in your stomach. Plus." She sighs. She's tired, in a way I have never seen her before. "I am in a lot of pain in that area anyway. Sometimes it feels like the surgery for the pregnancy and the tube was, like, yesterday, not a month ago."

I crawl my hand closer and find her fingers by feel alone, linking them with mine. My heart twists sickly. I hate thinking of my magic witchy flower girl friend in any kind of pain at all.

"I asked my care team about it. I was reading some forums of people who've had ectopic pregnancies and this surgery before. It sounded like they were all recovering faster and easier than me. So I talked to the doctors. And they said I can't compare. That everyone's different. Everyone's situation is different. I'm recovering at the pace that I am because my body got even more weak because of the rejection and the infection. I was on oxygen again. It was terrible, Araceli."

I squeeze her hand, tightly. She's trembling.

"And because of the malnutrition. That means it takes my body longer to recover. It's not at full strength." I roll over, so I can see her, her profile as she lies on her back next to me; so I can rest my lips lightly against the bare skin of her shoulder and breathe her in. "This was one of the worst times ever, Celi. I think it was really a wake-up call. For both me and the care team. That my nutrition fucking sucks." I see tears spilling down from the corner of her eye and down her temple. "Eating by mouth just isn't enough for me. My appetite feels lower than ever. The stimulants make me feel gross and sometimes I don't think they even work that well. Forcing myself to eat like that is just too hard. It's been a struggle for my entire life and I'm so tired of it, Celi. I want to be able to put that down. And even when I do manage to do all the fucking work of just putting food in my mouth and eating it. The fucking pancreatic insufficiency means that my body still isn't getting the fucking nutrients." She wipes her eyes hard with her free hand, so hard it's gotta hurt. "And if I don't eat, if I can't eat, I am going to die."

Mira gives my hand a last squeeze, and then she forces herself up into a cross-legged sitting position. I can tell it hurts; she winces as she folds her legs, touches her lower belly lightly.

"I'm sorry," she says. "The pain gets worse throughout the day. And I get super tired."

"Honey. The fuck are you apologizing?"

She cries. I hold her through it. I stroke her hair. I pluck a tissue from the box on the bedside table and wipe her face. I rub her back. I tell her to let go, to let it out. My heart cracks every time she sobs. This love is the best thing I have ever done, and the hardest.

"I'm sorry," she says again, once she's calm enough to speak. If she were mine, and if I were that kinda woman (I ain't, okay), I would spank her. "I'm sorry. This is the shadow work I have to do right now. I have to let go of the part of me that still wants to make it work. That wants to eat like everybody else. That's a false story that it's time for me to put down. It hurts and it's gonna take me a hot minute. But I am letting it go. I have to." She sucks in a deep breath, pulling her shoulders all the way up to her ears, then letting them lower. "I should be grateful," she says tiredly. "That a G-tube is even a thing. My pancreas really, really sucks right now, Celi. I am taking so many enzymes for it. It's basically starting to give up on its job. I'm lucky they've invented some other way I can eat. Otherwise, how would I keep myself alive? So I should be fucking grateful."

I kiss each of her cheeks. She clings to me and kisses my mouth. I taste the salt of her tears. I'd like to drink them, to drink her.

"You also get to be angry," I tell her. "And hurt. And sad. And grieving. And tired. And however else you need to feel."

She nods. "I wish I could get up and just be totally okay with this stupid fucking tube." She begins to cry again, almost silently, just little hitchy sobs as she continues to speak, wiping her wet red eyes. "I wish it weren't taking me this long. Because I know that it's important. But I am just not there yet, Araceli. It is still so, so hard for me. This fucking tube. It sucks."

I lean forward and press my lips to her forehead, a hard and lingering kiss.

"Tell me what sucks about it," I say.

She quirks a brow; there's my sassy girl. "How long you got?"

I laugh. She does too. "I got all night, baby girl. Actually, give me a second. Let me go pee."

"I'll come with you," she says.

She sits on the edge of the tub while I pee. I wash my hands and do the same as she pees. She groans as she starts going. "I've been holding it more than I should," she says. "My stomach hurts when I go. The scar pulls."

"Mira. Honey."

"I know," she says. "There is so much going on in my body right now. It's terrifying." She's out of breath as she stands up and wipes herself. "I know how worried Andre is. And I don't even tell him all of it." She gives me a wry smile. "Sorry I'm dumping all of it on you."

"Nope," I say firmly. "I am your best friend, Miranda. You get to lay it all on me, baby."

After she washes her hands, I wrap my arm around her waist and help her back to bed. She's starting to fatigue, I can see it, and I wish I knew what she needed more: to talk, to eat something (by mouth? by tube?), to try to sleep? I decide that, since I ain't no doctor and she ain't no child, the only thing I can and should do is listen to what she says she needs.

We sit cross-legged again, and I squeeze her knee. "So tell me what sucks about the tube?"

She sighs. "Everything? It doesn't feel good. It hurts. I'm tired of it already. I'm terrified of it getting infected. Sometimes I wake up in the middle of the night because I'm having a nightmare. Where it's started attacking me from the inside. With an infection. I don't want another fucking external thing in my body. I don't know how I'm going to handle another piece of daily management. I have to clean the area. I have to flush it out with water before and after I use it. Every single time. If I have it long enough, eventually it has to be replaced. If it ever does get infected, that's a whole other thing."

She pauses for a breath. "So I think I'm resentful. That I let go of the daily lung-clearing routine. And got used to having that extra time in my life. And now this. It's not as hard or time-consuming, I will say that. And, unlike the lung-clearing, which only I could do, and no one could help me with, this someone else can do for me. Andre has already told me." She presses her lips together. "That if I want him to do some of the feedings. And the care of the tube. That he will. I said I'd think about it. Truth is, I want him to. I'm so tired, Celi. Of just being alive, being a person. I want to keep doing it. Being a person. For a long, long time, if I can. I love my life. Still. But for right now, at least, I'd love some support with all this daily management. Maybe long-term. Maybe just till I'm feeling stronger. But…"

She rubs the back of her neck. "What is that? Asking my husband to help feed me. Maybe for the rest of our lives. Like, what is that? And yes, I know some inter-abled couples where one partner caretakes or helps caretake for the other. But I can feed myself. I just don't know if I can handle it. Doesn't that make me selfish? Or lazy? Or, like, ungrateful? And how is Andre gonna feel? Will he still see me as his wife? Will he still find me sexy? When I don't want to feed myself and I'd like him to do it for me?"

I open my mouth, already hesitant, because all of this is way beyond your girl Celi's (limited) areas of wisdom. But Mira continues speaking. What wisdom I do have tells me that what I really need to do for my girl right now is let her speak.

"And this sounds kinda out there, but… I feel like I don't understand how to use the tube? No. That's wrong. I mean, I know how to physically use the tube. I have been using it. A little. I guess… as horrible as this sounds… I don't know how to feed myself. Truth is, I have never successfully fed myself. I've been malnourished and underweight and physically weak because of it my entire life. I don't get the same hunger and appetite signals as other people around me—I'm starting to realize that. I like food, but only some of it, and only sometimes, and only in small amounts. But I need more nutrition than that. It's clear that eating by mouth is just not enough for me. I will have to get comfortable with feeding myself as much as my body needs through this tube. Maybe for forever. I don't know yet.

"And that's not even getting into the logistics of the thing," she continues. "If I spend long enough with someone, or go out for long enough, I will have to explain to someone about the G-tube. I'll probably have to use it in front of someone at some point. I have to tell everyone close to me, like Marco, and Hassan, and my mom, and Andre's family." Her eyes fill with tears. "And Paloma." The tears spill over. "When people see it or see me using it, they're gonna stare. They're gonna ask me questions. That's gonna make me feel like shit." She rubs her eyes. I wipe her face with a tissue again. "I'm already feeling so much. Sad and angry and resentful. I feel shame. Because I feel like I should be able to do this: feed myself. Normally. Like everyone else. But I can't. Like, this is normal for me. It's gonna feel like shit when other people don't see that."

"Fuck those other people," I say.

She blinks her wet, clumped lashes at me. "Easier said than done."

"I know," I say. "I'm sorry."

She shrugs. She looks down at her hands in her lap—or, maybe, down at the tube in her bare belly. "I'm worried about sex too," she says, her voice soft. "How sexy am I gonna feel, feeding myself through this tube?

Having Andre do it? What positions are gonna feel good? Am I still gonna be a sex person?" She sobs out loud. "I've loved being a sex person lately, Celi. I've always been a sex person on the inside. Now I've gotten to be one on the outside too. How am I still gonna be a sex person now?"

Heart thudding, I let myself trail a hand along her breasts. It makes her gulp in a shaky breath, then sigh. And it takes everything in me not to go further, to clutch her breasts in my palms, to slip them out of that tiny clinging bra and hold them, to roll her juicy nipples between my fingertips.

"Miranda," I say. "You are most definitely still a sex person."

She laughs. I feel like a fucking superhero, making my girl laugh.

"Andre and I haven't had sex yet," she says.

I blink. "You are still recovering," I say.

"We haven't even kissed," she says. "You are the first person I've kissed. Since I went to the hospital."

"I'm honored," I say, and mean it.

"I haven't felt very sexy," she says, looking down again.

"*Claro que no*, baby," I say. "You've been in pain. You've been recovering. It will come back. When your body's ready. When you're ready."

She nods. "I guess I'm just worried that it'll look different. Feel different. Sex, for me. Compared to how it was before."

"It might," I say. "But there are so many ways to be sexy, Mira. To have sex. To be a sex person."

She smiles—then her smile fades into a gradual look of intensity. "I've wanted to kiss you like what we've been doing today since I was ten years old," she says.

"*Igualmente*," I whisper. My pussy clenches so hard for her that I'm scared I'll come, just sitting in bed looking into her eyes.

"I think we should maybe eat something?" she says. "Before we go to bed. I want to sleep next to you, Araceli."

"Okay," I whisper. "I do too."

First, Mira flushes her G-tube out with water. As she prepares what she needs, a bowl of water and the feeding syringe, I ask her if she'd like me to give her privacy.

She smiles. "Since when have we given each other privacy?"

I shrug. "I dunno. I just…"

"*No te preocupes,* Celi. If it grosses you out, you do not have to watch."

"It doesn't gross me out," I say, rolling my eyes. "I just wanted to make sure. That you were comfortable. With me being here."

She rolls her eyes right back. "I want you here," she says, with gentle emphasis.

So I sit next to her while she flushes her tube with water, pumping it in with the syringe. There's something tender about watching her do this for herself, the care she takes of herself; and also, I gotta be honest, something sexy about her calm, efficient competence. Maybe she doesn't feel all the way there yet. But I can tell that she will get there.

Then we eat together. I warm up some of the *moro de habichuelas* that her *abuela* brought over a few days ago. Mira sits with me at the table and eats some of her liquid nutritional blend through the tube. We talk and laugh so much while we eat, just like we've done during thousands of meals in all sorts of places—her mom's place, my mom's cousin's place where I grew up, school, McDonald's, Crown Fried Chicken, the Chinese joint a couple blocks from our middle school, PB&J sandwiches on a bench in Fort Tryon Park, hospital cafeterias, even the occasional fancy restaurant over the years. We ate Thai food and dozens of tiny donuts at her wedding reception going on two years ago now. Well, I did, and the other guests did; Mira had just gotten over being really sick then, pre-transplant, a horrible lung infection. I watched her; she only ate a few bites the entire night. So there are a couple things different about our meal tonight. But the important thing is that we are alive, and eating together. My best girl is smiling, she's laughing. There are so many dark forces that tried to keep us, her and me, from being here together tonight. But tonight, there is only light around us. I probably don't, but my girl has got angels.

After dinner, while washing the dishes I notice Andre's "world's most expensive blender" on the counter. "That a blender?" I ask her.

"Yep," she says. "In case I wanna blend food and put it into the tube."

"How do you feel about that?" I ask her, glancing at her over my shoulder as I scrub a spoon.

"Dunno." I see her shrug out of my peripheral vision. "Kinda stupid. Like, I can't actually taste food that goes into the tube. So how is there a difference between this stupid nutrition thing and, like, champagne and caviar?" She laughs. "But at the same time." Her voice wavers. I turn off the water and turn to her, to see her. She's gazing at nothing, eyes filled with tears. "Maybe there is a difference. Maybe it'll feel different, knowing

I get to put actual food in there, not a blend that comes in a fucking can. That even if I don't want to eat by mouth, or I can't, I can still eat the food everyone else is eating." She wipes her face. "Andre was just trying to give me options."

I nod, hard. "You got yourself a good egg, baby girl."

She laughs. "Don't I know it."

We decide to make vanilla milkshakes. Mira says she will try putting hers in the tube. I blend our shakes. She takes a video of the blender spinning and rumbling. She asks me to take another one with her phone as she feeds the shake to herself into her stomach with the tube. She sends them to Andre. He responds within minutes with an audio message. She lays her phone on the table and taps the little arrow to play his message.

"That is so great, baby!" he says. "Thank you for sending me that. I hope it goes okay. I hope everything's going okay. I love you, hummingbird. Say hi to Celi for me. Text me if you need anything. And try to get some sleep, okay?"

"Ah, *tan dulce*," I say.

Mira blushes, like the young girl she was when she first met Andre.

While we have our milkshakes, Mira turns out the lights and flicks on her rainbow color-changing electric candles, arranges crystals on the tabletop, and does a card pull for each of us. She has a new tarot deck I ain't never seen before, an erotic tarot with provocative imagery. She also has several pieces of raw clear quartz that look expensive, and a black obsidian pyramid that she sets in the center of the table.

"Paloma gave me these," she says, of the new things.

"Have you spoken to her?" I ask, playing with the corner of the card she pulled for me, the World. The image is of a glorious black woman in a pink dress made of stars, perched atop the world up in the clouds. The World symbolizes wholeness, completeness, the fulfillment of a journey and the immediate beginning of a new one.

Mira shakes her head. "I am not ready yet."

She sits up on the counter while I wash the milkshake glass and the pieces of the world's most powerful blender, in the otherworldly glow of her candles. In one way it seems like she might have gotten a second wind, a new burst of energy; but I know that she has to be exhausted. I finish the washing. She flushes her tube out with water.

I step closer to her. She spreads her legs to make room for me. Instantly my heart begins to pound. How far are we going to go, my best friend and

I? I still don't know. I only know her lips, a brand-new kind of knowledge, as I kiss her in the flashing rainbow-tinted darkness.

She puts her hand on my chest. "Is your woman gonna kill me for kissing her girl?"

I shake my head. "No. We ain't all process-y like your girl. But Skye and I did meet in a sex pod. So we have talked about it. She actually has a relationship kinda like ours."

"She does?"

I twirl a lock of Mira's hair around my finger. "Yeah. She came to New York from Detroit with a friend of hers. They probably would have been a whole thing but the friend was all confused about her sexuality when they were younger. In denial or some shit. Anyway, they finally hooked up a few years ago. They're still tight. They kiss sometimes. Have sex occasionally."

Mira's eyes search mine. "You okay with that, *nena?*"

I nod. "Totally. You know how I do, Mira. I never expect my lovers to drop everybody else just because I came along." I tuck the lock of hair over her perfect tiny golden seashell of an ear. "That ain't how love works in my world."

Her eyes grow shiny in the electric candlelight. "Have you been with anyone else? Since y'all got together?"

I shake my head. "Well. We did go to a sex party once. I kissed a girl. That's it. And now." I squeeze her hips gently. "I'm making out with the girl of my dreams. Waiting to see when I'm gonna wake up and realize this was all just a dream."

"It ain't a dream, Araceli," she says. "I'm real. I promise." She gives me a wry smile. "Now who am I in this scenario? The one who kept us from getting together because I was confused and in denial about my sexuality?"

I suck my teeth. "Nah, Miranda, c'mon. I dunno, girl." She turns my face back towards hers with her hand on my cheek. "*Tal vez nunca fue el momento correcto pa' nosotras.*"

"*Y ahora aquí estamos,*" she says.

"*Y ahora aquí estamos,*" I say.

"*¿Acuéstate conmigo?*" she asks.

"Of course," I say.

We get ready for bed together. We've done this before too, but tonight it's charged with an unmistakable new energy of desire and anticipation. In the bedroom, Mira takes off her clothes and changes in front of me. This we have done thousands of times in front of each other. And we've always looked, wondered, desired. But it's never made me tremble quite like this before, seeing her lush, perky tits with coconut nipples, her big silky bush that I've had dreams about. She puts on one of her tiny little nightgowns. It's the kind of thing that would be so easy to lift aside in bed, to slip my fingers between her legs and feel her, make her feel good. Is she up for that tonight? Am I?

I take off my T-shirt and get into bed with her in my leggings and soft bra. She turns off the bedside lamp and we find each other in the dark, for the first time, this thing I've longed to do every time I got into bed with my girl, smelling her almond-oil hair and wanting her. I pull her into my arms and she climbs on top of me. I almost die; her loose breasts graze my body, I can feel their warmth, their heaviness. We kiss until she's out of breath.

I wrap my arms around her, turn us over, lay her gently on her back on the bed. "Mira, honey," I say. "Don't push yourself. Your body's still recovering. Yeah?" I kiss her cheek, lie down next to her, both of us looking up at the ceiling. She nods, next to me. I say, "Kissing is all I really feel ready to do anyway. For tonight, at least."

"*Lo que quieras*, Araceli," she says. "All I want is for you to be happy. That's all I've ever wanted."

"Same," I say. She presses her lips to the side of my face.

"If we're doing this," I say, "we're taking it slow."

"*Dime que tenemos tiempo*," she whispers.

"*Claro que tenemos tiempo*, Mira," I tell her. "We have our whole lives. I am not going anywhere."

We're quiet for a few moments. Mira's hand creeps closer to me. She lays a gentle, tentative hand on my belly. I breathe into it. My whole skin feels electric.

"Okay if touch you like this?" she says. "Just here."

"Yeah," I whisper.

Her hand caresses the round rise of my stomach.

"Your belly is so beautiful," she tells me. "I've wanted to touch you here my entire life."

Tears come to my eyes. It occurs to me that, if we do this, if we really do this, a whole new universe will open up between us. I will get to know her in a whole new way, meet a side of her that I never have before.

We breathe together for a while longer. I hear her breath start to get ragged. I roll over.

"Mira. Are you okay?"

Her eyes are big in the dark. She shakes her head.

"I'm trying really hard not to be," she says. "But I'm in a shit ton of pain."

"Honey," I say. "You're safe. It's me. I got you." I touch her cheek with my knuckles. "What do you need, baby?"

"My pain meds. I don't want to need them, but I do. It's already so hard to sleep. So fucking hard with the tube; I'm trying to train myself not to sleep on my stomach." She sits up. I do too. "Maybe you could also bring my guitar? I'll play you a song. It'll make me sleepy. Right now I'm too excited to sleep."

I bring Miranda's pain medication and a glass of water and her guitar and a pink guitar pick. She takes a pill and a long sip of water. She crosses her legs and places the guitar gingerly in her lap, careful not to let it press against the G-tube. I watch her tune the instrument, tilting her head to listen to its voice, twisting the little knobs at the top of the neck. On the long, long, long list of shit that I know nothing about is musical instruments. I do know, though, that Mira is a fucking incredible musician.

She plays a song I have never heard before. It's a strange one, y'all. It's all raspy and yell-y with an even, hypnotic cadence, punctuated with sudden screams. The lyrics are poetic and twisty. I have to close my eyes and listen hard to follow the thread of the song; I can tell it has a story, but at first I can't puzzle it out. The song is about how all life is interconnected. At one point I think it might be a mother singing to her children. Then I think it's about deep time; about emerging from the depths of the ocean. Mira's voice gives me shivers.

She plays it once, then twice when I ask if she can play it for me again. Finally I open my eyes and say, "What was that?"

She smiles and plays the original song for me on Spotify. It's called "Oceania," by Björk, some white chick I've never heard of before. My third time listening, the mystery finally unlocks: sung from the perspective of ocean, it's about how all living beings emerged from its salty depths.

"It's an etiological myth about why our sweat is salty," I say, as excited as I used to get in class at NYU when I knew the right answer to some philosophical puzzle when no one else did, not the prep-school girls and boys, not the children of British lords and Saudi princes—just me, Celi Henriquez, a girl from nowhere and nobody. I was smart, I realized.

My best friend laughs. "I'm so glad I lived long enough to hear you say that sentence, Araceli," she says. "That right there is worth the price of admission."

I brush off my shoulders. "Glad I could make it worth your while."

"When you talk like that it makes me want to fuck you so bad," she says.

"Um," I say. "Okay, girl. Wow."

She flutters her lashes. "Too much?"

"Not at all," I say. "I mean. Just please go slow with me, tigress. Be gentle with me."

"Of course, *nena*," she says. "I love you."

"I love you too. And I love this song. It ain't like most white-people songs."

She laughs. "I had a dream about while I was in the hospital," she says. "I heard it in my dream. While stingrays were flying in the sky."

"Of course you did," I say. "My little witch."

We pee one last time and go back to bed. I lie awake. I know I won't sleep until Mira is sleeping next to me. I listen for the gradual deepening of her sweet breath. She is so loved that her husband and her brother gave her their lungs to put in there. I love her so much it could shatter me. I don't wanna leave her tomorrow. I want to marry her instead, or marry her also, or whatever—who cares how it happens, I just need that to move from my fantasies to my present—and stay here with her forever.

As I lie there, though, I find myself also dreaming of our apartment on the Upper West, Skye and me. I think of sunset over New York on the balcony, our glasses of very, very cheap wine. I think of the savings account we opened together. We put at least five dollars a month each into it. This girl has never had a savings account before. When we get enough money in there, Skye is gonna rent a car and we are going to drive all the way down the coast to Miami. Skye's mom took her there once, the only vacation they ever took when she was a kid; she wants to take me to the beach, to eat *ropa vieja* in Little Havana. I've never been to Florida before. There are so fucking many places I have never been. I think of our bed, how Skye creates experiences there, just for me: with her strap-on, with silk ropes tied around my ankles and wrists, with massage oil and her strong hands when I have been a very good girl. I love our spicy-sweet, kinky sex. I love giggling together as we try to be quiet in our crowded but very safe home.

For years I'd linger as long as I possibly could wherever Miranda was. I did not want to go back home. It wasn't home; it was a site of pain, a place to escape. I'm realizing that home is now someplace I want to go back to, someplace I long for. I think about the World card Miranda drew for me, its paradox, its push and pull, its cycle of fulfillment and starting again. This doesn't mean I love the girl breathing deep next to me any less, not even a fraction less. I want her just as bad. It's just that my life expanded. The spell she cast for me, for a happy ending, came true. I ain't as good of a witch as her. But I send my intention into the world. What do I need to do, what kinda spell do I need to cast, so that she gets hers too?

I remember a discussion we had in an existential philosophy class once, in my sophomore year. I loved those debates, I felt so awake, I felt so present, I felt so clicked into place, like this improbable philosopher girl had finally landed exactly where she belonged. In this particular class, we debated the question of whether anything lasts forever. Can anything last forever? For all of our discussing, we never came up with an answer.

Now, the rest of it is a hard, hard night, y'all.

Mira wakes up in the middle of the night, sick. I'm only sleeping lightly next to her—my mind and body do not allow me to sleep deeply, not when I'm the only one Mira can count on right now if anything happens to her. So I wake up when she does, stirring in bed.

"You okay, *mami*?" I whisper to her.

"Araceli," she whispers back. "*No me siento bien*." Her hand cradles her stomach. "I think I'm gonna throw up."

I help Mira to the bathroom, where, for the next two and a half hours, she's violently sick. She vomits, over and over again, until nothing's coming up but bile. She shits. Eventually, she's shitting and throwing up at the same time, while I hold the tiny trash can that usually sits next to their toilet up to her mouth.

During one of her brief periods of calm, both of us sitting huddled on the bathroom floor, she says, "You can just leave me here to die, Araceli."

"Miranda. *No seas ridícula*."

"No. Really. Just go on without me. I can't continue." She drops her head on my shoulder.

"Are you too sick for me to spank you, little girl?"

She laughs. Then she clutches her stomach. "Oh, fuck. I think I'm gonna throw up again."

She throws up till her stomach muscles ache. I get a washcloth and wet it with warm water and wipe her face. I can't think of anything else to do to help her feel better. "Do you want me to call Andre, baby?" I ask her.

"If I'm too gross for you to stay with," she says, *"te puedes ir."* She starts to cry. "I would understand."

"Mira. Oh, my God, Miranda, no." I pull her into my arms. "You are not too gross."

"Yes, I am," she sobs. "I'm disgusting and I'm gross and no one's ever going to love me again."

"Mira. Wow. You are fishing for compliments so hard right now, *bebecita.*"

"Stop it!" she wails. "I am gross. *Debes irte.*"

"I am not going anywhere. And you are not gross."

I kiss her on the mouth, hard.

She pulls back, smiling. "Eww," she says.

"Be quiet," I say.

"Celi." She looks at me with scared eyes. "My stomach hurts."

"Honey." I stroke her hair. "Should I, like, call your doctors? Should we, like, go to the hospital or something?"

"No!" she screams, so loud I jump. She seems so weak right now, I'm shocked she can make that kinda noise. "No." The tears stream harder, faster. "No. No. I don't want to go back to the hospital. No." She clings to me. "Araceli. Please don't make me go."

"Baby girl. *¿Estás segura?*"

"Yes. I mean, no. I mean, please, Celi, please don't make me go. Please."

"It's okay, Mira. It's okay, honey."

"Please don't make me go, Celi. I'll do anything. Please."

"I'd never make you do anything you don't wanna do, baby." She presses her face into my chest. I hold her as tight as I dare. "I'm just worried about your stomach, honey."

She pulls back to look at me. "It'll be okay," she says. "I just need to stop shitting and throwing up. And go back to sleep. I just need to be in my own bed, okay? Don't call anyone. No doctors. No hospital."

"All right, *mama.*"

It's my worst nightmare, y'all. And it ain't because she's "gross"—don't let her make you think that shit, okay? She isn't gross. She's my girl and I love her. It's because she's sick and she's stuck here alone with me, the most clueless person on the planet. I have never taken care of anyone before. I have no idea what to do. I'm so scared I'm gonna fuck this up that I'm shaking inside. Am I gonna do the wrong thing? Am I gonna hurt her? Is something gonna happen to her because I have no clue what the fuck I'm doing?

I stay with her till it seems like her stomach is calm enough for her to go back to bed. I take her there, practically carrying her. I ask her what she needs. "I should probably drink some water," she says, so tired she can barely speak. I bring her some water and hold the glass to her lips while she drinks it.

"Do you think you can sleep, *colibrí*? I think you need some sleep."

She nods.

We get under the blankets, try to sleep. She's naked now, her nightgown long since abandoned on the bathroom floor, and she's trembling and crying. I ease her into my arms, hoping that my touch will comfort her. She cries, soaking the cups of my bra. I hold her until she cries herself to exhaustion and falls asleep. The sky is lightening now with the first deep blue fingers of dawn.

I wake up what feels like three seconds later to the sound of her moaning. Instantly alert, I turn over to find Mira trying to sleep on her stomach. I give her a push as gently as I can back onto her back.

She wakes up. "Oh, fuck, I was trying to sleep on the tube, wasn't I?" she mumbles.

I nod and give her another little nudge.

"Ow," she says, and turns over. She starts to cry again. My heart sinks. If this girl cries any more, I am legit scared that she is going to break something.

"Araceli," she says, turning those big, wet eyes on me. "*Estoy harta de dormir así.* I'm tired of this tube already."

"I know. I'm so sorry, baby." What am I supposed to say to that? Is that the right thing to say?

"Celi." She closes her eyes. "How much longer do you think this is going to last?"

"What, baby? The tube? I—"

"No, Celi baby, not the tube." She opens her eyes, looks at me. "Maybe I'm tryna fool myself. But I already know about the tube. I already know I'll have to wear it for the rest of my life. I mean my life. How much longer do you think all this is going to last?" She looks away. "I'm really tired already. How much longer do you think I'll have to be alive?"

I open my mouth but no words come out. I'm past the edge of my experience here, long past the point where I know what to say to fix this, to make it better. I'm kinda guessing, actually, that nothing I could say could possibly make this shit better.

So I turn and curl into her. I tuck myself to her side and hold her gently, one arm banded under her breasts. She hugs my arm, clutches it. Slowly, again, her breathing evens out, and she falls asleep. It's almost morning now. It's the first night we've ever spent together, just me and her with no one else around—not Andre, not her family, not somebody's roommate in the NYU dorm room I used to occasionally crash—and it sucked horribly. But it was also amazing. And best of all, we survived it.

When I wake up the next morning, Mira is gone. She's not next to me in the bed. I sit, but then I hear that new song by Rauw Alejandro and Selena Gomez playing from the other room, at a very low volume, Miranda singing along softly in her perfect voice. I flop back down. She's okay.

I force myself outta bed. In the bathroom, I pee and brush my teeth and splash some water on my face. Yep, your girl looks about as rough as she feels. I pull my T-shirt back over my head, slip my phone into the side pocket on my leggings, and go find her in the kitchen.

If you didn't know what all happened last night, you'd think nothing happened to my girl Mira at all. She's sipping tea and eating toast with butter. She's reading something on her phone and combing her wet hair at the same time. She's wearing a T-shirt from Harlem Renaissance Ballet, Auntie Lisette's school, and pink leggings, and she smells like vanilla. She must have gotten up early and showered and washed her hair and made breakfast.

"Hey," she says, putting down her comb and her phone. "Morning."

"Morning," I say.

"How are you?" she asks. "Want some toast?"

I sit down at the table with her and take the other slice of toast off her plate.

"I'm okay," I say, through a mouthful of toast. "How are you?" Up close, I can see that her eyes are puffy and red, physical evidence that last night really did happen.

She shrugs. "I'm okay. Celi, listen." She sighs, plays with the handle of her mug. "I'm really sorry about last night."

I shake my head. "Nothing for you to be sorry about, baby."

"No," she says, emphatically. "I just want you to know. I didn't really mean all that stuff I said last night. Or, like, I did mean it in the moment. I felt awful. I was so tired. I still am tired. But it doesn't mean I don't want to be alive anymore." She shakes her head. "I definitely still want to be alive. I was just tired. And really, really sick. And saying how I felt out of that. So. I'm really sorry for what I said."

"Miranda," I say. "You really don't have to apologize with me. You're safe with me. Safe to tell me however you feel."

"Thank you," she says. "I want you to feel safe with me too, Celi."

I almost laugh. She's been my safe place for almost my entire life. "I do feel safe with you."

She nods.

"Are you feeling better?" I ask.

"Yes, a lot better," she says. "Do you want some tea? Let me make you some tea."

"You don't have to—"

"Please don't treat me like I'm broken," she says, standing up. "Let me make you some fucking tea."

"All right, *mi reina.*"

Mira makes tea, one of her witchy blends that tastes like an enchanted garden. We drink and toast more toast and wash some strawberries from the fridge and eat them. She looks at her phone. I look at mine. I have about fifty trillion text messages from Skye. I show Mira a picture she sent me, of some early spring flowers she saw on her morning walk around our neighborhood.

"Oh, my God, Celi," Mira says, "that is so sweet." She nudges me. "Go home to your girl."

I put down my phone. "I thought Andre wasn't coming back until the afternoon."

"He isn't," she says. "But I'm seeing the look on your face when you just look at her messages." She turns off the music that's been playing quietly in the background. "I think you should go home to your girl."

I finish my slice of toast. "Will you be okay alone?"

"That's just it, Celi." She spears me with a look. "I haven't been alone at home. Not for more than five minutes when Andre took a walk or went to the corner store. He hasn't left me alone. At all. I haven't been on my own." Her eyes get wet, but she fiercely blinks the tears away. "I'm scared. Terrified. Of being on my own. With the tube. With my… my lungs, honestly, since my body tried to reject them." She wipes her face. "But I can't. I can't never be alone again. Right? So I need to practice. I need you to go home to Skye. And I need to practice staying here, by myself, till Andre comes home."

I look back at her. "Are you sure that's what you need?"

She nods. "I'm very sure. I'm scared, but I'm sure. If I'm gonna keep doing this, which I am, I have to get stronger. I have to."

"You can text me or call me if you need anything," I say. "I don't work until late this afternoon. I can come back."

"I'll be okay," she says.

So I get ready to leave. I brush my teeth and poop and take a shower and wash my hair. Mira hangs out with me in the bathroom the entire time. My heart starts to hurt. I am going to miss her. I am going to worry about her. Is she going to be all right? She sits on the bed while I get dressed and put on one of my wigs, a bouncy bright pink bob. I don't let nobody except my closest people see my real hair.

Mira comes and embraces me from behind. I look at the two of us in the mirror. So does she. She turns my face towards her and kisses me. I turn in her embrace so I can hold her, kiss her properly.

"I don't want to be finished with this," I tell her, breathless and feeling a little undone when we pull back.

She shakes her head, slowly. "We are so not finished with this, Araceli," she says. "We're just getting started. I think you're wise." She squeezes my hips. "Let's take this slow."

"Are you gonna tell Andre?"

"Yeah. You know he and I don't keep secrets from each other." She rolls her eyes. "Well, I don't." She sighs. "Are you gonna tell Skye?"

"Yes," I say. "We've talked about this kinda thing. A bit. We're cool with it."

"*Bien de bien*," she says. She looks at me till her face changes, becomes more serious. How do I even explain this? Mira and I have been best friends since we were four years old, when we did a puzzle together on our very first day of school. But we've never had the kind of friendship where we can read each other's thoughts, where I know what she is thinking. Maybe because of Mira's witchiness, or because of all the differences separating us, or maybe because of the erotic energy that has pulsed between us like an electric cloud, there has always been some part of her that has been essentially unknowable to me. I wonder if she will become more known to me, or only deeper and with more layers, if we continue this new part of our relationship.

"I'm really gonna miss you, Celi," she says finally.

"Me too." I cup her cheek in my hand, stroke her skin with my thumb. "We have time," I remind her.

"We do have time," she says.

I leave her with a kiss at the door, but I do not go home to Skye. If I did, I could entice her to take a nap with me, we could cuddle and drift off together in our bed for a couple of hours; neither of us has to be at work today till the late afternoon. Since I slept for about five seconds last night, that sounds like a fucking amazing idea. But I decide not to do that. Instead, I give Andre a call.

"Celi, hi," he says. "Is Mira okay?"

"Yes, she's okay, I'm sorry."

"It's fine," he says. "She just texted me. Saying she wants to spend some time on her own. So she's okay, right?"

"Yeah, she's okay. It's just—could I talk to you, Dre? Like, in person?"

"Sure," he says, real easy, like he says most things. "You sure everything is okay?"

"Yep," I say. "I just—I want to talk to you in person. 'Kay?"

"Okay," he says.

"Okay. So can we meet someplace? I don't gotta work till later, so I could meet you. Where you at, bro?"

"I was just gonna head to my favorite coffee spot," he says. "It's near Columbia, so not too far away. But I could also skip it and meet you someplace closer? Where are you and Skye now? Eighty-something?"

"No, don't skip it, baby," I say, already heading for the 1 train. "Columbia's perfect. I'll come meet you there right now."

"I'll text you the address," he says, and sure enough, my phone pings while I'm holding it. Gotta love a man who does exactly what he says he's gonna do.

Half an hour later, I'm walking through the sparkling clean glass door of the coffee shop, slipping my mask on. Indoor dining just reopened last month, around the time Mira got sick, and the bougie Columbia folks are taking full advantage of that this Saturday morning: every single table in this place is occupied. Andre waves me over to his tiny round table for two.

"Hey," I say, peeling off my mask.

"Hey, Araceli," he says. He glances up at my head. "Cool wig."

"Thanks," I say. "Cool hat."

It's a little chilly inside the coffee place, and he's wearing a multicolored knit winter beanie on his very bald brown head. I keep my hoodie on, tug it close to myself. He says thanks.

He wraps his hands around his coffee cup. It's definitely one of those fancy, expensive, dark and rich coffees that comes from, like, Ethiopia and takes ten minutes to order because it has a lot of adjectives. "Tell me what you want," he says. "I'll go get it for you."

I shake my head. "No. You don't have to get me nothing, Dre. Ain't this one of them places where everything costs at least ten dollars?"

"Yeah, it is a bit expensive," he says. The corners of his mouth turn down. "My mom gave me a hundred bucks. I already put it into our account. Then Mira texts me and says, *go get the expensive-ass coffee.*"

I smile. "She tryna get rid of you for a couple more hours."

"I understand that she needs to feel comfortable staying on her own," he says. There's a big *but* there, but he doesn't say, it, 'cause he's a good guy. "All right, come on. What do you want?"

"I don't want nothing, Andre. I came here to talk to you. Not to drink all your mom's money away on overpriced coffee."

"Am I a piece of shit?" he asks. "Taking my mommy's money and spending it on overpriced coffee?"

I laugh, though I probably shouldn't, I think he's being all vulnerable and shit. "Andre, come on. You're twenty-three years old. You're supposed to take your parents' money." He looks even worse then, so I suck my teeth and say, "Come on. If I had a mom, I would totally let her give me money, dude."

He tilts his head. "Let me get you something, Araceli."

I sigh, take my phone out my pocket and Google their menu. "Get me a matcha latte," I say.

"Hot or iced?" he asks while getting up.

"Iced, please. Thank you."

"Don't thank me," he says. "Thank my mother."

While Andre gets my ten-dollar matcha latte, I scroll Instagram and glance around the coffee shop. It's all pretentious and minimalist, everything—tables, chairs, ceilings, walls—made out of wood. There are fancy coffee contraptions everywhere. Your girl Araceli will definitely never come to this place again.

He comes back with my iced matcha latte, which tastes like milk and grass. "All right," I say. "I need to talk to you."

He puts his phone on the table. "Mira texted me," he says. "You two kissed?"

My face gets tight and hot, then tingly and cold. I knew he'd find out, I even suspected we would talk about it—ugh: talking about shit—but none of that could prepare me for the reality of actually having to talk about this shit, and literally hours after it happened. All right, so hear me out, y'all: we figured out so many inventions as a human race, when we gonna invent something that has complicated emotional processing conversations for us? I'm gunning for that.

"Yeah," I say. I put my phone on the table too. "We did. You cool with that?" I sigh, looking at his good boy face. Andre is a brother, I guess. He a cool guy. He's my friend and my best friend's husband. But he ain't like me. And he never will be. Andre and me inhabit two different worlds: parallel but separate. "I mean." I sigh again. "Are you all right? Are you, like, okay with this?"

His face softens into a small smile. "I hope neither of you is gonna front like this was a surprise," he says. "I always thought you would hook up someday. The surprise is that it took this long. There's been sexual tension between you two since, like, day one, hasn't there?"

I spin my cup between my hands, watching the ice bob, rotating in the pale green liquid. I take a sip. I don't not like processing shit because I don't have emotions, okay? It's because I have too many. And letting them out reduces me to a trembling mess. And for most of my life, in most of the places that I've been, it hasn't been safe for me to get vulnerable like that.

"I've always loved Miranda," I say. "And I always will."

"I know," he says. "Me too. So I just want her to be happy."

"Just want you to know," I say, glancing up at him. "I don't do cis-boy fantasy shit. I'm a old-school sapphic. I don't perform my love for guys. So I will never be down for you watching us or nothing like that. If we even get to that; we taking it slow. I ain't up for a threesome neither. I'm not into masc people. Please don't even ask me for no details. I ain't here to feed your fantasies."

"Araceli." He opens his mouth, closes it, opens it again. "I wasn't—I didn't—I mean, I don't—"

"Yeah, baby, I know you don't," I say. "Just wanted to make myself clear. And yes. I know I'm a bitch."

"You're not." He smiles again. "Araceli, you're not. You're protecting what's happening between you and Mira. I get that. I respect that."

"And I also just want her to be happy," I say. "So I need to talk to you about some stuff. About her health."

"All right." He nods. "Is she okay?"

"I mean, yes. I think so. I just feel I need to share this with you. And be honest." I take a deep breath. I focus on his eyes, which are all steady and warm and deep. If Mira had to get married and build a life with someone who isn't me, I'm glad it's this dude, out of all possible human beings. "She wasn't feeling well last night, Dre. She woke up in the middle of the night, all sick. I got up with her and I was trying to, like, help her. Eventually she seemed like she was okay, so we went back to bed and started falling asleep. But then, she was like…"

Fuck, I hate crying in public. I bend my head, letting my bright pink wig cover my face, falling into my eyes. I do everything I can inside to try to keep these tears back.

Andre's fingers nudge mine on the tabletop. "This okay?" he says.

I nod.

He takes my hand, squeezes it, hard.

"Fuck, Andre." I tilt my head back. "Like I thought I was okay with this. Like, legit. Or not okay with it. But like I could handle it. Mira told me this thing, and then she was all, *I'm sorry, I don't wanna burden you, I want you to feel safe with me.* And me, I'm all like, oh, it's fine. And when I was with her, I did feel okay. Because I wanted to be there for her. I wanted to be her safe place. But, Andre…" Despite all my best efforts, a couple quick tears escape. I dash them away with a napkin with my free hand. "*Fue muy duro.* What she told me."

"It's okay, Celi," he says. He allows a half-smile. "Or, no, it's not okay. This is hard. And it's okay that it isn't okay."

I let a few more tears go—gratitude, this time, because my perfect, perfect girl got herself such a good egg. "Well. She'd been like really sick but then she was feeling better. So we went back to bed and tried to go to sleep. Then she looked over at me and said, 'Celi, how much longer do you think this is going to last?' And I thought she was talking about the feeding tube. So I'm all like, 'Uh, I dunno.' And she was like… 'No, I don't mean the tube. I mean my life. How long do you think my life is gonna last? I'm really tired already. How much longer do you think I'll have to be alive?' Yeah. That's what she said. And me, I didn't know what the fuck to say. Honestly I didn't think there was anything I could say. So I just, like, hugged her. And…"

Andre doesn't say anything, just looks at me and keeps holding my hand. So I continue.

I take a deep, heaving breath. "So that happened. Last night. And I'm sorry for telling you. If I'm, like, betraying her confidence. I never wanna do that. I just thought that… you should know. That someone should know. In case she needs, like… help? So. Am I already fucking up this whole entire thing?"

Andre lifts my hand, squeezes it in between both of his for a second, then lets it go. "There's nothing for you to be sorry about, Celi," he says. "This is hard. Like we said. And the only really important thing is that Mira's okay. Like we also said. So we're figuring it out." He shrugs, looks away for a second. "I mean. I'm no expert. But I'm pretty sure that, if she says something that scares you or makes you cry, the right thing to do is talk to someone about it. In case she does need help and there's something we can do for her. But also… for you." He focuses on me again. "It's really, really hard to hear shit like that."

I look down at my half-empty tea cup, miserably. "Has she…" I swallow. "Does she say stuff like that to you? Sometimes?"

"She has said stuff like that before," he says. "Yeah. Not very often. Only a handful of times ever, I'd say. And it's only when she's really sick. And tired. I try to understand. The daily management… I know I can't, not really, but I try to understand. So, yeah, sometimes. When it gets to be a lot. She sometimes talks about being too tired to keep doing this forever. She says she wants to keep doing it, she loves her life, she loves… our life." His voice breaks here. "But sometimes she says she's exhausted and she doesn't know how long she can keep doing it. And this was a lot, Celi. It was so much. The pregnancy, the surgery. The lung rejection and the infection. She had to go on oxygen and she hated that. Thought she might be past that. They're worried about the possibility of CF diabetes. She's worried about taking on more daily management for that. And the G-tube…" He releases a pent-up breath, lifts his arms, cradling the back of his head in his joined hands. "It's a lot. I try to be understanding when she expresses those feelings. Of being tired. Of feeling overwhelmed."

"Okay," I whisper. I reach up and squeeze his arm. He drops them, places his hands on the table again. "Do you think she's actually, like… suicidal?" I wish I weren't scared of saying the word. I wish I knew more. I wish I knew the difference between "actually suicidal" and "expressing feelings of exhaustion and overwhelm related to the daily management of a chronic, complex illness." Is there a difference? How the fuck would I know?

But Andre, who at least has years more experience than me facing this with Mira on an intimate, daily basis, shakes his head. "I don't think so, Celi," he says. "We've talked about it. When she's feeling stronger and more rested, she always says very clearly that she isn't suicidal. That she loves her life and wants to keep doing it. Mira has been living with this since she was five years old. No one knows better than her how she feels and what she needs. I'm here to trust her. And to support her."

"Though she be but little, she is fierce," I whisper.

He smiles. "Exactly," he says.

"Yeah. Right. But still." I nudge his arm. "I don't wanna, like, minimize what she's going through. The bigness of it. Let's be real. Do you think she has the support she needs right now? Like I know that I have no idea how to be all the support Mira needs right now. Do you think she's getting that?"

"I don't know," he admits. "Probably not."

I pick up my phone. I have no clue what I think I'm going to do with it, but I'm a girl in 2021; my phone is my number-one weapon against everything in the world. "Has she been talking to her therapist? Maya?"

He shakes his head. "Not since she got home. I asked her about it. She said she's not ready. She'll reach out to her when she is."

"Have things been going okay with her?"

"With Maya? I think so. She loves Maya."

"Maybe we can gently encourage her," I suggest. "To talk to Maya."

"She did talk with the counselor at the hospital," he says. "She said she didn't want to, but it did help."

I nod. "Does Mira have any CF friends who live with a feeding tube?"

"Not any close ones, no," he says.

I turn my phone on. Still don't know what I'm going to do with it, but it's here: a link to the outside world, people out there who can help our girl in ways that we cannot. "Maybe we could find some," I say. It makes me a little scared, just saying it, but for her, I am willing to try. "We could help in ways that we can. We can find resources for her. Then we can leave it up to her if she wants to reach out to them or not."

He nods. "It has to be her decision. She knows what's right for her."

"Of course," I say. "We both trust her." I scroll through the notifications on my phone, looking for what, I don't know. "And," I say. "I don't know if this is, like, a thing. But is there someone she could talk to about the… ectopic pregnancy? I don't know shit. But I'm a little scared that's getting, like… lost in the shuffle." I put my phone down and focus on him, though it ain't easy. "Everyone's talking a lot about the feeding tube. And maybe that's where she needs to be right now. 'Cause I dunno jack shit about a feeding tube, but if she's gonna need it forever—oh, she said that too, by the way, that she believes she'll be living with it forever—then that's gotta be a big-ass deal. But." I swallow. I don't want to, I want to laugh or drink or make sick jokes, but I stay in the moment because I am a strong and classy-ass bitch, and I show up for my people. I look into his eyes. "Pregnancy loss is a big deal. A big fucking deal."

He nods. He looks really tired. "Yeah," he says. "It is."

"So do you think there's, like, a person?" There I go again, picking up and fiddling with my phone like it's gonna come to life and solve all our problems. "Is there someone she can talk to who specializes in this kinda shit? Like, someone she don't have to explain that an ectopic pregnancy that's threatening her life ain't a baby. Someone who already gets it. You know what I'm saying?"

"I think so," he says. "Someone she can talk to who's pro-choice and pro-abortion and pro-pregnant-person's-rights. Who understands the context. Who knows about pregnancy loss."

"Right," I say. "That. Exactly, that." I nudge him. "You know anybody like that?"

He laughs. "No. But we can try to find somebody. Then, like you said, we gently put it in front of Mira. Then she decides."

"Then she decides." I nod. I squeeze my phone, unaccountably excited. "Oh. Shit. Andre, I'm gonna text Marco. He's premed. He do, like, internships and shit." I turn on my phone. "He knows medical people. Don't he? Yeah. He does. I'm gonna text him. And ask him. If he knows any people."

Andre nods. "That's a good idea. Marco is premed. He might know some good people." He watches me open my text thread with Marco and start texting. We don't talk much—now that he's with Hassan, and I'm with Skye, and we're both with really good people, we don't hook up just for comfort no more, but that was definitely a thing for a long-ass while— but for Mira's health y'all can bet your ass that I will text my ex. "He got into med school, you know," Andre says.

I look up. "Did he? Nah, I didn't know. That's cool. Congrats, Dr. Marco." I send off the text. "May your savior complex serve you and your future patients well." Andre chuckles. "Where did he get in?"

He shrugs. "I'm not sure."

And that's enough about my ex for one day, folks. I put my phone down, facedown this time.

"I'll start looking on some of the CF forums and blogs and CF YouTube," Andre says. "I've talked to some really cool people on there. Both CF-ers and their family members and partners. I think I can give Mira some options of people to talk to."

I nod, hard. I remember what Mira said yesterday, about having options. "Yes, that's what we'll do," I say. "Give her options."

"Then she decides."

"Then she decides." I drink the last sip of my matcha latte. Yep, I will never be spending ten dollars on this shit again. Mira's tea is better anyway. "Andre…" I tug on the ends of my hair. I look around the café. When does talking about vulnerable shit ever get easier? Never, I bet, just to make this whole human experience that much more fucking delightful. "Okay. So. Last night Mira says those things. This morning she's all like, *I didn't mean them. I was just tired and sick.* Oh, wait, did I tell you? She was all throwing up and stuff. Having, like, diarrhea."

He nods. "She told me. This happens sometimes. It's a thing. She's okay. She gets it out of her system and gets some sleep and she's usually better after that."

"Wait, really? You sure? I was so fucking worried, Dre. I was all like, should we take you to the hospital?"

"And she was all like, *no, I'm fine, no hospital, no doctors, please?*"

"Yes," I say. "Exactly. But you don't think she actually needed to go, did she?"

"No," he says. He allows a small shrug. "Mira has spent a lot of her life in hospitals. Sometimes we make that calculus. Like, is this something we can treat at home? Is this a situation where we can call her care team and they can talk me through something? Or is this serious enough to pull her out of the flow of her life, where she's been feeling better, and take her back to the hospital and that whole life?" He touches my hand gently. "You know?"

I gaze at him, like I'm seeing him for the first time. I've known Andre a long-ass time, okay. I know every muscle and every inch of his male ballet dancer's body. We danced together for more than a decade. He's lifted me and thrown me in the actual air and caught me again, in front of a whole audience. We danced salsa once for a show, I was maybe fifteen so he was sixteen, and every time we rehearsed, he would get an erection, because the choreo had us rubbing our bodies all up on each other. (It ain't sexual, okay, y'all? Dance is just really physical. It's just bodies.) So I've literally had this dude's penis on me, like, multiple times. But I kiss his girl, like, once, and now it's like a whole new chapter's opening between us.

"Wow," I say. "Thank you for sharing that with me. I definitely get that."

He nods.

"Okay. So. We have this truly awful night. She wakes up. Early. I find her in the kitchen. Eating breakfast. By mouth. Doing shit on her phone. And this girl is acting like ain't nothing happened. She apologizes and explains about what she said. Then, like, twelve seconds later, she is practically kicking my black ass out the door." Andre laughs; I nudge him. "*Dime la verdad*, Dre. Do you think she all right? Do you think she didn't feel good and she was just tryna get rid of me?"

"Araceli." He twists his mouth, and you can just see it, how this nice guy is tryna figure out how to tell me something he think I ain't gonna like. "Could I ask you a question? If you don't wanna answer, you don't have to."

I scoff. "Course I don't, not if I don't want to."

"Right," he says. "All right. Listen. The... kissing and stuff you did. Was that all last night? Like, before Mira felt sick?"

I nod. "There was no 'and stuff,' though, okay? We did not hook up. I am taking things slow with her."

"Okay," he says. "Well, when you kissed. Was that last night?"

"Before she got sick, yeah," I say.

"Then she got sick?"

"Yes. We went to bed, we made out a little, we fell asleep because I am not ready to do anything more than that with her yet. Then she woke up and she was sick. I helped her. Next morning, she kicking my ass out. Now I ain't tryna take it personally. If Mira wants time alone, she should have it. I'm down. I just. I wanna make sure she's okay. You know?"

"I know," he says. "Okay. Celi. Listen."

I nod. "Listening."

"It's okay that I tell you this?"

I roll my eyes. "How am I supposed to know when I don't even know what it is yet?"

He sighs. "Okay. Here it is. Mira does this sometimes."

"Does what?"

"She gets close to someone, she pushes them away."

"Oh," I say. I feel my shoulders lower. "Okay."

"I might be overstepping here. And I'm sorry. I only think I know this 'cause she's told me before. With her illness, she wonders how many people she should be getting this close to."

"Because she's going to hurt them."

"She thinks she's going to hurt them," he says. "She does it to me. Still. But we've been together so long we're able to talk about it honestly. We'll, like… share something really vulnerable. She pulls away. She says something about her dying. And I am not good with that, Celi, okay." He rubs his hand over his face. "It sounds like you were awesome last night. Listening to her, not trying to find something to say to make it better. I think that's such a healthy, and supportive, response. Me, I just get upset and find it really hard to listen to her. Not when she talks about suicidal thoughts. I mean when she talks about her illness taking her. Someday. 'How this story ends,' she calls it. Leaving me behind." His eyes get wet. "I wish I were better. At being there for her like that. And I'm working on it. For her. But it's really hard for me."

"Shit. Baby," I say.

"Yeah," he says. "She does it with me. After our entire lives together. She did it with Paloma. Paloma wanted to, like, make things official, I guess. Be each other's girlfriends. Mira told me she had this whole conversation with her. About CF, about 'how this story ends.' About how she doesn't know if she should be forming more connections with people that she will have to leave behind."

I swallow. "What did Miss Paloma say?"

He smiles a little at this. "Miss Paloma took it like a champ, I guess. She said she's in love with Mira and what they have is worth it and she wants to be together."

I shrug. "All right."

"Tell me to fuck off if I'm overstepping," he says—and, duh, obviously—"but I don't think Mira has spoken to Paloma since this all happened? It's probably none of my business and I'm being a dick. Fuck if I know how to… poly. I don't talk to Paloma like I talk to you. We're really more dance colleagues than friends. But I just feel like… Mira's holding Paloma at arm's length right now? More than usual, I mean."

I laugh. "Course she is, bro," I say. "Miss Paloma is… different." And she is. If Andre and I are different people living different lives, Paloma and I are two different species, living on two separate planets.

"She is? Can I ask… how?"

I shrug. "How not, bro? She's older. She's, like, a real adult and shit. She front like she 'part of the community,' like your mama would say, but Paloma is an Oreo."

"Araceli," Andre says.

"No. Do not full-name me, brother. Paloma be swanning around this world with all her long hair and all her money. Come on." I suck my teeth. "Boy. You know. She Miss Paloma."

"All right," he says finally. "I think I get what you're saying, Araceli."

"You know you get what I'm saying, Andre. So there's all that. Plus she new. You and me, and Marco, we're Miranda's OGs. We got her back. We hold her down. We always have, and we always will. You know me. You know I don't trust nobody. I think it's good if Mira chooses to take it slow with Paloma. Hell, with me. With anyone. This world is mad ugly, Andre. You can choose to be in it. But me, I think you should also choose to take care of yourself."

He nods. "Boundaries," he says.

I laugh. "If you want the white-people definition, then yes. Boundaries."

"Boundaries are important," he intones, like any one of a million white-people wellness influencers on Instagram.

I let myself laugh, then I sigh, long and hard. "Andre. My brother. Do you think we're doing the right thing? I love her. I don't wanna do her wrong. Ever. Do you think we're doing the right thing?"

"Celi, I don't have any answers." He spreads his palms, showing me his hands are empty. "I don't know jack shit. I just got lucky and met the best woman ever. I've loved Mira my entire life. I try to do good for her. There's no guidebook for this. No textbook."

I laugh. "And you know who wrote all them textbooks anyway."

He nods. "White people. And you know me. I'm just trying to live my life as far away as possible from white failurism and all its hatred and fear. So how do I love her and help her take care of herself and get us both closer to happiness in a way that's not fear-based or white-failurist or patriarchal or capitalist? Like, how can we do that in community?" He laughs. "Wow. I'm sounding like my mom. I'm sorry."

"Nah, babe," I say. "I mean, ain't nobody perfect. But I bet your mom taught you some good shit."

He nods. "I mean, maybe one or two good shits."

I laugh.

"So I don't know anything," he says. "So I figure I'm going to make mistakes. And say the wrong thing. And fuck up sometimes. And it's gonna be really imperfect. And hard. Because no one has ever done this before. Because we're making it up as we go along. But together." He squeezes my hand again. "I love you, Araceli. I'm sorry if I haven't told you that. And thank you for loving Mira. She's everything to me. I couldn't imagine anyone better to do all this with than you."

"Ah, boy, come on," I say. "You know I love you too. And I don't know jack shit either. So I guess we a good match."

"Hey. Wasn't it one of those old-school philosophers who said that the best thing to know is that you know nothing? Socrates, yeah?"

I laugh. "Yeah. Socrates."

"There you go. A philosopher, just like you."

I buff my nails on my hoodie. "Andre, Socrates ain't nothing like me."

He laughs. "That's probably true."

"But look at you. I think you may be a philosopher too."

"Araceli, I am not a philosopher. I am just an accountant."

"An accountant in love. Practicing radical love."

He laughs. "The title of my memoir."

"Nerd." I feel such a surge of love for him, it almost knocks me down. "Where'd you stay last night?" I ask him. "Did you hang out with your friend Dan?"

He shakes his head. "No. Dan's a nurse. We all talked about it, but eventually I said I was scared of bringing all those germs home to Mira. Her immune system's vulnerable right now. And Dan works in a really high-risk environment." He looks around us. "I was uncertain even coming into this coffee place. You know? I haven't been to a coffee place or a restaurant or anything for an entire year."

"It's been a fucking difficult time," I say, waving my hand. "I think you been doing amazing, Andre."

"Thanks," he says. "But Dan and I talked for, like, three hours on FaceTime last night. He actually fell asleep talking to me."

I laugh. "He okay, working in a hospital?"

He shrugs. "He's okay. He's young and healthy. Black and brown people are being hit disproportionately by this shit. Somebody has to be out there helping, Dan says. And he's glad it's him."

I nod. "Okay, he definitely does not suck. So did you stay with your mom?"

He sighs. "Yeah. My sisters came too. They all wanted to see me, see how we've been doing. My dad made fried chicken and collard greens and cornbread. That was really nice. I tried to talk to my mom a little bit. But you know how she is. We're trying. My sister Angela has been going to this gym in New Jersey. Gyms and stuff have been reopened there for a bit, I guess. Angela's big into weightlifting and stuff, it's awesome. So she invited me as a guest at her gym. I wasn't sure, 'cause, you know, germs, but Angela took my phone and texted Mira and Mira was like… of course. So we went super early this morning, when they opened, and there was legit no one else there. It was amazing. Fuck, I've missed going to the gym."

"I'm really glad you got to go," I say.

"Thanks," he says. He tilts his head. "Do you think I should feel guilty, Araceli? That I so enjoyed getting out of the apartment for a night?"

"Oh, my God, no," I say. "You and Mira both need time for yourselves. You… like… I don't even know, boy. Just… are you, like, taking care of yourself properly? And shit?"

He laughs, though this shit ain't funny. "I don't know," he says. "I'm trying. But not really. Work is a lot at the moment."

"Could you take some time off?"

"I think I could, yeah. I need to look into that."

"Yep," I say. "You do. I know you gotta make that cash money, bro. But don't let the capitalists take all of you. 'Kay?"

"I won't," he says.

"You got somebody to talk to, bro? Not like Dan or your mom. I mean, like, I dunno, a therapist?"

He shakes his head. "I know therapy helps," he says. "But I've always struggled with it. For me. I guess I've internalized everything my mom always said. About therapy being, basically, like…"

"White-people shit?"

He laughs. "Yeah. Not necessarily in those words, but yeah. But I know. I've learned so much from Mira about that." He looks down at his hands on the table. "But I'm thinking of… Mira and I saw this, like, relationship coach? On Zoom. A few times, before all this crap happened. And it actually was really helpful. For me, to talk to somebody. So I'm thinking of reaching out to her again. To see if she would see me privately." He shrugs. "I haven't talked about it with Mira yet."

"You should," I say. "You know she'd be all over that, bro. You doing your… non-failurist, non-patriarchal self-care and shit."

He laughs. "I know. I will." He touches my hand. "How are you, Celi? Are you doing okay? And Skye?"

"Andre, honey, this girl is living the dream. I have an awesome, safe place to live. I have a day job that doesn't even suck. I'm doing boudoir shoots at least a couple times a month. I think folks wanna reconnect with their sensual side since the pandemic. Or some shit. But they are good, good money. My agent's tryna find me more opportunities. And Skye? She's good." I let myself smile. "I ain't never been in love before, Dre baby. Not like this. Skye makes me wanna do all kinds of shit. You know what I'm saying?" He nods, looking happy for your girl, like a good friend should. "I think I finally get what it's all about. The whole being-in-love thing."

"I couldn't be happier for you, Celi," he says. "It couldn't happen to a better person."

"Boy. You gonna make me blush."

His phone flashes with a text. I can see it's a group text, *accountancy team*, it says. "Just work," he says, flipping the phone over. "I should start heading home, though. Let me text Mira. See what she's up to."

I watch the glow of the phone on his face as he texts her, our girl, the woman we both love. No one never taught me this. Case you didn't know, I didn't have no family who taught me nothing, except how not to be a person, I guess. But I learned in my own tiny, ratched life that love means a lot of things. Love is what's between Andre and me, two very different friends coming together to create a community where none else existed. Love is what I feel for my work. Love is what will be there between me and

Marco, always, me and the first person I ever made love with. I love Skye, in a way that I didn't think was even possible for somebody like me. And then there's Mira. And we have a love that isn't like anything else.

"Hey, Andre?" He finishes his text, slips the phone in his coat pocket.

"Yeah, Celi?"

"Your… the." Now, there's a great start, y'all. I lick my lips, swallow. "Your. Um. I'm sorry. I'm really sorry, Andre."

Little lines appear between his eyebrows. "Sorry for what?"

"Your. You know. Your… ectopic. Thing? Wow. No. Your… not-baby? I'm really fucking sorry. That that happened to you two."

"Araceli," he says, eyes pained, "don't worry. It's okay."

"No, I'm not sure it is okay," I say. "Nah. I'm pretty sure it's not okay."

He nods, once, an acknowledgment, I suppose, of the general not-okay-ness of this seriously fucked-up shit.

So, that was a fuck-up. And, so, here is your girl, coming to you hot. Here is your girl Celi, trying again.

"Andre," I say again. "I realize that words might not be that helpful in this case. And maybe I'm not using the right words here. If so, I apologize for that. But I am so sorry. I am so sorry that you and Mira lost her pregnancy. I'm so sorry that happened to you two. I'm not sure how you're feeling about it. But I just want you to know. That if you need to talk to a friend. Or if there's some other way I could help. That I'm here."

Andre nods. He wipes tears from underneath both eyes. "Thanks," he whispers. He tells me he loves me. I say, "I love you too."

And I think, damn, this girl fucks up—a lot. But here is one time, one time maybe, when I have done the right thing.

Later on in the month of March, Hassan comes to visit me. Hassan is a chef, and his love language is food, and so he brings me all kinds of homemade dishes. He brings an enormous casserole dish filled with macaroni and cheese, which is my favorite food. It's so heavy his bicep muscles pop out when he slides it into the oven. The smell of the melting cheese and softened pasta is so good as it cooks that my stomach grumbles. That's a sensation I haven't felt since before I got sick. When he takes the pan out, the surface is golden-brown and bubbling, the edges browned and crispy. He's also brought me two dozen tiny, tiny yellow cupcakes with pink frosting and painstakingly made pink edible butterflies on them, dusted with edible glitter.

"The actual fuck, Hassan?" I say, when I see these. "How dare you just bring these over to my place, *así de así*, like it ain't nothing?" I pick up one of the tiny cakes. "Hassan. These are fucking art."

Even his ears are red. "This is the fruit of a deal with your brother," he says.

"A what?"

"I'm on a pastry-making course at a culinary school," he says. "Marco made me a deal, you understand. He said he would only allow me to help him more with his finances if I also agreed to spend some of the money on something that makes me happy." He nods towards the cupcakes. "Hence, pastries."

"Well, thank Marco for me," I say. "Your deal is making me happy too."

"I'm glad to hear it," he says.

He also brings me a bouquet of blushing pink roses. They're delicate but strong and fresh as newborns. They smell like a whole entire rose garden. They're everything springtime. I touch the edges of their curling pink petals with my fingers.

Outside in the world, it's springtime. The cherry blossoms are starting to bloom, the pink and white delight of every New Yorker. And me, I ain't been outside since the day I got home from the hospital a couple weeks ago. (What is time?) I know I need fresh air. I know I need to go for a walk. I'm scared I might actually forget how to use my legs. The days I used to, briefly, call myself a runner feel like a century ago. But I am not ready yet. Just getting out of bed every morning continues to feel like a major feat. Some mornings, actually, I don't even get out of bed. I just lie there and put liquid nutrition into my tube at twelve PM.

Everything he brought is so beautiful, it brings tears to my eyes. I start to cry.

"Miranda?" The look on his face is so tender, so concerned, it makes me cry harder. "Sweetheart, what's wrong? Are you quite all right?"

"Nah," I say, shaking my head. "No, Hassan, I am not quite all right."

His arms kinda flutter at his sides.

I burst out laughing, snorting through my tears. "Hassan. Boy, you so ridiculous. You can hug me. I ain't gonna break."

He reaches out and hugs me, tight.

I stroke his hair. It's thinner and grayer than it was before this pandemic began, but he still has a beautiful head of curly salt-and-pepper hair. He and my brother would make some beautiful babies—you know, if that were, like, a thing.

"See?" I whisper. "Flesh and bone. I ain't made of glass. You can hug me, baby."

He squeezes me. I cry harder.

Andre comes into the kitchen. "Are you okay, baby?"

"I'm fine." I pull back from Hassan, wiping my face. Andre hugs me too. Then Hassan hugs us both, one of the best three-way hugs this girl has ever been in.

"I'm gonna go do a little bit more work," Andre says. "I'm just doing a half day today." He puts his hand on his stomach. "Then I'm gonna come out here and help you two eat all that food."

"We'll save you some," Hassan promises.

No one, except for Araceli, knows about the G-tube, not in any detail. They know I had one in the hospital, but I haven't told anyone else that I've brought it home with me. (I guess Andre's folks know, but they don't count, y'all know that.) It sits, uncomfortable and itchy, under my loose T-shirt like an ugly, shameful secret. My eating continues to be a giant fucking mess. As the days go by, I get more and more used to not eating by mouth anymore. I only chew and swallow something that sounds really, really good. I don't do nothing, so I don't need much fuel. I squirt as much liquid nutrition as I feel like I need into my tube, and I do nothing all day. My life sucks.

It feels so weird, eating by mouth again. It's like I have to relearn to chew, the hard feeling of teeth against teeth, my tongue a wet muscle in my mouth. The mac and cheese is warm and soft. I remember being the girl who used to like this food. I feel it settling in my stomach. It hits different than the liquid through the tube.

I eat as much macaroni and cheese as I can manage. Hassan and I eat a cupcake each. He eyes his for a long time before putting it into his mouth.

We talk about stuff. He's finally almost done with his next novel. He's working on the cookbook he sold, about cooking at home during the pandemic. The graphic novel is selling really well. Netflix is starting production on the *Fifteen* miniseries. He's cooking at this fusion Mediterranean restaurant in Hudson River Park downtown, Thalassa Atlantic. Some days, he says, it's warm enough for people to eat outside.

"I'm looking into what I need to do to get my green card," he says.

I put down my fork. "Hassan, you are? Brother, that's amazing! What great news."

He smiles, a little shy. "Yes," he says. "All of my people are here in the US. This is where I belong now, I suppose."

"Course it is."

"Alex graduates this semester, can you believe this? She starts her political science PhD immediately after. So she will be here another seven years or so, for sure. After that, we will see."

"And I hear she's dating someone now, so…" I spoke to Alex recently; she called me on FaceTime and we talked for two hours, till I was too tired to keep talking. Alex is one of those people who just cannot stop talking. That suited me fine. I basically sat there and let her talk, her stories about classes and exams and her job at the campus bookstore and her friends and volleyball practice and volleyball games and going on dates in downtown Santa Barbara on sun-drenched weekends lulling me into a fugue state. I fell asleep and had a dream that night. I dreamed that I was in a classroom, writing something on a whiteboard. I could hear the squeak of the dry-erase pen, smell its chemical fragrance. It made me think. My college experience would not look one thing like Alexandra's—obviously. But it made me wonder, longingly. Could there still be some way that my G-tube and I could put on a backpack and start all over again at City College this fall?

"Yes, this is right," Hassan says. "This summer I have a trip planned out to California to meet this person that Alex has been seeing."

"I had a CF friend who lived in California," I say. This was a friend of a friend, the oldest person with CF that I (kinda) knew personally. She passed away last week, aged forty-three. She had a ten-year-old son. I went to her virtual memorial. Her son and husband seemed sad, obviously, but there was also a lot of laughing and remembering her cool, fun, very full life. She liked to kayak and ski and she did stand-up comedy. (Those hobbies sound like my personal nightmare, but you do you, good sis.) Forty-three sounds like both a billion years from now and tomorrow.

Hassan pushes his plate away. "How are you, Miranda?" he asks gently.

Part of me wants to scream. Another part wants to cry. But what I actually do is say, "Dunno. I'm starting to, like, miss stuff."

"What sort of stuff?"

I shrug. "I miss going to the thrift store. I miss the grocery store. I miss the frozen aisle, how it's so cold over there it makes you shiver. I miss going to the museum. I went with my friend Araceli and her girlfriend not long before I got sick. I don't miss going to work. Not yet, anyway. But I do want to feel good enough to go back to work. Sometime."

"Can you go to any of those places?" he asks, again gently. "Perhaps a short outing?"

"I guess I could." I turn my face away. "But I'm not ready yet. I feel like me and my lungs need more time. It was so scary, Hassan." I take a deep breath. I can still do that, at least. "The rejection episode. The infection." I sigh. I don't want to talk about it anymore.

"Perhaps you will go when you are ready."

"Mmm-hmm," I say. I'm starting to think about my bed: how soft it is, how quiet, how no one bothers me there. I want to go back to bed. It's an effort to focus and stay present with Hassan.

"Miranda." Now he takes a deep breath. "May I share something with you?"

I force myself to look at him. This sounds important. "Yeah, sure," I say.

"Next week," he says, "I am going to a program to get treatment for my bulimia."

This wakes me up, okay. "You are?"

He nods, once. "I am." He looks down at his hands on the tabletop. "This has become unsustainable. It has only gotten worse. I have been living with this eating disorder. Living around it. Now, so has Marco. This is not how I want for either of us to live. So, I am going. I do not want to go. I'm an old guy who's been sick with this for a very long time. I feel… quite foolish." He sighs. "But I am going."

I reach out and squeeze his wrist. He wears a silver bracelet, a present from my brother on their wedding day.

"Hassan," I say. "I'm super proud of you."

He looks away, embarrassed. "I feel very stupid. I don't know how I'm going to manage this. Perhaps I should not go."

"Nope. You're going. You deserve to get better, Hassan."

"*Inshallah*," he says.

"How long is the program?"

"It's just two weeks," he says. "Extremely intensive. There are longer stays if this is not effective. Or if I need longer to integrate new habits. But I am just starting with the two weeks." His voice shakes. "To say that I am not ready is a vast understatement, Mira. Every day I think about calling them to cancel my spot."

"Hassan. Baby. Please go." I squeeze his wrist again. "Promise me you'll go."

"I am going to try," he says.

I look at his red eyes. "Well," I say. I stand up. He watches me stand, wondering, I bet, what the fuck I'm doing. "I see your two-week bulimia treatment. And I raise you one gastrostomy feeding tube."

I lift my T-shirt so Hassan can see the tube in my belly.

"Oh, very cute," he says, which surprises me, makes me laugh. "What is this, sweetheart?"

"This is my feeding tube." I touch it gently. I realize this is like when I showed Hassan and Marco my tattoo, except less badass and sexy. Then again, hey, y'all, maybe it is badass, and even just a little sexy, the lengths I'm willing to go to keep staying alive in my bizarre-ass life.

"It's a gastrostomy tube. I had to have surgery to put it in. We call it the G-tube."

"Hello, G-tube," Hassan says. "How long will you need to wear it?"

"The rest of my life."

I sit down.

"The tube, it supplements your nutrition?" Hassan asks.

I almost wanna cry, y'all. Here's somebody who gets it, even a little, without me having to explain every single fucking thing!

"Exactly," I say. "I've been so underweight because I don't get enough nutrition from eating by mouth. Because a, I have no appetite and b, pancreatic insufficiency. Which means that my body doesn't absorb nutrients when I eat by mouth anyway."

"Hence, the tube," he says.

"Hence, the tube," I say.

"I'm sorry, was it insensitive of me to bring you food?" he asks, brow furrowed. "I am sorry, Miranda. I did not know about your new G-tube."

I shrug. "I know. I can still eat by mouth if I want to. I just save that for food that tastes good, that I actually want to eat. To taste, I mean. I'm trying to shift to getting my actual nutrition through this tube. But it's hard, though." I sigh, deeply. "I am not there yet."

"That would take time," Hassan says, carefully. "Shifting the entire manner in which you eat food. And experience food. And think about food."

"And prepare food," I say. "I miss cooking. I like cooking better than I like actual eating."

"You might still cook?"

"I will," I say. "I'm not ready yet. I think I'm… I don't know." I heave a breath. I'm close to tears, now. "I'm mourning, I guess. I'm—I'm grieving."

"What are you grieving?" he asks.

"The false story that I had to be like the people around me," I say. "The girl I was, always taking my eating pills, trying to do my best. My body, that didn't used to have a tube attached. My old lungs, I think. It's been a whole year with these new ones and they are objectively better. But the old ones and I went through a lot together. I got up every morning and took such good care of them. They got me to almost twenty-one, which people were saying they wouldn't. I was born with those lungs. For, like, some reason. I never even said goodbye."

"Maybe you can still say goodbye," he says.

"Yep. Maybe. I'm grieving that I used to think I could have a baby someday," I say. "Conceive and carry and birth a baby, I mean. Andre's baby. But I don't think it is safe for my body to do that. If we do ever do that, it will have to be some other way."

He nods. "There are all sorts of ways," he says, "to make a family."

"Ain't that true."

Andre comes into the kitchen again. "Hi, baby," I say.

"Hi," he says. He comes over to me, lifts my face, and kisses me.

"Have some macaroni and cheese," Hassan says.

"And some cupcakes," I say. "They're awesome."

Andre sits down, takes my plate of macaroni and cheese and starts eating it.

"We're talking about my G-tube."

His eyebrows lift. "Are we, now?"

"Yep. I'm trying this new thing. It's called talking about my feelings."

He laughs. "Ten out of ten recommend," he says, around a mouthful of food.

I stand up. "I think I'm going to put some food into the tube."

"Go for it," he says.

So I feed myself through the tube. Andre asks me if I need any help, and I say no, so he just chills and keeps eating. Hassan, though, watches. I let him. It feels good, to be watched. Hassan eats another cupcake, tentatively.

"What's it like, making yourself throw up?"

"What?" Andre says. "Why are we throwing up?"

Hassan and I laugh.

"I have an eating disorder," he explains. "Bulimia. It's an eating disorder that involves binge eating and purging."

"Oh," Andre says. He looks at Hassan. "I'm sorry, bro. I didn't know that."

"Almost no one knows that," he says. He looks at me. "Next week I'm going to a two-week treatment program. I was just telling Mira. I don't want to go."

"Bro, you should probably go," Andre says.

"I know." He sighs. "I will go."

"Hey," I say, "listen. I have a surprise for you."

His eyebrows lift. "You do?"

"Yes," I say. "Listen. Wait. Can you use your phone at this treatment place?"

"I get one hour of phone time a night."

"Perfect. Listen. Can you spare me, like, a half hour of your phone time every night? The other half hour you can have phone sex with Marco or whatever y'all need to do."

"Oh, yes," he says. "I am going to feel so sexy, receiving inpatient treatment for bulimia for two weeks."

We all laugh.

"Okay, listen, baby." I take a deep breath. "When I was in the hospital, I finished my story."

"You did?" Hassan says.

"You did?" Andre says, at the same time.

I feel proud of myself, okay. It ain't all that often that your girl surprises people.

"I did. I didn't feel well enough to actually write, so I dictated it to myself on my phone. But I figured out the ending."

"Mira, you did it," Hassan says. His eyes are wet.

"I'm so proud of you, Mira," Andre says.

"Thank you," I say. "Hassan, this week I'm gonna type up the story. I'll get it printed and give it to you. You can take it with you to the treatment place. And read it. It has ten chapters. So the first night you can give me your overall impressions. The next ten nights we can discuss the chapters. Then we can talk about the thing as a whole. I'll edit, meanwhile. Based on your notes. And we can talk about your treatment."

"Will you use your G-tube?" he asks. "And let me know how that is going?"

Damn, do I really wanna promise all that, y'all? But I look at Hassan looking at me, and I know I have to.

"Yeah, sure. We'll talk refeeding methods."

I expect him to laugh, but he stays serious and says, "It will help me. Knowing that someone else is also healing in a similar way."

I sigh. About a good forty percent of me does not want to do this. The other sixty knows I have to. It ain't perfect, but I decide it's good enough. It has to be.

"Deal," I say. I reach out my hand for him to shake.

"Deal," he says, and shakes it.

My and Andre's first real, grown-up date, when we went out to a restaurant alone without a group of friends, and ordered appetizers and food and desserts, and looked into each other's eyes across the little table, and held hands, and afterwards we got drinks at Starbucks and sat in Washington Square Park cuddling and making out on a bench, was on March 31, 2014. We ate Thai noodles and sat there sickeningly, dizzyingly in love in the restaurant's back garden. It was a Monday and just warm enough after school to eat outside. I was fifteen, Andre was sixteen. A little over five years later, we had our wedding reception at that same restaurant, dancing on the cobblestones in their back garden.

June eleventh is our wedding anniversary. That's the day we celebrated last year, and we'll celebrate this year, and every year ever, in the way that the world understands.

But before that, there was March thirty-first. We've also celebrated that day, though not in any type of a flashy, showy, Instagram-worthy way. I am not having my best time right now. I am not at my fullest capacity. I'm still hurting and confused and not sure what comes next or how I will get there. I feel winded, knocked flat. I am reduced, stripped down to essentials, if even that. What remains when even everything inside seems to have been taken away?

What's left of me, though, is going to celebrate today. It ain't gonna be pretty. But I am gonna do it. What's gonna be left for me is love. What's left for me right now is tenderness.

Early in the morning, when it's still dark out, on this steamy spring day that's going to be rainy and mild, Andre wants to hold me. I don't feel like someone who gets to be held. I don't feel cute, or adorable, or lovable, or delicate, or tender. No, I feel swollen and bruised and like I've been cobbled together from a bunch of rusty spare parts. I'm metal and clunky. I have lost my shine. And Andre wants to hold me. He pulls me into his arms, holding me whole. And I feel every cell in me trembling, struggling against this tenderness. This isn't happening on the outside. On the outside, I am still in his arms, so still I can feel the slow, heavy, hydraulic splat of my heartbeat exploding my ribcage. No, this struggle is on the inside. My inner being crumples in fear, turning its face away from this lavishly offered tenderness. After everything I've been through, it's hard to imagine that I could be deserving, that I could be accepting, of such warm, luscious, uncomplicated tenderness.

After breakfast we sit together on the couch. Here we are in our little living room, half sunken underground. There's the clock on the wall, keeping a time that, these last months, has meant almost nothing. There's the coffee table lined with my morning medicines, Andre's work laptop, a box of tissues, just through there is the tiny kitchen table that we have only just left, but which we can still see, no separation. There has been so little separation between our selves and this small home over the last twelve months, like we have grown into it, like it has grown into us, two fruits baked into a bittersweet cake. Andre pulls me into his lap. I am so light, I am small, I fit there perfectly. I still feel two selves removed from my body, despite its persistent attempts to remind me of the gross, throbbing weight of it. I still don't feel like a girl who gets to be held, cradled in the lap of her lover.

I try to sink into his embrace, till I feel my heartbeat on his. I press my face to his neck, wanting to inhale him. His arms bracket me, hold me in place. I like their tightness, I need it, scared otherwise my organs might spill out around me.

A long time of silence goes by. Eventually, in the ticking, I say, "Do you wish we could go somewhere?"

Andre rearranges our bodies so that we can look at each other, me at him and him at me. His dark eyes grow serious, like I have said something worthy of thought and consideration. Finally, he says, "Sure. Sometimes," and I like his honesty.

"I was scrolling Instagram and someone had posted a video of Hawaii," I say. "The ocean was so blue, the sand was so pale, almost white. People were surfing, their skin was all sparkly from drops of water. It kinda made me want to go to an island."

"I'll take you to an island, if you want to go," he says, in an earnest tone like he'd pack our bags and book us a flight now if I said I wanted.

"Okay, *papi*." I squeeze his shoulders. "Someday."

"Someday," he says.

I swallow. "Do you still think I could travel somewhere?"

Lines of concern appear between his eyebrows. "Mira. Of course you could."

I bury my face in his shoulder. He holds me tighter. "Are you tired of our apartment?" I whisper.

"No," he says. He rubs my back. "Are you?"

"I know I should go for a walk," I say. "I'm just not ready yet."

He strokes my hair. "Are you tired of me?" he asks.

I pull back. "Wow. Andre. Boy. No." I hold his face in my hands. "I don't know how I'll ever have enough time with you."

Andre asks me if I want to take a bath together. This is the kind of thing we always do on this day, allowing ourselves the sweetness of a random, sudden, midday bath, our wet, naked skin together an indulgence that has no meaning or purpose other than love. Today I wonder if I can allow myself that: that decadence of physical love.

We run the bath with bubbles and take off our clothes. We haven't really been naked together, not intentionally, since I got sick. After making sure that the plug on my G-tube is closed, so no water can get in, we step into the bath. I imagine I'm a delicate, elegant lady hundreds of years ago, that soaking in a hot, bubbly bathtub is a daily part of my life, the way I relax my body before retiring to my chamber every night and going to sleep. I fantasize my illness something distant and romantically sick like from an old storybook, a rosy-red, blush-cheeked consumptive young woman, warm and limp; I fantasize that he could take me to the sea to breathe good air, make me well again. I feel so far from that in reality, so gritty and unromantic, that I let myself daydream. Andre big-spoons me. His fingertips graze my shoulders. It helps me drop back into my own body, slowly.

I feel him draw in a breath. "Can I touch you?" he whispers.

"Yeah," I whisper.

His fingertips skim down between my breasts. They touch my scar. It's been a year, more than a year. Andre and Marco have both had one-year follow-up appointments; everything looks good. I feel my breathing change, in a way it hasn't since before I got sick. His hand slips under the water, cups my belly. My breathing gets ragged, deep.

"This okay?" he asks.

"Okay," I say.

His fingers trail and trace my belly. It feels sensitive in a way it hasn't since the surgery. It's felt hard, metallic, plasticky; for the first time now it feels warm and skin-like, rushing with blood.

"Mira," he says.

His hand drips water over my breasts.

I gasp. I haven't felt anything like that in what feels like forever.

"Is this okay?" he says, touching my breasts lightly, circling their shape with his hands.

I nod, too breathless to speak.

He cups my breasts. He takes their weight in his hands, feeling them. I feel cool air under them as he supports them. Water laps and sloshes gently around us. He rubs rings around my nipples with his thumbs until they get firm and hard.

"Oh, my God," I whisper. It feels like the first time I'm being touched.

In response, I feel his penis firm and harden, lengthening against my back.

With one hand, he keeps hold of my right breast, gentle but firm, cupping it. With the other, he travels down my body, finding the cloud of my pubic hair in the water. He plays with it, running his fingers through it.

"I want to kiss you," he says.

"Kiss me," I say.

He turns my face back towards his so we can kiss. It's our first real kiss since everything changed. I remember kissing like this on that bench in Washington Square Park that March evening as it got cold and dark but we were warm, our lips wet together, the hard ridge of his insistent erection between us. It wasn't long ago, I guess, but I was a teenager then, a girl, a girl who didn't have my scars yet, a girl who hadn't had a lost pregnancy.

Our bathroom sink is leaking, a slow, infrequent drip. I know how to fix a leaky faucet, but I haven't yet; haven't felt strong enough to. I will, soon. I hear the drops of the water against the porcelain and my body's like that faucet, gathering wet at a slow but inexorable pace.

I pull away, gasping. My heartbeat's so fast it feels dangerous. "Can we get out?" I say. "It's really hot. I think I'm overheating."

Andre lifts me out of the bathtub. He dries us both and wraps me in a towel and carries me to the bedroom. On the bed, he dries the area around my G-tube carefully, making sure it's dry. Yesterday there was some fluid leaking out of it, but we told my care team and they said it was just normal drainage. It was scary, though.

We sit on the bed naked and Andre combs my hair. This feels like the most activity I've done since I got home from the hospital. It makes me feel a little guilty that it's this kind of aimless, indulgent tenderness and not something badass or efficient and productive. My neck moves in response to his gentle tugs of the comb. I wonder if it's okay to feel both horribly, disgustingly sad and also grateful. Yesterday I looked in the mirror and saw that I have gray hairs, like a lot of them, scattered silver strands along my hairline. My whole body has reacted in sympathy to everything that's happened to me.

Andre gathers my hair into a low, puffy ponytail, ties it loosely. He kisses the back of my neck.

"I want to comb your hair down here too," he says, a gasp in my ear, his breath hot in my ear. He gives my hair a gentle tug. I feel the speed of his heartbeat against my back, the stirring of his penis.

"Okay," I say. I'm a little nervous, in that gentle, delicious way. We have never done this before.

Andre uses my hair serum, a little between the teeth of the comb, as he draws it through my curls. He's gentle with the little snags and tangles, but this hair is so intimate and close to my body, I definitely feel them, the pull of each one tugging my labia. I sit with my knees parted and him between them, and he keeps looking between my lips at my clit peeking through and panting.

"This is so fucking beautiful I want to come," he says.

"Andre," I say.

"Can I touch you more?" he says. "I want to touch you everywhere. I miss you."

I feel tears sting my eyes.

"Fuck," he says, touching my face. "Mira, I'm sorry."

I shake my head. "I'm sorry. I miss you too. I miss me."

"We're right here," he says, touching my chest.

"Touch me," I say.

As promised, he touches me everywhere. His hands are intentional, giving me pressure, anchoring me, reminding me. He rubs my feet. He kneads my ass, pressing it with his thumbs. I start to feel like maybe a person again, not a robot or a cyborg or a doll. My shoulders are pinched and tight.

"I should learn massage," he whispers. "I could give you real massages."

I find myself laughing. "You do not need to learn anything else for me, Andre," I say. "This is a real massage."

He laughs too. "It wouldn't only be for you, Mira," he says. "This is for me. This is so fucking hot. I'm, like, close right now. I'm going to come."

He skims my ribcage. I ask him, "Can you touch the tube?"

He touches it, lightly.

"You can touch it," I tell him. "I want to be a sex person again, Andre. I've always been a sex person. You know that."

I've started to cry. He puts his hand over the tube. He smiles down at me. "You do not have to be a sex person right now if you're not ready, Mira."

"I want to be a sex person again sometime soon," I say, "but I can't until I can feel sexy with this feeding tube."

He laughs. "I find you and this tube very sexy," he says. He bends his head and kisses it. It's a light, gentle kiss, but, oh, I feel it all throughout my body.

I take his hand. "Can you touch me here?" I whisper. I put his hand on the scar on my lower belly.

"Sure," he says. But his voice is shaking. His hand is, too, when he touches it.

"We…" Am I gonna be able to get this out? We're both shaking.

"Does it still hurt?" he asks. "Here?"

"Yeah, sometimes, a little," I say. My breath hitches. "I'm healing."

He starts crying too.

"We…" I gasp pathetically. "We made a… a fertilized egg."

"Our poor fertilized egg," he says.

"It's okay," I say.

"It's okay," he says. "Or, I don't know, you're okay, Mira. There is only you. You're safe and you're okay and you're going to heal. That is all that really matters."

He hugs me, tightly. I say in his ear, "Thank you."

He pulls back. "If we had had a… a viable pregnancy," he says, "if you had wanted it. I would have been down. I mean, I would have been scared. But also excited. To do that with you."

"Same," I whisper through tears.

"I also would have supported you if you didn't want it," he says. "This is your body."

"This is my body," I agree, "and I don't think it can do a viable pregnancy, Andre. I don't think that happens for me."

"That's okay," he says. "I love our perfect life."

And, well, y'all, some days you get a feeding tube put in. Other days, the same you gets to hear a sentence like that.

Andre touches my scar more. He lowers his head and kisses it. He kisses me all up and down my body: my navel and the soft hair under it, above and below the tube, the tips of my breasts, my shoulders. Between us, my pubic hair dries in lovely, satiny curls, unmatted and perfect, a sweet-smelling cloud. Andre comes just from our bodies rubbing together, crying out in my ear a tortured release, his cum dripping all over my torso.

"I missed having you on me," I tell him.

"Oh, God," he says, crushing me to him.

"Ow," I say. "Baby, you're kinda crushing my G-tube."

"Fuck." Panting, he loosens his hold on me. "I'm sorry," he says.

"It's okay," I say. "We're learning."

He smiles, smooths his hand over the baby hairs on the top of my head. Some of them are gray. "We're learning," he says.

"Do you still recognize me?" I whisper. "Like, am I the same?"

"I definitely still recognize you," he says. "But no, you are not the same." He shakes his head. "I'm not the same either, I don't think."

"If you knew all this would happen," I whisper, "would you still have done it?"

"Mira," he whispers, with all that infinite tenderness I woke up this morning so fucking afraid of. "If I'd known what this would feel like, I would have done it sooner."

It's April now, and I haven't seen Paloma in almost two months. Maybe I can reasonably make excuses. I mean, I did almost die. But I didn't, and I've continued trying to be a person, best as I can. At some point, my free passes have to run out. If I'm going to keep playing this game called life, I can't shut out all the other players on my team indefinitely. I'm going to have to face her.

I'm terrified. I am not the person I was two months ago, when Paloma saw me last. Maybe she had just begun to understand that I have a chronic illness, that I live with and around it, and so do those closest to me. I feel cruel, just imagining telling her that I now have even more conditions around which I have to shape my daily life. There's the obvious fact of the G-tube. I'm starting to be able to see forward to a time when it won't feel like a giant silicone monster about to swallow my life, but just a tiny tool that helps me continue to live my life, and which (yes) I should be grateful for. But I am not there yet. And I do not want to talk about it to Paloma. I do not want to explain it to her. I don't want to show it to her.

Invisible but just as invasive are these new fears I live with. They've seeped into every corner of my day, a creeping black sludge. Sometimes when my new lungs breathe I am afraid of them. What if they turn on me again? The doctor said the ectopic pregnancy was probably caused by my IUD. They're uncommon no matter what, but more common with IUDs. If I could, I would just have the thing removed; one less external device in my body would do me really good. But pregnancy is too risky for my body for me to live without contraception. I neither trust condoms that much nor want Andre to wear one. So there's still a piece of plastic in my uterus. I get that my chances of ever having an ectopic pregnancy again are hovering somewhere right around winning the lottery. But understanding on an intellectual level that the risk is low, that the likelihood is low, is not the same as feeling safe again. When will it feel safe to have sex again?

I guess that doesn't matter yet, though, because I don't feel ready to have sex anyway, neither physically nor emotionally. I don't feel sexy. I'm scared to see Paloma in this state. Before, just looking at her made me feel so fucking sexy, it made me feel like I was sex itself, luscious and combustible. Now, Andre can comb my fucking pubic hair and come all over me, and my girl Celi can curl up next to me in bed with all the perfect curves of her body, and I still don't feel ready to do anything more than kiss. I think I only even let them take me that far because I trust them so damn much, because there's so much more between us than sex. Paloma and I built the first foundation of our relationship on sex. Will she still want me when sex is something I simply cannot do? I have no idea when that part of who I am will reawaken.

I cocoon myself in blankets in bed to call her. I'm shaking. We've texted. We've spoken on the phone once, for just a few minutes, and I even told her about the pregnancy. But it's time for me to either reinvite her back into my life, or let her go. I've been the world's worst polyamory married girlfriend, and I know I have.

"Hello?" she says.

"Hi," I say.

"Mira," she says. I close my eyes. Just her saying my name brings it all back, like it was decades ago and not weeks: holding hands in Central Park, dancing in her living room, being inside her while I wore my strap-on. Will I ever wear that cock again? Will she feel the same inside, if I am able to fuck her again? Will she feel different, because I am different?

"Paloma." I take a breath—and hear that she is crying. "Oh, sweetheart." I grip the phone. "Oh, *mami. No llores. Dime que te pasa.*"

"Nothing," she whimpers. "*Me haces falta. Yo preocupo por ti todo el tiempo.*"

"Paloma," I say.

"How are you, Mira?" she says. "How are you feeling? Are you okay? How are you recovering?"

I sigh. "I'm getting there, *mami.*"

She sniffles. "I'm sorry I'm crying," she says.

"It's okay," I say.

"*Yo pienso en ti en cada momento,*" she says. "It's so good to hear your voice."

"Yours too, baby," I say. "*Oye.* Can I see you? I miss you too, *mi nena. Quiero verte.*"

"Of course you can see me, Mira," she says. "Anytime, anywhere. I can come over? For a little while? Or for as long as you want. Whatever you need, honey."

I take a deep breath. I didn't go on oxygen again, and fight off that fucking infection, and lose a fallopian tube, and gain a gastrostomy tube, to do shit halfway. If Paloma and I are doing this, then we are doing it.

"I'd love for you to come over," I tell her. "I'd like to ask you to stay a weekend with me. If you'd like to." Paloma has never slept over at our place before.

"I would love that," she says, right away.

I continue. "Andre will be here," I say. "Honestly I don't know what that looks like with sleeping arrangements and whatnot. I'm still recovering from everything and I haven't been able to think that far ahead. Maybe it's something we can all talk about and figure out together."

"Of course," Paloma says. "That's how this is done. There is no rulebook, Mira."

I nod. "I have no idea how to do this," I tell her. "I don't know what this all looks like."

"That's why we're figuring it out together," she replies. "I don't, either."

"Okay," I say. My voice shakes. "*Oye.* I'm… I'm not… I mean. Paloma." I draw in a shuddery breath. "I guess it wasn't that long ago. But I'm not the same like I was before. Some… things have changed. I can tell you in person. And—show you. But I am not all the way recovered. I am not all better yet. So, I…"

"Miranda," she says tenderly, so tenderly it brings tears to my eyes. "You don't have to do anything. You don't have to be anything. I just want to see you. Just exactly the way you are."

"All right," I manage to say, around my swimming eyes and trembling lips.

"I miss you so much, *mi sirena.*"

"I miss you too, honey. I'm looking forward to seeing you." I burrow deeper in my blanket cave. "I should go. It's late. I haven't been sleeping that well. I should try to get some sleep."

"Yes," she says. "You need sleep."

"Yeah," I say. "I'll text you in the morning? We'll figure out a time?"

"Please," she says.

My heart nearly leaps out of my throat. "I love you," I tell her, the words feeling like stepping one foot out onto a rickety bridge, trying to span the gap between who I was and whoever it is that I am now.

"Mira," she says, in that voice like honey. "I love you too."

The Friday that Paloma is supposed to come over, Andre calls out from remote work because he has a migraine. He has suffered from migraines since he was a teenager, painful, hypersensitive periods where he can't stand any noise or light or movement, and can only manage to lie still in a dark, quiet room. He goes to the bedroom and shuts the lights and pulls the blinds and gets into bed, the covers over his head.

I haven't had the apartment to myself like this, quiet and solitary, for ages. Even though I feel both tired and somehow jittery, being the only one up while Andre rests makes me feel like I should do something. I dust and wipe down all the kitchen surfaces and scrub the toilet. I think about mopping too, but my energy feels sapped. This is the most physical activity I've done since I got out of the hospital, by far. Our place is already pretty clean, though. It's yet another thing Andre has been taking care of for the past almost two months. As a CF-er, I learned at a very young age that a clean environment is one of the best things for my health. And as a homestead and kitchen witch, taking care of our place every day is part of my spiritual practice. I sit down at the kitchen table and look around our tiny, clean apartment, feeling calmer than I have in a long while, that small sense of satisfaction that comes from having done one good thing in the space around you.

I go into the living room and sit down on the couch, wrapping myself in a blanket and resting my head against the cushion. I look at the apartment door. When will I feel ready to step out of it again?

I must doze off, because I'm awakened in a haze by a text on my phone. It's from Andre: *I miss u.* I put the phone in my sweatpants pocket and pad through the apartment. I open the bedroom door as quietly as possible, stopping before it reaches the point where it always creaks. I slip into the darkened room.

Andre is burrowed in bed with his phone, its bluish glow on his face. He must be feeling better, if he's able to look at the screen. I get into bed with him. He turns over briefly to put his phone on the bedside table.

"Hi," he says. "I missed you."

"Hi," I say. "I missed you too." I caress his chest. I imagine he's naked under the covers; often when he has a migraine everything feels like it hurts, so he takes off all his clothes. "How are you feeling?"

He looks at me with soft eyes. It's been so long since I was the one feeling better, stronger, of the two of us, able to be there for him, to ask him how he feels.

"I'm feeling much better," he says.

"Did you fall asleep?"

"I don't think so," he says. "It hurt too much. So I just rested." He closes his eyes.

"Do you want me to tell Paloma to come a different day?"

He opens his eyes. "You don't have to do that," he says. "I'm okay."

"All right," I say. "We're just gonna hang out anyway. Keep this low-key."

He nods.

"Do you need anything?" I ask him.

He shakes his head. "Nope. Only you."

I cuddle closer to his body. He extricates himself from the tangle of blankets so our bodies can meet, opens his arms so I can fold my face into his chest. He holds me tight. I feel him breathe me in, deeply. I hook one leg over his, drawing us nearer.

I feel the unspeakable delicacy of his penis, the juicy round firmness of his balls, against me. He's warm and soft. Sparkles erupt in my body, a gentle shower like glitter. Finally I can breathe deep into my lower belly, feel the very bottom of my breath there. In a brilliant spell of sex magic, ever since Andre and I touched my lower belly scar like a week ago, the pain there has lessened. It's not all the way gone. Your girl still has further to go. But it feels like a promise, a glimmer: I can see my way towards a time when I can take his cock deep, or firm my lower abs as I run the last stretch of a mile, or feel myself wet as I put on the strap-on again. It won't be today. But it is coming.

"Mira." He pulls me back gently by the hair for a kiss. "I love you so much."

"Me too," I say. I touch his mouth. "Are you hungry? Could I make something for you?"

His eyes brighten; that's all the answer I need.

Andre puts on a pair of boxers and we go into the kitchen. As I take out a pan and a mixing bowl and the butter, it don't feel like coming home, not quite, not exactly. Nah, it feels like setting your feet on the path towards home, maybe. It feels like being lost in a dark, rainy forest, at dusk, and seeing the lights of your home way off in the distance. And you're tired and tapped out and in pain and feeling pretty shitty, but you see it, the lights calling you home, and you think maybe you can make it a little bit longer, and so you keep on going.

For my inaugural meal since returning home from the hospital, I make something super simple: blueberry pancakes. We have a box of mix that's technically expired, but only by two weeks, so it's gonna be just fine. And we have fresh blueberries, because Hassan has some sponsorship deal with a subscription box for fruits and veggies, so he's been having boxes sent to our place. (I just love the YouTube influencer life for Hassan, with his sweaters and Egyptian-British accent and silver fox persona, don't you?) I prepare the mix with milk and melted butter and a little squeeze of vanilla extract instead of water, though, 'cause I still gotta go kitchen witch on y'all, even when I ain't operating at one hundred percent.

Andre tries to help me, but I say, "Sit down. Let me," in a voice that I'm not sure if it's commanding or sweet.

I make two perfectly round blueberry-studded pancakes. We listen as the batter hits the thin layer of hot oil in the pan and starts to sizzle gently. Their edges have that perfect crisp thinness, browned and just slightly crunchy. The berries have bled their sweet little indigo hearts into the golden cakes. The pancakes are perfect, objectively and aesthetically beautiful. And I have no desire to eat them at all. I plate them and hand them to Andre. He thanks me with slightly shiny eyes. He offers me some. I say, "No thanks, baby." I see the way he's looking at me, so I take out the blender and blend some blueberries and milk, sit down at the table with him and pump the mixture into my tube. I don't want to, I don't feel like it, but I do it.

Andre takes a shower and puts on basketball shorts and a Black Panther T-shirt. I haven't showered today and I slept in this cami and sweatpants. I should really try to be more of a person before Paloma comes over. But I just can't. There's also probably something a little calculated in this choice: if this girl wants to be a real part of my life, she'll have to take the real me. At the last second, though, when Paloma texts to say that her Uber just turned onto our street, I pull a flowered hair wrap over my hair. I am just not ready for her to see me with all my new gray hair, weeks before my twenty-second birthday.

Paloma arrives as usual, at once so familiar, so her, it's like I must've seen her yesterday, and at the same time her presence is so intense and concentrated it overwhelms me. She's in soft leggings and an oversized bright orange T-shirt proclaiming that the Mets were champions of the NL (National League, maybe?) in the year 2015. She has six bags with her, one of which is her weekend bag, and the other five contain food I'll either struggle to eat, pretend to eat, or watch her and Andre eat, and other gifts for us, including books, a bouquet of flowers, crystals, sports magazines for Andre, candles, a weighted blanket, and a heating pad. The gifts are wonderful and beautiful and entirely too much. I hug her for about five minutes straight at the door, feeling her every curve, breathing in her Chanel No. 5 or whatever expensive thing, realizing I missed my girl way more than I accounted for. The truth is, I missed her more than I wanted to. She and Andre hug for a long time too. They kiss lightly on the lips, mouths closed. He says something in her ear that makes her laugh, and they kiss again.

So I'm already feeling all shaky and weepy when we go into the kitchen together and Paloma shows us all the gifts she brought, taking each one out of its bag and explaining the whole story behind its provenance. (I think Paloma, as an ancient history person, would be proud of my use of the word *provenance,* which I learned in the one archaeology class that BMCC offers; it refers to the place of origin of an object.) I start to cry when she shows me the weighted blanket and describes how one night she was eating ice cream and watching reruns of *Shark Tank* and saw this blanket advertised and thought of me and ordered it immediately. I don't want to cry, I want to stop before she notices and it becomes a thing, but I can't stop.

"Oh, Mira," she says. "Miranda. Can I hug you?"

I nod, now crying too hard to speak.

Paloma hugs me tightly. In her arms, I only cry harder. I feel out of control, unable to stop. I also hate that Andre's standing there awkwardly while we hug. He hasn't seen me cry like this since I got home from the hospital. I haven't been able to.

When we finally pull back, Paloma's crying too, wiping her eyes. She's giving me a look that almost scares me.

"Yeah, how about I let you two talk," Andre says, looking between the two of us. "Mira, baby, if you need me, I'll be watching *The Mandalorian* in the bedroom. With my headphones. On a very high volume."

Now, we all know that your girl Mira's clueless when it comes to, like, nerd shit—but even I know that this has something to do with *Star Wars.* So I look at him and say the only thing that can be said in a situation like this one, which is: "May the force be with you."

Andre and Paloma and I stand in silence for a beat. We're all crying, to varying degrees. But then we look at each other and burst into laughter.

He takes me by the shoulders, bends his head and kisses me. "May the force be with you, Miranda," he says.

"Have you watched season two?" Paloma asks.

He shakes his head. "Dan and I are watching it at the same time and then discussing each episode over FaceTime."

Wow—I still ain't thrilled that Andre and Dan discussed his new anal experimentation before he and I did, but I am glad he has a BFF to talk nerd shit with, so I don't have to.

She nods. "Let me know what you think of episode five when you get there," she says.

"No spoilers," Andre says warningly.

She flutters her lashes. "Wouldn't dream of it, Dre."

Andre goes into the bedroom and shuts the door. I sigh deeply and pick up the beautiful blanket. I still feel all shuddery. I wrap myself up in it and curl up on one of the kitchen chairs, my legs pretzeled underneath me.

Still looking at me with a combination of angry hurt, sad accusation, helpless confusion, and now a grudging sweet fondness, Paloma sits at the table with me. She sinks down gracefully, hair flowing behind her.

I pick up one of the chocolates she brought, sitting in its box on the table, unwrap it, put it into my mouth. I let it melt on my tongue. "Whatever you gotta say to me, girl," I say around it, "just say it, okay?"

Paloma crosses her arms over her giant beautiful breasts. I'm feeling about as far from sexy as a person can right now, but I still have to admit that I missed those breasts. She stares at me another moment. Then she uncrosses her arms, takes a chocolate too, unwraps it, and chews it thoughtfully.

"You've been through some shit, Mira," she says finally. "Are you sure you have the space to hear how I've been feeling right now?"

I shrug. I take another chocolate, just to give my mouth something to do. I want to kiss her, also to bite her. She's a naughty, insolent, bad little girl. I want to punish her.

"I'm not all the way recovered, no, if that's what you're asking," I say. "But I ain't made of glass, Paloma. You won't break me. You can talk to me."

"Are you okay?" Her eyes get shimmery. "I don't wanna make this all about me."

"No, I'm not okay, Paloma," I say bluntly. "But I also have no desire to make anything all about me. So you wanna talk, then talk."

She nods, nods, then nods some more. She looks away. She folds our empty chocolate wrappers neatly into squares. Then she says, "You really hurt me, Miranda."

I cuddle myself tighter in her blanket.

"You shut me out." Her lower lip starts to tremble. She bites it. "We have this amazing weekend. You fuck me like I don't think anyone's ever had me before." I close my eyes for a second, I have to, looking at her flushed, open, vulnerable face is too much right now. "Then, next thing I know, you have Andre texting me…" Her eyes flash towards the bedroom door. She lowers her voice to almost a whisper. "You have Andre text me to tell me that you're in the hospital. That you're really sick."

Her voice catches. I wipe my wet face with a corner of the blanket.

"A rejection episode? A lung infection? You were on oxygen, and the… the…"

I just look at her.

She looks at me. "And I had to get updates from Andre," she says. Her cheeks bloom bright red. I want to slap them. "Mira. I was so worried about you. I had no idea what was going on with you. If you were okay."

She presses her hand to her mouth, to try to stop herself crying. "If there was anything I could do. If I could be with you."

"Paloma," I say. I sigh. How can I want her so much, still be so drawn to her, and already be so tired of her that I just want her to leave? "I was not okay. There was literally nothing you could do. They didn't even want Andre there. Because of the virus. So, no. You couldn't come see me. I mean, it's like you said. My body tried to reject my new lungs. They're thinking it might have been triggered by the trauma of the ectopic pregnancy. I woke up in the middle of the night in unbearable pain. I was bleeding all over the bathroom floor. Andre had to scrub it all off the floor. Okay? They did emergency surgery to take it out. And one of my fallopian tubes. Then I was just lying there for weeks, trying not to die from the lung stuff." She sobs out loud. "So it's not like we've been having a party over here without you, Paloma."

"I know that," she says, almost shouting at me—really, though, does she? "But you've been back home for a while since then. You've been well enough to see your friend Araceli. I saw you two posting pictures on Instagram. I know you've seen Marco and Hassan. I ran into them at the Westside Market near Columbia and they were telling me how you are. I had to hear from your brother-in-law how my girlfriend was doing, Mira. Because you shut me out."

"Paloma." I cover my face with both hands, extricating them from the blanket.

"You tell me you want to be my girlfriend," she sobs. "You tell me you love me, Mira. Then you shut me out. You want to see everyone except me. And I'm just worrying about you and thinking about you all the time. But I know you've been through so much so I can't say anything. Just wait until you decide to let me back in again." She spreads her hands. "Do you know how much that hurts, Mira?"

"Paloma. Sweetheart. *Mi reina. Mi nena.*"

"Mira," she says.

I push the blanket down to my shoulders. "Can we go sit on the couch instead?"

"Why?" She sits up straighter, alert. "Are you okay? Are you in pain?"

I shrug. "I am still in constant low-grade pain because of the surgery and all of the shit," I say. "But I just wanted to go to the couch so you could get under this blanket with me and I could cuddle you, *nena.*"

"Don't you use all your sex magic to make me stop being mad at you, Mira," she says sternly, but she also gets up, and her breathing is also a little heavier. "I am still mad at you."

"Okay, *nena.*" I get up too, and draw the blanket around me, and head into the living room. She follows me.

On the couch, I invite Paloma into my blanket cave and I put my arms around her. She rests her head on my breasts.

"All right, baby girl," I say. "So you are being really selfish right now. Selfish and childish."

She makes a noise of protest.

"Shut up," I say. "Let me talk now. Like you said, I've been going through some shit. I almost died, Paloma. I was literally fighting for my life. I give Andre my phone when I can't talk to anyone. He updates everyone. So they know I'm not dead. If I do die, he'll be the one who has to let everyone know." I pause. "When I die, I mean."

"Mira," she whimpers.

"Shh," I say. "So I didn't die. This time. So I came home and now I have to relearn how to be alive. I have almost no energy. Because of everything that happened. So all of my energy goes to just getting out of bed and feeding myself and trying to be a person again. Yes. I did see Araceli. My best friend since I was four. Oh, and, story for another time, but we kissed. Anyway. I also saw Marco. Actually, I haven't seen him, because he's interning at the hospital this semester and he doesn't wanna expose me to all the germs. So I actually just spoke to him through that door. And I did see Hassan. My brother-in-law. Paloma."

I tug her hair. Obediently, she looks up at me with her tear-stained face.

"Paloma, I don't have family like you do." Her face crumples. I take a breath. "What I mean is, I don't have a wonderful mom and dad who love me and support me and take care of me financially and emotionally. Like you do. I don't know how much you know about our mother." Paloma just looks at me. Am I really going to cut this half-healed wound open too, when I've already told her about the pregnancy blood all over the floor and there's still the tube to get to? "Well. She's an addict. Heroin, when she's really fucked up. Alcohol when things are semi-normal."

"Mira," she whispers.

"Oh, God," I say. "Please don't look at me like that, Paloma. I can't take that shit. Please don't start thinking badly of me. Or of Marco. Or of my mom. You don't even know her."

She shakes her head. "I don't… I wasn't… I'm not…"

"Okay." I nod. "There's more to her than that. I love her and she's amazing. And she's also really sick. And that made our childhood, well, pretty fucked. She was neglectful and a trainwreck and very emotionally abusive to Marco. He's still messed up over it. I am too. But anyway." I shake my head. "All of this is to say that, now that I'm not a child anymore, things are better because I'm able to distance myself from my mother. It also means she's not really a part of my life anymore. Not like she was when I was a child and dependent on her for shit. But my illness is a complex one. I can't manage it on my own. No one does. So I have help. From Andre, mostly. He takes on a lot for me. Most guys his age aren't even married at all. Let alone to a sick person who requires care. But I lean on Marco and Celi and even Hassan a lot too, Paloma. Do you think that's easy for me? To finally actually be grown up, to get married and leave my mother's house, and still depend on other people just to help me stay alive?"

She shakes her head.

"No. It's not easy. It's intimate and uncomfortable and hard. I feel angry and resentful and exhausted. Sometimes I just want to scream that it's not fair. It isn't fair. Andre is feeling burnout and trauma of his own and probably even a little compassion fatigue. Things are weird with me and him and Marco because they donated me their lung lobes. Which I can't even keep safe. But anyway. Paloma, I have a lot going on. I know I said we were girlfriends. And we are. And that I love you. Which I do. But that shit is hard, okay? It's a lot. It takes time for me to grow enough closeness with somebody to lean on them like that. You and I…" I touch each of her cheeks. She's lovely and vibrant and earnest and sweet and she's very precious to me. I want her, and I want all that she represents for my life.

"I love you. Very much. And I want to get there with you. But we are not there yet." I shake my head. "I am sorry that I shut you out. I am sorry that I was distant and unresponsive. I'm sorry you had to worry about me. But right now, this is the speed I can move at. I missed you and I wanted you and I'm sorry. And I'm here now."

"Mira," she says. She stirs in my arms, stretching up so she can kiss me. I kiss her gratefully, again not realizing how much I missed her lips until I've tasted them again. "No. I'm sorry. You're right. I'm selfish and immature and I have no idea what I'm doing." God, I wish sixteen-year-old Mira could hear her saying that. "I'm sorry. You're right, again. It does take time to build that kind of closeness. And if you'll have me, I want to keep trying."

I fist her hair in a knot and kiss her again, hard. "I'm right here," I repeat.

"I'm right here too," she says. "God. I'm so sorry. I made this all about me and my feelings. When it should be about you."

"Nah, baby." I use the knot of her hair to tilt her head so I can kiss her neck. It's smooth and flushed and pretty and her pulse is fucking wild. If I weren't beyond depleted right now, I would fucking devour this woman. "I'm actually glad you called me out, Paloma. Ain't no one been calling me out on my shit lately. Everyone's been treating me like a piece of glass. Which I am not. I fought for my life. And I won. You can tell me how you really feel." I kiss her perfect trembly lower lip. "It takes a lot more than that to break me."

She touches my mouth. "You're so strong," she says, reverently.

"Sometimes," I say. "Sometimes, I'm also really, really weak."

She nods.

"But you can talk to me," I say. "I love you and I wanna build something with you, Paloma. It might be on a slightly different timeline than some other people who are not dealing with my shit. But I am here for you. I am here for whatever's growing between us."

Her eyes glow up at me, my earnest, romantic, fairy-tale girl. "I am here too, Mira," she says. She puts her hand over my heart, feels it beating. "I am right here."

I look at the clock on the wall. It's only seven PM, but I am exhausted. My scar is throbbing.

"I know it's stupidly early," I tell her, "but I think I need to lie down now."

"Of course," Paloma says. "Can I go with you? Cuddle with you?"

"Sure," I say.

I get ready for bed. I'm feeling so tired that I imagine I'll sleep straight through the night. Paloma and I trade places with Andre: we get onto the bed; he kisses me good night and relocates to the living-room couch with his laptop and enormous headphones and Baby Yoda.

I am not ready to tell Paloma about the G-tube yet. And I sure as fuck don't want her to find out by accident, spooning me in bed and feeling its silicone curve. So I tell her, "I've been sleeping on my back. With a pillow next to me. That's the most comfortable thing. I'm still feeling a little tender."

She gazes at me with wide, trusting doe eyes that break my heart. "Okay, Mira," she says. "Whatever you need."

I place a pillow on my right side, as a buffer. On my left, Paloma cuddles up to me tentatively. She nuzzles her cheek against my bicep. "This okay?" she whispers.

"Better than okay," I whisper back.

I haven't been comfortable at all, not even for a second really, since the hospital, and the worst is when I'm trying to sleep, unmoving and with no outside stimulation to distract me from the aches and itches and pains firing in different parts of my body. But right now I feel soothed by Paloma's sweet smell, her breath and her cheek on my arm, the abundant curves of her next to me. It's a pleasant surprise, how fast I feel myself sinking into sleep.

I wake up later, alone in the bed. It's full dark outside now, late. A squinting glance at the bedside clock tells me that it's five minutes after eleven PM. I hear the clink of plates in the kitchen; I think that's what woke me. I take a deep breath and feel it against the tube, reminding me, as it does every time I awaken, that it exists. I reach a hand gingerly under my shirt and feel it, and the skin around it, to see if it's swollen or tender or painful. What if it gets an infection again? What if it eats me? What if I am not able to hold onto my lungs this time, what if my body attacks them and we lose? I don't know that I can go through what I went through, not again. I whimper to myself. Why am I not better yet? Shouldn't I be feeling better by now?

"Okay, now tell me how you really are, Andre." Paloma is speaking quietly in the other room, but our place is so tiny, if a conversation is going on anywhere, you can hear it from anywhere else. They must be eating a very late dinner together. I didn't eat dinner, and I don't want to.

"I don't know, Paloma," he says, sounding a little irritated. "I'm okay. I'm fine." I can even hear him chewing aggressively. Mouth still full, he says, "Some stuff at work is really bothering me right now."

"Like what?" Paloma says. "Is everything okay?"

"I mean, everything's okay, it's just… Wait. You know Mandee, right?"

"Yes, I know Mandee," she says.

"Well. I was chatting with Mandee. She works in finance too. She's management-level at Chase. We've been talking about how I could maybe advocate for myself better at work. And, like… I don't think I have been? As well as I could have?"

"Yeah, I mean, that's really challenging to do, Andre," she says. "It takes time and practice."

"I mean, yeah," he says. "But. Also." There're some plate-clinking noises. I realize I'm barely breathing, trying to listen in better to their conversation. I know Andre's been talking to Mandee about work, but when they get on Zooms together, I deliberately tune out. I'm so sure that I won't even understand what they're talking about, so sure that I'm worthless in the world of work, that I can't even hear them over the roaring silence of my own insecurities.

"Also," he repeats. "There's this guy on the accountancy team. Ryan. We started at the same time. Same graduation year. Same age. Same job title. But, you know, I finished my basic degree early. Because I started at Baruch with a bunch of college credits. So I stayed an extra semester to get a special certificate in tax accounting. Plus I have a whole extra year of internships that Ryan doesn't have. Anyway, point is, I'm actually more qualified than he is. But you know what I found out last week?"

I assume Paloma is shaking her head.

"When Ryan started, he negotiated a higher salary than what they were offering. And they said yes. When I started, I just saw the number and felt excited and said sure. So Ryan is making more money than me. For doing the exact same job. Just because he advocated for himself. And I didn't."

"Is Ryan white?" Paloma asks.

"Yes," Andre says, "he is. And, P, I mean, I don't begrudge him the money. I mean, good for Ryan. Right? Who isn't married and doesn't have medical bills and lives at home with his mom and dad in Brooklyn."

Fuck, I think. And this is why I usually don't listen when Andre talks about work. I want to cry now. I want to pull the covers over my head and stop hearing, and start feeling sorry for myself. This is when I'd normally start making this all about me: how I'm a burden on Andre, how he could be living the finance bro life like white-boy Ryan right now, living at mom and dad's with no bills and no responsibilities, spending all his cash on weed and video games, if it weren't for me. But, for once, even though my ass is lying in bed eavesdropping instead of bravely and presently listening to what he has to say, I shut up my inner voices and just try to hear him.

"Anyway." Andre sighs. I can see the way he shrugs when he sighs like that, shoulders up towards his ears and back down again. "It's not about Ryan, really. It's about me. I'm feeling feelings of… what's the therapy word here? Feelings of shame, I guess. Because we could be doing better. For me doing the exact same work. But we're not. Because I didn't even think to negotiate and stand up for myself. I honestly wouldn't have even thought of doing that, Paloma."

A chair moves. "I'm going to have a beer, do you want one, P?"

She sighs. "God. Yes. I'd love one." The fridge opens. "What kinds have you got?"

"I've just got this IPA from a microbrewery in Brooklyn. You're going to love it, Paloma. It's super hipster."

She laughs. "Am I really all that hipster?"

"I don't know," he teases her, "are you?"

They clink their bottles together. "Oh, that is good," Paloma says.

"See, I told you." He sighs again. "Anyway. So. That's the Ryan situation. But I'm trying to be, like, positive here. Instead of bitter and failurist. This is why Mandee is awesome, though. I'm talking to her on Monday after work and I'll see what she has to say about all this. She gives great advice. And she, like, gets it. And this is why mentorship needs to be a thing, a real thing, in the black community. When I feel more settled and older and like I know what the fuck I'm doing, I want to do for somebody what Mandee's doing for me."

"I think you already know exactly what you're doing, Andre," Paloma says.

"Nah, P, I…"

"No, dude, seriously. I respect you so much. I think you kick so much ass."

I can just see his look of embarrassment. "Okay, P," he says. "Thank you."

They eat and drink for a couple minutes in silence. Then Andre says, "I told her about what happened with Mira. Like, not all the details. But yeah. What it's like. With work and… that."

"What did she say?" Paloma asks gently.

"Well. She told me that when she transitioned, and also some times when she's had flare-up episodes and crap with her lupus, she had a home health aide. Like, someone who came to her place and helped her with, like, shit. And I said no, we're okay, in the physical-care aspects at least. The care team asked us about that at the hospital, and we said we're okay. We've got it."

"Do you?" Paloma asks.

"I mean, I think so," Andre says. "Mira said she doesn't need anything that she can't do by herself. And…" His voice catches. Paloma murmurs something to him, so low I can't hear it. "And, if she does need something, as long as you don't need to be, like, a medical person to do it, like as long as I won't hurt her, then I will do it. I want to do that for her. You know? She and I, we've always been there for each other. That's why we got married, you know? So we could take care of each other forever."

"You two have the sweetest love story," Paloma says.

"Thanks," Andre says. "That's what I'm really proud of, you know? Not so much my job. I mean, I like my job. I like where I'm at. But it's what I'm building with Mira. That's what really matters to me."

"You're a good guy, Andre."

"I try," he says. "Shit's been really hard lately, though. I'm thinking of trying to get some time off. You know? Some significant time. A week? A couple weeks? Even a month? Like it would be so nice to not only be really present for Mira, like really talk to her, make sure she's okay, but also get my own shit together. You know? Because my head is not together, Paloma. I feel like I'm faking it. Bullshitting my way through the day. I don't wanna live like that. So it would be really cool to have some time. To take a breath. To deal with my shit."

"Is it, like…" She pauses. "Any shit you wanna talk about?"

He sighs. "I don't know, P. I don't mean to be a dick. But, like, not really?" They both laugh. "I'm sorry. I just haven't even faced it myself yet. What's happened. How I'm feeling about it. It's heavy shit and I'm not there yet."

"I understand," she says. "But do you have someone to talk to?"

"So Mira and I saw this relationship coach a while ago. Marcela. I really liked her. I guess I liked having someone to talk to? So I recently booked some sessions with her. For just me. So maybe I can get there. To dealing with and talking about some of this crap. Because I am not doing my best right now. And you know I want to. For Mira. And for me too. So."

"Andre. Honey."

"Fuck. I'm sorry I'm crying."

"The fuck are you apologizing?" she says. "You can cry. Cry."

"I'm sorry," he says, "I'm also trying to poly better."

She laughs. "You're trying to what?"

"To be a better member of our… polycule? You and me and Mira. If you two are a thing, and if you love her, then we are on the same team, Paloma. Fuck. Sorry for the corporate metaphor. You just can't escape work, can you? I just want us, you and me, to be friends, to feel a little close to each other, if you and my wife are a thing. Does that make sense? Is that, like, okay?"

"That makes perfect sense," she says, her voice a little rough, with emotion, I think. "And it's better than okay. It's perfect."

"Marcela, this coach, she's also a poly relationship coach, apparently. I researched all her shit before we booked our sessions with her. She's in a throuple herself, with two men. They've all been together for like five years. I mean, I don't want to be in a throuple. But if Mira has other… lovers, then I'd love to be able to be tight with them. If I can. Like, friendship-wise. So I wanna work on that."

"You are working on a whole lot right now, my friend." Paloma sighs. "Are you sure you're okay?"

"It is a lot," he acknowledges. "And I'll be okay. But I'm exactly where I want to be."

"Okay," she says. There's silence for a few moments. "Andre, can I ask you something?"

"Sure," he says.

"Do you think this is all… too much?" I can see her making an all-encompassing gesture, elegant and balletic. "I mean. Everything Mira's going through. Everything you're both going through. And also trying to, like… poly, as you put it? Is it too much, all at once? I mean, I know we don't get to make decisions for Mira. She decides what's right for her. And I am here for whatever she wants. So probably I'm being kind of a dick here. But I'm still gonna ask. Do you think we're all taking on too much?"

Andre doesn't answer right away, 'cause he's all thoughtful and considerate and shit like that. Then he takes a deep breath and says, "Paloma. I know all this scary shit happened when you and Mira were at the beginning of building your thing. And it was some really scary shit. For me, too. But Mira has been managing this illness since she was five years old. Since before I met her, actually. My wife is all about still living her life. Doing her thing. CF is one of her things. And it always will be. Like she always says, it's in her literal DNA. So if she started something with you, P, it's because she wanted to. And she is all in."

"I am all in too," Paloma says softly. "Can't think of anyone better to poly with than you, Andre."

"Same," he says.

"Honey," she says, "I think you should try to take some time off from work. I think that pause would be really good for you."

"I know," he says. "It would be. You're right. Well. I'm gonna talk to Mandee about it on Monday. With all her health stuff, and when she transitioned, she has a lot of experience getting the time off for herself that she needs. I'll see if she has any advice."

"I'm really glad you met her."

"Yeah, me too," he says. "She's really cool."

Paloma yawns, loudly. They both laugh.

"I'm sorry, baby," she says.

"Don't be," he says. "It's late."

"Drinking beer makes me sleepy," she says.

"Do you want to go back to bed with your girlfriend?"

"I don't know," she teases back, "should I?"

"Yeah," he says, "you should. Your girl might wake up and miss you."

"She's very sweet," Paloma says, "in the middle of the night."

"She is," Andre says.

All this sweet shit makes me want to fall back to sleep, just so I can wake up again next to her, groggy and warm and wanting to cuddle. I close my eyes and try to sleep again.

I wake up in the morning, next to Paloma, feeling much better. First of all, this is probably the best sleep I have had since before I went to the hospital. So I'm waking up in that calm, steady, slow-heartbeat way you do when your body and mind have actually had enough sleep, and you don't feel achy-eyed and irritable and like you just wanna smack somebody. So there's that. Second of all, did y'all hear everything Andre and Paloma said last night? I'm aware that nothing is perfect. I'm aware that nothing is fixed. But I was also reminded by hearing their talk last night that I am one lucky girl. I have some amazing people in my corner.

I ease myself out of bed. Paloma is still sleeping. On the living room couch, buried under about ten blankets, Andre is also still sleeping. It's rare that I'm up before him. He's an early riser.

I take a long, hot shower. I wash my hair, put some serum in, let it dry loose. It feels glorious to have clean hair. More complicated is how I feel when I take a few long moments to look at myself, at my hair, in the mirror before I step out of the bathroom. If I go out there like this, sometime in the next little while, my girl is gonna see me with my new gray hair. I'm still scared. I want to remember that I earned this gray hair, that I lived long enough and did something hard enough to get it, every strand. And I guess I do. But I also tear up, because I'm in my early twenties and I have gray hair, a lot of it, and Paloma is almost a decade older than me and has perfect, long, thick, lustrous black hair. Every time I doom-scroll Instagram, all I see are the other twentysomething girls, wearing bikinis, posing in pretty places with their cute boyfriends or girlfriends, gearing up for a hot vaxx summer. And that just ain't me. That is not my life.

I can't hide in my bathroom forever, so I creep out. My guy and my girl are still asleep. So I go into the kitchen. I light some of the candles and arrange some of the crystals Paloma brought me around the room. I spritz the bouquet of flowers she brought me, pink and yellow spring tulips. I turn on the lavender air humidifier. I drink a glass of orange juice and reply to some of my text messages: my CF friend Jess, Mom and *Abuela,* Marco and Hassan, Araceli. I swallow some of my morning meds by mouth; I pump my pancreatic enzymes into my body through the tube. There— now I can live for another day. Maybe it's not what the wellness and self- love folks on Instagram might suggest. But it's hard. Remembering what Andre said last night, that what he's most proud of is what we're building together, and what Paloma said, that she's all in with me, that makes it easier to keep doing this daily routine that I am truly so fucking tired of. If it were just me, if I were alone, I honestly don't know if I could keep bothering. But I will do it if it means I get to keep showing up for my people.

Andre wakes up, goes into the bathroom for a little while, then comes into the kitchen to find me cooking. "*Hola, mi reina*," he says, and squeezes me and lifts me from the floor and kisses me, and I don't mean like a little good-morning kiss, y'all, I mean this man kisses me properly.

"Oh, okay," I say, touching my lips as he puts me back down on the floor. "Good morning, then."

"Morning," he says, with a sexy little smile that, three months ago, before my body started feeling like a scooped-out melon, would have had me naked for him in seconds. Now, I feel a little glimmer inside, and I'm grateful for that.

"Sorry I'm making these blueberry pancakes again," I say. "I know we ate them yesterday."

He gives me a look that clearly says, *I ate these, girl, you did not,* but he doesn't say it out loud, which is nice.

"But we have so many blueberries," I finish.

"Why are you sorry?" He kisses me again. "These pancakes are amazing." He squeezes me. "And how about you actually taste them today and see for yourself?"

I roll my eyes. So much for that, then.

Paloma comes into the kitchen just then. She's clearly brushed her hair and her teeth and put on a silk robe over the tiny cami and silk sleep shorts she slept in, and she looks like a visitor from another, way more elegant and put-together, planet, crash-landed in our tiny basement kitchen.

"Good morning, *ma sirène*," she says. "Good morning, Andre." She kisses each of us.

"Morning," I say. "I'm making blueberry pancakes."

"Amazing!" she says. "Can I help?"

"Sure," I say.

I put on a reggaeton playlist and we all make blueberry pancakes together. It's all sweet and awesome and fucking kitchen-table-poly aspirational, until I have to sit down and try to eat some of this food. I have not been eating solid food much at all lately, okay. I've been putting enough liquid into the tube to a, stay awake and b, keep Andre from giving me side-eye. Like I said, I have two amazing lovers, but your girl remains just a little bit fucked up. I eye the blueberry pancake on my plate. I feel both slightly nauseous and completely un-hungry. But I know I have to eat it. So I look at them happily eating and I think about Hassan, who completed his two-week in-patient bulimia treatment (and apparently only made himself throw up once during the fourteen days, which, he told me, is a win for him right now) and I focus on the taste of the food—soft, slightly crunchy golden cake; fat, hot, sweet blueberries—and I make myself eat.

While Andre's washing dishes after, his phone brightens with a text on the table. "It's your sister," I tell him, glancing at it. "She's inviting you to the gym. You should go," I say, firmly.

"It's a really nice gym," he says, all dreamy, like one of those memes that says to get yourself a lover who looks at you how Andre looks at good gym equipment.

"You should go," Paloma and I both say.

We all laugh.

"Are you two trying to get rid of me?" he asks, turning the water off and turning around to look at us.

"Yes. Paloma is planning to initiate me into an ancient goddess religion today, Andre," I explain. "We must cleanse the premises of all masc energies."

He laughs loudly, turns back to the dishes. "*Bien de bien.* I will take all of my masc energies to the gym and lift weights with my sister."

So Andre and his masculine energies get ready to leave. At the door, he kisses me and says, "Mira. Please eat today."

I want to smack him. "Yes, sir," I say.

"Mira," he says. "Can you, like, not?"

"Do not *Fifty Shades of Grey* me, Andre," I say.

"I'm sorry," he sighs.

"Andre," I say. "I am doing the best I can."

"I know." He hugs me, kisses the top of my head. "Can we talk about this later?"

"Sure. I can't wait to talk about my fucking gastrostomy tube more."

"Okay." He kisses my forehead a last time and lets me go. "I'm going now." He looks past me to where Paloma is scrolling her phone on the couch, pretending not to eavesdrop on our shit. "Bye, Paloma."

"Bye, Dre. Have a good workout."

"Yeah," I say. "May the force be with you."

He laughs in a way that lets me know we are gonna be okay. "May the force be with both of you, young Jedis."

Paloma and I sit together on the couch and scroll through our phones. When she gets up to go to the bathroom, I text Andre: *Sorry I was being a big baby about the g tube. I know my eating is fucked & I'm sorry. I will do my best today and yes we can talk about it. I'm gonna do better I promise.*

He writes me back instantly. *You are doing amazing and I love you. You are not a big baby, you're my brave queen. I'm sorry I was a pushy dick. You're my perfect girl and I miss you already.*

I melt into the couch. *I love your pushy dick,* I write back.

Ohhh okay, he writes back, and the blushing emoji.

Paloma comes back from the bathroom. I toss my phone facedown onto the couch and say, "Paloma, baby? Can I talk to you about some stuff?"

Her face goes alert. "Of course you can, baby girl."

We go into the kitchen. This feels like a kitchen kinda talk, the place where I feel comforted and in my magic, and also where I have something to do with my hands. I play with crystals, rolling them around in my fingers, arranging and rearranging them on the tabletop, as we speak.

I start with a big sigh. "I'm sorry our weekend is turning into one long processing session," I say.

"No, Miranda." She squeezes my knee. I look at her perfect nails, a shiny iridescent pale white, against my ratty leggings. "I'm totally here for it. For whatever we need right now."

I close my eyes. "I missed you saying my name the way you do."

She whispers my name in my ear. I shiver.

"I'm right here, baby," she says.

"And I'm sorry I'm not, like, going anywhere," I add, opening my eyes. "I've just been at home. I need to be home right now. I'm sorry I'm so boring."

"Also no." She rubs my thigh. It feels good, the most sexual touch I've had in days. "Baby. You are not boring. I missed you so much. So, so much." She combs through my hair with her fingers. I remember all the grays and freeze but she just keeps stroking my hair till I feel warmer, calmer. "This is all I want. To talk to you, hear your voice. Look at you. Touch your hair. We can talk and listen to music and cook together and do some witchy stuff. We'll pull cards for each other and do a candle ritual." She squeezes my earlobe gently. "That sound okay?"

My eyes get wet. "That sounds perfect," I say.

I take a deep breath. "When I was in the hospital," I begin, "they were really worried about my nutrition. About my weight. So every night..." My voice is trembling. I hate this. "Every night when I was in the hospital, they gave me a light sedative. To put me in to what they call a twilight sleep. They gave me a little surgery to place a feeding tube in my stomach. So I could get nutrition directly. And every night they fed me liquid nutrition through the tube."

"Did it… did it help?" Paloma asks.

I nod. "Some. My weight gain is slow. It's related to the pancreatic insufficiency. It doesn't make enough enzymes to break down the nutrition in food and, like, feed me. It's a pretty big problem. So my care team decided that I needed to take the tube home with me. And so…" I stand up. My heart's pounding so hard it makes me feel sick and dizzy and I think I might pass out, or throw up. But I lift up my giant T-shirt so I can show Paloma my tube.

"So, this is it. It's called a gastrostomy tube. G-tube for short. I've got a syringe that attaches so I can feed myself."

Paloma looks at the tube. Her looking at it is, of course, nowhere near as bad as I thought. "Thank you for telling me that," she says, looking into my eyes again. "Thank you for showing me your G-tube."

"Of course." I sit down.

Paloma takes my hands, squeezes them. "Do you feel like talking about it?"

I nod. "I'd like to. If you have any questions about it, I want to hear them, and answer them."

It's almost funny, how calm and mature I'm fronting on the outside, while on the inside I am scream-crying.

"Okay," she says. "Thank you." She sits back. "So you… feed yourself through the tube?"

"Yeah. Sometimes."

"What… goes in there?"

I smile. "I have a liquid nutritional blend that I can put in there. It's medical food. Meaning, it's not for swallowing by mouth. It's specially formulated by my care team with the exact nutrients that I need. It's meant to go directly into my tube. But, actually, I can put anything in there that I want."

"You can?"

"Yep." I point to Andre's stupid new blender in a corner of the counter. "You just blend it up and you can squirt it into your tube."

"Oh… okay," Paloma says. She's cautious. And I get it. What, exactly, do you say to your new girlfriend about her feeding tube? "That's… cool?"

I shrug.

"Can I ask you a really silly question?"

"Go for it, *nena*."

"Can you, like…" She looks away, then back at me again. "Can you taste the food somehow? That goes into the tube?"

I try not to laugh at her question, but I do. "Nope," I say. "There is no tasting with the gastrostomy tube."

"But you… this morning you ate some pancakes, right? So you can still…"

"Yep," I say. "I can still eat by mouth. If I want to. It's just…" I sigh deeply. "Food is complicated for me, Paloma, okay."

She nods. "I noticed," she says. "Do you want to tell me about it? I'd love to hear it. I want to know you more, Miranda."

"I know you do," I say. I tug my hands through my hair, and for a tortured minute, my conflicting desires war with one another. There's my desire to bring her closer, and my desire to push her away. There's my desire to reveal and to conceal. There's my complex feelings for this woman, churning together with my shameful feelings around food.

"So, it's complicated. I like food. I do. I like the way it tastes, the way it smells. I love cooking food. But I'm finally realizing, and coming to terms with, how I don't really feel about food the way other people do. I have such low appetite. I don't really crave food. Eating is hard for me. There's a lot of reasons for it. I have a lot of digestive issues related to CF that make eating difficult. I used to hate the obsession with it when I still had my old lungs and just the constant lung infections and illnesses—like, was I taking in enough fat and calories to support my body through the lung-clearing routine and all the calories you burn trying not to die from infections? I hated that. Hated my food and calorie intake being monitored. I hated feeling like I was being forced to eat more when I just didn't want to. I hated the frustration of it: not wanting to eat, feeling sickened by food, but eating it anyway 'cause I knew I had to, taking my stupid appetite stimulants, and still not gaining weight. Because of the pancreas thing. And…"

I look her in the eye. "This is not a CF thing. This is a Castillo family fucked-up thing. As you probably know, we did not have much money growing up. For a variety of reasons. Including generational poverty, institutionalized racism, the high cost of having a chronic illness, and how expensive my mom's addictions were. But anyway. My mom and my brother always tried to make sure that I had food. Like, sometimes they would choose to be hungry so I could have food. Which I didn't even want. And my body couldn't absorb. So that made me feel like crap. And fucked up my relationship with food even more. Wow."

I let out a deep breath. My body is coursing with adrenaline.

"I have never said any of that out loud before," I tell her.

She grips my hands. Her touch anchors me.

"Wow," she agrees. "That's a breakthrough, Miranda. I'm honored I was the one you shared it with. Thank you for trusting me."

"Thank you for listening," I say. "So, it's fucked up. The G-tube should help with some of those issues. The physical ones, anyway. But I still have so much emotional shit to… untangle. I know I'm still not using it as much as I should be."

"Can I ask why not?" Paloma asks, still cautious.

"I don't know. Guilt? Shame? Fatigue? Letting go of the story that someday, getting better means becoming like everybody else. When it doesn't." I shake my head. "Andre's been talking to some other G-tube users online. I've been chatting with a couple of them. A woman with CF in her thirties who's been using hers for years. She was telling me she goes out to restaurants where they know her and blends her food and eats it there with everyone else using her tube. I mean… I can't see me doing that, but I love it for her. And I've been talking to this lady whose eight-year-old daughter has CF. She recently got a G-tube put in and she's feeding her and teaching her how to use it. She told me she's feeling relieved. 'Cause now her kid will get the nutrition she needs and some weight gain. So that's cool."

"How does it make you feel?" Paloma asks. "Talking to them?"

I shrug. "Not as good as it should," I say. "Like I'm happy for them. I'm glad there's people out there who've found a way to still live great lives this way. People who just have a G-tube and it's not their, like, whole fucking life. It's not all they think about. It doesn't define them." I shake my head. "I am just not there yet. I'm not sure what will get me there. Facing all my shit, probably. I'll get there. Just not, like, today."

I rest my head on the table.

Paloma strokes my hair. "Sweetheart. Are you all right?"

"I guess so," I mumble. "I just can't talk about that any more for now. It's exhausting me."

"Of course." She rubs my back. "That was a lot, Mira. I'm really proud of you. Thank you for telling me all of that." She leans down, kisses my head. "What do you need right now? What would feel good for you right now?"

I lift my head. My eyes prickle with tears. "Could you comb my hair?" I ask her. "And pull a tarot card for me and give me a reading?"

She takes my chin and kisses me on the mouth. "Of course I can," she says.

We go into the bedroom. I sit between Paloma's spread legs and she combs my hair. The serum is still there, silky and thick on my scalp and coating the strands of my hair. Paloma works it through with the comb. We share one breath: drawing it in as she comes to small tangles or kinks, letting it out with grateful release when the teeth of the comb move smoothly through. Then she brushes my hair. She uses a kind of satisfying force. I feel the charms on her bracelet on her right wrist knocking lightly against my skull as she starts her strokes at the top of my head. She brushes my hair until it's smooth and soft. While she brushes, she whispers sweet things into my ears. She tells me how pretty I am, how good my hair feels, how it's the color of one of those shaken espresso drinks at Starbucks, all deep brown and rich and then shot through suddenly with gold; this makes me laugh. My scalp tingles, and I feel pleasantly tired. It's been a while since I had an orgasm, or even thought about having one, but I feel sort of like the way you do after a violent and long-needed orgasm, languid and swelled, heartbeat heavy and thick as syrup.

Paloma has brought me a new tarot deck, because of course she has. It's maybe the most beautiful deck of cards I've ever seen. Its aesthetic is cosmic and celestial, with a moody color palette in black, gold, lavender, royal purple, and pink. The figures are all represented by voluptuous naked women with brown and golden skin. She says it was designed by a witch friend of hers who funded it via a Kickstarter, because of course it was.

I say I don't know what question I want to ask the cards, so Paloma just shuffles and says, "Miranda Marcela Castillo asks if her guides have any wisdom for her today."

She pulls for me the Star, reversed. The image on the card is of a woman bending down to pour one vessel of water into a flowing stream, and simultaneously another one onto the ground. Her dark purple box braids flow out behind her. Twinkling pink stars surround her.

"What do you think it means?" I ask her, blinking at the card from past her shoulder. I'm sitting behind her now, as if I want the protection of her body and her aura between me and the cards, which I have not consulted for guidance since I got home from the hospital. I have one arm held tightly around my girl, holding her close. I can feel her breathing.

"Well, the Star is about your divinely guided purpose in this life," Paloma says. Her voice is husky. I don't know if it's from the mysticism of the tarot or because of how I'm holding her, or both. "It's about your natural brilliance."

"Do you think I've forgotten it, maybe?" I nuzzle her shoulder with my lips.

"What?" she whispers.

"My divinely guided purpose," I whisper back. "In this life."

"I don't know, Mira," she says. "Have you?"

"Do you think I have dulled my brilliance?"

"I…"

I sink my teeth into her shoulder.

"Mira," she sighs.

I stroke her round breasts, her round stomach.

She twists around to look at me, panting.

"Touching you is probably all I can do right now, sex-wise," I tell her, against her lips. "I'm not there yet." I touch the top of her thigh. She bends her leg up at the knee so I can give her juicy inner thigh a proper squeeze. Her breath hitches for me, my responsive girl that I missed very much. I want desperately to be her sex person again, to get all wet for her, to say her name, but it's not time yet.

"Oh, Mira," she says. "You touching me again is so much. It's everything."

"You feel so good." I put my lips, my tongue, to the side of her face, her ear, her neck. I pull her earlobe between my teeth.

"I missed you so much," she says, with a noise almost like a sob.

"I missed you too, *nena*." I rub her navel with my thumb. "I'm so sorry."

She leans her head back against me. "Don't be sorry, baby," she says. "Don't worry. I understand. Everything is okay."

I want to stay in this with her. I want to be able to keep touching her. I want to make her feel good. I ghost my fingertips over her nipples. They feel so good, so tangible. She whines for me. A jolt goes through me. But it isn't enough. My arm loosens around her. I lean back against the wall behind the bed, panting, and not in a good way.

Paloma turns around all the way to face me. She cups my cheek. "Mira? Are you okay?"

I shake my head. "Not really," I say truthfully.

"Oh, God," she says. "What's wrong, baby? Can I do anything?"

"Think I'm just dehydrated," I say. "I should drink something."

"Yes," she says. "I'll go get you something. What do you want? Some water with ice?"

"I'll go with you," I say. "Let's go sit in the kitchen."

Paloma puts her arm around my waist and we go to the kitchen. She sits me down. "Tell me what you want, *sirena*," she says.

"Could I have orange juice, please?"

Paloma finds the orange juice in the fridge and a glass in the cupboard and pours it for me and places it in front of me. I thank her in a soft voice. She shakes her head quickly, a silent signal that I do not need to thank her. She watches me while I drink the juice slowly. There's a new awareness, a new understanding, in her eyes that was not there before. She doesn't say anything, but somehow I know what realization she's come to: I am really sick. It's not that she didn't know it before, or didn't believe me; but there's a difference between hearing stories about it and having to carry me to the kitchen and give me orange juice to revive me after touching her body sapped all my energy. She pours herself a glass too. She moves around the kitchen, assembling a plate of snacks, a combination of stuff she brought yesterday and stuff we had lying around: chocolates, crackers, chips, little cubes of cheese, an apple that she quickly slices. She puts it on the table between us and starts eating a piece of cheese. I'm not hungry, but I nibble an apple slice to look more normal.

"Are you okay?" she asks me.

"I don't know," I say. "I mean, no. I'm not, like, in any immediate medical danger. But I'm still working on being okay." I swallow some apple. I want to cry, but I won't. "Is that okay?"

She smiles faintly. "Of course it is."

"I don't want to talk about my shit anymore," I tell her. "Tell me something about you. Something good. How is your research going? Your teaching?"

Paloma tells me the latest about her dissertation. She has a new reader, a formidable theorist from the women's and gender studies department at Columbia. She says that the professor's critiques are sharp, "but they're going to make my work stronger." She's teaching two online undergraduate courses this semester, one about women in Greek myth and another about Minoan and Cycladic art, one of her favorite topics. Hearing about her classes makes me feel unbearable longing.

I ask so many questions about her classes, about whether she thinks Greek myth is inherently misogynistic or if she thinks a feminist reading of it is possible, about what it feels like to teach nineteen-year-olds about her favorite art, that she smiles and says, "Have you heard back from the school you applied to?"

"Paloma," I say. "I have something to tell you." My voice shakes.

She squeezes my wrist. "Honey? What is it?"

"It's nothing bad. I just…" I take a deep breath. "Yes, I heard back. I got in to the program. And I accepted. So I am. Going back to school."

"Miranda." Her eyes glitter as they search mine. "You are?"

"I am."

"Mira!" she says. "I am so proud of you. Back in school is where you belong, Mira." She shakes her head. "They are gonna be so lucky to have you. I'm jealous of whoever's going to get you. That mind of yours. Your intelligence. Your philosophy. All your questions."

"Oh, girl. Stop." I nudge her foot with mine under the table. "I'm so worried about it, Paloma. I'm terrified."

"Of what?" she asks.

I laugh. "So many things. I love studying. I love learning. I love writing. And I like being in the classroom. But I'm so shy there, Paloma. I'm painfully shy in front of people like that. I struggled with that so much when I was just doing my associate's. This is a more advanced degree. At a four-year school with, like, regular students. I'll be older than them. Not much, but a little. And my experience is going to be just… so different from theirs."

I'm tearing up. Paloma picks up my hand and kisses it and says, "They need your perspective, Mira. You're going to be exactly where you belong. The other students are going to learn from you."

"You think?"

"I know," she says. "God. I wish I could have you in my classes. I mean, not really." She laughs. "You're my girl. You're my lover. I want you so much. I'm just jealous of whoever's gonna get to have you like that. In a way that I can't."

I'm so in love with her suddenly that my throat hurts. I know I try to push her away. But it's only partly to keep her from getting hurt. She could hurt me too, profoundly. And it ain't just in the usual, and utterly terrifying, way that any and all of our little human hearts are capable of being hurt when we give them away. The likeliest ending to my story is that I leave this girl behind. And I will miss her so fucking much when that happens.

But, for now, there's September to think of.

"Thank you," I say. "I'm also scared about the finances. I love so much about school. But I'm so against the whole machine of student loans. My family is in a lot of debt already. Mostly because of my medical bills. So is it ethically right for me to go back to school, at this point in my life, and probably incur more debt?" I shake my head. "I talked about it with Andre. I think he's more excited about me going than I am. And I also… talked about it with Hassan."

So, here's how this whole thing happened. Hassan went to his inpatient bulimia treatment. As planned, we talked every night about my story. We got to the end, the new ending I wrote by dictating it on my phone while I was in the hospital. Hassan gave me notes to make my story stronger. He also told me that he cried, reading my character Tina's story while he was trapped in the most awful place ever. He said that wanting to know what happened to her, wanting to know how her magic would turn out, kept him going over those two weeks when he wanted to give up.

I saw it so clearly then, y'all. I knew it. I knew that, even if all I have left are the four years it's gonna take me to do this degree (three, I'm hoping, if enough of my associate's credits will transfer over), I'd want to spend them writing stories, sharing them, making them stronger.

I told Hassan, "I got into the creative writing program."

And he said, "You're going. You are a writer, Miranda. This is where you should be. If you need me to, whatever your scholarships do not pay, I will pay for you."

"Are you sure?" I whispered.

"I am so sure," he said.

"Can I think about it?" I said.

"Take the money," he said. "Save your brainpower for your classes."

What would it feel like, to let him give us money? He said he would pay for my school, and that he would like to help us pay down a lot of our debt as well. Andre could take time off work and not worry about it as much. The other day, we found out that the cost of our internet is going up, and that when our current lease period ends, our landlord is raising the rent by a hundred dollars. I'm planning to start writing and translating for LWP again, I'm well enough to do that, but if we weren't in so much debt, I could at least maybe stop working at Anthropologie. We could travel, if and when I'm well enough to do that. We could save. I could go to school and not be in debt. I hate knowing that so many other broke girls like me can't go to school debt-free, or at all, because they happen not to have a family member with random money, but maybe if enough of us rise, we can make a world where anyone can go to school who wants it. I don't know how, but I believe in magic and miracles. I think we could make that world.

"Hassan offered to pay my tuition," I tell Paloma. "Whatever my financial aid won't cover."

"Let him do it," she says. "Hassan is a Netflix big shot now. A *New York Times* bestseller."

"You think I should?"

"Of course I do," she says. "That's what money is for, Mira. For helping your family. It doesn't mean anything if you don't use it to help your people."

I nod.

"This is the best, Mira," she says. "I love this for you. I can't wait to hear every detail. You'll get out of class and I'll take you to bed and take off all my clothes and just listen to you. Hearing about you in class like that is gonna make me so wet for you."

I can't stop laughing. It's the most I've laughed in a long time.

"Thank you for being excited for me, Paloma," I tell her.

"Of course I am!" she says.

"I love you so much," I tell her.

"Oh, sweetheart," she says. Her cheeks are flushed, eyes sparkling. "I love you too."

"I want to take you back to bed, Paloma," I whisper. "Right now. I don't know how much I can do. But I really want to touch you."

"Mira…" she says.

Then we hear Andre's key in the door.

The moment's broken, at least for now. We hold eyes for a meaningful second, letting each other know silently that we will take this conversation up again later.

Andre and Paloma and I prepare and eat food together. Hassan's also been sending us Hello Fresh boxes, since he has a sponsorship deal with them too. We make probably the simplest recipe ever, *cacio e pepe* pasta and a spinach and mozzarella salad. While the water boils for the pasta, we play a candle magic game, all three of us, the rules made up by Paloma: we ask a question of the candle, close our eyes, and see what color it's flashing when we open our eyes—my rainbow electric candles cycle through three colors, red, green, and blue. In our game, red means no, green means yes, and blue means maybe. We only ask light, playful questions—will we have a hot summer, will the Mets be in the postseason (maybe, says the candle), should Paloma take this online watercolor painting class she's been eyeing (yes, the candle says)—but there's a deliciousness to this that goes deeper than our questions would suggest, sharing this game not only with Andre but in the circle of energy and experience that we're creating together, the three of us. I don't often share my witchy stuff with Andre. I don't know why; maybe I'm projecting a lifetime of my brother teasing me and dismissing my mysticism as unscientific onto my husband, which isn't fair. His eyes glow when Paloma tells him to ask a question. He closes his eyes earnestly. And he's excited to see, and to discuss, the candle's responses. It makes me think I should invite him into my magic more often. He's so sweet it makes me hurt.

The water boils. We pour the pasta in, stiff spears of spaghetti that rattle against the pot. They soften in the extreme heat of the water, becoming pliable, tender things, long, smooth ribbons that chase each other in the whirlpool created by our stirring. I lean over the pot to feel its warmth on my face.

When the pasta is finished cooking, we toss it with butter, salt, pepper, lots of pecorino cheese, and some of its own cooking water. Meanwhile, Andre makes the salad.

Once the food is done, I take a close look at it. Grated bits of cheese cling to the spaghetti, still steaming. The beautifully tangled noodles repose in small pools of melted butter and punchy black pepper. Bright, crisp spinach nestles beside creamy white pearls of mozzarella. The food is lovely. But I don't think I can eat any of it, not right now, and not by mouth.

So I measure out the exact amount of liquid nutrition that my care team recommends for a meal. I wash my hands and flush out my tube in preparation. I attach the syringe. I feed myself through the gastrostomy tube while Andre and Paloma eat. I watch them eat and enjoy the food. Andre looks at me feeding myself with an expression of approval and relief that I do not miss. Paloma steals glances over at me while trying not to look like she's staring. I say, "It's okay. You can look, baby," and after that, she watches me with curiosity and an interested kind of arousal that I also do not miss. I wish I could say that everything's perfect, that I'm cured, that with one transformational eating experience, I have now accepted my G-tube and am ready to go forth into the world with it, healed. But y'all know it don't work like that, right? What I get right now is the distant suggestion of a day when I will feel better than I do today.

After lunch we sit together in the living room. We chat about a rotating constellation of delightfully random topics. Sometimes, relaxed but also tired from balancing my shaky, tentative recovery and my lingering pain with more activity than I've had in months, I doze off, curled into the softness of the couch. We take turns going to the bathroom. During the moments when one of my lovers is away from the room, the other one takes the opportunity to cuddle me, to kiss my mouth, to whisper things to me. This makes me feel like an adored, treasured thing, a secret lovingly kept.

Andre asks Paloma if she still does her podcast. "Sex Never Sleeps?" she says. "Not much, since the pandemic, but I would like to get back into it. Why?" She lifts her eyebrows at him suggestively. "Would you like me to interview you?"

"I don't know," he says, looking away.

"I've barely ever listened to your podcast," I admit to her. "It felt weird, having this crush on you and hearing you talk about sex with other people."

She smiles. "You never have to listen to it if you don't want to, Mira."

"No, I'd like to," I say.

"I'd love to know that you're listening, if you want to," she says.

We talk about podcasts we sometimes listen to. Paloma and Andre both like the same Mets baseball podcast. I like listening to affirmations and visualizations and a couple of good astrology podcasts.

"Andre, baby, what zodiac sign are you?" Paloma asks.

"I'm a Capricorn," he says.

"Course you are, baby," she says, nodding. "God. That makes so much sense. You're all grounded and organized and protective and successful and basically, like, a total king."

He laughs. "Um, thanks."

"Andre is all Capricorn," I confirm, gazing over at him. "Total black excellence and win-all-the-time goat-fish energy." I don't say it—I've discussed this point at length with Celi, though—but Andre's mom Lisette is also a Capricorn. That goat-fish energy expresses very differently in him, but a lot of his shadow side comes from his mother.

"But you two are only focusing on my goat side," he argues, sitting up straighter. "Capricorn is a goat-fish, right, Mira? You've made me read about my sign so many times. The fish side means that I'm sensitive and emotional and I have a big, like, inner life. Right?"

"Right," I agree. "All that is definitely part of who you are too."

He nods. "Paloma? What sign are you?"

"I'm a Gemini," she says. "June first."

"Of course you are," I say.

She tosses her hair. "Classic Gemini. Social and curious and intellectual and I talk too much."

We all laugh.

"No wonder you two work so well together, though," Paloma says, pointing between Andre and me. "Two earth signs. All grounded and loyal and consistent and building shit together."

"We try our best," Andre says, looking at me with so much warm love that I basically, like, die.

"What about Gemini and Taurus?" he asks. "How are you two together?"

Paloma and I look at each other.

"Gemini and Taurus are very… different," Paloma says.

"But we're attracted to each other's differences," I say.

"That's right," she agrees. "Taurus is all devoted and passionate about shit. I have a new interest, like, every week. So I really like her focus. Seeing that excites me. And Taurus is… sensual. I love that." Her skin flushes slowly as she says all of this.

"And Gemini is… really vibrant," I say. "Sparkly. That excites me. I love sparkly things. Gemini is… charismatic. Magnetic. So inspiring to just talk to and listen to. I can't get enough."

"Mira," Paloma says.

"Why do I feel like you two are not really talking about zodiac signs anymore?"

"Oh," I say, "we're not."

"Well." Andre stands up. He leans down to kiss me on the forehead. "In that case I am gonna leave you two to flirt with each other astrologically. Or whatever you're doing."

We all laugh again. I'm shocked at how smooth and natural it all feels, how not-awkward.

As soon as Andre leaves the room, Paloma gets up from the armchair to sit with me on the couch. We sit cross-legged, facing each other. Our knees graze.

"Mira," she says. She reaches out for my hands. I reach mine back. She laces our fingers together. "I read the journal you gave me. I read it every single day when we were apart."

Fuck if that isn't one of the most romantic things I've ever heard. But I also feel my face get hot, remembering some of the utterly explicit things I recorded in that journal.

"Did you like it?" I whisper.

"Like it? Mira." She shakes her head, closes her eyes and puts her hand to her chest. "I adored it. I was obsessed."

"I've never had sex dreams like the ones I have about you, Paloma. You're my fantasy. Then you're here and you're real and I can barely stand it."

"The things your words made me feel..." She lets go of one of my hands, trails a finger down my forearm. "You are a fucking amazing writer, Miranda."

"That turns me on so much," I say. I feel like I'm glittering. "Knowing I made you feel something."

"Oh," she says, "you definitely made me feel something."

"You're so beautiful," I tell her. I unjoin our other hands, so I can cup her face. I trace her lips. Her breath is heavy, lifting and lowering her breasts. "You are all pink. I want to lick you all over."

"Mira." She sighs. "Am I being, like, too much? I'm sorry. I just get close to you and my body starts reacting. You're right; I'm like a fucking magnet with you."

I smile. "Why the fuck you apologizing, girl?"

"I'm… I just…"

"Are you wet for me?" I whisper.

"Mira," she says. She closes her eyes. "You know I am."

"Yes, I do know," I say. "I can smell you from here."

She gasps softly.

I touch the middle of her little silk sleep shorts, facing directly towards me. "Can I?" I whisper.

She nods. "Yes, please."

I hook a finger under the silk and tuck it to the side. I only let myself have a glimpse of her—her glorious cunt, wet glistening in her folds, prettily swollen for me—before I straighten her shorts neatly again.

"I'd like to touch you, Paloma," I say softly, "but I'd have to take it slow."

"We can take it as slow as you need to," she says. "Or we can just sit here and talk. Like this."

I put my thumbs onto her nipples. At first, I just rest them there, letting them lie, letting her absorb their weight and warmth. Her nipples are beaded and erect. Her breathing deepens under my hands.

"This okay?"

She takes in a ragged breath. "Oh, my God, please," she says.

I start rubbing her nipples in slow circles. She says my name.

"Do you want to just sit here and talk?" I ask.

"I mean, no," she says. She draws another shaky breath. "I…"

Andre comes into the room. I give her nipples a gentle press, tilt my head at her. She nods. I continue touching her.

"Shit," he says. He walks through the small room, heading over to the table by the door where we drop our keys and stuff when we first enter the apartment. "I'm sorry. I was just coming to get my other earbuds 'cause the other ones, like, died." He glances at us. "Yeah. Sorry."

"It's okay," we both say.

"Do you want me to stop?" I ask. I circle Paloma's breasts, taking the entirety of their weight in my hands. She moans, trying to cut the sound off, to stop herself, but she can't. She shakes her head.

I look at Andre.

"I mean… no," he says. "You don't have to stop. If you both… don't want to."

He comes a few steps closer and stands and watches for a moment, while I stroke my girl's perfect swollen nipples. I look at her face. Her mouth is open, lips wet, breath deep and shuddery.

"Paloma," Andre says. "You, uh, you're… wow."

She opens her eyes, licks her lips, and laughs. "I know," she says. "I know." She looks at me. Her look's so deep it makes me shudder. "Your wife is torturing me."

"I mean… fuck," he says. "Yes. I can see that."

"I'm sorry," she says. She's nearly panting now. She's so good, I want her so much, I am doing whatever I can to gather the strength to put my girl on her knees and fuck her.

"Don't be sorry," he says. "Thank you for letting me see this. But I am going to go back into the other room now. If that's okay?"

"Andre, baby," I say. "Whatever you want to do, or don't want to do, that's okay."

"What she said," Paloma manages.

"Thank you," Andre says, and goes back into the other room.

"Now, where were we?" I whisper to my girl. "Oh, right. Did you just wanna keep sitting here, letting me torture these pretty nipples, or did you want something more?"

"Mira." She squirms for me, pressing her thighs together, giving herself the touch she's craving.

"Can I see what you've got for me?" I ask.

"Of course you can." The words end on a moan.

I slide the damp silk to the side again. She's so wet I bet Andre can smell her from the kitchen.

"Mmm." I let myself make the noise my body wants to make, seeing her like this for me again. "You're so pretty, baby. Look how wet you are. You are fucking swollen, honey."

"I know I am," she says. She pulses her thighs together, opens them, peels her cunt open for me again. Her clit visibly pulses, diamond-shaped, purple with blood. "I'm aching for you, Mira."

I lean close, rest my chin on her shoulder, whisper into her ear. When I inhale to speak, I smell the musky sweetness of her sex. "Does this pretty clit need me to touch her? Make her feel better?"

"Mira." She grips my arms. "Please touch me. I need you to touch me."

I take her into the bedroom. By the time we get to the bed, she is legit whimpering for me. I embrace her. She's trying to hold onto me and take her shirt off at the same time. I hold her tighter, though not as hard as I want to, as I would if I were feeling stronger.

"I can just feel you throbbing from here," I tell her.

"God," she says. "I'm so ready it almost hurts. Baby. Miranda. Please."

We get her out of her clothes. Peeled out of the clinging silk, she's a revelation, warm mahogany skin and her smell and the smoothness of her against my skin and against my lips. Holding her naked again, I realize once more how much I missed her. I didn't let myself miss her, not beyond a distant, almost polite sensation; I didn't let myself miss her with bodily specificity, like the birthmark on her belly, or a faint scar from stitches on her knee when she was seven (I asked, and she told me the story), or her cute and battered toes, which are nothing like what those shiny pink pointe shoes would suggest on the outside. But now that I have her again, the physical reality of her, she hurts, coming back in to me, like how a numb limb tingles as the blood rushes back into the vessels.

Faced with her nakedness, how wet she is, how obviously ready, I don't feel inclined to move as slow as I thought I'd need to. There is no slow. I hold her close and thumb her clit, like I did with her nipples minutes ago. With no distance between us I can feel her every reaction: whimpers as quiet as a breath, the shake of her limbs, the crash of her heartbeat on her ribcage. It feels impossible not to turn my hand so that it's like I'm cupping her whole body, and slip a finger inside her, and two, especially when she starts to ride my hand to the knuckles, and we fuck her together with a pent-up and tender savagery. Her breasts bounce. She tells me what I'm doing to her, tells me how good I am, says my name to the squelching sound of her vulva. She drips into the center of my palm, between my fingers, down to my wrist. I feel the warmth of the crease of her ass. When I'm feeling better I want to touch her there, to smell her. I want to use my tongue. I make her come three times. By that point her clit feels pulpy and hot. I restrain her and smear her mouth with what I made come out of her, making her taste it.

"Oh, my God, Mira," she says. She licks my palm.

I'd forgotten how messy it is between us. I will do whatever I can to keep this.

Paloma's crying once it's over. My adrenaline is rapidly wearing off now, but I hold her and soothe her. I kiss her eyelids and smooth her hair against her head. My hand aches from fucking her so good, a wonderful feeling. I put my lips to her temple, where a slender thread of her pulse beats beneath the thin skin. I remember being in the hospital, the sick-sweet smell, missing her orchids. Her body is so strong in my arms, muscles that could overpower me, muscles that have danced entire narratives in ballet, taught a decade of dance classes in sweaty studios. This evening she lets me hold her, like a doll of a girl that I could comfort.

Paloma unfolds herself from my arms after a long time. Shadows are entering the room. There are dried tears on her face, her eyes red and the skin splotchy. "Mira," she says. Her voice is rough. She rolls onto her back, threads her hands over her belly, looks at the ceiling. "I need chocolate," she says.

I laugh. The mood between us feels both sad and delightful. "All right, *nena*," I say. "Let's get chocolate."

She sits up, rubbing her eyes. "Do you want me to touch you too?" she says. "What would feel good for you, Mira?"

I lean close and kiss her. "I am not ready yet. Touching you was what I wanted today. Chocolate sounds pretty good too right now."

When we emerge from the bedroom, Andre is in the bathroom. Paloma finds some of the chocolate truffles she brought in a shopping bag, puts them on the kitchen table. I start brewing some tea.

Andre comes out of the bathroom, and Paloma goes in. He goes into the bedroom immediately, closes the door. I sit down and rest my head briefly in my hands. My scar is starting to hurt, like it does every evening, sending me to bed early, cutting off some of the things I might like to do with my day. Paloma comes out of the bathroom. The water boils. I get up, and Paloma bumps my hip with hers. It actually hurts a little, that's how tender I feel, but I feel embarrassed to say anything, so I don't. "I can make the tea," she says. "You relax."

I go into the bathroom. Nothing looks dirty, but I need to do something with my hands to soothe myself, so I wipe down the bathroom surfaces with Lysol wipes. My stomach's hurting. While I sit down on the toilet and take a shit, I think about Paloma in here: the way it's a little hard to pee after you've come that hard, how the toilet paper comes away from your skin gooey and thick and wet with your lingering juices. Imagining this makes me feel a combination of jealous, sympathetic, and aroused. I wash my hands, which still smell like her, and tie my hair into a bun.

In the kitchen, Paloma and Andre are eating chocolates and drinking tea. This is a blend I made from ingredients I ordered from one of my online witchy stores: decaf black tea leaves, dried orange, cocoa bits, lemon, calendula, sunflower petals. Paloma's truffles, large and smooth and each one decorated with a colorful pattern—pink chocolate stars or tiny red roses or deep indigo swirls—pick up the dark, subtle notes of chocolate in my tea. I eat three of them, remembering how chocolate melts in the heat of your mouth, how it sticks sweetly to your back teeth.

"I can't believe you made this tea yourself, this is amazing," Paloma says.

She's tired and slouched at the table and emotionally wrung out, but still finds space to compliment me. "You are such a kitchen witch."

Andre smiles over at me. "She is, isn't she." His eyes are red; I think he's been crying. My heart squeezes, though not as hard as it would if I were at my full empath capacities.

During a quiet moment as we sit there eating chocolate and drinking tea, and the night gets later, I pick up my phone from the tabletop and text Andre. He feels his phone vibrating in the front pocket of his hoodie, slips it out, and reads my text with a small smile: *Are u ok baby?*

He replies: *I'm ok. I love you.*

I love you too, I write back.

Paloma looks at both of us and smiles but doesn't say anything.

"I think I've gotta get some sleep," I tell them.

"Sleep sounds amazing," Paloma says, longingly.

"I'm already falling asleep sitting here," Andre says. It's been a long and emotional day for all of us.

"I'll go on the couch," he says.

"Hey," I say. Tears burn behind my eyes. I do my best to keep them back. "Y'all can shoot this down if it's, like, a ridiculous idea. But I was really wanting us to have a living-room slumber party. I wanna sleep on the floor with a bunch of pillows and blankets."

"Will the floor be all right for you, baby?" Andre asks.

"The floor will be fine," I say. "The tube doesn't really hurt as much when I lie on it anymore. And I feel like I'll be less likely to roll over on it on the floor anyway." I sigh. "I just want to sleep on the floor in the living room. With both of you close by."

"All right," he says. "Let's do it, then." He stands up. "P? You in?"

"I'm in," she says, and stands up too.

We all get ready for bed. I feel really good, my two beautiful lovers in their cozy sweats helping me pile pillows and blankets onto the living-room floor. "I'm gonna go on the couch, if that's okay," Andre says. He nods at Paloma. "I think P wants to cuddle you, hummingbird."

She laughs. "I mean, he's not wrong."

We turn off all the lights. From the couch, Andre says sleepily, "Mira? Can you play one of those sleep visualizations?"

So I grab my phone and find one of my favorite sleep visualizations, the one where you're guided to imagine that you're climbing down a set of crystal purple steps from the crescent moon and down into your bed. The woman's voice leading us in the visualization evokes the comfort of a rainy night when you are warm inside: rhythmic, steady, childlike, nostalgic. As promised, Paloma cuddles up to me in our nest of blankets on the floor as we listen. I wonder if the feelings and images called to my mind by the visualization are the same that Andre and Paloma are imagining. I know that they are not. What a kind of magic, I think as I fall asleep, that we can all listen to the same words and make out of the same raw materials three completely different creations.

When I wake up in the morning, Andre's gone; he's left me a text saying he's going for a run in Fort Tryon Park. Paloma's in the bedroom, attending her Zoom yoga class; through the closed door, I hear the instructor's voice emerging softly from the small speakers of her phone or maybe her iPad. I've slept for a thousand years and I'm all alone. I burrow myself back down into my blankets and decide to sleep some more. I remember a doctor I used to have as a kid, an old guy who retired years ago now, who used to say that sleep cures everything. It's another of those mornings when, though I can't quite say I feel all better today, I can see my way towards a day when I will.

When I wake up again, it's to the sound of the front door to the apartment closing. I sit up. Paloma is holding a huge brown paper bag of food.

"Morning, beautiful," she says. "I ordered some Uber Eats for us."

"Thank you." I clear my throat, blinking my bleary eyes and pushing a hand through my hair. "Fuck. What time is it? How long did I sleep?"

She furrows her brow, shakes her head. "You needed the sleep," she says.

I go to the bathroom and take a quick shower and put on a long nightgown. I'm just not ready to pants today. I find my guy and my girl eating eggs and bacon together at the kitchen table. Paloma's long, loose, perfect hair is wet along the back of her T-shirt. Andre has also recently showered and smells fucking amazing, shampoo and aftershave and the whole thing. I'd like to curl up on his chest and just inhale him for an hour or two.

They both get up to kiss me. They ask me how I'm feeling, if I slept okay, if I want something to eat. I sit down with them and do my best to eat a little. I take my morning meds, by mouth and through the tube.

Sometimes I wish I wouldn't have these thoughts, but I don't know how to stop. I imagine some day in the fairly distant future, when I will not be here anymore. Will Andre and Paloma be here for each other? Will they comfort each other? Will they remember me together?

After breakfast, Paloma tells us she should be getting back home. She says she has a Zoom meeting with an art history colleague of hers who wants to write an article together, an early online class tomorrow morning that she should prepare for. "Baby girl," I say, "you go do your thing."

"It was great having you," Andre says. "Text me if you still wanna get in the studio. I'm sorry we haven't had a chance to do that yet."

"Dude, please," she says. "But yeah, I'll text you."

At the door, Paloma hugs me for a long time. I let myself relax into her hug, instead of worrying if I'm holding on too long, or clinging too hard, or if she's tired of me. I mean, I'm a big hugger, y'all, and I know that not everybody is. But I press my face into Paloma's shoulder and she strokes my hair. She whispers to me that she loves me.

I pull back, so I can see her face. "I love you too."

"Thank you for inviting me," she says. "For having me here."

"I already can't wait for next time," I tell her. "Text me when you get home."

"My Uber's probably here," she says, and looks at her phone, and it's one minute away. As she leaves, I hold the edge of the door and watch her walking away, and I stare down the empty hallway and to the stairwell even after she is gone. I have not left this door since I got out of the hospital. We've even done my follow-up appointments via telemedicine, because my care team decided that my healing at home where I'm comfortable and avoiding germs was more important than any tests or other shit they could do in person. I have quite literally been halfway underground for a month now. And maybe I've needed to be. But soon it will be time for me to get out of here.

In the apartment, I wash the dishes and clean up the kitchen. I fold the blankets in the living room and put them in the closet. Andre's all like, "Can I help you do stuff?" But I say, "Nah, baby. I got energy for the moment. Let me do some shit." So he's like, "Okay," and sits at the kitchen table half watching me and half reading a Colson Whitehead novel.

I go into the bedroom and strip the bed. I stuff the sheets into the laundry bag. I wonder if I'm feeling up to a trip to the laundromat. I wonder if I want my inaugural trip back out into the world to be around the corner to the laundromat.

In the kitchen, Andre is still reading, pausing to hold the book in one hand and wipe his eyes with the other. "Hey," I say.

"Hmm," he says.

I take the book from him gently. "Talk to me?" I say.

He sighs. I sit down with him.

"I'm sorry I, like, walked in on you and P last night," he says.

I shake my head. "You didn't, baby. You live here. I mean, this is literally your apartment." I gesture around. "I don't even work. You work and pay for all of this so I can have someplace to live."

He stares at me for a long moment. "Wow, Mira, no," he says. "Just… no. First of all, you do work. You're not working at the moment because you are recovering from a huge medical crisis. Are you actually kidding me, Mira? And second. You are my wife. And, like…" He shakes his head. "Can we actually talk about how fucked up that is later?"

"Uh," I say.

He wipes away more angry tears. "I'm sorry I did that," he says again. "I want your thing to be yours, and about you, and not about me. I want it to belong to you."

"It does." I shrug. "It's okay, Andre."

"I don't want to be a voyeur with you and P," he says. "Do you think she's mad at me for that?"

I probably shouldn't, but I laugh. "No, Andre. She is not mad at you for that."

"I don't want to do that again," he says.

"We'll have better boundaries if and when she's here," I say.

"Okay," he says. He rubs his hand over his head. "Also I feel like I'm flirting with her sometimes? And it's weird?"

"Does it bother you?"

"Not really," he says. "It feels kind of fun to just talk to her like that. And not have it be anything except flirting. And knowing that she is making you happy. It's just… Do you think it bothers her?"

"Not at all," I say firmly. "I think Paloma likes flirty talk too."

"All right," he says. He stares at me some more. I wait. Finally he says, "I heard you two yesterday."

"Did that bother you?"

He shakes his head. "No. I liked it," he whispers.

"I like knowing you can hear," I say. "I think she does too."

"Does that make me fucked up?" he asks.

"God. Not at all," I say. "I love that."

"I sat here," he says, "here at the kitchen table, and I got hard, listening to you two."

I'm nervous, with what I'm about to do, because it's a new thing. But it feels good, really good, to feel alive and awake enough to be trying a new thing again, and with my man that I've been with for so long.

"What did you hear," I ask, "that got you hard?"

"Fuck, Mira," he says. He casts his eyes away, remembering. "I heard a lot of stuff," he says. "But I think what mostly did it was listening to her say stuff to you."

"What kinds of stuff did she say?"

"You know what she said," he says, his voice low. "You were there."

"Yeah, I know," I say. "But I wanna know what you heard, Andre. What you remember."

"She was telling you how it felt. What you were doing to her."

"What was I doing to her? What did she say? Can you tell me what you heard her say?"

He blinks at me. I am different, right now, and he is too.

"Well, she was saying, 'You're fucking me so good, Mira.' And, 'You feel so good in me. You're so good.' She was saying *oh, my God* and asking you to please fuck her harder."

My temperature rises, hearing him say the things she said to me in his voice.

"That was so hot, Mira. Hearing her say those things to you. I wasn't sure if I should. But I got it out and started touching myself. Here at the kitchen table. Hearing to her talking so dirty to you. I was so turned on, knowing you were fucking your girlfriend in the other room."

"How did it feel?"

"It felt good," he says. "Naughty, but in a good way. Maybe a little guilty."

"Did you come?"

He nods. "I came. I was wiping myself off with napkins at the table. I've never jerked off at the table before."

"That's fucking hot, Andre. I love that."

He just looks at me more. He shakes his head slowly. "I haven't done it since, you know, before," he says. "Jerked off. I haven't wanted to."

"That's okay, baby," I say.

"Is it?" He lifts his eyebrows. "You don't think I'm, like…"

He trails off. He doesn't have to say anything more, though; this is not the first time we have had a version of this conversation. At times throughout our years together, Andre has expressed worry that he isn't as obsessed with sex as maybe he "should" be, or as he imagines other guys are, that he doesn't want it or think about it every second or get hard effortlessly and constantly. He asks me if I think there's something wrong with him.

"No," I say. "I think you're wonderful. You're everything to me. Our life hasn't been all that sexy lately. So you haven't been in the mood. That makes sense to me. There ain't nothing wrong with you, *papi chulo*."

"I'm sorry our life hasn't been that sexy lately," he says.

"Why the fuck are you apologizing right now?" I say. "You are tryna make me spank you."

"Whenever you're ready," he says, "I want to make you feel good again, Mira."

"You will," I say. "You remember March thirty-first. We're starting to do some stuff again, ain't we? Slowly."

"Slowly."

"But you touched yourself again," I say. "That sounds like a big deal."

"It was," he says. His voice shakes, and I love him, I love him so fucking much, for being willing to be here with me in this. His eyes get wet again.

"And when you're ready," I say, "I want to make you feel good again too, baby."

A couple tears spill down his face. "You do make me feel good, Mira," he says.

"You know what I mean."

"You're right," he says. "Slowly. When we are both ready."

"We have our lives together," I remind him, and me. "We've been through a lot."

A few more tears escape. He wipes his face with a napkin. "No fucking kidding," he says.

"I'm right here." I reach out for his hand. He gives it to me, and I squeeze. "For whatever you need."

"Mira," he says, just my name, but the way he says it, it says everything.

The next day, after work, Andre's mother calls. He takes his phone into the bedroom and closes the door. I am sitting with his laptop at the kitchen table. I am trying to write an article for LWP again. It's an easy one, one of those listicles that entice you to click through them. But it's the first work I've done since I got sick. It's slow going. But a little flickering flame of yearning low in my belly is keeping me going. I still don't feel great. I still don't feel as restored and recovered as I'd like to be by now. But I want to be a writer again. What I write today ain't gonna be brilliant. It ain't gonna be perfect. It's not going to win any awards, okay? But I am writing today. And that makes me a writer.

I can hear Andre's voice, deep and slightly annoyed, from the bedroom, but not what he's saying. I put on his headphones and turn on Maná, a Mexican rock band that Auntie Carmen used to love. Last night after I hung up from Paloma, I was practicing one of their songs, *"Ángel de Amor,"* on my guitar.

I'm about a third of the way through a draft of my list when the bedroom door opens. Andre doesn't come out, though; I hear the creak of the bed as he climbs back onto it, the rustle of the covers. Unlike your girl Mira, Andre is not a nap guy. I don't think he's going to sleep for the night either. That can only mean one thing. His mom was a jerk to him. I save my work, pull off the headphones, and go into the bedroom to check on him.

He's lying on his stomach under the covers, burrowing, only his head visible. He's also crying, silent tears into the pillow. There's been a lot of tears at our place these last couple days. Not many of them have been mine. I mean, I guess I ain't much of a crier. It used to hurt, back when I had my original lungs and my nose was always fucked from colds and infections. I'm a little worried this time, though. I haven't really cried yet for everything that happened to me—not even the fertilized egg and its sad little heartbeat. It feels like the sort of thing I should've had some big, epic cry for, screaming and wailing in an empty house all by myself, only my broken heart for company. But I haven't.

I sit on the bed next to him, put my hand on the back of his head. "Hey," I say.

He turns onto his side to look at me. "Hey," he says.

"Everything okay with your mom?"

A couple of tears spill out. "No," he says.

"Mi nene perfecto." I stroke down to his neck. "What did she say?"

He sighs. He sits up in bed, pulling a pillow into his lap and wrapping his arms around it. He is still my perfect boy, still the twelve-year-old who kissed me in his bedroom and stole my little preteen heart.

"Nothing much," he says. He wipes his eyes hard. "I guess I was just trying to tell her how I'm feeling about… stuff. She wasn't hearing it. She basically told me to, you know, get over it. I made the big mistake of telling her that I've started seeing Marcela for sessions. She was just, like, *hmm*. You know how she's always been about, like, therapy and stuff. Then I made the much bigger mistake of telling her that I think the way we look at therapy in the black community needs to change. She… did not like hearing that. Then, instead of shutting up, like I should have, I started to cry and I said that I think it's a way of honoring the ancestors and their struggles. That I get to focus on my inner world and healing my emotions. Lisette… did not like hearing that either."

"*Mi amor. Mi vida.*" I slide closer so I can hug him, tightly. I feel the stupid G-tube, between my T-shirt and his hoodie. I pull back. "You know how proud I am of you? You are fucking slaying at this whole life thing."

He laughs, which makes him cry more. "I shouldn't let her stupid crap bother me this much anymore. I'm twenty-three and still letting my mom make me cry."

"Yeah. That's because you're a fucking king."

He laughs harder. "Am I, really?"

I hug him again. "Yes. You are."

"You're everything to me, Mira," he says in my ear. "I can't do any of this without you." He squeezes me. His arms shake. "Please don't ever leave me."

"I am not going anywhere, baby boy."

I give him a last squeeze and pull back. I shift around so I can sit next to him, leaning my back against the bedroom wall behind us. I feel winded, overtired.

"Are you okay?" he asks me, rubbing my shoulder with his thumb.

"I'm fine, baby. How are you?" I put my hand on his thigh. "I'm sorry your mom couldn't really hear you. But I can. You know that, right? If you wanna talk about everything you're feeling, you know I'm here, don't you?"

"I know," he says, with a sigh. "I just… I'm just…"

"Please don't Marco me, Andre," I say. This means that it isn't okay for him to decline to talk about his feelings with me in a fucked-up, patriarchal effort to "protect" me. "I'm your partner. Your wife."

"I know that," he says. "And I promise not to Marco you, baby. I need you. You know that. There is no literal way I am getting through this without you. It's just that… I am all fucked in my head right now, okay, Mira. I think I need to talk to Marcela more. I need to take a second, take a breath. All this shit has just been… so much." He lets out a deep breath and, with it, more tears. I wipe them away with my thumbs.

"All right. *Bien de bien,* Andre. As long as you don't forget that I'm here. Whenever you are ready to talk about the shit. All the shit. I'm here."

"I don't forget you for a second, Miranda," he says. "You're my girl."

"And you are my perfect boy." I cup his face. "And it's our shit. All of it."

He nods. "Am I, still?" he asks. "Your perfect boy?"

"Fuck yeah you are," I say. "You're the exact same boy I fell in love with. Only better."

"Thank you." He brings my arm to his lips, kisses me where the hummingbird tattoo is. "Mom said to tell you hi."

"Mmm-hmm," I say. "Tell Lisette hi."

"Mira," he says, "I'm sorry Mom was a jerk about your G-tube."

I shrug. "*No importa nada,* Andre."

"It doesn't?" he says. "It didn't upset you?"

I shrug. "Nah, it ain't nothing," I say. "You know, compared."

"Compared to what?"

"Boy," I say. "Your mom don't like me. Her being insensitive and ableist about my feeding tube is a minor symptom of a much larger disease."

"What?" he says, his eyebrows drawing together. "You think my mom doesn't like you?"

Can y'all believe this boy sitting here looking legitimately surprised right now?

I laugh. I shouldn't. But I have to. "Andre. How long you been knowing me? I know you smart. Don't front like you didn't realize your mom despises me."

"Mira," he says. "My mom doesn't despise you."

"Fine," I say. "Homegirl low-key hates me."

"Mira. C'mon. Stop. She does not low-key hate you."

"Fine," I say. "She hates me for her perfect baby boy."

"Mira." He closes his eyes, rubs his hand over them. He looks at me and says, "My mom does not think I'm perfect. And you know that."

I shrug. "She's a difficult woman," I allow. "But she legitimately doesn't like me, Andre. Your whole family doesn't like me."

"Mira," he says. "What?" I can't believe that such a smart guy as Andre is so floored by this totally obvious truth. He touches my shoulder. "My family loves you. How could they not? You're, like, fucking perfect."

I laugh again, loudly. "I… can't even begin with all the ways that ain't true, boy."

"Mira. What the fuck? Really. Why in the world wouldn't my family like you?"

"Um. 'Cause I'm sick? 'Cause they're scared I'm gonna die and leave you widowed at a young age? Because you gave me a lung. You gave away part of your actual self to your sad, sick, hopeless little girl. Who's gonna die anyways."

"Mira," he says. There's so much hurt in his eyes that I stop that line of argument.

"All right," I say. "And 'cause I don't have a job. I didn't go to real college. Like literally every member of your family. I'm a fake writer. I don't do nothing. I can't even pop out your babies."

"Mira," he says.

I guess I should, but I can't stop.

"I'm ghetto as fuck. I grew up in the projects, Andre. My mom is an alcoholic and a drug addict. She used to do sex work sometimes to pay for all my shit. And Marco is… well, you all know Marco. My family is a bad movie, Andre. We're a stereotype. We're, like, why the stereotype exists."

"Mira," he says. "I love your family. Your family is not a stereotype. Your mom… I know she isn't perfect. But I love her too. She's smart and she's strong. I don't mean to defend her. Or to bypass all the crap she did that hurt you. But maybe she did what she could at the time to take care of you. I love Marco. He's my brother. You know that." He nudges me. "Why are you saying horrible things about your family?"

"I'm not," I say. "Or, I am. But what I'm saying is how your family sees me, Andre."

"That is not how they see you," he says. He's crying now, hard, for real.

"Whatever, fine," I say. "I can't even, Andre. Lemme just stop right there. I can see that I'm hurting you."

"Yes," he says. "All this shit you're saying, it's hurting me."

"Fine," I say. "I know you got enough to deal with. I will stop saying shit that's hurting you."

I lean my head against the wall and close my eyes. I'm so tired I could just fall asleep and never wake up again. My breath comes shallow. I feel the tube abrading against my skin with every inhale. I wish I could rip it out.

"Mira, honey?" Andre gives my shoulder a gentle shake. "Are you okay, baby?"

I shrug. "I'm really tired, Andre."

He presses his lips together. He looks at me, expressionless, for a long moment. Then I see him allow a whole flood of anger to come into his eyes.

"You're tired," he says, "because you don't eat."

"The fuck?" I say. I'd, like, yell, but I'm too tired to.

"You're tired because you don't eat," he repeats, more strongly this time. He strokes my hair. The touch is so loving, but his eyes on me are still so fucking angry. "You had that tube put in so you could get more nutrition, Mira. So you could get stronger and get well again." He touches my cheek. "Don't you want to get better?"

"Of course I want to get better," I say. "I'm just so tired, Andre."

"You're tired because—"

"Yeah, I heard you the first two times. I'm tired because I don't eat."

"Now you're saying it too."

"Oh, my God, no," I say. "Nope. You do not get to mansplain my illness to me, Andre."

"Sorry," he says. "I'm sorry. But can you not use mansplaining as a way to shut this down? Can we, like, figure this out?"

"I don't know," I say. He wants to figure this out? I have to wear a feeding tube and it's stupid and uncomfortable and I hate it, and I'm tired of it and everyone's going to stare at me and laugh at me and ask me ten zillion questions, including his mother. What is there to figure out?

"Don't you want to figure this out, Mira? Don't you want to get better?" he asks me again.

"Andre. Of course I do."

"Because you scare me, sometimes." He leans away from me. "I get scared sometimes when you keep saying you're tired, Mira. Are you tired of… all this? Are you tired of being alive?"

I'm gonna be honest with him. I have to be. "Yes, sometimes, I am tired of being alive," I say. "Because just for me to stay alive every day is a whole lotta management, baby. And it has been since I was five years old. So excuse me if I get a little tired of it sometimes. Because it's a lot."

"I know it is," he says, except no, he really doesn't. "I just want to be here for you."

"I know. And I want to be here for you too. We're partners, Andre. We're a team."

"Are we, really?" he says. "You say you're my partner. You're my wife. You say you want to be here for me."

"I do!" I say.

"Okay!" he says. "Then you know what I need from you, Mira? You know how you could really be here for me? Make things easier for me?"

"No!" I say. "How?"

"You could eat!" He seems to realize we are yelling now, takes a ragged breath, lowers his voice. "You could fucking eat. Because I can't work. I can't sleep. I can't focus on anything. I can't feel anything. I can't do anything except worry about you. I worry about how much you're eating—or not eating—all day, every day. I worry about your energy levels and how tired you say you are. So, if you want to be my partner and be here with me, then that's what you could do, Mira. You could use the fucking G-tube and fucking eat."

"I'm trying, Andre!" I say. "I'm trying. But this G-tube is hard for me. You know it is."

"I know it is," he says. "But, like…" He pauses, sighs. "All right, Mira. You said you wanna hear all my shit."

"Yes," I tell him. "I do."

"Okay. Then I have to tell you this. I'm sorry in advance for how it's going to sound."

"It's fine," I say. "Just say it."

"If you're sure you actually wanna hear my shit," he says.

"Oh, my God! I'm not fucking made of glass, dude! Words don't kill me! Just fucking say it!"

"When you don't eat," he says, "it doesn't even feel like you're my wife, Mira. I feel like you're my kid and I have to force you to eat. I actually had a dream about it one night. A nightmare. I dreamed that I was literally force-feeding you. And worst part? It felt good. So maybe it wasn't a nightmare. Sometimes when I talk to Daniela, the lady with the kid who has the G-tube, I'm actually jealous of her, Mira. Because she just hooks up the syringe and feeds the girl herself. Sometimes I wish I could do that with you."

I take another one of our pillows and hug it to my chest, let it take my weight. I feel the stupid, stupid tube pressing against it.

"Fuck," I say. "That's… fucked."

"I know," he says. He's breathing like he just finished sprinting ten miles. "I'm sorry, Mira. I'm really sorry. I love you and I'm sorry. I want to make this better. I'll do anything to make this better for us."

"I love you too," I say. "I'm sorry too. But I really am trying. And I really am tired. I'm… resentful, I guess. I resent that, on top of everything else, I now have another element of daily management to deal with. Eating was already a huge struggle for me. Now I can't just, like, as your mom so nicely put it, regular eat. I have to flush out my tube and get some liquid and attach the syringe and feed myself and flush it out again and check the stoma every day. And that's just here at home. What does it look like if I have to do this out in the world somewhere? How is it gonna feel for me when people stare or laugh or ask me a million questions? I don't want to find out. But I have to. So it makes me tired. And resentful. And that is why."

"Mira," he says. And with just the way he says it, my name, my intuition knows that something is coming. This is why we got married, why we love each other, really: to shift things for each other. We did it because we are ready to go to places together that maybe no one else is willing to go. I can see it in his eyes: we are going somewhere now.

"I have an idea," he says. "You can shoot it down immediately if you hate it."

"Okay. Lay it on me."

"I don't know how you're gonna feel about this," he says.

"You will soon. 'Cause I'm gonna tell you. As soon as you tell me what it is."

"Okay," he says, with a deep breath. "I don't know if you'd be okay with this. But I'm hearing that you are tired and resentful of the tube because it's more daily work and management for you. And I get that. You have had to take on so much. And it sucks. But this… here is a thing I could help you with." He touches my wrist gently. "You get to decide this, Mira. But I am willing. If you are. To take care of your G-tube. To… to feed you."

"You want to… take care of my G-tube?" I repeat. "Feed me?"

He nods. Now that he's gotten it out, he almost looks excited. "Yes. Whenever we're both home. It will be my responsibility to flush out your tube. To measure out the nutritional liquid or whatever else you're eating. I will put it in the syringe and feed you. I will check your stoma. If there are ever any issues with it, if you're comfortable with this, I can come with you to appointments and find out whatever I need to know to make things better. You won't have to do anything at all. With this one thing, I can share the management with you, Mira."

"Andre," I say. "Baby. This ain't one small thing. This is eating. Yeah? That thing you're supposed to do three times a day, every single day, for your entire life? I can't ask you to take over feeding me."

"You're not asking me," he says. His eyes are actually glowing, can y'all believe this? I think he thinks this is a good idea. "I'm offering. I want to do this for you."

"You… do?" I say.

"I do," he says, firmly, no weirdness, no hesitation. "I'm your husband. I want to take care of you."

"This is not… the way husbands usually take care of their wives, Andre."

"Fuck the way things are usually done, Mira," he says. "Since when have we done anything the way it's usually done? The way things are done is fucked anyway."

"True," I murmur. "It's just… it's a lot."

He shrugs. "You've been cooking for me for years," he says. "You've fed me so many times. Your mom and grandma have cooked for me so many times too. Now I am going to feed you."

I'm starting to cry. "I don't know that it's… the same thing."

"I don't know," he says. "But it's still eating. It's still making sure that the person you love is fed."

"But if we start doing that, will you… will you still see me as your wife?" My lips tremble. "Will you still love me and find me sexy and want to fuck me? Or will you start seeing me as a child? As a… medical patient or something?"

"No, I don't think so," he says, shaking his head. "It's because you're my wife that I want to take care of you like this, Mira. I would never want to do this with anybody else. And I will always find you sexy and want to fuck you, little bird. Always."

"Are you sure?" I whisper. "Because I can't trade that. Our sex. Not for anything, Andre."

"I'm sure," he says. "I actually…" He casts his eyes down. "I'm sorry. I swear I don't have a medical or illness fetish or anything. I think you know that. But I think I will actually find it sexy. In a way. Feeding you, I mean. Making sure that you are fed. That you are taken care of. That you allow me to help take care of your body. That you trust me enough to allow me to do something so intimate for you."

"Damn," I whisper. "Boy. That's hot."

"I told you." His eyes flicker. "Plus I won't have to worry as much anymore. I'll know you're eating. Because I'll be feeding you myself. That alone is going to make me feel like I could be a sex person again."

"Hmm. You are trying to Christian Grey me. Aren't you, Sir?"

He smiles. "Little bit. Maybe. Honestly, though… can I tell you the truth, Miranda?"

"*Siempre.*"

"What I'm trying to do is Marco you."

"What…?"

"Let me explain," he says. "I'm sorry if I shouldn't have. But I was talking to your brother. He was telling me about Hassan. About him trying to recover from his eating disorder. About what works and what doesn't. And he told me that, if he feeds Hassan, like literally sits him down at the table and feeds him with a spoon, or from his hands, then he'll eat. And he won't purge. I know you and Hassan are not going through the same thing. Not even close. But it got me thinking. First of all, that we are all going through shit. Every single one of us. Because it's a sick, fucked-up world. And the people who get better are the ones who say fuck it to the way things are usually done. And do what works for them. I want to be that brave, Mira. And second, I just thought we could try it too. I want to try it. Feeding you."

He's quiet then. He has made his case. Now he watches me, waiting to see what I am gonna say.

"Well," I say. "It ain't the worst idea I've ever heard." I tilt my head. "Question. Would you ever be into, or open to, me feeding you too? Like, Marco-style."

"Like…?" he says.

"Like you sit there. And I feed you. With a spoon."

I am not sure what he's gonna say to this. But he says, "Yes, I would be open to that, Mira. It actually…" He squirms on the bed. "It actually sounds kinda hot. Giving up control like that. Letting you feed me."

"I would take care of you," I say.

"I know you would." He wipes his eyes. "You have taken care of me since day one, Mira."

"*Igualmente*," I say. "And honestly it would make me feel better. About needing to be fed. Needing you like that. Knowing that I'm not the only one."

He shakes his head. "You are not the only one, Mira. I need you in ways I don't even think you realize."

I touch his chest.

"So," he says. "It's not the worst idea you've ever heard, huh? Does that mean you'll think about it?"

I shake my head. For a second he looks crushed, until I say, "I don't need to think about it, baby. I want to go try it. Right now." I start to get off the bed.

"I love you so fucking much," he says.

So we go into the kitchen. Somehow, I feel both calm and maybe more scared than I've ever been of anything. I'm calm because this is Andre. He's been by my side through everything. Two months ago, he held me while I gushed blood out of the center of me, wailing and screaming until the ambulance came. Almost two years ago, he married me when I was too sick to even have sex on our actual wedding night. I know he'll take care of me. I know him. But I'm scared because I know that there's another me waiting on the other side of this experience. And I don't know her—not yet. I'm scared of her. Do you think she'll be cool?

I sit at the kitchen table and take off my shirt. I fold it neatly, place it on the table. Andre flushes out my tube with water. He measures out the recommended amount of the liquid nutrition. He sits next to me, hooks up my syringe, and starts to pump the liquid through. We don't speak. We don't need to. I watch him closely: his lovely, serious face, the calm competence of his hands, the little sleek muscles in his perfect brown forearms moving underneath the dark hair. I got some hard shit, y'all. But I also got this.

I sit there and breathe and feel myself fed. It's funny, the G-tube; like I told Celi, even though you're not eating by mouth, you can feel yourself becoming un-hungry, becoming satisfied, as the food goes directly into your stomach. He looks up at me, to ask silently if I'm okay. I nod. I feel perilously close to those tears I've worried I have not cried, epoch-making, diluvian. I don't cry them, though, not yet, not here. Maybe it don't feel sexy or like softcore medical fetish porn just yet. (Stay tuned, though, folks.) But it does feel like, for once, I am exactly where I am supposed to be.

It's a Tuesday in April. I woke up with Andre's work alarm and I made an omelet and he ate it and fed me through the tube. I drank a cup of tea and took my meds. While he started work, I went into the bedroom and listened to music while doing some arm exercises with my little pink one-pound weights. My stick-figure arms are just sad, y'all. But maybe if I was able to get stronger before, I can do it again.

Now it's late morning. I lie in bed and work on an article on my phone for a little while. I want to work on a new short story, but I don't feel ready yet. I text with Celi who's at work at Babeland, with my other friend Carolina who I haven't seen in, like, years. She's been going through a bad breakup. I find some funny TikTok videos to send her. I take off my shirt and send a few shirtless selfies to Paloma.

I put my shirt back on. I close my eyes and try to rest. But I am not tired. I am at least not as tired as I was. Also, the sunlight out the window keeps undulating on the warm canvas of my closed eyelids, in red and gold waves. It's beckoning me. I sit up in bed. I feel suddenly like I will die if I do not get outside into that day.

I go out into the kitchen. It's noon, and Andre is just taking off his headphones and putting them onto the table. They had an eleven thirty team meeting.

"Andre?" I say. "Would you like to take a walk with me?"

A slow smile spreads over his face. Fuck, that's the most beautiful thing I've ever seen, even more so than the sunlight still winking at me from our half-sunken windows.

"You want to go for a walk?"

I nod. Pure excitement wells in my belly.

"Fuck yeah, Mira," he says. "Let's go for a walk."

He calls out for the afternoon from work. "When we get home," he says, "we're celebrating."

"How?" I ask.

"I don't know," he says. "We'll figure it out when we get there."

I put on my sneakers. I have not worn real shoes in weeks. "Do you think I need a jacket?" I ask Andre.

"You definitely do not need a jacket," he says. "It's seventy degrees outside right now."

"Oh, fuck," I say. "That's perfect."

"It is perfect. Come on, baby. Let's go."

We leave the apartment with Andre's hand on the small of my back. We lock our door. He slips his arm around my waist as we take the stairs from our basement unit up to the lobby. I haven't walked up any stairs in all these weeks. Tears sting my eyes when we reach our lobby, with its strange, bubbly, cracked black-and-white-tile floor, its narrow corridor, its wall of dull metal mailboxes. There's ours; a tiny slip of paper inserted into the little window says *Castillo-Lee.* That's us.

"Hello, mailbox," I whisper.

Andre opens the door for us and takes me outside.

I have not been outside in more than a month. My legs are shaky. I've probably started to forget how to use them to walk in the real world. I'm unused to all the sunlight; I should have worn my sunglasses. Fresh air feels weird inside my lungs. Everything is loud and close. I'm sure I have whatever vitamin deficiency you get when you don't get enough sunlight.

But it is also the most glorious spring day that has ever been made. Sunlight glitters over my neighborhood. Flowering trees are in bloom. I feel the day's warmth glowing on my arms, bare in my oversized T-shirt, turning the hair on my arms to gold. I forgot the world's beauty.

After removing myself from the flow of this outside world for so long, do I still even belong?

We walk slowly. We start with a walk around the block. But I don't feel tired; I feel excited. We walk past the laundromat. We walk past the McDonald's, where the smell of fries floats out on a salty cloud. We walk past the bodega. Andre stops and buys a chocolate bar. He gives me half of it. I accept; we eat it while we walk. I don't feel rejected by this world, by my neighborhood that I ignored for so long. I feel welcomed by the world, by the day.

Andre asks me if I want to walk more, and I say, "Fuck yeah."

We walk to Dyckman Street. The vendors are out! Men are selling Yankees hats in every color of the rainbow. Women in housedresses are selling bracelets and *chancletas.* There's the Dominican bakery. There's the shoe store. It's called Gemelos, which means *twins.* I've always felt like that's some kind of sign from the universe—of what exactly, I am not sure, maybe that I belong here. There's the CVS. We stop in and buy toilet paper. I use my Apple Pay, which I have not tapped in months. There's the bench where I sat with Skye and Araceli in February, or possibly one thousand years ago, when I was a different woman.

It's there, standing in front of our bench, that I start to cry. My best friend has met one of the great loves of her life. We looked at old objects made out of gold. We sat there and ate sandwiches. I did something that day that I don't have to do anymore, that I never have to do again if I don't want to, which is force myself to eat food that I do not want to eat. Maybe then, maybe even then, strange cells were multiplying in me. That warmish afternoon, I didn't know it, but a heart was knitting itself inside of my tube. It could have killed me, but it didn't. I feel Andre holding me up as I let myself cry. I think mournfully about my mother. I haven't seen her in, like, a year. I am not just a *gemela* anymore, Marco's little twin sister. I am a big sister too. I've been the world's worst big sister; I haven't even met our girl yet. Was I, am I, a mother, too? I mean, I don't think so. I don't feel like it. But I was a something.

It still ain't the big tears, okay. I am not there yet, if I ever will get there. This is just me crying a couple tears out on the street in front of a goddamn bench, on my first trip back outside in a month. Andre folds me into his chest. He holds me, silent and understanding, while our neighbors stream around us. Everyone is out enjoying the world's most perfect spring day.

When I feel calmer I pull back and say I want to walk more.

"Okay, little bird," Andre says. He takes my hand and we walk more.

When we return to the bodega, the one nearest our apartment, Andre stops again, this time to buy me flowers. "What for, *papi*?" I ask. I'm still tearful, that is, full of tears—*llena de lágrimas.*

"Nothing," he says. "I'm just really proud of you, Mira. I love you."

"I love you too, *nene.*"

He picks out for me a bouquet of big luscious roses, so classic in what they are and what they mean, but so New York City bodega in their vibrant orange color. It's been so long since I have seen such bold color. They make me cry. Their fat, edge-curled blooms look good enough to eat.

"You like them, baby?" he asks me.

I bury my face in them, sweet strong rose perfume and cellophane paper. "I love them," I say.

I gather them into my arms. And I walk my roses slowly home.

One of my first outings out in the world again, other than going for walks around the neighborhood with Andre, is to see my therapist, Maya. I have not seen her in person since before the pandemic. I'm excited to see her, more excited than folks probably normally are to see their therapist. But, like I've told y'all, Maya ain't your typical therapist. I will say that there is a thread of anxiety, of nervous anticipation, woven in with my excitement, though. 'Cause, for all her atypical awesomeness, Maya Harris is still a therapist, y'all, with all those therapist's tricks of forcing you to face that which most terrifies you.

Pero ya, I'm excited to get up in the morning with a plan and a schedule and someplace to be. I'm excited to put on real clothes—I wear a loose, lightweight rainbow sweater and comfy leggings, but still, it's regular-person clothes—and cute sandals. I even polished my toenails last night, a light lavender. I put on eye makeup—no lip, since I'll be wearing my face mask in the Uber and in Maya's office. I'm excited to put my phone, a journal and a sparkly pink pen, a bottle of hand sanitizer, a raw piece of amethyst that Paloma brought me, my wallet, a pack of tissues, my painkillers, and an extra face mask into my mini backpack. I haven't packed my bag to go anywhere in so long. I missed this tiny, everyday act of self-care: making sure that you have what you need with you, wherever you go.

I'm excited to kiss Andre on the curb as my Uber arrives in front of our building; for the first time in ages, I am going somewhere while he is staying home. He opens the door of the black SUV for me and helps me in, closes the door behind me. He goes back inside of our building. I slip on my face mask. My Uber starts to make its way downtown. And for the first time in all these weeks, I am alone, in a place that is not our apartment.

I'm excited to arrive, to be in Maya's office again, with her cheerful abstract art on the walls, the glass bowls of crystals on her desk. She's wearing a beautiful long hot pink dress and the tips of her Afro are dyed pink. Tears prick my eyes when I see her.

"Miranda Marcela Castillo, as I live and breathe," Maya says. "It literally could not be better to see you, girl. May I give you a hug?"

"Of course you may," I say, all choked up. I lean over her wheelchair and hug her so hard I practically fall into her lap.

I sit in the chair on the other side of her desk and we both cry a little.

Maya plucks a few tissues for herself and then a few for me, passing them to me. We both pull our face masks down a little and wipe our wet faces.

Maya picks up a few sheets of paper from her desk. I cringe, hard, when I see that they're a printout of the email I sent her last night. When I booked this appointment, I texted Maya and asked if she'd be willing to read an email where I would explain everything that's happened to me lately, so I wouldn't have to spend my entire session giving backstory, and we could start to get somewhere. She said sure.

That fucking email I wrote last night has gotta be one of the hardest things I've ever written, harder than my City College application, harder than that article on redefining sex for Latinx Wellness Project, the one that made Paloma cry. I had to describe my new relationship with polyamory, that I'm now a married woman who also has a girlfriend. (There is also Araceli, yes, but that's so new, so private between the two of us, that I'm not ready to talk about it with anyone yet.) Obviously, I had to put into words what happened to me that night shortly after Valentine's Day. I didn't go into all of it, and I didn't go into any graphic detail. Writing is healing, y'all, for sure, but it's still too close to me for the inclusion of intimate detail to be anything except re-traumatizing. Maybe someday I will be ready to write that experience with closeness and specificity. But today is not that day.

I did, though, tell her about the ectopic pregnancy, and its removal. I wrote about the rejection episode and my long, long recovery. (I did not write about the G-tube. We're gonna play show-and-tell today instead!) Did writing that email feel, like, cathartic? I guess it did, maybe, a little bit. Seeing it written there in black and white, by my own fingers, made it feel less scary, less of a nightmare that I am still living and more of an experience that I have had. It's starting to feel like, if not something that I could forget about or move on from, then something that I can incorporate into the things that have happened to me.

"Is that my email?" I whisper, pointing at it.

"Yes, Mira, it's your email." She looks at it briefly, flipping through the two pages, then puts it down again. "All right. Where would you like to start?"

Like all the best therapists, Maya likes to focus on clear intentions and do the work. I dig it. I mean, this shit hurts enough without dwelling and stretching it out and fucking around. I prefer my therapy to be like the classic band-aid analogy: tear that shit off quick, make something fucking unbearable hurt less.

"I have something to show you," I say. "It's on my stomach. Okay if I pull up my shirt and show you?"

"Go for it," she says.

I lift my shirt, tuck it under my chin, and point. "This is my gastrostomy tube. G-tube for short. It helps supplement my nutrition."

"How is it working for you, Mira?"

I pull my shirt down. "It's a process," I say. "But better than when I first got it. There have been some… developments since I first got it put in back in the hospital."

She nods, writes something down in her notebook. "Tell me about them?"

"Yeah." I'm trembling, but I am going to say it. "I was struggling with it. Andre saw that. He offered to take over the management of the tube for me. What do I mean by that? He takes care of the tube, meaning he flushes it out with water and he checks the stoma, the hole where it's inserted in me, every day, to make sure it's not getting infected. I had my first in-person follow-up appointment the other day, he came with me and listened to everything the doctors had to say, asked a bunch of questions. It was nice, having him there. I haven't brought him along to many CF appointments over the years. I wish I had. And, well. I'm kind of stalling, aren't I?

"The big thing, Maya, the big thing is that… well, Andre has taken over feeding me. Through the tube. He gets the liquid nutrition ready—there's an exact amount they recommended for me, so I can get the nutrients I need and put on a little weight safely. Or sometimes he blends real food, I mean like chewing food, for me in the blender. Whatever it is, he puts it in the tube and pumps it into me. He decides. He decides what I eat. He feeds me on a schedule so I don't skip meals anymore. I trust him completely to do this for me. I trust him more than I ever trusted myself when I had to force myself to eat by mouth. I mean, I wasn't even really using the tube. I don't know why. I just wasn't, Maya. But now I am. I've gained two pounds and everyone's really happy about that. I feel better. Stronger. I have more energy, feel more awake. I mean, I'm probably always going to be tiny. Being a sexy fertile goddess woman just ain't in the cards for me. But if I can get healthier, then that's more than enough for me."

Maya writes down some stuff. She looks up at me and nods, real calm, like all this ain't nothing. This is why I love this woman, okay.

"Tell me more about how you feel about this? About Andre taking over feeding you."

I nod. I still feel nervous, but calmer, I am easing in. "It's been, like, I don't know? A couple weeks now? What even is time anymore? But anyway. Honestly I like it, Maya. I like it better than I thought I would. I like getting to just sit there and get fed. I like not having to worry anymore. About forcing myself to eat. About feeling crappy or guilty when I couldn't eat or didn't have an appetite like the people around me. I love that there is an aspect of my daily life management that someone can help me with."

"Can you tell me how it makes you feel emotionally?"

I feel myself touching the place where my tube-removal scar is, on my lower belly, a kind of grounding in my new body. I probe my heart, look into it, cautiously. But I know that, here, I am safe. "It makes me feel… happy? Yes. Happy. I like having that quiet time with Andre a few times every day. We laugh and talk about random shit. I feel like we haven't laughed and talked about random shit in a long time. Not since I got so sick. It's all been about that, about my recovery, or about the big scary emotions we're both having about it. But when it's tube feeding time it's like… getting back to who we were, before all this happened. Kinda. And it makes me feel… seen. Taken care of. I feel calm and centered and loved."

"Are these ways that you want to feel, Mira?" she asks me.

"Yes," I say, easy. "I like the way this is making me feel. Except… shouldn't I be feeling guilty about it?"

"What do you mean?" she asks.

I sit back in my chair, rubbing my bony little elbows with opposite hands. "I mean, I was really worried about it at first, Maya. About making Andre take on more shit for me. But he kept saying I'm not making him do anything. This was totally his idea. He offered. I'm the one who wasn't sure. And I keep checking in with him, you know? Asking if he feels like it's too much. If he feels like I ain't his wife anymore, but his, like, medical patient or something. And he's always like, no, no, he likes exactly where we're at, he's happy he gets to take care of me like this, he loves how I trust him to do this for me, he enjoys tube feeding time too. Sometimes he eats too, and then we're eating together, you know, like a normal couple. Sorta."

"I think you and Andre are a very strong couple," Maya says.

"Thank you," I say. "But, like. I still feel guilty sometimes. I still worry. Like the other day I was watching this YouTuber I follow. He's a wheelchair user and his wife is also his caregiver. He can't physically feed himself so that's one of the things his wife does for him. And I'm watching them and I'm starting to feel bad, Maya, girl, you know? Because it ain't like I can't physically feed myself. I just emotionally don't want to. And I'm putting this thing on Andre. This physical-care aspect that I could be taking care of for myself."

Maya writes a few things. She looks at her notes. She takes a breath that I recognize as a calming, grounding one.

"You mentioned that you weren't using the tube at first," she says. "That you don't know why. Would you feel okay digging into that a little deeper?"

I take a deep breath.

"Good girl, Mira," she says. "Deep breath. You're safe. You're here."

I nod. "Yeah," I say. "I was feeling guilt."

"Guilt about what, honey?"

"Guilt that it takes so much management for me to just stay alive." And here are the tears; they're coming. "Guilt that I couldn't just eat like everybody else. Honestly? I was scared of eating. Scared of what would happen if I ate for real and got myself stronger. 'Cause then I'd have to face up to shit! There'd be no more running from all the shit that I gotta face."

"Can you tell me about some of that shit, Mira?"

"Yeah. Like the ectopic pregnancy. How are we both feeling about that? I ain't even touched all that yet. And I think that's what's standing in my way. In our way. From being intimate again. From me continuing to be a sex person like I really want to be. And going back to school! Like I put in the email, I said yes to the writing program. That's three years where my life is really gonna change. And now it also means fitting that around my tube feeding time. And yes, I am prepared to work on doing it for myself if our schedules don't always allow us to do it like this. I've come too far to turn back now, Maya. To give up now."

"Does having Andre feed you help you feel empowered to keep going, Mira?"

"Yeah," I whisper. I dash tears away with the edge of the sleeve of my sweater.

"Can I say some things?" she asks.

"God, please," I say. "Please say some things. Lay that wisdom on me, good sis."

She laughs. I love her big, lovely laugh.

"Mira," she says. "You deserve to take up space."

All right, that's it, y'all, I'm crying.

"You deserve to take up space," she says again. "Your health deserves to take up however much management it requires. You get to decide what that management looks like. You do not owe anyone anything. You do not owe the world any attempts to be like anyone else. You do not owe the world any false story of what health looks like. If the space and management you need right now is for Andre to feed you, and he wants to do it because he loves you and you are partners in life, then that is fucking awesome. Do that. You do not need to judge yourself as physically unable to eat to deserve, and to ask for, and to receive help in this way. Because health isn't just physical health. You know that, Mira. And if there comes a time when you have to shift to doing it for yourself, or finding some other way to make eating happen, then we will all work together to support you in doing that. We practice wellness as a community. This is your community, Mira. And there is no one like you, girl. We want you and we need you here. As long as it feels right for you to keep being here, because your life is yours and you get to make all the decisions about it, then your community is here to support you in doing that. Whatever it looks like."

I just sit there for a few seconds and steep myself in all my feelings like tea. I soak in all this woman's wisdom. I've missed her presence so much. I cry, and let myself feel the crying. She hands me tissues, and I even slow my system down enough to feel the delicate softness of the tissue against my cheeks. She got the fancy kind of tissues, the ones with lotion somehow magically threaded into their silky fibers. I thank her.

She nods. "We've got a little time left," she says. "I do want to give you some tools and exercises and resources and things. We can do that at the end. So for now… Mira, would you like to maybe tell me about Paloma?"

I feel a little glow inside, and know it's reflected, in my face and in my aura, just at hearing her name. "Okay," I say.

"Miranda," she says, grinning back, "there's that beautiful smile. I missed seeing your pretty smile, girl. Can you tell me about what's behind that smile?"

"Sure," I say, feeling myself tingle at all my edges. "So, Paloma's my girlfriend. She's so great, Maya. She's so smart and fun and funny and sexy. She's so vibrant, so excited about things. She loves doing stuff and trying new things. I mean, I always liked her, you know? Like I wrote in my letter, I've had a crush on her for a long time. But this is something else entirely, you know, Maya? I didn't really know her then. I liked an idea of her, I guess. But now I know the real her, and… it's better between us, more magical, than I could have even dreamed."

"That's beautiful, Mira," Maya says, still smiling. "And yes. There is often a world of difference between nurturing a crush and an idea of someone and sinking into a real relationship with that person. Can you tell me what it's like to be exploring polyamory as a married woman?"

"Sure," I say. I'm so glad we decided to end our appointment talking about this and not about my G-tube and all the other shit. Now I feel like a flower. "It's unexpectedly great. And it's so great because I'm doing it with, like, the best people in the world. Paloma's all mature and knows what she's doing and just constantly vibrates at the vibration of love. Ya know? And you know about Andre by now. He's been doing all this reading to educate himself. He's been talking to Paloma and building a closer relationship with her. Not because he's romantically or sexually interested in her. But because he wants us to all be on the same team if she and I are building something."

"How does that make you feel?" she asks. It's that cliché question, y'all, but damn if it doesn't work.

"It makes me feel fucking awesome," I answer. "It makes me feel important and loved. I mean, my husband consistently becomes more and more awesome all the time. That makes me want to be a better person too. The best version of me that I can be. This whole experience is making me fall in love with him more. Something I don't even think I believed was possible."

I pluck another soft lotion tissue. This time, it's tears of love, though, y'all.

"It ain't all perfect, though, Maya," I say, after I've wiped my face delicately. "Polyamory definitely has some… logistics. Figuring out the sex stuff has been a little bit awkward."

"What do you mean?" she asks.

"Well, Andre and I have also been exploring going to bed together with other women. In threesomes. I mean, not lately. Before. Anyways, a while ago, Paloma actually offered. To be with both of us in a threesome. If we wanted. I personally would have been all over that. But Andre… definitely did not want that." I shake my head. "He's been very clear that he sees Paloma only as a friend, and a dance colleague, not romantically or sexually. While Paloma is very… open. I am too. We've all spent some time together. Especially since I got sick and, honestly, he and I don't really want to be away from each other. So they've done some… flirting, I guess, which Andre says he likes but also feels a little weird about. And he's seen and heard me and Paloma do some sex stuff. Which he found sexy but also weird."

Maya nods. She writes in her notebook. "It makes sense that polyamory would require adjustment and logistics and communication," she says.

"Right," I agree. "But like I said, they're both awesome. And they love me. We're figuring it out. I'm so lucky."

"Is Paloma aware of what you've gone through the past few months?" Maya asks.

"Yes," I say. I rub the back of my neck. "That's probably been the biggest challenge between us. Me trying to open up and be honest with her about my health. While also not dwelling on it or bringing myself down by playing the lifespan game. Which I hate. And her, I guess, just trying to navigate what it means and how it feels to be with someone who has a chronic illness. It's hard for her, I think. So I try to be… compassionate to that."

"And how does it feel for you?" she asks.

"It's never easy for me to have to explain it all to a new person," I answer. "I hate it when she feels sad or scared about losing me or angry on my behalf because of what my illness makes me go through. Because it hurts me, seeing her like that, feeling like I'm the cause of painful feelings for her. But the more I think about it, and the closer I allow myself to get to her, the more I'm realizing that's all part of love. Of love for her and me, anyway."

"What is part of love for you and her?"

"I was reading this spiritual book recently," I say. "It said that part of love is the acknowledgment of impermanence. That this life we have doesn't last forever. That love means accepting also loss. Or at least living side by side with the fear of loss. And the book said that's why love is brave, actually. Choosing to love is brave. Because when you go all in for love, you are signing yourself up for loss. And that's fucking terrifying. Ain't it? So we are both scared."

"But you're choosing to love anyway?" she says.

"But we are choosing to love anyway," I affirm.

My mother, Gloria Isabela Castillo, nee Rodriguez, was born in New York City in 1978, to a Dominican mother and a Puerto Rican father. She was a remarkably smart little girl who loved school.

When she was twelve years old, her dad, my grandfather, raped her.

She told her mother. My mom's mother, my grandmother, went to her husband and said, "*Mi hija y yo, nos vamos.* And if I ever lay eyes on you again, I will kill you."

Gloria, my mother, and her mother, my grandmother, left New York. They went back to the Dominican Republic. My grandmother went to work at her mother's hair salon; that would have been my great-grandmother. My mom tried to go to school, to do the right thing. But she'd had a hurt from which she would never properly heal. It's like when you break a bone, you know? Set it incorrectly, and it just never grows back right. You need the right doctors, the right placement, the right technique, the right medicines. My mom, she didn't have any of that when she needed it, when she was a little girl who did not yet know how to heal herself.

When my mom was sixteen, she met our dad, Miguel Castillo, at a party on the beach. Gloria and Miggy were two of a kind, twin flames, two star-crossed Leos who fed each other's fire. They were both super smart and loved school and books and learning, dreamed of going to college and immersing themselves in the scholarly world, but they also both loved alcohol and drugs and partying.

My grandmother said to my mom, "Don't be stupid when you're so smart, Gloria. You can make something real out of your life. But if you get pregnant, I will throw you out. I'm not raising any more babies."

Six months later, my grandmother passed away after a swift and brutal battle with breast cancer. They had no money for treatments. My grandmother died at home, my mother trying to take care of her.

When my mother was seventeen, she got pregnant. They wanted their kid to have US citizenship, like Gloria did (and Miggy did not), so she dropped out of school and went to New York. As soon as she turned eighteen, they got married. They had zero money and nowhere to go, so they moved in with my mom's father, my grandfather, for a brief period. (That went about as well as you'd imagine.) They left after an awful fight in the middle of the night and spent the next couple months couch-surfing with randoms around Spanish Harlem and Washington Heights. My mom had a miscarriage. They lost the baby.

Gloria and Miggy were heartbroken. They knew they were pretty fucked up. They didn't have family or money or jobs or even a real place to live. But they had love. They loved each other, they loved their baby, and they'd wanted it, very much.

They got their GEDs. My mom got a job at Target, my dad a job shelving books at a library in the Bronx. At work my mom met her BFF, Carmen Castellanos, who was studying linguistics at Lehman College because she wanted to preserve ancient Mexican languages. Gloria and Miggy got an apartment, the place in the Bronx where my brother and I would later grow up. Things weren't perfect. They were always, always struggling to get and stay sober. They fought, a lot. They wanted to love each other, but, because of all of their wounds, they didn't really know how. When my mom was twenty, they decided to get pregnant again. And, almost right away, they did, and it was twins!—a girl and a boy. They felt thrilled and excited and terrified, all at once.

The last time my parents ever spoke, they were having a screaming, shouting, crying argument one night. My mom was seven months pregnant. The next morning, my dad was killed in a collision between a car and a truck, riding his bike to work. The two drivers died later at the hospital. My dad died instantly.

My mom wasn't sure how she would go on. She felt she had lost the love of her life. But she was also about to give birth. Her friend Carmen, whom she leaned on a lot during those years, said, "*No estás solita,* Gloria. You and I will raise these babies together."

On May 20, 1999, at 8:02 in the morning, my mom gave birth to my older brother, Marco Michael Castillo. Ten minutes later, at 8:12, she had me, Miranda Marcela Castillo.

Gloria was heartbroken and broke and had no family and was still always trying to maintain her sobriety. She was twenty-one years old. And she was a mother.

She and Auntie Carmen traded off working shifts at Target and taking care of Marco and me. My mom decided to go for her dream, which was to go to college. She enrolled at Lehman College and declared a double major, English and psychology. It would take about twelve years, till Marco and I were thirteen, but eventually my very smart and hardworking mother would earn her bachelor's in English and psychology with a minor in linguistics, as well as her master's in social work. When Marco and I were fourteen, starting high school, Mom got a job as a guidance counselor at a school in the Bronx, at which she has always been brilliantly successful. She gives the students she works with the kind of tough love that has them writing her emails years later, thanking her for the positive impact she had on their lives.

When Gloria was twenty-six years old, and two years sober, her five-year-old girl was diagnosed with a scary fucking disease called cystic fibrosis. She had never heard of it before. She learned that CF is a genetic disease, that she and her husband, unbeknownst to them, were both carriers of the CF gene, passing one copy down to their son, and two copies down to their daughter. She learned fucking fast that CF is an expensive and complicated disease to have. She promised that, no matter what, she would take care of her daughter. She would take care of both of her kids.

And the hits just kept on coming. A year later, Auntie Carmen was diagnosed with breast cancer. Her fight with cancer was years long and drawn-out, full of remissions and relapses. My mom relapsed with heroin, a monstrous addiction she hasn't fully kicked to this day.

Carmen died when Marco and I were twelve. Mom felt, again, gutted, like she had lost the love of her life. But she had a daughter and a son. So she kept going, for them. My *abuela,* my dad's mom, came to New York from the DR to try to help her. We weren't, and aren't, a perfect family, but we fucking try.

Teachers started to tell Gloria all kinds of things about her son: that he was brilliant; that he was a once-in-a-lifetime student; that the school had never seen anyone like him. Doctors told her all kinds of scary shit about her daughter: that she might not live to twenty, or maybe thirty; that CF costs something like $40,000 per year to manage; that I needed to be on the lung-donor list because my lungs were going to fail. What the fuck was my mother going to do?

Now, I'm sure y'all wanna hear more stereotype stories, more trauma-fetish tales from the projects, so we could fit your idea of what my family is supposed to look like. And, like, yeah, I could tell more of those. I could tell, like, thousands of those. Do you wanna hear more about how my mom started doing sex work online, and sometimes offline too, to make extra money? Does it feel good, in a sick kind of way, to hear about how she hit Marco and yelled at him and told him sometimes, when she was really drunk, how fucking much he looks like our father? Maybe you want to hear about her drug dealers following me home from school.

And, well, that happened. And I could tell it all fucking day.

But I could also tell how my mother raised us with so much love. No one taught Gloria that. Her parents sure didn't tell her they loved her every day. But Mom did. She told us she loved us. She said we were smart and strong and beautiful, that we were gonna do great things in the world. She said we were going to do things that she couldn't do, or our dad, or our grandparents or their parents; she used to say that we were going to do things that no one in our generations had ever once done. She used to say that our ancestors dreamed us up. She taught us Spanish. She taught us to talk about our feelings. She told us that there are a thousand different ways to love. She taught us that sex is something to enjoy, not to be ashamed of, and that we could come to her at any time with literally any question. (And we did, y'all, okay.) She taught us that gender is a social construct and that we got to be who it felt right for us to be. She complained about our friends and girlfriends and boyfriends, but she also cooked hundreds of meals for them and invited them over at times when they had no place else to go. She said she'd support us in anything we chose to do, as long as we were happy. She took us to museums and baseball games and Olive Garden and church on Sundays. We laughed and shared secrets and watched movies and created traditions and made up shit, made up all the shit, as we went along.

Mom saved my life. She saved me, over and over again. I would not have survived this without her. She helped Marco get to the place where he is now, about to graduate college and go to medical school and become more successful than anyone in our family has ever been. My mom is a deeply fucked-up person. She got dealt a fucked-up hand with few resources to heal from it, in a cycle of generational poverty and institutionalized racism and addiction. I have had to draw boundaries with her and distance myself from her and all of her shit in so many ways. In so many ways, I have deliberately created who I am in exact and intentional opposition to who she is.

But she is also my mother. She is my mother, and I have chosen to love her. My mother has always been a source of ongoing grief for me: grief for the way I wished she would be, or the way I wished our relationship would be. It's in my love for her, then, that I first learned that to love is to live side by side with grief, with loss. But my eyes are clear when I look at her; I have wrestled my shadows: if I am to love her, then I have to love who she is, not who I wish she would be. I have to love her, grief and all.

Mom and Marco and I, the original trio, have not been all together in over a year. I haven't seen her in months and months; I don't even remember when. We arrange to meet at the apartment where *Abuela* has been living with some friends, while they are all out, at work. My grandmother, who doesn't have papers, works at a nursing home. Those places have been hotspots of the virus during this pandemic, so I haven't seen my grandmother either; since the transplant, whenever we talk, she always says she don't wanna expose me to no extra germs. Marco is gonna graduate from college and go off God knows where for medical school and become a doctor, someone I won't even recognize, and, *así de así,* my whole family, it'll be all broken up.

We're all late; like I've told y'all, punctuality, unlike the gene that causes cystic fibrosis, is not part of the Castillo family gene pool. Mom texts us when she arrives at the apartment, which is up in the Heights, ten minutes after the time we said we would meet. When I get there, fifteen minutes late, my twin hasn't arrived yet, so it's just my mom and me.

I start to cry the moment I open the unlocked front door to the apartment and lay eyes on my mother, standing in the middle of the living room. She's the prettiest, with her creamy skin and light brown eyes and waist-length wavy dark hair. Marco and I really don't look much like our light-skinned, black-haired mother, with her eyes the color of tea. We got our father's tightly curled hair, his mocha eyes, his much darker skin with a splash of hers, milk in black coffee. Genetics is funny, ain't it?

Mom starts crying too when she sees me, and we've got a good hard *llanto* going as we fall into each other's arms by the door. Mom grips my arms. She runs her hands up and down my back, my sides, making sure her girl is here, she's whole. It's stupid, I know it is, but I think about the baby I'm never going to carry, the way that I am never going to be a mother, not in the way my mother is—raw and bloody and whole, *de las entrañas.*

"Mira," she says. "Mira, honey." She squeezes my two Afro puffs, one in each hand. "*Mi hija. Mi nena perfecta.* I missed you so much, baby doll."

"I missed you too, Mom," I say, and it's the truth.

Mom kisses me all over my face. She squeezes me hard. We sit down on the couch in my grandmother's house, I take off my shoes and cuddle with her, letting my mom wipe the tears from my face and kiss my cheeks and untie my hair and stroke my scalp with her perfect long fingernails. My mom ain't perfect. Y'all know that. It brings up complicated feelings, seeing her again. But I gotta say I'm also grateful, so grateful, for how good it feels to let her soothe and take care of me again. For me, at least, despite everything else, and whatever it says about me, there just ain't nothing like having my mom rub my back and tell me everything's gonna be okay.

"How are you feeling, *nena*?" she asks me. We gaze deep into each other's eyes. Mom is beautiful, but she don't look so good, you know what I mean. There are new lines all over her face, her eyes are red and deeply shadowed. I wonder what she sees when she looks back into my face. I see my own face every day; what does it look like to someone who hasn't seen it since I got my new scars?

"*Estoy tratando*, Mom," I tell her with a sigh. "How's the baby?"

Mom gives me a faint smile. "She's good, honey. She's asleep in the bedroom."

"I—"

We both get a text message then. It's from Marco, in our group chat, saying that he's getting in the elevator to head up to us. Mom says she's gonna run to the bathroom and check on the baby for a second. I stand up once she's gone, my heart pounding in my ears as I wait for my brother.

Marco opens the door. "Mira," he says. "Oh, my God, Mira."

Just like with me and my mom, we rush into each other's arms. But we do it hard, almost painful, almost a tackle. As my brother holds me I wonder what it must be like to be one of his soccer teammates, hardy and not breakable, receiving his hard, pummeling, celebratory hug after a win, crashed against his powerful chest like a wall. I put my face into his chest and smell him, spicy deodorant and oceanic aftershave and a girl's perfume that smells like bubble gum and, if I inhale hard enough, a lingering trace of sweat in the fabric of his T-shirt; and I feel him, his pec muscles against my face and his shoulder blades and the ropy muscles in his arms and the lean spareness of his body. We pull back and look at each other. Marco holds my face in his hands, tipping my chin up so he can look at me good. We'll be twenty-two soon and he feels like he is able to put on muscle now in a way that he couldn't when we were teenagers. He's grown up. He'll only get stronger, thicker and more solid, turning a healthy and well-maintained twenty-five and thirty-two and forty-seven.

Marco tries to smile at me. His lips are trembling. His long hair is piled on the top of his head in a curly bun, glossy wet from a recent shower. He's wearing a little eyeliner and dark blue nail polish. He's the cutest.

"Mira," he says again. "I missed you so much, baby girl."

"I missed you too, *nene*." I grip his biceps.

"How are you? Are you okay?" His thumbs stroke my jaw.

"I don't know," I whisper. I shake my head. "No, not really."

Marco bends his head and kisses my cheek. He turns my face gently and kisses my other cheek, this time slow enough that I can feel his wet lips. Finally he centers my face in his hands, lowers his head again, closes his eyes and places a kiss on my lips with his lips. He lets go of me and looks at me with his big pretty tear-filled eyes. He looks scared and sad and grateful and full of joy and full of grief. To show him it's okay, everything's okay between us, I rise to tiptoes and kiss him also, lightly but fully on his mouth with my mouth.

He hugs me again, crushing me to him. I feel a kind of elation, hugging him again, a jolt so strong in my whole body it's like sexual. I mean, it's not; we lack the language to talk about any kind of powerful, transformative love that ain't sexual. But, also, I mean, come on, y'all. Are you even really from a fucked-up family if you haven't thought about what it might be like to fuck your brother? I'd ask him not to be gentle with me. And maybe then I'd finally feel like I ain't a little glass doll, like I'm strong and whole enough to take whatever shit this world throws at me.

Mom comes into the room then, and I watch them hug and kiss on both cheeks, and Mom touches his hair and says it's gotten so long, he's the prettiest boy in the world. We all go sit on the couch together, me sandwiched between Marco and my mom. He and I watch each other with our usual fascination. He's wearing his favorite old white T-shirt that he's had since high school, and which now clings very lightly to all the muscles in his torso, and a cute pair of shiny royal blue track pants with a white stripe up the side. He takes off his sneakers to curl up on the couch with us. He's wearing two different socks, one gray, one white.

"You're wearing two different socks, *nene*," Mom says.

Marco rolls his eyes. "Really, Mom? Can you not? Chill."

"*No me hables así.*"

"Ma, *por fa*,'" I murmur to her.

Marco hugs me, hard, against his side. He plays with my earring, a blue druzy crystal in the shape of a teardrop. "These are so cute, *nena*," he says.

"Thanks." I give my other earring a flick. I almost say that they were a gift from Paloma, but at the last minute I remember not to. Mom doesn't know anything about Paloma and me. And I'll be keeping it that way, okay. Mom would be just fine about the poly stuff, 'cause she cool like that, but she's never liked Paloma. Her negative energy and judgements would pollute this beautiful, perfect thing I've got going on with my girl. So my mom just ain't invited to this particular party.

I decide to distract and shut everybody up by lifting up my shirt to show them my gastrostomy tube. Mom touches it gently, looking at me with so much love that it stings my eyes with tears. Marco looks at it intensely. I keep my shirt lifted up so he can look at it as much as he wants. They ask me, like, mad questions, but this is my family, the people who helped keep me alive at times when I couldn't do it myself. They've seen everything I've got, so I decide it's all right.

"Andre has been helping feed me, through the tube," I tell them. "You know how all this crap is. It's really nice to let him take care of this one thing."

"Wonderful, that's great, baby," my mom says.

"Yeah, that's hot," Marco says, with a flutter of his long eyelashes.

"How is Andre, baby?" Mom asks.

I shrug. "You know. We're trying. It's been a lot, *sabes?*"

"My sweet girl," Mom says, massaging the back of my neck.

"Mira," my brother says, his voice trembly, "I am so sorry. So sad for you and Andre. About the…"

"Thanks, Marco Polo," I say. "And it's all right. Long as you don't call it a baby."

They both nod.

"Are you okay, *nena?*" Mom says gently.

"Not really. They had to do an emergency surgery to take it out. And one of my fallopian tubes. It had a heartbeat, you know?" I hear Marco inhale sharply. "The ectopic pregnancy, I mean. It could've killed me."

Mom murmurs a prayer.

"I talked to my care team," I say. "They're saying it's never really gonna be possible for me to have a viable pregnancy, carry a baby."

"I'm so sorry, Mira," Marco says.

"You're here, you're safe," Mom says. "*Eso es lo que importa.*"

"*Exacto*," Marco says, nodding.

I hear them—and I want their assurances to be enough to blot out my grief. But, for right now at least, it is not enough. It still hurts, ridiculously, way more than I feel like it should. Shouldn't I be able to let this go, to move past this?

"All right, *mi gente*," I say. I pull my shirt down. "That's enough Mira trauma stories for one day." I turn to my mom. "Mom, you have to tell Marco and me how you are. Really." I nudge her. "Tell us what's been going on. For reals."

Mom turns and looks at Marco. She looks at me. She casts her eyes towards the bedroom door, pulled ajar. Her new baby is asleep in there. Her lips are tight with grief. I feel tired and broken, before I even know what she's going to say.

"I haven't been doing all that well lately, *mis bebés*," she says finally, with a sigh.

I look at Marco on my other side.

"Where have you been staying, Mom?" he asks her.

"With some friends," she says, evasively. "*No quiero que mis bebés preocupen por mí.*"

"Mom. *No somos bebés*," Marco says. "And that ship, *mi vieja*, has sailed." He flicks his wrist. I swallow a laugh. "*Ya basta.* Come on, Mom. Tell us where you've been staying."

"*Ya te dije*, Marco," she says. "I've been staying with some friends."

"What friends?"

"Stop treating me like a child," she says.

"Then talk to us!" Marco says.

I shove him into the arm of the couch. "If you two start yelling, I will legit walk outta here," I say. Mom and Marco both turn to me in surprise. Yeah, I ain't the same meek little Mira who left home a few years ago. "I am still trying every day to get better from this shit and I do not have neither time nor energy for y'all pulling this type of bullshit."

"*Ya*, Miranda," Mom says. "Language."

"Mom," I say eloquently, "please."

"We're sorry, Mira," Marco says. He strokes my upper arm. "All right, Mom. Fine. Whatever. Don't tell us where you and our sister are staying. Or if you two are safe. Whatever. It's fine. But at least tell us, 'cause it was our home too. You don't have the apartment in the Bronx anymore, do you?"

Mom shakes her head. If we're wanting her to explain further, we'd better not hold our breath.

"The baby's father…" I say, tentatively. "He ain't in the picture, is he, Mom?"

She shakes her head. "No, baby," she says, "he isn't."

"You told me he signed away his rights, *verdad?*" Marco says.

She nods.

"What the fuck?" I say; and Marco says, "*Pendejo.* Like, who does that?"

Mom sighs.

"Are you still working?" Marco asks. She pauses, then nods. He and I share a quick look—what did that pause mean? "Are you healthy? Sober?" he presses on.

Mom starts to cry. She buries her face in her hands. Marco looks at me with big eyes, hurt and angry. I sigh and slide closer to her and put my arm around her shoulders. She leans into me. I close my eyes and, for a moment, wish myself anywhere but here. I think about Paloma. I think about being at home with Andre. I think about splitting a small fries at McDonald's with Araceli. I think about playing my guitar. Sometime soon I will be someplace good, someplace better, someplace that is not here.

In the bedroom, the baby starts crying.

Mom stirs in my embrace. I let her go. She gets up, goes into the bedroom, wiping her face. Marco stands up, starts to pace the small room angrily. I curl up small on the couch and pull my phone out of my hoodie pocket and just hold it. Its sleek smoothness comforts me, the knowledge that, even if I don't turn it on, just its existence means that I am connected to the outside world. Seriously, how did kids even survive fucked-up families before phones were invented?

Mom comes out of the bedroom holding her crying baby. "I'm going to warm her up a bottle," she says.

Marco holds his arms out. "*Bien.* Let me hold her."

"All right," Mom says, and hands my twin the baby with, like, zero fucks given that Marco has never held a baby in his life, knows nothing about babies. But of course he takes the baby with perfect calm expertise and cradles her against his shoulder. He rubs her back to soothe her and talks to her gently while Mom goes into the kitchen with her diaper bag. Silent, unable to speak, actually, I track Marco's movements with my eyes, as he paces the floor, now holding our baby sister.

Mom comes back into the living room with a bottle.

"Can I feed her?" Marco asks.

Our mom's face softens into a smile as she looks at the two of them. "Sure," she says.

I tuck myself as close as I can into the corner of the couch, pressed against the arm. Mom and Marco sit with me again. Mom helps Marco get the baby situated in his lap and hands him the bottle. The baby is already trying to take it.

"It's easy," Mom says. "Magda's a big girl now, she pretty much does this all by herself."

The baby grasps the bottle with her chubby little hands. Marco's just kinda there for supervision as she feeds herself. We watch her pursed rosebud lips as she drinks the milk. She pushes the bottle away when she's done.

Mom takes it and puts it on the coffee table. "Magdalena," she says, "this is Marco. He's your *hermano mayor.* Can you say hi to Marco, baby girl?"

"Mmm," the baby says.

"Oh, wow!" Marco says. "Does she talk now, Mom?"

"She makes some sounds," Mom says. "She's hitting all her milestones on time."

"That's good," Marco says. He's gazing at the baby, cuddling her close, giggling as she pats his cheeks with her hands. "Oh, my God, Mom. She's so cute. She's so sweet." He bends his head, kisses both her cheeks and her forehead. "Look at her. *Ella es perfecta.*"

I look at my mom looking at Marco and the baby. Her eyes are wet.

"Mira," Mom says, and my eyes dart back to her face. "Would you like to hold her?"

I open my mouth. I know what I'm supposed to say. I haven't officially met my baby sister yet. I've barely even looked at her. (Marco told me when he met her last year that she looks like me. I'm kinda trying not to look, but she is right next to me, and yeah, me and this girl are definitely sisters, all *morena y negrita,* and just look at her big puff of curly hair. I don't know who her dad is, but clearly my mom only fucks with dark-skinned brothers, and I ain't mad at her, all right.) I should hold her. I should say hello to her. I should start letting her know me. I have to start behaving like a normal ass person, starting now.

I risk a look at Magdalena. Marco's now helping her stand up on his legs, her dimpled bare feet on his thighs, holding her little torso firmly.

They're gazing at each other, giggling at each other, half in love already. Part of me aches to say yes. But there's something in me, something big, violently recoiling, screaming at me to say no.

"Okay," I whisper.

Marco smiles at me. Mom smiles too. This means I am a good girl; I have given the right answer, made everybody happy. He picks the baby up, starts transferring her to me. She makes a gurgling sound. I put my arms out. I wrap my fingers around her warm, wriggly, solid, surprisingly strong middle. I brace my arms, preparing to lift her onto my lap.

But then, suddenly, something inside me snaps. I want to. I want desperately to continue to maintain the charade that I am normal, that I am healed. But I can't. All four of our hands holding onto our baby sister, I burst into tears. And these are not cute, sweet, sentimental tears because our girl is so adorable. Nah, I'm sobbing, feeling every reverberation in my core like earthquakes.

"Mira!" Marco says. "*Nena,* are you okay?"

"Mira, baby." Mom squeezes my shoulder.

The baby looks at me and starts crying again too.

"Oh, God," I moan. "I can't hold her, Marco. I can't. Look! Just look! I'm upsetting her!"

Mom plucks the baby out of Marco's hold. I get up from the couch and run blindly into the bedroom. I close the door behind me and fling myself onto the bed with extreme emo teenage drama. I press my face into the blanket. It smells unfamiliar, because this is a fucking stranger's bed. My grandmother's friends, a couple, whom I've never met before, sleep here. And here I am, streaming my eyes out and dripping my nose all over their bed. Thinking about how pathetic I am only makes me cry harder.

There's a knock on the bedroom door. I lift my head. "What?" I ask miserably.

Marco comes in. He shuts the door quietly behind him. He joins me on the bed, sitting cross-legged. I drag my sad sack of a body to a seated position as well, leaning my back against the wall behind the bed. I put a pillow in my lap, a soft barrier between me and literally everything else in the world. My head throbs from the crying. My eyes are in fact still leaking. My scar and the area around my G-tube ache, that's how hard the sobs were from my belly.

I hug the pillow. "*Soy tan grosera,*" I say. "Look at me, on some rando's bed."

Marco laughs. He reaches over, squeezes my leg. "Are you okay, *hermanita*?"

"No, Marco Polo, I am not okay." I scoff. "I couldn't even hold her."

The tears start up again in earnest.

Marco looks at me with wet, glowy eyes. "What can I do, Mira? Tell me what I can do to support you. To be there for you."

I laugh, a mean and nasty sound. "Marco. Wow. There is literally nothing you can do for me right now."

He hangs his head.

"I could barely even look at her," I whisper. "I'm so messed up."

"Mira," he says. "Mira, baby, you're not. You've just… been through an awful thing. You've been through so much, and for right now, maybe you need to focus on you. On whatever it is that you need."

"Please don't tell me what I need right now," I say softly. I wipe my eyes. They're getting swollen, painful to the touch. What I need is to get out of here.

"I am so fucking mad at her," I say suddenly, the words feeling like gravel passing out of my throat. I didn't even realize the emotion until I had named it. "I can't believe her, Marco. She went and had another baby." I'm trembling. "Our mom went and had another baby when she cannot even take care of herself." My breath feels like a bellows. "Our mom, Marco, who fucked us up so bad." I nudge his knee. "Don't you remember what it was like? Growing up with her?"

"Mira." He crosses his arms. "Do you think that I could forget?"

"Is she gonna grow up the way we did?" I whisper in a hiss. "MP. No. She can't… we can't…"

"Mira," he says. "Honey. Are you breathing? *Respira profundo.* You're scaring me."

Even though he's pissing me off, I stop, focus for a few seconds on breathing deeply.

"And she's fucking using?" I continue in the same angry hiss. "Is this woman literally shooting heroin when she's taking care of an infant? Marco."

He comes closer, hugs me hard. "Mira," he says. "You're shaking. Are you okay?"

"No, I am not okay." I break into tears again. "Marco. I'm so angry at her. I can't believe she did this. I can't believe she had another baby."

"I know," he whispers into my ear. "I'm so angry at her too. And we're gonna figure this out." He strokes my hair. "We are going to figure this out."

"How?" I say. "Marco. We—"

Our mom bursts into the room then. We break apart, like we've been doing something wrong.

"Miranda." Mom has my phone. I stand up. What the hell is she doing with my phone?

"Mira," she says. "Why is *la chica esa* Paloma texting you? She is sending you naked pictures!"

I lunge for her and grab my phone. "Mom!" I scream. "What is wrong with you? You cannot just look at my phone like that!"

"*Lo dejaste en la mesa,*" she says. "I just saw it. *Ahora dime.* Why is this woman texting you naked pictures?"

"I am not telling you anything! How dare you! You cannot just look at my phone, Mom!"

"I can look at your phone anytime I damn well please!" she says, now yelling back. "I still pay our family phone bill, *nena desagradecida.*"

"Then stop!" I scream. "Andre and I can fucking take care of it. Like we take care of everything."

"Does Andre know you're sexting with this woman?"

"*Por Dios,* Mom. Yes! Yes, he knows! We've been doing polyamory. Conscious nonmonogamy."

"You've been seeing other people?"

"Yes," I say. I'm panting. My heart is throbbing so hard in my belly and chest that it hurts with every beat. "We have."

"Why didn't you tell me?" she asks.

"Because I knew this is how you'd react," I answer. I start to cry again. "I need something that is just mine, Mom. I need you to just let me live. And I need you to focus on your own life. Marco and I are grown up, okay. And you've just had another baby. You need to get your shit together and take care of her."

"*Cómo te atreves,*" she whispers.

"Mom," Marco says.

"Nah," I say. "No. Nope. I am outta here."

I storm through to the front door. I call Andre. He picks up right away. The second I hear his voice, I'm crying again, so hard I can barely speak.

"Mira?" he says. "What's wrong? Where are you? Are you safe?"

"Hi," I say. "I guess I'm safe but I'm not okay. I'm still at my *abuela's* place. I hate my family so much and I have to get out of here. Can you please come get me?"

"I am already on my way," he says. "I will be there in like ten minutes."

Andre came down to Washington Heights with me, knowing things with my mom would probably go to shit. He's at a coffee shop a few blocks away, drinking one of his expensive coffees. I'm so grateful for him right now I could lie down on the floor and dissolve.

Marco comes into the living room, where I'm standing right by the door. I slip into my *chancletas*.

"Mom is crying in the bedroom with the baby," he says.

"Wonderful," I say.

"Are you leaving?"

"Yep. Andre is coming to get me."

"All right. Good." He sighs. "Mira, I'm sorry."

"Don't apologize. It ain't your fault, MP."

"Yeah." He sighs again. "I'm gonna try to talk to her a little more. Make sure she has a ride back to wherever the fuck she's staying. I need to get out of here too."

"Sorry for leaving you here."

"No." He shakes his head. "You need to focus on you right now."

"I'm gonna go outside. Andre is at some coffee place just a couple blocks away. So he'll be here soon."

"Be careful," Marco says.

I roll my eyes. "Goodbye, MP. Text me, okay?"

He gives me a last hard hug. "Text me when you two get home safe."

I go downstairs and wait for my husband on the sidewalk. He's there within minutes, half running to reach me. I want to throw myself at him like a drama scene from a movie, but I feel so weak I have to settle for my version, which is a gentle hug.

"Hey," he whispers. "You okay?"

I put my face against his Mets sweatshirt and inhale him, his aftershave and deodorant and the sugar and caffeine smell of the coffee place. "No," I whisper back. "But now I will be. Please take me home."

Andre gets us an Uber home. I don't think I've ever been more grateful to open our door and go inside. There's our home, quiet and clean, a bouquet of sunflowers in a pink vase on the coffee table, my tarot cards and crystals on the kitchen table, the lavender air purifier bubbling merrily away. No one is yelling. No one is hurting themselves or each other or violating each other's boundaries. Everyone and everything is safe.

I don't know if we will, but if Andre and I ever have a kid, this is how we will raise them: calm and quiet and loving and safe. I ain't sure of much, y'all, but I can promise you that.

I'm too tired to do anything except go into the bedroom and lie in bed. Andre comes with me. He strokes my back. I know everyone's been encouraging me to talk about how I feel about everything that's happened. And, I'm realizing now, deep in the heart of me, that I've been reluctant not 'cause I don't want to. I do want to talk about how I feel. I always do, I always have. Honestly, I am scared. I am scared of what I have to say. I am scared of all of the feelings that are gonna come pouring, bubbling, out. You know that one closet you got, where you stuff all of your shit? You're scared to even open the door, all shoved shut against the bulging weight of all of your shit, because then all your crap will come tumbling out, and you won't have any choice. You will have to deal with it, one way or another. This is how I've been feeling about all the scraps of my emotions these past weeks, compacted behind a door inside my heart.

Also, you know how, when you're all in your feelings privately, and things have a certain taste and texture and look a certain way? And then, you tell somebody else, and they don't react the way you imagine they will, and suddenly everything looks different to you too? Well, I am also scared of that. If I start to be honest about how I am feeling, then Andre will be honest too, and not only will I have to deal with my own recently unearthed shit, I will also have to face his. And I do not know if I am ready.

But as I lie here on our bed, hurt and exhausted by my family's shit, with him tenderly stroking my back, the silence begins to gnaw at me. I have reached a point where it's gotten more painful to hold it all inside than it will be to speak, to face what we've got coming for us. And, like I told Maya, I did not come all this way, and get these fucking new lungs, and fight for them, and fight for my life, to turn back now.

I sit up. "Andre," I say, "I think we should have a baby."

He narrows his eyes at me slowly. I can see the confusion descending over him bit by bit. "Wait. You think we should… what?"

"I think we should make a baby," I repeat. "I know we can't, like, have sex and conceive naturally. But, like everyone's saying, there are so many different ways to have a baby. To create a family. I think my eggs are perfectly healthy. We could explore surrogacy. Or other ways. Point is, I think we should have a baby." I take one of his hands in both of mine. "I want to make a baby with you, Andre."

Andre looks down at his hand in my hands. "Mira," he says. He sounds like he's in pain. Already my heart is sinking. I was scared this might not go the way I had dreamed, and I'm starting to think I may have been right. "I…" He looks up at me. I am there, ready to meet his gaze. "I don't think I can do that," he whispers finally.

"But," I whisper back. I will not cry. I won't. I don't want to. I don't want fear of hurting me, of making me cry, to influence his feelings and responses right now. But my eyes are stinging, bad. "Why not?" My voice cracks as I say it, and I feel awful, like a hurt child, not a woman capable of being a mother to a child herself.

"Mira," he says.

I'm a dick, yeah, but I don't even let him speak. "But you said." I try to temper my voice, to sound open and curious instead of whiny. "You said, on March thirty-first, you said that, if we'd been pregnant for real, you would have been open to it." And there it goes; with these words, this memory, I am starting to cry. It's been a hard day for my poor swollen eyes. "So then… what… why…"

"Mira." He squeezes my hand, then slips his hand out of mine. "If God, or nature, or the universe, or who the fuck ever had given us a baby, then yeah, I would have done it. I would have been fucking scared, and still not ready, Mira, but I would have decided to see that as a gift, and I would have…" His voice cracks here, and oh, fuck, is it awful. "I would have done it with you, hummingbird. I would have supported you, whatever you wanted to do, however you wanted to do it. I would have tried my fucking best to be whatever you needed. And I would have done anything, anything I had to do, to be a father to our baby."

His voice breaks again. We are both crying. It hurts so bad. I want to make it stop. But I know I can't. I've crossed a threshold and there is no going back to a past that is gone.

"I don't know how good of a job I would have done," he says, wiping his eyes. "Because I'm too young and I have no clue what I'm doing and my own shit is really, really not together. But you are my wife, Mira. And that would have been my kid. And I would've done anything…"

I know I'm continuing to be a dick here. He's hurting, he's crying in front of me, and I know what I'm going to say is gonna hurt him worse. But I can't stop myself from saying it.

"So, what you're saying is that, if we accidentally got pregnant due to, like, God's will or whatever, then you'd have a baby with me?" Fuck, it sounds even worse coming out my mouth than it did rattling around like jagged metal in my head, bruising up my brain. "But you're not open to intentionally trying to make a baby with me?"

"Mira," he says. "Why are you doing this?"

"But that doesn't make any sense, Andre," I say. "Either you're open to having a baby with me or you're not."

He opens his mouth, closes it. "I don't even know what to say to that, Mira."

"But it's true," I say. "And, Andre, it isn't fair." I'm biting my lips, trying to keep the real, painful, breathtaking sobs from getting out. "What if I can't get pregnant accidentally due to the universe just dropping a baby into my fucking womb? Like, what if that's not how it gets to happen for me? What if I need a little help? What then, Andre? Then you're not open to trying to have a baby with me—"

"That is not what I am saying," he says, his voice somehow both soothing and angry. "What I am saying, Miranda, is that I am not ready for that. It is not the right time. Not right now."

I start to cry harder. "So you get to decide when it's the right time for me to have a baby?"

His eyebrows lift. "If you want to have a baby, Mira, I can't stop you," he says. "It is your body. I am only telling you that I am not ready to have a kid. To be a dad."

"So, what? You want to leave me?"

He squeezes my wrist. I'm shaking.

"Mira," he says. "I don't want to leave you. I will never leave you. I'm scared you want to leave me."

"I don't want to leave you," I sob. Fuck, I am messed up. "I want to have your baby, Andre. I love you."

"I love you too, little bird," he says. "So much. I am just not ready for us to have a baby. Not right now."

"I hate my mother so much." I squeeze my eyes shut, immediately mortified. Did I really just say that? And yeah, I mean, it's true, but why the fuck is that coming out right now? "Look at her, having another stupid baby when she can't even take care of herself. How could she?" I drop my head into my hands. "It was awful, Andre. She was there with her dumb baby and Marco was all half in love with her, and me? Boy, I couldn't even look at her. Like, Mom asked me if I wanted to hold her, 'cause Marco was, and I couldn't even do it, Andre. I just burst into tears like I ain't got no sense and I ran outta the room. Marco had to come and rescue me. As usual."

"Mira," he says, tenderly. "Baby. You do not have no sense. You're perfect. You are healing."

"Fuck that," I say, which, I mean, best answer ever, right? I rub my eyes angrily, impatient with their constant stream of tears. "I want to make a baby with you, Andre."

"I'm sorry, Mira," he says, shaking his head. "I am not ready. I can't do that right now. It would not be right."

"Why not?" I ask tremulously. I ask the question like I'm scared of it (which I am), like it's a step venturing into a dark wood where I am not sure what I will find.

"I am not ready," he says, for about the ten billionth time. "Things are a lot for me at work right now, Mira. I feel like I am just starting to learn how to advocate for myself and handle shit and, like, be an actual professional person. I'd love to get a couple promotions before we start thinking about a kid. It would be cool to save more. Feel more stable. And, I don't know. I mean, I love this place. I like our neighborhood. I'm so glad I was able to hold onto this place on my own even after I didn't have roommates anymore. But is here where we wanna raise a baby? I don't know, maybe we want something… bigger?"

"Andre," I say. "We don't need a fancy job or to be rich or have a huge place to have a baby."

"That's not what I'm saying," he says.

"You know how I grew up. I mean, sure, my mom is a trainwreck. Today's, like, exhibit A of that shit. But I still love my life. I'm still so glad my mom had me. You don't have to be rich or have a huge house to have a kid, Andre. That isn't fair."

"Like I said," he says, "not what I'm saying."

"Then what are you saying?"

"I am saying that I want to feel more stable. I want to have my shit together, Mira. I want to be someone our kid would be proud of. Okay?"

"Andre." I mean, what do you even say to that? "You're the best. Our kid would so be proud of you."

He shrugs. "I don't know, Mira. Sometimes I'm not proud of me."

"Baby," I whisper.

"Mira," he says. "I feel too young. Too unprepared. I can't do this yet. I am not ready."

"We are not that young," I say.

"What? I am twenty-three. You are not even twenty-two. In what world is that not young for having a baby?"

"I don't know," I mumble.

He just looks at me. I know what he wants me to say, but I ain't gonna say it. I just stare back at him. Finally I say, "All I know is, we love each other, Andre. We're married. We got married when I was barely twenty. You were cool with that. I think we are ready. And I think we should do it. We should have a baby."

He gives me a look like he can't even believe me. I don't feel good about it, or about anything, but I cannot seem to stop. "Getting married is one thing, Mira," he says. "We're adults. I mean, we're young, yeah, but we're adults, we can take care of ourselves, we can make decisions for ourselves knowing the score. A baby is… a whole other person, *mi reina*. A whole other soul. You probably are ready for that level of responsibility. You're way more mature and emotionally together than I am. But I am not ready to be responsible for somebody else's life. Not when I barely feel like I'm handling mine."

I have to laugh at this one. "I really don't know in what world I am more mature or emotionally together than you, bro. I don't have a job. I have no money. I couldn't even hold a baby today. And I called you crying to come get me 'cause my mommy was mean to me and I was sad. I literally have trouble feeding myself."

His eyes are starting to get wet again. "You handle your shit, Mira," he says. "I know this is on the list of ableist shit you hate hearing. So I'll just say it once and then shut up. But you are the strongest person I know."

"Andre—"

"Can you just let me?" he says. "Shit happens to you that would literally kill most people. But you are still out here. Trying to do your thing. And I love you so much. I love you more literally every day. And I…"

"This shit did almost kill me, Andre," I remind him. I've given up now, tears are running down my lips, salty when I lick them away.

"Yeah, you think I didn't know that?" His lip trembles. He bites it, hard. "Mira. When I went in the bathroom that night." He points in the direction of the bathroom, in case I forgot where it is. "And I saw you there, bleeding. I almost had a heart attack. I thought, tell me what I can do. Tell me what I can do to stop her having to go through this. Let me go through this, whatever it is, instead of her. Except I couldn't, yeah? So then you go into the hospital. I can't even go see you, be with you at first. You had to have that surgery by yourself. Then, the rejection episode. They weren't sure they were gonna be able to bring you back, you know that, Mira?" He sobs openly, and I make myself look at him, even though it hurts, even though I don't want to. "I had convinced them to let me be there with you by then. And I think it was 'cause they were worried you didn't have much time left. Okay? At one point one of the nurses even asked me. She asked me if I had a support system, if I had someone I could call to come get me, to be with me, if we. If we lost you. I broke down crying. There in the hallway. Sitting on the floor. It was… not a good moment, Mira.

"Part of me felt stupid. So stupid. I remember years ago. I remember when you were sick when we were teenagers. That time the hospital priest came and prayed with us because they thought you weren't gonna make it. And it was awful. It was the worst thing ever. And I wanted to die. But this? This was worse, Mira." He grips my wrist again, needing to reassure himself, I think, that I am in fact still here. "It was worse because we aren't kids anymore. It was worse 'cause I was alone. That other time, all the other times, your mom was there. Marco was there. This time, there was no one for me to ask. I mean… if something happened to you, if some decision had to be made… I was gonna have to make it. So I felt stupid. I'm your husband, baby. I'm your man. I'm supposed to take care of you.

"The night before our wedding, because you're stronger than me, you reminded me. You told me that while you believe in miracles and you're open to them, the likely ending to this story is that you die before me. You die young. You asked me one last time if I was willing to walk into this with you knowing that. And I said yes. And I meant it, baby. Then we said those vows, made those promises to each other. Then, the second something happens, and you trust me to be there for you and take care of you like I promised you, I was scared. I was so scared, Mira."

The only thing I can do right now is hold him, so that's what I do. I hold him close and let him cry. I get so many good things. I get so, so many good things, y'all, and you know that. But me, I also get this. And I ain't gonna run from it neither. I walked into this with my eyes open too, you know.

"Andre," I whisper to him. "You did take care of me. You do take care of me."

He shakes his head.

"Oh, honey, yes, you do. What's wrong with you, boy? You literally feed me. Every single day. You think I don't know how hard that is? How much that is on you?"

He pulls back. "I'd do anything for you that I had to, Mira," he says. "Anything."

"Right. 'Cause you are a fucking king. But also don't you lie to me and tell me it's easy. That it ain't a lot on you."

"Fine, Mira, yeah," he says. He looks into my eyes, and I feel like, for the first time in a long time, we are truly seeing each other, he and I, this man I've known since he was a kid. "It is a lot. I mean, I am happy to do it. I love you. You're my wife. I'd do this and a lot more. And I know you'd do it for me too."

"In a heartbeat," I confirm.

"But it is a lot, Mira. It takes all my love. All my attention. All my care. While I'm also trying to handle shit at work and deal with my parents and feel whatever it is that I'm feeling. Which I am doing a really shit job of."

"Baby," I say.

"No, really," he says. "I haven't even looked at how fucked I feel right now. But I will. 'Cause right now, you have my whole heart. All of it. Let's focus on feeding tube time. Let's get you into school and settled there. Let's focus on us and maybe having sex again when we feel like we can do that. And when I do stop being chicken shit and actually let myself feel my feelings, I am going to need you, okay?" He looks right into my eyes, lets me see him crying. "I'm still lost and hurt and scared and I have no idea what I'm doing. I need you. I am not that good, okay, Mira? I am selfish. I want you. I need you. I am not ready to share you with a kid. Not now. So. Can we wait a while? Till we—till I—feel like my shit is more together?"

I nod.

"Can I tell you something else?" he says.

"You can tell me anything," I say.

"It was also worse this time, much worse," he says, with a very deep breath, "because you were pregnant. I'm sorry if I'm saying the wrong thing. Or feeling the wrong thing. I know that this was not a baby. Not a viable pregnancy. I know that this is your body. Not mine. And whatever

I'm feeling pales in comparison to what you are feeling. And that's how it should be." I put my arms around his neck.

"But," he says. He slips his arms around my waist. "I'm sorry. But I feel like I am grieving our… lost pregnancy. Our… fertilized egg. Or whatever. I don't even know what to call it. How to talk about it. All I know is that I feel sad. And empty. I didn't even know you were pregnant. I had no idea. We only found out when, and because, you were losing it. And you were in danger. Which also makes me feel scared when I think about it. And angry. And… all kinds of things. I don't even know. I don't know how to… say goodbye? Or grieve? Or, like, move past this?"

I just nod. Fuck if I have any answers to any of this. I'm past the point of saying anything. All I can do now is listen and hold him and be here.

"I still have nightmares about it," he whispers, putting his forehead close to mine.

"Oh, honey. About what?"

"About how I…" His voice shakes. "How I had to clean the blood off the bathroom floor." He looks away, though his arms are still holding me. "I didn't want to do it. But I knew I had to. So I did. And that was from our…"

"Andre," I whisper. "Baby. I am so sorry."

"I…" he says.

My phone rings.

"It's okay," he says, letting go of me. "See who it is."

I find my phone on the bedside table. It's Marco. I slide my finger across the screen. "Hello?"

"Mira," he says. "You didn't tell me when you two got home safe."

I roll my eyes and trust that my twin can hear it.

He sighs. "Listen," he says.

"Oh, God. What is it?"

"*Oye.* Okay? Mom is here. And the baby."

"Here, where?"

He sighs again. "Mira, Mom and Magda are here at my place. With Hassan and me."

"They are? Why? Is Mom not…? I mean, is the baby safe?"

"I don't know," Marco says. "I mean, I think so. I think Magda is okay. She seems okay. But, Mira, Mom was really upset. She was so upset. I started to get worried. About if she'd be okay to take the baby. Back to, well, wherever the actual fuck they've been staying. So the only thing I could think of to do was bring her back home with me. Both of them. She was so upset she didn't even argue. She just came with me."

"Wow." I lock eyes with Andre. "Well. Are you okay? And Hassan? And Mom and the baby?"

"Yeah, I guess," he says. "We're fine."

"Do you… need anything?"

"Nah. I don't think so. You just focus on you, okay, Mira?"

"MP, come on," I say. "Your place is a studio. It's small for you and your man. Are y'all okay, with Mom and the baby there?"

"We're fine."

"I mean… what's the game plan? How long are they gonna stay?"

"I have no idea," he says. "We'll have to see. We'll figure it out. But for now, they're here, and our sister is safe."

"All right," I say. "That's good. Will you please keep me posted? Let me know if you need anything?"

"Of course I will keep you posted, *nena*," he says. "Look. I better go now. I'm gonna make sure Magda has everything she needs. All right?"

"*Te amo, hermano*," I tell him. "Thank you."

"*Te amo*, baby girl," he says, and hangs up.

"Oh, fuck. So he said…"

"Yeah," Andre says. "I heard. So, can I ask? What happened with your mom today?"

I sigh. And, not for the first time in my life, and probably not the last neither, my mom and all her shit hijacks a moment in my life that was supposed to be mine.

Andre and I have found a counselor who specializes in pregnancy loss. (Yeah—just saying it makes me die a little inside, but I did say this would be a demon-wrestling session, didn't I? Like, this ain't gonna be pretty, folks.) We went back and forth a little bit, wondering if maybe we should go the full medical route, find a psychologist or psychiatrist with, like, university degrees and shit. But then we decided we didn't want to spend any more time thinking about insurance, intake forms, possible diagnoses, or any of that other shit that y'all know has colonized such a big part of my life. So we searched for and found this counselor, Ava, on Instagram.

I know, I know. What can I say? I can only maintain that the internet is our modern-day magic. It's our quest, our holy grail; it's our dragon and our cave. It's our salon, our meeting place, the campfire around which we sing songs and tell stories. And, like all magic, throughout every age, it has its strengths and weaknesses, its moments of incomparable splendor right alongside its black hexes, its dark shadows. But we reach for it, we take it as it is, for what else do we have left in this depleted, unromantic world, aside from magic?

Ava describes herself as a mystic doula: she guides people and couples through the process of conscious conception and childbirth, and, at other times, through the shadow of the valley of pregnancy loss, miscarriage, infant and child death. We read her profile dozens of times. We look at her website together. We scour years' worth of her Insta feed and her blog posts. We listen to her podcast at our kitchen table. We scroll down to the bottom of her site and find her testimonials. We dig up some of her old clients on IG and DM them, asking respectfully if they'd be willing to share about their experiences with Ava. All three couples respond. They say that working with Ava was difficult, but worth it.

I'm not thrilled about how much money this woman charges. Andre, who's typically fairly open-minded, is a little worried about just how esoteric she comes off, calling herself a "mystic doula of life and death." But, ultimately, we both decide we are willing to give it a try.

We message Ava, start chatting with her. The next day, she offers us a "free discovery call to see if it would be a fit for us to work together." The day after that we have our call. (I do love how fast these Insta healers be moving, y'all.) I'm mostly quiet during the call. I talked about this with Andre beforehand; I asked him if he'd be okay with taking care of most of the talking, asking and answering questions, during this call. He said of course. So I do about ninety-five percent listening on our discovery call.

Ava talks about her process. She says she typically begins with a session or two of traditional Western talk therapy, just so she can get our backstory in the simplest and most straightforward way possible. Then, she says, she enters the form of a vessel, so that she can channel for us the kind of healing we most need right now. She says she draws on a repertoire of practices like chakra balancing, rituals for grieving and letting go, aura cleansing, yoga and other somatic methodologies, breathwork, crystal therapy, tarot and astrological healing, all of which she says she's trained in. Most of this shit is, as y'all know by now, right up Miranda Castillo's magical alley. Andre is perhaps a shade more skeptical. But he knows that we are both lost when it comes to grieving here, or letting go, or facing death, or whatever the fuck we're even supposed to call it. In fact, I think, most of our world, whether it's the medical field or regular therapy or even our relationships with our friends and family, is pathless and clueless when it comes to processing, facing, and dealing with death. We know we need a guide. And we know it will have to come from something outside of our usual experience.

We set up a session with Ava. She has a room in a yoga studio in Midtown where she does her work. We ask if we can meet with her in person, and if she'd be comfortable with us not wearing face masks during our session, as long as we bring negative virus test results with us. She says yes.

The day of our session with the death doula arrives. The moment I open my eyes, I remember, and I begin to wonder. I squeeze my eyes shut immediately, wondering if, by just refusing to open my eyes and begin this day, I can keep its events from happening. See, here's the thing, my peeps. I was not out there tryna get pregnant. I had no literal clue I even was pregnant—not until I was actively, and traumatically, and perilously, in the process of becoming un-pregnant. And whatever it was, it had already grown a heartbeat sometime before I was even aware of its precarious, star-crossed existence. How can I say goodbye to that heartbeat, to which I'd never even said hello? I didn't seek or ask for that pregnancy. And so, becoming un-pregnant felt not like a loss that belonged to me or came from me, but like yet another medical drama that happened to me, and over which I had no control.

I mean, how does my strange loss even compare to the loss of a pregnancy that someone longed for, and planned, and awaited, and prayed over, and deeply, tenderly wanted? Like, do I even get to be sad here?

This, though, this session with the doula—this is different. This Andre and I did plan, and seek out, and wait for, and agonize over, and want with a bittersweet desperation. We have paid for it already with money, and I know that, before day's end, we will have paid for it in tears. This is me taking ownership of my hurt, my grief, this stupid and horrible fucking thing that has happened to me. I didn't ask for that heartbeat. I didn't ask for this grief. That made it easier to just push it away. But now, today, I am going to bring it closer. And that shit is fucking frightening. I didn't choose to say hello. I am, though, going to choose to say goodbye. That I don't want to do this is a giant fucking understatement. I've done some shit I didn't want to do before, plenty of times. But this shit is up there, way up there at the top of the list.

I don't want to get out of bed.

But I do. Andre and I, we do. I feel pretty fucking alone, I gotta say. But I have just enough magic left in me to feel like my ancestors, many, many women who came here before me, who got up on days when they didn't want to get up, and did things they didn't really wanna do, are getting up with me.

We Uber to the yoga studio where Ava holds her sessions. We take the world's narrowest, most rickety elevator up to the fourth floor, where the yoga-looking guy with a man bun at the front desk points us in the direction of Ava's room.

The door's open, and there she is, sitting cross-legged on the floor with a pad of paper in her lap, writing. Every few seconds she reaches up to toss her curly hair out of her face. Andre and I look at each other. I sigh silently. He reaches up, knocks on her open door tentatively.

She pops up out of her sitting position. "Andre? Mira?" We nod. "Hi! I'm Ava! It's so lovely to meet you both. May I shake your hands?"

We nod again.

Ava shakes both our hands. Her handshake is warm and firm. I can't help but observe her: she has enormous energy, a super intense aura that cannot be ignored. She's a small woman, maybe only a couple inches taller than me and nearly as slim (which is a feat, lemme tell you, 'cause y'all know I am tiny), but her energetic impact is concentrated, like a powerful medicine compressed into a tiny pill. She has hair somewhere between light brown and dark blond, in a springy cloud of curls bouncing off of her head. It gives her the appearance of being electrified, like she stuck her finger in a socket, came out with magical powers. Her skin glows, that pretty light brown color that the cute mixed girls have, y'all know what I'm talking about. She's wearing black leggings and a tiny, tight mint-green tank top, socks and no shoes, like she just finished a yoga class here at the studio. I'm not sure of her age, but I'd say she can't be any older than thirty-five.

"Would you like to sit down?" she says, walking past us to close the door behind us. "You can sit anywhere you like."

We sit on white cushions on the floor; they look like the kinda thing you'd sit on to meditate at a yoga class. I rest my back against the thick, sturdy leg of a table behind me. It's a massage table, with a face rest at one end. The room is full of all kinds of yogic and esoteric shit—a rack of colorful rolled yoga mats, boxes of incense sticks, a display case of small bottles of essential oils, a mini fridge with a glass door full of bougie drinks like kombucha and watermelon juice blended with apple cider vinegar. My head hurts just looking at everything, just taking in Ava's overwhelming energy. I want to go home. I lean my head back against the table leg and wish myself anywhere but here, hard.

Ava sits down on the floor with us. She asks if we can begin by taking three deep breaths together. I wanna be like, no, but of course we both say okay. "You're invited to close your eyes, if that feels okay for you," she says. "You're safe here."

I gotta say, I'm shocked at how the energy in the room changes as Ava leads us in three deep breaths. It's like the oversaturated energetic brilliance of the space is instantly turned down, going from neon flashing lights to a faint, soothing, barely-there light blue. I put my hand on my lower belly and feel myself breathing there.

"Okay," Ava says softly, and we open our eyes. She gives us a gentle smile. Even her halo of curls around her head looks calmer. "Hi, Mira. Maybe you can tell me a little bit about what brought us here today." Maybe she sees the look on my face—y'all know I don't like being called out, and y'all know that I am in no way ready to be here today—because she says, "I like to hear from the person who was carrying the pregnancy themself, first, if I can. Maybe, if you are feeling safe, and ready, you could tell me what you experienced in your body."

I look over at Andre with a sigh—'cause, like, do I have to? He takes my hand. We rest our clasped hands on my thigh.

"All right," I say. "I had an ectopic pregnancy. I didn't even know I was pregnant. Not until I lost the pregnancy. I was bleeding out. I had to be rushed to the hospital. Andre couldn't even come be with me, not at first, because of all the pandemic restrictions. You know? So they performed surgery to remove the pregnancy, and they had to take one of my fallopian tubes, which was where the pregnancy had implanted. So, like I was telling you during our call, I have cystic fibrosis. I had a double lung transplant a little over a year ago. That makes pregnancy pretty dangerous for me. So all the trauma caused a rejection episode. That's where, like, your body, your immune system, attempts to attack your transplanted organ 'cause they don't recognize it. We were able to get that under control.

"And, well… a lotta other shit happened. That I frankly don't have the energy to get into right now. 'Cause it's a lot. And I have a fairly extensive team. Yeah? Lots of people, helping me do and deal with and process different things. But I'm here. Tryna deal with the fact that I did lose this pregnancy. Which I didn't even know I was carrying."

"I'm very sorry this happened to you, Mira," Ava says, and though they're the usual words you often hear, she says them so sincerely, so simply, they do hit a little different.

"Thanks."

"How long ago did this happen?" she asks.

"Mid-February," I say.

"May I ask you some more questions?"

"Okay," I say, like, yeah, I came here, didn't I? So hit me with your best shot.

"Sometimes," she says, "when we experience something extremely complex, it can help to distill our feelings down to their simplest essence." I nod—fine; I'm willing to try this. "If you could describe your feelings about what happened in one word, Mira, what would it be?"

"Resentful," I say, right away. I had no clue this particular word was gonna come out. But it comes out like a punch, something quick and with stunning clarity, singularity, and force. I feel knocked back, a little bruised. But I also feel shockingly better: like the blow was to my stomach, that it purged something from me, dislodged a blockage, released a poison.

Ava nods, like this makes total sense—and, I gotta say, the validation helps. "Can you tell me more about that feeling?" she asks.

I nod. "Like I said, I didn't even know I was pregnant. So I was just... blindsided. By this thing over which I felt like I had zero control. And I'd been doing really well. I was doing all kinds of new things that made me happy. The lung transplant had made a big difference in my health. And then—this. I felt resentful. I didn't ask for this. I want to get back to my body and the way it was feeling. I want to get back to sex and intimacy, which I haven't felt able to do since this happened. And you know what else really sucks about this?"

"What else? Tell me, Mira," she says softly.

"I've always wanted to have a baby. Andre's baby." He squeezes my hand. And here come the tears. I knew they were coming sometime today. "So it's not like I didn't want a baby. I do. I still do. But that wasn't a baby. It almost killed me. And. It forced me to face a truth I kinda knew but wasn't ready to accept yet. While I was in the hospital recovering, which took weeks, I talked with my doctors and they told me they don't think it will ever be safe for my body to carry a baby. So. It's like not only did I lose this pregnancy that I didn't even know about or ask for and which wasn't a baby, but I also lost the chance to ever have an actual baby. And it all makes me feel like I'm living in a surreal nightmare. Because I didn't have anything in the first place. But I lost it. And I lost all my theoretical chances in the future too. And I don't know how to come back from that."

"You can come back from that, Mira," Ava says, with a kind of conviction that, I gotta say, does make me feel better. Sometimes, when you are feeling weak, you really do need to lean on the vision of someone who can see clearer than you can.

"You have come back," she adds. "Here you are, Mira. You're right here."

"Right," Andre says, softly but clearly. He gives my hand a squeeze. I turn my head and look at him. And, yeah, sometimes you just need the people around you to remind you that you are real, that you are grounded on earth and still have your physical existence, that you are here. I am here.

"Thank you for sharing that, Mira," Ava says. "There's a lot we can work with there, to help you and your body heal." I nod, and whisper okay. She turns to my husband. "Andre? Can you tell me what your experience was of everything that happened?"

I sit there on the floor of Ava's room in the yoga studio, letting the table behind me take my weight, holding Andre's hand, and listening to him tell this story. It's only the second time I've heard him share his version of what happened while I was sick. We were apart for a lot of it, so I know our two experiences were very different. It still hurts to hear, no less than it did that night in our bedroom when I told Andre I wanted to try to have a baby, but I also know that it was so complex, and so painful for him, that he's not done telling it, I am not done hearing it; neither of us is done processing it.

He talks again about the difficulty of not being allowed to be with me when I underwent the surgery, about the fear of losing me during the rejection episode. He articulates even more plainly that it felt harder this time than any other time in the past, because we are older, because we are married, he is my husband and I am his wife. "The more we share together, the more I love her, and the harder it is to even imagine losing her," he says, one of those statements, sweet as love and stark as death, that I'll replay in my head a thousand times, nights when I can't sleep. He shares about the blood all over our bathroom floor, how he scrubbed it on hands and knees, crying the entire time.

"God," I say. "I am so sorry you had to do that, Andre."

He holds my eyes for a long moment. His eyes are swimming in tears. He looks exhausted. I know I don't look much better. But I also feel a hint of the old us; I feel a strength in us, like we are two people who can depend on each other, who hold each other down, who hold each other up.

He shrugs. "I'm happy you didn't have to do it," he says. "Especially since you already had to…"

His eyes well up deeper. "I feel like we're here because I can't let go," he says. "I can't move past it. I can't forget. Mira and I haven't had sex since this happened. I know this sounds stupid, I know that it's wrong. But I feel like that's my fault. I want to make love with her again. Our intimacy is really important to me. And if we're both not there yet, then that's cool, I'd never want to rush it. But I'm scared. I'm scared that there's something wrong with me, you know? Like I'm never going to get back to feeling like that ever again. Even though I really want to."

"Andre," I say. "That is not stupid. It is not your fault, babe. But the way you feel isn't wrong."

He smiles sadly at me. "Isn't that a contradiction?"

"If I can," Ava says softly. We both look at her. "It's possible to hold two truths at once. Your feelings aren't wrong, Andre. But I think we can unearth a deeper truth here that can help you feel better."

He nods, tears on both cheeks, and I think, maybe, I love him more than I ever have: his honesty, his bravery, his willingness to go into this dark, difficult thing with me.

"Maybe it would help you to distill your feelings down to one word too," she says. She folds her hands in her lap. "If you had to encapsulate your feelings into one word, Andre, what would it be?"

"Guilty," he says, right away, just like I did. His word also has that same sudden plosive power and stark singularity, like a shot. I feel it land on my body, ponderously; and while it doesn't feel good exactly, there's something satisfying in its weight, in knowing that I have taken some of it from him.

"I mean," he says, beginning to speak quickly over a tide of tears, "I know it's not logical. I know it isn't right. I know I'm acting like I caused something that I actually had no power over. But I just keep thinking. I made that happen to her." He looks at me. "Like I gave that to you, Mira. Something I gave you, put into your body, hurt you. I know that isn't the right way to think about this. But I don't know how to stop. I am so sorry, baby."

"Andre," I whisper.

"I am so, so sorry," he says.

He begins to sob then, and I reach over and hold him. I tuck him against my side, feeling how hot his body gets when he cries. He relaxes against my body, letting me hold him, and letting himself cry. I look up and meet Ava's eyes briefly. Her eyes are wet, like mine are too. She nods, and I nod too, and I know that our session is over for today, we are not going to get any farther than this. But we also both know, we all know, that we have gone extremely far today, that we've traversed a distance maybe not of geography but of vast emotional landscape.

Ava asks if she can see each of us privately, so she can focus on some healing modalities she thinks might work for us. I have my solo session with her first.

When I arrive at her room in the yoga studio, she says she wants to work on a method called sacred geographical mapping. "It's a magical embodiment practice," she says.

"Okay," I say. I am down for all of the magical shit.

I sit on the table while Ava explains more about the modality to me. She says it's similar to reiki, in that she will work on my energy using hers, with no physical contact between us. She will scan my body's energy and my aura with hers, sending her energy out from herself like a wand, like a magical sensor seeking heat. She will identify any places that need attention or love or healing or restoration, and we will work on rebuilding them together, seeping past the gross body back to the source, the subtle energetic body. She will then map on me a brand-new inner geography: filling in empty places with love, redirecting any paths or streams that might've veered off their course, repairing ruptures and breaks. She says it's sort of like a surgeon, sewing tendons and skin back together again; "it's returning you to yourself," she says.

"I like that," I say.

I lie down flat on the table, face-up, not using the face rest—I don't need to, since I'm not getting a massage. This experience reminds me in some ways of when I got my first and, still, only massage, back on New Year's. I thought I'd changed a lot last year, that I had gone through something massive, unmatched. And I had. But I also had no clue of the enormity of what would happen this year. When I got my massage, I was upset with Andre for telling Dan about the whole anal thing before me. (Shit, remember that? That feels like five centuries ago now.) Back then, that felt like the worst thing in the entire world. And it was. It still fucking sucks. When I think about it, I can still reconjure the pain, fresh as if it were yesterday. It doesn't make sense, but no, it wasn't erased, or even eclipsed, by the pain of everything that happened after, even if my recent hurts are arguably, objectively, on a whole other level. Like I keep learning, pain is pain; it doesn't necessarily exist on a hierarchy. I hold tight to this realization.

Unlike during my massage, no part of my body is physically touched. I guess you could say I was passive during my massage, in that I just lay there and allowed the therapist to work on my body, but no, I could feel my body responding to every touch: offering a good, satisfying resistance here, melting into her hold there, moving up or down to meet her hands, breathing into the many places that needed to soften and let go. During this experience, neither one of us moves, and there is no physical contact between our bodies. It is all energy, the kind of subtle, mystical thing that cannot be explained, for which no concrete proof can be mustered for the haters, all them skeptics who are determined not to believe.

But I can feel it. I can feel her energy molding mine. I can feel the simple strength of her powerful good intentions. I feel her moving up and down my unseen body like a ladder, like the keys of the musical scale. I feel strokes like silk and velvet, soothing my long jangled nerves. And I feel my energy respond: eager like my little orchid flower limp and dry and hungry for water, emerging from my soul that's longing for beauty, exhaling itself till it's warm and malleable like clay. It's felt endless, this process, like I would never, ever get better. It's felt cruel, like being kicked when I'd only just gotten up. But it is a process, ain't it? Like, they call it that for a reason. Like, there ain't no big moment when it all comes magically together. Nah, the magic is all the tiny moments knitted together, into a tapestry that you hope makes some kinda sense.

My heartbeat slows. My whole body breathes out. It lets go of a heavy thing, something it barely even realized it was carrying, which it only knows it has to let go.

I feel dizzy after our session. Ava gives me a cup of cold matcha tea to drink. It tastes earthy, and as green as it looks. She also gives me, of all things, in a wooden box with a clasp, a blob of slime to play with. It gives my hands something to do, a set of specific textures on which to ground myself. It's moldable and stretchy, a purple color, dark like a plum when squished tight into a ball, pale when pulled thin. It's full of silver sparkles like scattered stars. It's pleasantly cold. It gives me a full surrender, contorting into any shape my hands can think up, and yet it's sturdy and firm, thick, retaining its own integrity, no matter what.

While I drink matcha tea and play with purple glitter slime, Ava and I sit down in chairs at a little table. She pulls out a pad of paper and a green pen and, while telling me about what she found in my energy body, draws me a diagram of it. I love my magical shit, y'all know that, but I have never had an experience quite like this one.

"I went up and down all your chakras," she says. She draws a vine, up and down, with seven little circles along it. "Are you familiar with the chakra system?"

I nod.

She meets my eyes, then looks back down at her paper to draw a symbol inside of each of the seven little circles. They are symbols I have never laid eyes on before. I have no idea what they mean.

"We cleared blocks in all of your chakras," she says. "Mira, by the way, I want you to know that you were a full co-creator in this experience. Your body, all your bodies—gross, subtle, energy—were there too, participating in the healing. Your spirit and soul as well."

I nod.

"Then I went into your womb space," she says, quiet but also super casual, 'cause, yeah, this is your girl's life now, energy healers all up in my womb space. "Your womb has a message for you."

"Does she now?" I quirk an eyebrow, a wry smile. "What is it?"

Ava smiles. "Just that she's here. She hasn't gone anywhere. She is still a part of you."

I nod. And that would be Mira and her womb, one; haters, zero.

"I went into the area of your fallopian tubes," she continues. "I went behind your scar. I checked on its length. I felt its healing. I felt how it is knitting itself together again, keeping you safe. And I just want you to know, Mira, that, even though they had to take one of your tubes, its energy is still there." I didn't know that I would, but at this, I feel myself begin to tear up. "The moment I entered there, with your body's and spirit's permission, I felt the energy of your entire reproductive system. The energy of your other tube is still there. I experienced it like a cone of sparkling energy, healthy and pink. And I just want you to know."

I start to cry harder; something in me knows that what's coming next is gonna be big.

Ava hands me a box of tissues. I put down the slime, pluck a bunch of tissues, press them gently to my face.

"Mira. I just want you to know that your energy of fertility is still one hundred percent intact."

"It… it is?" I blot tears from my face. "Even though… even though they told me that I can't carry a baby? And, like, Ava. Doctors have been telling me shit my whole entire life. Some of it's true. Some of it ain't. But this one?" I shake my head. "Ava, girl, this one is true. I can feel it. Down to the bottom of me. With my whole intuition. Carrying a baby is something that my body is not going to be able to do. This shit nearly killed me. I cannot ever do this shit again."

Ava nods. She looks calm, not put out, not scandalized. She smiles and says, "Even so, Mira. Even if you and your body never carry a baby in your womb. You are still fertile. Fertility is so much more than carrying a baby. Fertility is about being a site, a vessel, for creation. And you, there are so many things that you are going to create in your life."

I cry again. It still ain't the big, epic, cinematic crying. And, like, maybe we are never gonna get that. And that's okay. Today we get a soft, gentle, quiet crying, cleansing and almost pleasant like a spring rain.

"And I felt something else," she says.

I pull my tissue bundle away from my face. "You… you did?"

"Yes." She nods. "Mira, is there something in your… stomach area? Maybe around your solar plexus chakra?"

I nod. And—I dunno when your girl got so dramatic, but here we go again—instead of explaining in words, I just put down my tissues, sit back in my chair, and pull up my shirt. And, well, I guess I can't not explain at all, so I say, "This is my feeding tube. I have eating problems. So it helps me supplement my nutrition."

She nods. I pull my shirt back down.

"Okay," she says. "So I just want to say… thank you."

"Thank you?" I repeat. "For what?"

"I see you, Mira," she says. "I see your struggles. The hours. The hurting. The tears. I see all the hard work you've put in."

"Into… what?" I ask, surprise and confusion having stalled my tears.

"Into staying alive," she says simply. And my tears continue. "And so I just wanted to thank you."

"Why?" I whisper.

"Because the world wouldn't be the same, without you in it," she says, with a casual brightness. "You have come to many an impasse. But you haven't turned back. Instead, you've gone forward. You've forged forward, even when the path was hard. And you felt alone. And you weren't sure how you would continue. But you did. And you know who benefits? The whole world benefits, Mira. Because you are a witch. A fucking badass witch. I see you, Mira. You've come here to cast your spell. To work your magic. And I am so here for it."

We both look down at the paper on the table as Ava resumes drawing. She draws one cone of energy in about the place where my missing fallopian tube should be, in the diagram of my body. She draws another in my stomach. She draws a little heart right about where my heart should be, cute and childish as a valentine. She draws two lungs, two half umbrellas, flanking my heart, protecting it like two imperfect guards. Then she folds up the paper and hands it to me.

"You do rituals, right? Like you have an altar and everything?"

I nod.

"And you keep the cycles of the moon?" At my nod, she says, "Okay. Next full moon, you ritually burn this drawing at your altar. All right? That helps you let go of everything that's happened that no longer serves you. It helps you put down what's heavy that you no longer need to be carrying. And it helps the energy restoration and healing that we did today to become permanently mapped onto the sacred geography of your body." She looks at me, hard. "Everything that's happened to you, it's all a part of you, Mira. You carry every scar like landmarks on your sacred geography. The things you've been through, the things they've taught you, the things you learned—no one can ever take any of that away from you. So, integrate. Incorporate those things into you. Take the gems of wisdom they gave you. Take them into your future. And the rocks you chiseled them out of? Set them down. Leave them behind. They're heavy. You don't need to be carrying them around anymore, okay?"

"Okay," I whisper.

Three days after my first solo session with Ava, Mom sends a group text to Marco and me. It says, *I need to talk to you both.*

I wanna be, like, all healed. But I have to admit that my heart still freezes when I read these words. What new drama is Mom gonna be bringing to our lives this time?

Up until just the other day, Mom and the baby were staying with Marco. He sent me updates on her. She was meeting with students on Zoom using her phone; so it seems she is still working. She took care of the baby, who, he said, seemed healthy and happy and totally fine. There was no evidence, at least during the days when she was staying with him, that she was using or drinking.

He also got her to fill in some of the gaps about where she'd been and what she's been doing lately, simply by wearing her down, asking over and over again. She definitely bitched about it, accused him of treating her like a child, raised her voice—but got neutralized before things escalated, probably because Hassan is there too, and no abuser wants her shit aired to outside parties, you feel me? Better Marco than me, that's all this girl's gotta say.

Apparently, Mom got thrown out of her apartment. (Marco could not get her to reveal why.) For a short while, she and the baby were in a shelter. My heart froze when my brother called and told me this. I felt sick. I felt gritty with shame, imagining my mother and my baby sister with nowhere else to go in this city but a homeless shelter, in the middle of a global pandemic. He asked her why the fuck she didn't just come and stay with him. She said she felt too ashamed.

Eventually she said, "*Tengo que irme,* Marco. You and Hassan need to have your own space, your own lives."

"*No tienes que irte*, Mom," he said. "Stay. You and the baby, stay."

She insisted. Marco said, "*No te puedes ir* unless I know you are going someplace safe. *Con mi hermanita.*"

When she tried to argue, Marco said, "Mom. *Estoy en serio* here. I will do whatever I have to do. *No te puedes ir con mi hermanita* unless I know where you're going, and it's someplace safe."

Finally they negotiated that she would go and stay with Laisa, a friend of hers from work. Marco insisted on speaking with Laisa on a video call. This resulted in another argument, but Marco wouldn't give in. He spoke to Laisa, a young woman, maybe late twenties, who's a cafeteria worker at Mom's high school. She has a baby too, a two-year-old, and is also working on her sobriety. Would it be the best thing for the two of them, and their daughters, to be together? Marco and I discussed it, but we are not sure. (I mean, what the fuck do we know?) But, as I predicted, Mom and the baby staying with Marco and Hassan in their studio apartment was not exactly the best scenario either. So Marco escorted Mom and the baby on the train to Laisa's apartment on the Lower East Side. He cried, he said, when our sister clung to him as they said goodbye.

That was just the other day. And now, there's this text.

"What do you think it means?" I ask Andre.

"I don't know, Mira," he says with a sigh.

Mom, Marco, and I have a group FaceTime call. I haven't seen either of them since I stormed out of *Abuela*'s apartment that day. And y'all know what, I do not regret it.

I don't want to dwell on every detail of the conversation with our mom. I can't put that much energy behind it. Maybe it is, you know, one of those things that's too heavy for me to keep carrying.

Mom gets all weepy. She tells us how much she loves us. She says we're her blessings, we're her gifts, we're the only good things she has ever done. Marco and I are quiet during this part of the call. All of this we have heard before.

But then, Mom says some stuff she has never said before, not once in our whole lives, with the billions and zillions of things she has said to us.

She says, "I can't do this anymore. I have a problem. I have a real problem, Marco, Mira, and I can't keep going on like this." She glances off-screen briefly, where there's some noise, then back into the camera. "I'm sick. I am really sick. I have been sick for most of my life. And if I don't do something about it, it's going to kill me."

Marco and I are silent again. But this time it ain't in resignation. It's in shock.

"Sweethearts, I'm going to get treatment," she says. "I'm going to go to rehab."

I still feel stunned into silence. Our mom has never tried rehab, or any other kind of extensive, long-term treatment, before.

"But I have something to ask you," she continues. "A favor. I'm ashamed to even ask. But I have to. Because I have to get better. I…"

"You want us to take care of Magda while you're away," Marco says. His voice is flat, unreadable.

Mom pauses. Then she nods.

"Mom…" I say. It's basically the first thing I've said this entire conversation.

"Temporary custody," Marco says, suddenly.

"What?" Mom says.

"Temporary custody," he repeats. "Mom, if you want one of us to do this, while you're gone, then it has to be official and legal. We'd need temporary custody of Magdalena."

"What?" she says again. "Marco, no. Why? We're all family. Why would we need to do that?"

"Because," he says. "It needs to be official and legal."

"Why?"

"What if something happens to Magda while you're gone?" he says. "What if she's sick? Needs medical care? Whoever's taking care of her needs to have legal authority to make medical decisions for her."

"Marco *tiene razón,*" I say softly.

"We won't be able to do it if you don't grant us temporary custody," Marco says.

Mom sighs. "Fine," she says.

"I'll look into what we need to do," Marco says.

"Mira," Mom says.

"Yeah?" I say.

"Would you and Andre be able to take care of Magdalena for me? Just for a while?"

"Mom, I…" I look over at Andre, who's listening. His eyes are enormous. I look back at the screen with my mom and my brother on it. "I don't know," I say.

"Baby, please," she says.

"Hassan and I can do it," Marco says.

Mom shakes her head. "I have already imposed on you two so much," she says. "And Marco. You are about to graduate. You got into Harvard Medical School."

Wow, okay, this is the first I am hearing about that.

"School doesn't start until the fall," Marco says. "And we don't know if I'm going to Harvard. Hassan's job is here."

"You got into Harvard," Mom says again. "Harvard's your dream. You're going to be a doctor, baby. You and Hassan can figure it out. He can write another show for Netflix."

He laughs. "Yeah, no. It doesn't work like that, Mom."

"I got into school too," I whisper.

"You did?" Mom says.

"You're going back to school?" Marco says.

I nod. I feel shaky, sick. "Just City College. The creative writing program. I applied. I got in. I already said yes."

"You did?" Marco says.

"Mira, baby, I am so proud of you," Mom says.

"Yeah," Marco says. "That's amazing. I'm so happy for you, baby girl."

"Thanks," I say. "I mean, it ain't Harvard or nothing. It's just here in New York. And I'm not really working right now. 'Cause… you know. So, I mean, yeah, I guess. I could take her. Take care of the baby… for a while."

I glance over at Andre. His eyes are even bigger, if that is possible.

"Mira," Marco says.

"Marco Polo, c'mon. It's Harvard. You should totally, like, go. Convince Hassan. Find him a job down there. Go find an apartment in… where's Harvard at anyway? Boston, right?"

"Cambridge, Massachusetts," he says.

"There you go. Cambridge. Tell them yes. Move to Cambridge. Go do your thing, MP."

"Mira," he says.

"I'm sorry," Mom says suddenly. "It's just. You've always said you never wanted kids of your own, Marco. You got a vasectomy at age eighteen because you never wanted kids. And Miranda…"

"I've always wanted a baby," I whisper. "Always."

I feel Andre looking at me, but I don't look back. I can't, not right now.

"I don't want to burden you," Mom says. "With something you don't want."

"*Tengo que hablar con* Andre," I say.

"Yes," Mom says. "Talk to Andre."

I disconnect from the call; I have to. Mom is looking confused and hurt. Marco looks like he is about to cry. I want to lock myself back in that room with Ava, where I'm safe, where nothing can hurt me. How do you even know, I want to ask her, what is yours, and what does not belong to you?

"Mira," Andre says, as soon as I've left the call, coming to sit next to me at the table. "There's no way you're actually thinking of doing this, are you?"

"Andre," I say. "Does it look like I actually have a fucking choice right now?"

"You absolutely do have a choice," he says. "If you don't want to do it, you say no."

"I say no, and my baby sister goes into foster care? Or, like, my mom doesn't do treatment because she has no one to take care of the baby?"

"Marco said he would take care of her," Andre says.

"Marco is about to graduate and go to fucking Harvard."

"And you," he says, "are about to go to City College."

"Andre, Harvard is in fucking Boston. And it's his dream. He didn't go for undergrad because I was so sick then, when we graduated high school. So he stayed here. For me."

Andre shakes his head. "Marco made that choice. He stayed here in New York. For him. Now, if he wants, he can make a different choice."

"City College is in New York," I say. "And I'm not working. So I can make it work. For the summer. Or however long Mom needs me to."

"Mira," he says. "You are not working because you're still recovering from a major medical crisis."

"I know," I say. "But I'm doing so much better now. I can take care of Magda for a little while. I can handle it."

"I'm sure you can," he says. "But do you want to?"

"I don't know. Does it matter?"

"What the fuck, Mira?" He puts his hand over mine. His eyes are wet. "Of course it matters."

"Do you want to do this?" I whisper.

"Honestly? Not really. But I understand. It's your mom. It's your baby sister. You want the best for them. I get that." He takes my hand, squeezes it. "So, if you wanted to do this, if you felt like it was the right thing for you, then I'd be on board. We'd figure it out. But, Mira. Is this the right thing for you?"

I shrug. "I don't know."

"You're still recovering," he says. "You told me you couldn't even hold the baby. That you cried when you just looked at her."

I squeeze my eyes shut. "I'm tired of still recovering," I whisper. "I just want to be better already."

"If Marco wants to do this," he says, "I think you should let him."

I open my eyes. "What about Harvard?"

He laughs. "What about Harvard? Fuck Harvard. If Marco is really as smart as everyone says he is, he can just go to Harvard later."

I laugh too, even though nothing actually feels funny right now. "But Mom asked me to do this."

"I'm sorry for saying this," Andre says, "but I don't like how your mom idolizes Marco because of all of his school stuff. Like, he's smart, we get it. But you. You're smart and you're talented and you're fucking brilliant, Mira. And this is your time. If you don't think it's right for you to do this right now, then don't."

I can feel my heart starting to lighten in my chest, despite myself. "What about Magdalena? She's my sister, Andre."

"She's Marco's sister too," he says. "And he said he wants to take her."

"What about Hassan?"

"What about Hassan? I bet he's on board too, Mira. And, of the four of us, Hassan is the only one who has any fucking clue how to take care of a kid. He has a daughter, remember? Hassan is a grown-ass adult. You and me and Marco are in our twenties. If anyone is ready to take care of a baby, it's Hassan."

"I'll talk to him and Marco," I say. "See how they feel about it."

"How do you feel about it?" he asks. He strokes the back of my hand with his thumb.

"Shitty," I whisper. "I want to want to do this, Andre. I feel like I should. I'd feel horrible, dropping all this on my brother."

"You are not dropping anything on your brother," he says. "You do not need to protect Marco. From anything. It's his life. He makes his own choices. You make yours."

"And what about you?" I ask.

"You're my wife," he says. "We're a team. We do what's right for us."

"Would you want to do this?" I ask him.

"No, not really," he says. "I don't think we're ready. I think we're still grieving what happened to us. Or, I know I still am. We're figuring out the feeding tube stuff. I have so much shit with work right now. Going back to school is your dream. And I really want to see you do that. I think we have too much going on right now. I want you to be selfish, Mira. I want to be selfish too. I want you to do what feels right for you."

I nod, slowly. "So you think Marco and Hassan should take her, and not us?"

"Yes," he says. "I think Marco and Hassan are in a much better place

213

than we are right now to take care of a baby. And I think he wants to do this."

"I think so too," I admit. "He really loves her."

He shrugs. "I don't know much about taking care of babies, Mira. But I do know that they should be with someone who wants them, who loves them."

"I love her too," I whisper. "It ain't like I don't."

He nods. He strokes my hand. "I know you do," he says. What neither of us says, though we're both thinking it, is that I don't love her the way my brother does, not right now. I can't. I can't give her what he can, not right now. That sucks, and it hurts, but you know what? The clarity, the honesty, of that hurt feels better than trying to deceive myself, to force myself into a yes when my body and heart and intuition tell me it's a no.

"Okay," I say. I pick up my phone. "Let me call Marco."

I feel like I need comfort, so I get up from the table and go to one of my favorite places on earth to have this conversation, which is my bed. Andre comes with me, and then there I am, in my favorite place on earth, with my favorite person on earth. I call my twin.

And he says, "Mira, *tal vez* this is a conversation we should have in person? Could Hassan and I come over?"

"Of course you can," I say. "You know y'all are welcome here literally anytime, baby. When you wanna come?"

"What are you two doing now?"

I look at Andre, who nods and shrugs.

"Nothing. Y'all wanna come now?"

"Yeah," my brother says. "We'll leave just now."

"Y'all want food?"

"How about we bring Chinese?"

"You want Chinese, baby?" I ask Andre.

"Always," he says. Into the phone, he says, "Thanks, bro."

"You got it."

Two hours later, Marco and Hassan are at our place, with two huge bags of Chinese food. They are both wearing eyeliner and dark blue nail polish, which literally gives me so much life. I don't feel like sitting at the table, so we all sit on the living-room floor around the coffee table. Marco, Hassan, and Andre inhale large amounts of Chinese food. I feel too emotional to spend extra energy forcing myself to eat right now, so, meanwhile, as he's eating, Andre also feeds me through my tube. And maybe it sounds crazy, but it's the best feeling in the world, being fed, not having to do anything but focus on the (very hard) conversation happening around me; getting to sit there, in nothing but my bra and leggings, nobody staring or thinking I'm weird or asking me questions, my family all around me.

"Marco," I say. "I'm sorry. But I don't think Andre and me can take care of the baby. Not right now."

"Mira and I just have so much going on right now," Andre says, touching my hand. "I don't think it's the right time for us to take on something like that."

Marco chews a bite of spare rib, which is possibly his favorite food ever. He looks at both of us. He finishes chewing, wipes under his eyes with his knuckles. Hassan hands him a napkin.

"Yeah, of course, *nena,*" he says, obediently wiping his hands. "All the shit you've been going through…"

I feel Andre sit up straighter next to me. "We lost a pregnancy," he says. "That we didn't even know she was carrying. It was an enormous risk to Mira's health. There was a point when she was in the hospital that the doctors and nurses thought we might lose her; they were asking me if I had a support system in place if that happened. And I, like… lost it. So." He looks at me. I look at him, my brave, brave boy. How did I even get this boy, a ratched, messed-up girl like me? "That was a lot of shit to come back from. There's the tube." He points to it, just in case anybody missed the piece of silicone attached to a syringe sticking out of me. "We're focusing on making sure Mira feels stronger. Work is nuts for me at the moment. And Mira is going back to school in the fall." He says it so strongly, there can be no doubt about it: I am going back to school. "So. That's what's up with us. And I do not think my wife and I can also effectively take care of a baby right now."

There's quiet for a moment. Andre strokes my hair, looks at me with a fierce tenderness. "Am I being extra, *mi reina*? Is that too much real talk?"

I shake my head.

"Not at all, bro," Marco says.

"Thank you for telling us all of that," Hassan says.

My husband nods.

"Hassan and I, we are totally prepared to take Magda," Marco says. He looks at Hassan, who nods.

"Yeah?" I say. "Are you two, like, sure?"

They nod.

"Marco. What about Harvard Medical School?"

He shrugs. "I'll figure it out," he says. "I just feel like Magda needs us. Needs me. For now, at least. I feel like this is what I have to do."

"Yeah?" I say. "What about, like, I don't know, being a doctor and shit? I thought you were all about that."

"I have my whole life to figure that out," he says. "Magda isn't even one year old yet. I feel like this is the time when she needs me."

"Okay," I say. "I can see that, baby." I look at Hassan. "What about you, Hassan baby? And please be honest with me, okay? We are all family here."

He nods. He looks at his man. He looks at me and says, "What Marco says is right. We are both very prepared to do this."

"Be real with me, boy," I say. "Having a baby ain't gonna cramp your style or nothing? I know you already did the whole, like, dad thing. With Alexandra. Are you cool with having a baby in your life now? Were you looking to chill and enjoy all your new cash from your Netflix deal?"

"Mira," he says. He takes a deep breath. "The Netflix money is for our family. Magdalena is very much our family. And I..." He looks at Marco again, for strength, maybe. "The truth is, I got to spend some time with Magda while she and your mother were staying with us. And I... she..."

Marco smiles over at Hassan. He looks exactly like the heart-eyes emoji, gazing over at his man. "He was so sweet with her, you should've seen," he says. "She took, like, his whole heart."

Hassan smiles back. "The truth is, Mira, I have always, always wanted a family with your brother." He puts his hand on Marco's shoulder, squeezes. "I didn't think it would be possible for us. But perhaps it will be, even if just for a little while. I love him with a baby. I love us with a baby." He nods at me, definitively. "So, yes. Marco and I are very prepared for this and all that it entails. We are both, as Alex would say, all in."

I can't help grinning—they are just so sickeningly cute.

I still gotta play a little hardball with them, though. "Let's say, God forbid, something happens to Mom," I say. "Your temporary custody could turn into full, forever custody. I mean, we could discuss that if the time came. But she'd know you by then. You'd have a thing going. We have no other family. And obviously we don't want her going into the foster system."

"Obviously not," Marco agrees, vehemently.

"How would you feel if this temporary thing turned into you and

Hassan being her legal guardians forever? Is raising our baby sister like your own kid what you wanna do, MP?"

"If it's necessary, I'll do it in a heartbeat," he says. I'd say his conviction is so strong it's surprising, but really, it's not. This is the same kid, after all, who gave me part of his own body, just so I'd have a shot at a better life.

"Are you sure, Marco? You're so young. We're not even twenty-two. And I know this isn't what you imagined for your life."

"I am totally sure," he says, putting a hand on his heart. He looks at me. "But, Mira, are you sure? I mean, Mom asked you to do this. I don't want to, like…"

I shake my head. "Marco. No. I am in no way in the right place to be able to do this. You're the one who is. And c'mon. You know Mom. You're her golden boy. You're going to Harvard. You're gonna be a fucking doctor." I smile sadly. "She wants to manipulate us. Direct our lives. Make our decisions for us. She always has, *nene*."

He nods. No one can argue with the truth of this.

"All right," he says, with a ring of finality. "So you're cool with this, Mira?"

"Totally cool."

"Okay. I've already been looking into the paperwork we've gotta do. I'll call Mom."

"You want me to be a part of that conversation?"

He lifts his eyebrows. "You wanna be?"

I scoff. "Hell no."

He laughs. "All right. We got this. I'll talk to her."

"Keep me posted, okay?"

"You know it, baby girl."

"I have one more question," I say.

He tilts his head.

"You take her in. You fall in love with her 'cause she super cute or whatever. Mom comes back. But you're fucking attached. You don't wanna give her back. It hurts." I tilt my head back. "How are you gonna deal with that, MP? You ready for that?"

Marco sighs. "No," he admits, and, I gotta say, I love the honesty. "But I'll deal. I'll figure it out." He looks at Hassan. "It's not about us, Mira. It'll be about what's best for Magda."

He sounds like a parent already.

Marco and Hassan hang out a little bit longer. Then they get ready to leave. I say goodbye to Marco at the door, while Andre and Hassan talk about something in the kitchen. I hug my brother, hard, and when we pull back, we kiss lightly on the lips. Marco is stepping into a whole other dimension of his life. My twin is leaving me behind; he is going someplace that I cannot follow.

Marco has said, plenty of times, that losing me, living in a world that doesn't have me in it, will be the worst thing that can possibly happen to him. One day, that will happen, and he won't have me anymore. But he'll still have our baby sister. They'll have a whole family life together, that I will not get to see. That makes me feel so sad it's unfathomable. But it's also my life, which, as y'all know, ain't no tragedy. (Don't y'all start.) It's my life, neither all bad nor all good, but all fucking mine.

I hug Marco again, one more time. I hold my twin brother tight, even as I let him go.

Andre has also had two solo sessions with Ava. In the first, she gave him reiki, his first time trying that healing modality. I asked him how it went, how he liked it; he shrugged and said, "It was fine." In the second session, when he gets home, he tells me that they talked for a long time, and then Ava gave him a ritual practice to do.

"She told me I have to go out in nature and find three natural objects that I feel represent what we lost," he says. "Then I have to throw them in the Hudson River. It's a way of saying goodbye, I guess."

"What did y'all talk about?"

He shrugs. "Not that much. I feel like I was making her go around in circles. I mean, not on purpose. I just…"

"You just what?"

He rubs the back of his neck. "I spent a lot of time being really insecure. About my feelings. Like I was asking her if it was even valid, or, like, okay for me to feel sad about this."

"Of course it's okay for you to feel sad, Andre."

"Yeah," he says. "I guess. And feelings of guilt. Of helplessness. So she gave me this ritual to do."

"Do you want me to come with you?" I ask.

He seems to think for a moment, then shakes his head. "I think I'm supposed to do this by myself," he says.

So I have no idea how this ritual goes for Andre. I don't know where he goes to find these bits of the natural world. I don't know what he's looking for: if he leaves our house with some objects in mind, seeking them out with his eyes, or if he enters into it with no preconceived plan, open to whatever the world will bring him. I don't know what he finds. I don't know what objects or talismans or symbols would seem to represent what we lost to him. I wonder how he talked about it during their session: did he call it our baby or our fertilized egg or our lost pregnancy. I don't know.

I don't know how he feels when he finds these items; what spark of intuition lets him know that this is what he seeks. I don't know at what entry point along the river he tosses the items, or how it makes him feel afterwards. I only know when he leaves our apartment and I kiss him at the door. And when he comes back, he hugs me for a long time by our kitchen table. I lean my face into his chest, feel the strength of his body and smell the fresh air of outside.

"Are you okay?" I ask, clinging to him.

"I'm okay," he says.

"How…" I squeeze him hard. "How did it feel?"

He smooths the tiny baby hairs at my temple with his hand. "Mira, I felt so helpless," he says. "It felt good to do something."

Is it strange, how sharply our paths have diverged in this thing? We made something together, which we had no idea we had even made. I lost it in a way that made me feel so alone. Now he has devised a way of grieving it to which I was not present; I even think that part of the power of this ritual was my absence from it, his bravery in going alone. I gaze up at him, fathomless dark eyes that I know so well, and that I love more every day. And it strikes me more than ever, the essential unknowability of every person, how every person carries an ocean inside. Every person is a river, with a thousand banks and entry points, with lighthouses and docks and treacherous rocks, with talismans they bury deep underneath their waves in order to say goodbye.

A few days after his ritual to say goodbye, Andre feeds me at the kitchen table. I've sensed something shift between us since the ritual. In the way of magic, I couldn't have said exactly how, if someone had asked me to put it into words. It's a softening, maybe, a gentle narrowing of the space around and between us, like when you dim the lights in a room, casting it into a warm, intimate glow. The air has tightened between us, in a pleasant way, the light constriction of an embrace.

His feeding me feels more intentional today, not accidental or incidental, not just something we fit in around all of the other things we do in a day. We hold eyes while we do it. I'm in nothing but my bra and leggings, like I usually am for this process, but it feels different today: I feel extremely aware, in a sweet, delicious way, of the expansion and collapse of each inhale and exhale, stretching my bare skin, lifting and lowering my breasts, tingling with presence. After not long at all, I also notice that Andre's penis has hardened in his shorts, making a perfect and enticing bulge. The more that I look at it, the harder and longer it gets.

Andre finishes feeding me, flushes the tube out with water and detaches the syringe. He sees me seeing his erection. Our eyes start to flicker towards each other, with secret little smiles on our lips. I feel like a fifteen-year-old, flirting, the same one I was with this same boy, years ago.

Andre washes his hands; I wash mine. I lean back against the sink, watching him. By now his dick is a tentpole making a tent of his shorts.

"Uh…" I say. "You're, uh…" I cast my eyes down at his groin.

He smirks, at once proud and shy, and, I gotta say, this fucking makes me melt.

"Yeah," he says. "I guess I am."

"Are you… did you…" Fuck, have I completely lost any ability to talk dirty? I pause to take a deep breath. "Did that… turn you on?"

"Mira." His look on me is intense, and it feels so good, reminds me that my life has not always been and will not forever be recovery and appointments and barely being able to leave the house, that there is still for me romance and good drama and delight. "It turns me on every time."

"It… it does?"

That look he's giving me is making me lose my breath, y'all.

"Yes," he says. "Always. Every time. I guess I just didn't allow myself to go all the way into it."

We both look down at his penis. It's hard not to look at it, I gotta say.

"Why not?" I whisper.

He looks back up at me. "Guilt, maybe," he says. "Do I still get to feel good, after everything that's happened? And, I don't know, shame? Like, I didn't want you to think I was freaky, or sick, or illness-fetishizing? I didn't want to hurt you."

Maybe I shouldn't, but I have to laugh. "Andre, baby." I pull him into my arms and squeeze him, to soften the blow. "You never gotta be ashamed with me, baby. Your girl has a chronic illness. You know that. And I told you. This is what we got. This is what we're working with, baby boy. If you can't find me and my G-tube sexy, then I don't know where we're going, *mi nene.*"

"Mira." He takes my hand, presses it gently against the rod-like stiffness of his penis. It's warm through his shorts. Now, if that ain't a full sentence, then I don't know what is. I shiver, all over. "I find you, and your G-tube, so fucking sexy."

"Andre." I collapse against him, letting him hold me up. I feel weak, but in the good way, my bones liquid. I cling to his shoulders. "Can we go to bed?"

"Can we?" he says, and he lifts me straight up from the floor and takes me to bed.

In bed, we struggle me out of my bra, Andre out of his T-shirt. I press myself to him, so we can both feel my breasts against his bare chest. "Tell me why?" I say against his lips. "Why do you find it sexy? Why does it turn you on?"

"I mean, how could it not?" He grazes my lips with his. "You trusting me with your body like that? You letting me put food right into your body? And feed you?" Our lips graze again. "It's the hottest thing ever."

"Oh, *papi,*" I say. "*Mi perfecto. Mi viejito.*"

He puts my hand on his dick again.

"Oh, my God, yes," I say.

I pull off his basketball shorts and boxers, in one fell swoop. His dick springs free, attentive and eager. I put my hand on it, and he closes his eyes. It's warm and we're both so excited, I can feel the blood pulsing through his veins. I remember so vividly what it was like when we were teenagers, when we had to steal moments and each one was hot and necessary as bread, when getting to shove my hand inside his pants and feel his hard, damp penis, sticky with precum, left me gasping, grateful for oxygen. It's almost like we are returned to those times, a sense of reopening like springtime.

I take off my leggings and panties. Andre reaches into our bedside table for a bottle of lube and tosses it to me, and like that tells me what he wants. He wants to be touched, simple and old-school. I drizzle lube on him and take him in my hand. He lets out a deep exhale and nudges between my thighs with his knee. I open to him with a jolt of awareness, of memory.

He puts his two fingers between my lips and, for the first time since he found me wailing on our bathroom floor, finds me wet.

As we touch each other, I remember. Sometimes, we felt frantic, from whispered, fevered phone sex and long school days sneaking sexts between classes, naked selfies snapped in our bedrooms, telling each other what we wanted to do to each other. We had to find a place, any place, to touch each other. Sometimes it was Central Park, when it was almost dark out. Once—fuck, I remember it—it was on the bus, our school backpacks covering our laps, the bump and rumble of the ride making me more aroused. More than once it was in the single bathroom of some place, my hand curled in his underwear and his in mine, both of us panting. We'd be rushing, knowing we didn't have very long, and knowing we had to finish each other, we had to. My hand would come out wet from his cum. He'd bring his fingers to his face and deeply inhale, taking in what I'd left behind on his body.

It's like that now, a little bit, but without the rush and the struggle. We move much slower. I feel the luxurious suck of the lube between my hand and his cock, the lovely swollen shape of the head when I slide it, hard, all the way through my hand and back again. I touch his balls with my other hand, cup their weight, feel how they're both so vulnerable and so heavy. He touches me too, delicately at first, asking me if it feels okay, if it feels good, my labia swollen under his fingers. He kisses me on the temple and pauses, pulling away slightly to squeeze some lube onto his fingers. Then he puts them between my lips again and I draw in a breath at the clingy wet of it. I want to cry—everything's changed, I've changed, it feels good but I'm not getting as wet as I would have before all this shit happened, stroking his penis that's so excited it's jerking in my hand, feeling his breath flutter in his hard belly. But it feels so fucking good that I don't cry, I can't cry, I can only sink in to the experience and feel it, the warming of my intimate tissue, the erection of my clit until I can't take it anymore, I can't hold back. Coming feels so fucking good it's almost painful, turning me inside out with pulsing wave after wave.

It makes him come on me too, shaking, an eruption of musky cum all over my hand, up to the middle of his chest. I can't move, can't catch my breath.

We lie there recovering, clinging to each other, wet skins melded together. We both drift off into sleep, wake up again. "I missed you," I tell him. "I missed you so much."

"I missed you too," he says. "*Mi reina. Yo te amo.*"

"*Te amo, papi chulo.*"

He rolls onto his back, lifts me so that I am lying on top of him. I look down into his eyes, which are, like, serious as fuck.

"Ava and I," he says, "we talked about sex."

"Yeah?" I say.

"Yeah," he says. When we breathe, I can feel the gentle silicone press of my G-tube between us. "I was just telling her how much I want us to be able to make love again. And what I need to do to feel like I can do that again."

"All right, *papi.*"

"And," he says, "I thought about it a lot, and I think I know now. What I need."

"Oh, *de veras*? What is that?"

"Yeah," he says. "Mira. I wanted to ask you. If you would make love to me. I mean. I want you to penetrate me."

I trace his eyebrows with my finger. "You want me to penetrate you? With the strap-on?"

He nods against the pillow underneath his head. "Yes," he says. "I want to take it from you, baby. In my ass."

I drop my head, press my lips to his.

"Would you do that to me?" he asks, a little breathless from our kiss.

I kiss him again.

"Course I would," I say. "Whatever you need, I am gonna take care of you."

"Mira," he says. There's the sparkle of tears in his eyes, and relief, and the kind of fear that comes from going someplace you've never gone before, and gratitude. "Thank you," he says.

Andre and I go to the sex store together and pick out a new dildo for him, one that can be attached to my strap-on harness. It's brown and of a medium length and thickness. I look at it and handle it and try to imagine it, attached to my body, sliding into my man's ass by the strength of the thrusts of my hips. It scares me a little, but in a good way—thrills me, gives me tingles all up and down my body. I cannot deny that your girl feels like a total baller, walking up to the register and buying a dildo for my man, which I am gonna go home and fuck him with. Standing here, maybe I can't see my way to that just yet, but I trust that Andre and I will get there together.

"I don't wanna rush this, baby," I tell him when we get home. "I wanna take this slow."

He sits down with me on the couch. I open my arms to him and he cuddles in to me, resting his head against my breasts. I stroke his smooth head and his jaw and the softness of his earlobe.

"I think I need that too," he says, pulling back so he can look up at me.

I bend my head and kiss him softly on the mouth. I missed the warmth and ease of the intimacy between us. "I'm thinking I need some time to get more used to this dildo, and wearing it."

So Andre and I decide to do something I haven't done yet with the two other lovers I've penetrated with a dildo so far: we spend an evening together, naked, with me wearing the dildo on my strap-on harness. I have never moved through the world preceded by my big brown dick. I like it: knowing that the delicacy of my body is punctuated by my perpetually hard cock; that I have the power to choose how I walk through the world, how I present my body and how I use it.

We sit on the couch together and watch dirty videos on Andre's laptop. Now, it's been a hot minute since I partook of any porn, y'all. Unpopular opinion alert, but your girl Mira really loves porn. I love how, no matter what your pleasure or your fantasy or your predilection or your curiosity, you can find what you seek. I love how there is a style of porn for every disposition and mood. There's unglamorous amateur stuff shot on randos' iPhones. There are famous porn stars featured in glossy, well-lit videos with high production value. There's feminist porn with women's pleasure at the center. There are educational and instructional videos, full-length erotic films with both plot and smut. There's every kind of fetish, from feet to watersports to age play. When I had never so much as held another girl's hand before, I had watched a shit ton of lesbian porn; y'all can knock it if that feels right for you, but watching girls get each other off, and being so turned on by it, helped me feel like I really was my little queer self even when I wasn't ready to take that part of my identity out on the road just yet.

I love that I love porn. As you know, your girl Mira is not in many ways badass or edgy or subversive. I'm soft-spoken and kinda shy and scared of a lot of shit. I'm a little old-fashioned and pretty traditional. But I love dirty videos and dig me a good hard cumshot.

Andre loves that I love porn too. Honestly, I like it more than he does. Like many men who are feminists, he feels a sense of discomfort, maybe even of shame, at watching and liking porn. I just don't; I straight-up like it. So his enjoyment at watching me shamelessly indulge in porn is twofold. He's already hard, just with anticipation, as we sit down and he passes me his laptop so I can choose a video for us. I decide on a giggly video of naked white girls play-fighting with each other in a pink plastic pool full of soap suds.

Andre laughs in incredulous delight. "Oh, Mira," he says.

"You're welcome," I say.

He gives his penis a squeeze. "Yes, my queen," he says.

The video is everything it promises to be: naughty and campy and dirty and fun. The girls, with their perfect perky breasts with pink nipples, pierced belly buttons and tiny pointed hips, laugh and tumble around one another in the pool. They squeeze soap suds in their fists and throw them playfully at each other like summertime snowballs, they smear them over each other's skin. There are the occasional quieter, more soulful moments, where the camera focuses in on two of the girls, one opening the lips of another with her fingers, rubbing her clit with the soft white bubbles; the girl being touched tosses her head back as she comes, jet-black hair spilling down nearly to her ass. Maybe the best thing about the video is how it's shot: the pool is set on a lush, emerald-green lawn in full, luscious sunlight, gilding the women's flawless skin, making their soap bubbles, the wetness in closeups of their vulvas, sparkle.

Andre gets off on my enjoyment of the video. The visible throb and pulse of his erection, and knowing that it's caused by me, turns me on much more than the women and their erotic frolic. The fact that we are sitting here naked on the couch with twin erect penises keeps me so aware, so charged, that I bet I'd give you an instant electric shock if you touched me.

"Andre," I say.

"Yeah?" he says. He's a little bit breathless.

I gesture down at our penises. "Do you think this is how Marco and Hassan feel?"

"Mira," he says.

"Yeah?"

"Can we maybe not talk about your brother and Hassan right now?"

I have to laugh.

Then Andre puts his hand on my cock, and at the look in his eyes, the way he draws his tongue over his lips, I am not laughing anymore.

He strokes my penis, from tip to root.

"Baby," I say. I let my breath out with the word.

"*¿Te gusta eso?*" he asks.

"Fuck yeah," I whisper.

I reach out to pause the video.

He fists my penis a little firmer, sliding over its surface with his hand. He touches the underside of the head with his thumb. He presses gently down to my balls. It's the first time, I think, he's touching a dick other than his own.

"How does it feel?" I ask him.

"It feels good," he says softly, thoughtfully. He lets a slow smile spread over his face. "I like all the veins. A lot." He skims his thumb along one of the veins, a light, tingling sort of touch. It makes me suck in a sharp breath. "They're so sexy. I'm really into this dick of yours, Mira. It's so… lifelike."

I have to laugh, again. It is not the same kinda laugh as before, though, y'all.

"Yeah. I'm a real boy," I say.

He laughs too, and squeezes his cock, so for a moment, he's holding his in one hand, mine in the other.

"That you are, Mira," he says. He lowers his lashes. "Sir."

He continues touching me, gaining confidence with every moment of contact. Every moment is still infused with gratitude and glittery awareness and a gorgeous curiosity. He touches the slit of my cock, the thick root, the natural curve of the shaft, my brown balls in the cup of his hand. He runs his finger around the base of the head, where it flares with a thick ring of silicone flesh. He looks down at it with a kind of gentle reverence. I wonder if he's imagining, as I am, how it'll feel in the tightness of his ass when the mushroom of that head pops inside. The anticipation of that moment is nearly as strong as death: we know it's coming, we both do, it's inevitable, but how is it gonna feel when it really happens?

The delicacy and sweet tenderness of his touch, the care he takes with my penis, makes it feel like he is drawing with every pump of his hand a real connection between the dildo and my body. With his love he is fusing us together, my silicone prosthetic and me. He is animating my android. With the strength of his arousal he is making me whole.

"Mira," he says. "May I taste your dick?"

I did not see that one coming, y'all. But when he asks me something like that so nicely, how the fuck could I say no? And why would I want to?

"Of course you may," I say.

Andre gets onto his knees on the floor in front of me. I spread my legs to make room for him. He slides closer, hands on my thighs for leverage. He lowers his head over my cock. At first, he only takes the head of it into his mouth. He sucks it, experimentally but deeply. He lets more of it slip past his lips. Now he has a full mouthful, down into the top of his throat, of my cock. I want desperately to laugh. But somehow I know that impulse is just a front for my true, deeper desire. I have to stay in it. I have to let myself. I have to push through. And when my body wants to, I let myself moan.

Andre pulls back, holding only the tip of my penis in his mouth. He presses forward, taking it almost to the base, with a sound of resistance in his throat. But he, too, pushes through, bringing me deeper.

"Oh, baby," I say. "Oh, my God, that's so good. You are doing so good." I put my hand gently on his head. "Yes, just like that." He bobs his head up and down on me. "Yes. Like that. You suck me so good, baby."

He flicks his eyes up at me, gazing at me through his lashes while he holds my cock in his mouth. The look he's giving me, it's like a jolt right up the middle of me, making my clit tremble.

He pulls off, releasing me with a wet pop.

"Oh, my God, Mira." He rises from his knees a little shaky, sits down next to me again. I reach out and rub my thumb in a circle around his wet lips. "Mira," he says. "That is so hot."

"I know, baby. I know."

"Mira," he says. "Oh, my God, I have to touch myself, I have to."

He takes his own dick in his hand and looks down at it. His stomach hollows out with the punching power of his breath. He starts to jerk himself so fast the sight of his dick blurs in my vision.

I put my fingers between my legs and touch myself too. I'm wet. I mean, I'm not dripping, my hair isn't soaked. They wouldn't put me in no video for the theatric visibility of my wetness. I am not wet like I would have been before. I am not like I was before. Maybe I cannot be. Maybe what's erotic for me right now is accepting that. I feel myself. I am inside. And I am here.

We speed together, hurtling towards orgasm. And there ain't nothing cheap about this cumshot, y'all, mutual and violent; every second of it integral as mined gold, pulled from the depths and hard-won.

And now, if all that weren't enough—later, after we've come, and basked together in a sweaty afterglow, later, I go into the bedroom and catch sight of myself in the full-length mirror. The light is on in the room and there ain't no hiding from my self, from the image I create in this moment. We've decided that this is enough for tonight, this is so much, a whole chapter in our story in itself; the moment of penetration will have to come later. I am about to take my dildo off. But first, I have to look at it.

It ain't easy, looking at myself tonight. I'm gray-haired and silicone and scarred. There's the tube in my stomach, the undeniable protrusion of my detachable penis. It's been in my husband's fist, and in his throat. I have a salpingectomy scar. I own two other people's lungs. I have been patched together, so skillfully, so necessarily, that I am starting to blur the lines between what is naturally me and what I have absorbed into myself like a single-celled organism. I am not single-celled. I ain't no amoeba. I exist in community.

I look at myself hard, though seeing myself ain't easy. I commit myself to memory. Then I take my dildo off. It is part of me, though. I know; I can put it on again, whenever I need to.

As I thought it would—we have built up some momentum here and do not want to abandon it—the moment arrives soon. I feel in us a push and pull between the spontaneousness of desire—the way we all sometimes wish that sex would be, all heat and rush and unbearable excitement and explosion—and the need for intentionality. What we are about to do is new. It is sacred. It's going to change us. And that needs to be approached with some care, you feel me? I have never had anal sex before. But it does not strike me as the kind of thing you just jump into for the first time, with no preparation, no warmup.

On a warm Friday morning, Andre and I wake up together. He's decided to take the day off from work. He wakes up hard, like his body recognizes too that this is time outside of time. Our bodies are drawn to each other under the covers, natural as magnets, in a way that they haven't been since that night when he found me bleeding. Our lips find each other. Our kiss softens everything. It returns us to our very first time; it returns us to the kind of curious prepubescent exploration of each other's bodies that we used to do before we were even sure what sex was. He kissed me for the first time before I had gotten my first period; I was with him when he used to check between his legs for signs of his first downy black curls of pubic hair, when he worried that his penis hadn't grown big enough. (He still worries that sometimes now, I know. And all I can say to that is that it ain't true, y'all. I find his brown penis and its elegant upward curve utterly perfect, okay.)

Our kiss makes me wet: its morning slowness, its deliberate sensuality. We slip off our clothes under the sheets like a secret. He caresses my nipples, tangles his fingers delicately in my curly bush. He plays with my clit with his thumb with so much patience, so much care, for so long, as long as it takes me to come today, that it brings tears to my eyes, makes me feel cherished.

When I reach between our bodies to take his penis in my fist, he wraps his fingers around my wrist, tenderly but firmly.

"I want to save it," he says. "If that's okay?"

There's such trust, such vulnerability, such openness to this experience that we're gonna have in his eyes that I think I fall in love with my man all over again, just like that.

We get up and take a shower together. It's both awkward and incredibly sensual. Maybe it is so sensual, really, because of its awkwardness: it ain't staged or smoothed around its edges. It's real and it's us. There is still a way and a space for us to be sensual, in our tiny shower whose tiles need to be scrubbed, with my tube between us and our still tentative rediscovery of each other's bodies. The water is warm and all around us, making our skin slippery and soft. The sound of the shower in the deep echo of the bathroom makes me feel like we might be the only two people on earth. We hold each other close, a silky layer of soap between our bodies. As I soap his penis in both hands, I think about how, later, I'll be wearing one of these too. Even though neither of us has said it, we both know, somehow, that today is the day. We are going to do this. And this is how there is a sharp blade of awareness slicing through the undeniable tenderness of this April morning.

I made overnight oats last night, which we eat for a late breakfast with sliced fruit. I tell Andre I'd like to eat by mouth today; he says, "Okay, *mi reina.*" I also say, "Can I feed you, baby?" I hold his eyes for a long, meaningful moment, and, my beautiful man, he doesn't let go of the gaze for a second.

"Yes, please," he says.

It's the first time we're doing this, too. We sit side by side at our kitchen table. There's a bowl of tumbled crystals in the center of the table. Marbled green and blue stones echo the earth they came from. There are white stones, translucent and milky. Sand-colored stones stand like little mountains. I think my favorite are the unearthly, lunar purples, their color a gentle suggestion of mysticism. I feed myself, and I feed my husband. He takes easily and well to being fed, opening his mouth placidly every time I touch it gently with the spoon. It's quiet in the apartment, the bubble of the air humidifier and the swish of cars outside.

"You like this, baby?" I ask him.

He swallows and nods. "I like it," he says. "It makes me feel… like, tender, but in a good way." He looks at me through his lashes. "I like doing things like this with you, Mira. Things I wouldn't do with anybody else. Do you like it?" he asks me.

"Yes, I like it," I say. "I like watching your throat while you're swallowing. Knowing that you're getting fed."

After we eat, we binge-watch several episodes of a new Netflix series that takes place at a ballet school. It's brutal and dark (like many pop-culture things about ballet tend to be), and unrealistically hypersexualized, but it has great music and brief flashes of almost transcendental dancing; the cast, all professional dancers, did the dancing themselves. I watch Andre watching it. His eyes track the dancers across the screen as they move. I don't know how he could watch them and not want to dance himself. If I could dance the way he can, I would never give it up.

As we watch, we also slowly, and without words, lose pieces of our clothing. Andre takes off his shirt. I take off my socks and slip my bare feet underneath his thighs. I take my shirt off too. He starts finding excuses to brush his hand or the side of his arm against my breasts. I sift my fingers through his chest hair, touch his hard little nipples. He slides off his pants and is then in only his underwear. When I start letting my fingertips linger between his legs, feeling the gradual firming of his cock, he pauses the show we're no longer watching.

"All right, little bird," he says, wrapping his hands around my waist. "Come here, you."

I laugh as he lifts me up and puts me down so that I am straddling his lap, facing him. He laughs too, and it feels so good, laughing together again. I cup his face in my hands. As we draw closer to kiss, our lower bodies also magnetize together; I feel the warmth of his burgeoning erection pressing against my center. The wet of our tongues together hypnotizes us both. We begin to rock in to one another. I can't help but whimper as my clit, insistent even through the layers of our remaining clothes, finds the hardened bulk of his penis. You know, I wish I could say it were gone—but it isn't. It's still here—the pain, I mean, that I've been living with since that day in February. It's quieter now, though, an ache far beneath the surface, as I roll my hips against my husband's, seeking the friction between us.

"Mira," Andre whispers between kisses. I feel the warmth of him rising up to meet me. "Are you gonna take me to bed?"

"Course I am," I say.

He's the one who picks me up and physically carries me to our bed, but we both know that, tonight, he's the one who's getting taken. We take off the last few pieces of our clothing. Andre helps me put on my strap-on penis. I like this, a lot: him helping me into the dick that he's going to get fucked with.

I wear it while we lie side by side, touching each other slowly, so I can get used to it. There's a gentle weight to it, a learning curve in the way it bumps and grazes his erect, lengthened penis. This may be new for us, he may have kept this from me for a while, but I know this boy. This close, he cannot hide from me. I can almost smell the nerves on him. It emboldens me. He looks at me with big, longing eyes, and short breath, telling me I will have to be the one to take him by the hand and lead him into his next right step. I am ready.

My featherweight caresses of his penis, my holding of his balls in my hand, leads to delicate brushes of my fingers between his cheeks. Nervous, and shy, he doesn't open them for me right away, does not yet spread his legs to peel his cheeks apart and let me touch more deeply. As we enter this experience, I feel that we are both in control, holding the reins of this horse together. I like his slight tremble, the quickening of his breath, in the midst of our nearness: he trusts me, even someplace new. Somehow, despite the way I do not fit in anywhere in this world, I have gained this man's trust. I hold his eyes and focus and gentle my hand. I pour all of the love that I can into my touch. I stay in it, thumbs whispering against the smooth skin of his ass cheeks, until his breath smooths into a deep and even rhythm.

"Okay?" I whisper, so deep in his eyes I could fall in.

He nods. "Mira, touch me," he whispers.

I reach for the bottle of lube. It has become our new sexual talisman. I pour it all over my fingertips, like a recipe with the freedom to drizzle as liberally as you like. Andre is sliding his legs open for me. They are not as wide as they could be; he's still nervous, unsure. I will go as slow as he likes. Maybe the pleasure I'm sure is waiting for us will inspire him to trust, to open more.

I stroke him with the lube. It's warm and wet and his intimate skin gets slippery. I feel like a rocket rising, full of delicious pressure: his perineum softens for me, his hair clumps like wet eyelashes, his anus contracts as I paint little circles around it. I can't help panting, a silent moaning. I think he tries to hold on, to fight it, to hold himself rigid—but before long he can't stand the pleasure either, I see him breaking before my eyes, rock splintering with cracks, and he whimpers, a pleasure almost like pain, an animal sound. His chest heaves with breath; he'd been holding it. I put my fingertip directly over his pulsing hole.

"Mira," he says. He takes my hand, presses it harder against himself. This means, I know, he wants me inside.

We slide into a dance of push and pull. I seek inside with my finger. He breathes out, opening to me. His legs part further, feet planted on the bed for leverage, giving me more, like I desired. My finger enters his ring of muscle. We both groan. His eyes close. I adjust to how hot he is inside. He rocks onto my finger and grunts. The sound is so fucking primal I need to scream.

"Mira," he says. "More, please."

I give my man another finger. He's open and into it now, accepts it easily.

"Oh, baby," I tell him, "you are so perfect. Look at you. So beautiful."

He whimpers.

"You're taking me so good, baby. That's it. How does it feel?"

"Mira. I need more."

I lean forward and kiss his damp forehead. "You want me inside, baby?"

He nods.

I slide my fingers out, admiring how pretty and open his hole looks, all ready for my cock. He takes the lube and prepares my cock for me, for him, drenching it in lube. The bed is wet and sticky all around us. It smells like cum and my juices and the inside of his ass. On his back, he tilts his hips up to meet me. I hold his shoulders and feel him wrapped all around me like a vine. I press forward, and he helps me guide my penis inside. Like this, him parted and unfolded to me, closer maybe than we've ever been, I can feel the thump of his heartbeat thundering his chest. Maybe it's wrong, I don't know, but in this moment, just for a second, I find myself thinking of Paloma. I think of her silky long hair, how I can feel her heartbeat between the spongy tissue of her breasts, how it feels like her blood and her emotions are so close to the surface when I make love to her. Andre doesn't feel all that different to me right now, all wet brown skin and erotic trust and wanting me. In our sex I am becoming who I am.

I inch into him carefully. His breath is ragged. He makes a sound from the back of his throat when the head of my penis gains entry. "Okay?" I say.

He says, "God. Please." His head presses back into the pillow.

If you're counting inches between us, we do not get that far. I rock my way into him about half my length. I know that this ain't the last time, it's the first, when you have to build things from the ground up. Next time, I will learn to move my cock like an extension of who I am; next time, he will learn to open more, and things between us will soften and flower. For now, though, we find a breathless and shallow rhythm. I feel the heat of his taut testicles. My shaft takes the tightness of his hole. We apply more lube. I ask him if he feels okay, getting fucked for the very first time in his life; he laughs sweetly, almost tearfully, and it makes my heart ache. "It feels so good," he says.

I get tired before anything climactic happens. (What is the end, anyway, of anal sex with a strap-on, if there is one? This is another something that I will have to learn.) Andre helps me disconnect slowly from his body and lowers me to the bed beside him. His arms, too, are trembling.

I lie next to him, regathering myself and catching my breath, while he strokes his penis slowly. He makes a rattling groan when he comes, and it's a fucking torrent, that must have been so pent-up in his tight balls, splattering my stomach. This is so hot I can barely stand it; I squeeze my eyes shut as something very close to an orgasm rocks through me too, though I haven't been touched.

Later, when revealing my secrets, they'll ask me what it was like, fucking my man for the first time with my beautiful strap-on dick. And I will say, y'all know when you're looking into a mirror, but it's all cloudy and splotched? So you spray it and wipe it clean. Then you blink your eyes and look again. And then you can see yourself, your reflection so sharp and clear, it's realer than reality. That, I'll say—that's what it felt like, making love to Andre for the first time.

Our mom has left for her ninety-day inpatient rehab treatment (it's somewhere in rural Pennsylvania, apparently), and the baby is staying with my brother and Hassan. He signed the temporary custody agreement, so it's all official: he is Magdalena's legal guardian. It's dumb as fuck, but I feel nervous, getting dressed to go over and visit them for the first time. What's it gonna be like? I wonder as I tie two fluffy pink scrunchies around my Afro puffs. Will it be awkward? How will I feel, seeing my stupid brother pretending to be a parent to our little sister? How are he and Hassan handling everything? Will it hurt, seeing this physical evidence that Marco could be a parent in a way that I could not?

It's also my inaugural trip back on the New York City subway. I ain't been on the train in ages, I don't even remember when. I wear two face masks, a disposable one under my flower-patterned cloth mask from Anthropologie. Maybe I'll text my boss, see if she can put me back on the schedule. I couldn't be a mother, but maybe I can handle a few short shifts a week. On the train, as we rumble along the tracks downtown, Andre and I sit in the two-person seat in the corner, by the door. He insists on sitting in the outside seat, the one nearest the rest of the passengers on the train; I have to smile at this sweet attempt to protect me, however he can. I lean against him, my cheek against his powerful bicep, and read short poems from Rupi Kaur's latest collection while we ride. He takes my hand, laces our fingers together, rests our hands on top of his thigh. He puts in his earbuds. I hear the music playing faintly from the tiny speakers, some kinda rock music. Andre likes the randomest hipster music, y'all, emo indie bands that ain't nobody ever heard of, and I listen to all kinds of stuff. I can't even.

Andre puts his hand supportively at my lower back as we climb the train stairs and reemerge into the city, taking off our masks. He keeps his arm snaked around my waist as we walk. It's a beautiful sunny spring day. The two flights of stairs up to Hassan and Marco's third-floor walkup tire me out, but don't completely exhaust me. This is a win. Hassan opens the door for us when we knock.

"Mira!" He hugs me gently, holds me by the shoulders and looks at me. "You look lovely, sweetheart. What a beautiful shirt." It is cute, a rich blue with little pink flowers, a belt that ties around my tiny waist.

"She made it," Andre says.

"You did?"

I feel my face get warm. "Ah, it ain't nothing."

"Oh, yes, it is," Hassan says.

"Yeah, she made it," my man says again. "She bought the fabric and made it on the, like, sewing machine." He makes a motion with his hands that I guess is supposed to mimic using a sewing machine. I can't help laughing. We go inside. Andre and Hassan hug, clapping each other on the back. Marco comes into the living room, a kitchen towel thrown over his right shoulder. He hugs Andre and then me, holding me tight. We kiss on both cheeks.

"Everything okay, *nena*?" he says.

I nod. "Everything okay."

I guess I always knew it, but I'm realizing more than ever, now that I have the feeding tube and another way to eat, how many of our family and other gatherings center on food. I always found that hard; y'all know my eating is fucked. Today I don't feel capable of submitting to the vulnerability required to feed myself through the tube, so when we all sit down at Marco and Hassan's tiny kitchen table, in their narrow strip of a kitchenette in their studio apartment, I take a plate of food and eat by mouth with everyone else. I could almost say that ain't nothing changed here at all.

Except then I can't, 'cause my brother and Hassan have a baby, sitting with us at the table in her high chair. We talk, but she captures most of our attention. I still feel a little twinge that makes it hard to look at her, but at the same time I can't ignore her. As he eats, Hassan also reaches over and feeds her, with a little spoon from a jar of baby food, some shit that looks truly revolting, all orange and gooey and mashed. (I mean, if I thought regular food was gross and unappetizing all these years, damn, just look at baby food, y'all.) Magda seems to like it pretty good, though, ingesting about seventy percent of it while the other thirty ends up smeared all over her face. Marco wipes her face with a napkin.

"She's not drinking milk no more?" I ask them.

"She is, sometimes," Hassan says.

"We're starting to wean her off," Marco says. "She is almost eight months old."

"Okay," I say, nodding like I've got a fucking clue. "Cool."

"Mira," Hassan says. He gives the baby a bite of food while looking across the table at me. "Have you given any more thought to my paying for your school?"

I glance at Andre. "Hassan, baby, no," I say. I look at Marco. His brow is furrowed. I risk a look at Magdalena. She pushes her lips out, food dribbling down her chin. Hassan gathers it with the spoon, puts it to her lips again. "Hassan… I can't. I mean, y'all have, like, a baby." I feel hot and helpless, and suddenly just want to go home.

"Mira, no," he says. "We are doing all right. We are okay. I would still love to help you with your school, sweetheart."

I shake my head. "I can't. I mean, don't y'all wanna, like… I don't know. Get a bigger place, or something?" I gesture around.

Hassan looks at Marco, who shrugs. He looks back at me. "I don't know, sweetheart," he says. "We are okay here, for now. Especially so long as this remains… temporary."

This word hangs on the air. Marco and me, we've known our mom for our whole lives. Andre ain't too far behind that; he's no stranger to my mom's antics. Hassan is newer to this whole scene, but he smart; I'm sure he's caught on quick. There is no telling, not with Mom's history and track record, just how temporary this arrangement will be, or how things will turn out.

"Magda has everything she needs," Marco says.

"What about med school?" I ask him.

He rolls his eyes. "Girl. We talked about this. Medical school isn't going anywhere. But now's your time, baby. Take the money. Go back to school."

Now, I know that this ain't about Magdalena. It ain't about medical school. It ain't even about the money. This is all about me, y'all. This is all about the feeling deep in the pit of my stomach, a sensation that feels like sinking and liftoff all at once. This is terror, pure terror at taking my next step. Because if I remain in limbo, if I find every excuse in the fucking book, I'll never know. I'll never know what it feels like to be forced to trust myself. What if I take this chance, and risk Hassan's money, on all my supposed talent and drive as a writer, and it goes nowhere? I'll never know how much that hurts. I feel all their eyes on me. I even feel my little sister's eyes on me. I'll also never know, of course, how good it'll feel to grow beyond myself.

"Are you sure?" I ask Hassan, one last time.

This man does not give me an out. "I am sure," he says. "Miranda, we have talked about this."

"Yeah," I say. "But that was before y'all had a baby."

"We are perfectly all right," he says. "Let me do this for you. May I?"

I take a deep breath. Andre puts his hand on my back. "Okay," I say finally.

Hassan and Marco break out into smiles. I feel a little sick, my heartbeat racing, clammy sweat under my clothes. "Are you saying yes?" Hassan says.

"Yes," I say, shaky, but I say it. "I'm saying yes."

"Good." Hassan says it simply but with finality. "I will email you and we will work out all of the details."

We all finish eating. Hassan wipes the baby's hands and face. Marco plucks her from the high chair and holds her against his shoulder, walking her around the tiny apartment. Hassan washes the dishes. Marco burps the baby. He talks to her, replying to the little babbling words she says. He takes her into their bedroom alcove to change her diaper. We all meet again in the living room, where Marco hangs out on the floor with the baby, helping her practice standing up, holding her firmly around her chubby little waist. It's surreal.

My brother and Hassan seem so natural with the baby, almost as though she has always been with them. She seems to have blended seamlessly into their lives, like they were made for each other, as though there were something fated about all this. But me, in my life, I am careful with that kinda thinking, okay. As well as my brother and his man might meet this experience, for all the good all three of them might find in it, none of this was planned. Is this the workings of fate, or is this the trainwreck that is my family's life, striking again? I ain't no impartial observer, though, as y'all know. I am too close to this to have any answers.

The way I feel when I see my brother laughing with the baby, pulling her close to kiss her on the forehead, prevents me from entertaining any mystical thinking. I feel a clean and tangible hurt, the weight of an embryotic sadness in my belly, something with ultrasonic heartbeat and teeth, an ancient longing that doesn't have a name. My twin gets this: the messiness of a life, the tangibility of changing diapers and jars of baby food, the weight of a baby as he carries her the tiny distance between the window and the kitchen table. I get something much more amorphous: the free-fall weightlessness of trusting a dream. There are many ways to be fertile, indeed.

We don't stay long. At the door, I hug my brother again. "You okay?" I ask him, holding him by the shoulders. He looks a little more tired than normal, maybe, but mostly like himself.

"I'm good, Mira," he says. "I can do this. We can do this."

"Fuck," I say. "You are, like… a dad."

"Ha," he says. "Yeah. I guess I am." He tries to play it off, but I don't miss his look of satisfaction, of pleasure. Maybe my brother, improbable as it is, is exactly where he's supposed to be.

Hassan kisses me on both cheeks. "I can't even believe you're gonna do this for me," I whisper up at him. "I just… I can't…" My eyes sting with tears. "Thank you."

He touches my chin. "Don't thank me," he says. "Just go and write good stories."

"Okay," I say. "I'll try."

Not long after our visit at Hassan and Marco's, I have my last session with Ava. It seems strange to me that I could be finishing up my entire engagement with somebody I've only just met. But I also know that, with my life, I've taken a very different approach to relationships. Basically, I collect people, and I hardly ever let them go. I married my childhood love. I've had the same BFF since we were kids. I've been crushing on Paloma since I was a teenager. I'm also used to long-term healing relationships: I've been seeing my therapist Maya for years and I adore her; I've had my CF care team forever, and I trust them with my health and my body infinitely more than I trust my own mother. Your girl Mira mates for life. My circle ain't big, but it's really, really close.

So it feels a little antithetical (y'all like that word? I just learned it) to me that it's almost time for Ava and me to say goodbye. How much can you really accomplish in only a few meetings, especially when you're wrestling with the big topics like death and dreams and the self? But I get that Ava has a whole different approach from me. She ain't a therapist. She doesn't work with the deep time of the lifelong doctor. Ava works like a laser, on the collapsed timeline of the shaman. She's here to drop something on me and let me go. Not everyone's here for life; not every connection's gotta be permanent to be meaningful.

Or, you know, this is the shit I tell myself as I sit in the back of an Uber to my last session with her, trying to make myself feel better. I say these things to myself like a mantra, repeating the words like fingering smooth worry beads for comfort, telling myself that everything will be okay, that I will get what I need and take it with me, that there really is a point to all of this.

At my session with Ava, sitting with her on meditation cushions on the floor, I find myself telling her about the visit to my twin. I tell her about seeing my brother and his husband with the baby, their ease and effortless presence, their obvious joy, with her. I tell her about seeing Andre hold the baby, my little sister. They sat on the couch, Marco and Andre, and my brother handed him the baby and he held her. I felt a complex mass of emotions like tangled yarns: hurt and anxiety and peace and resentment and fear and jealousy and wanting and deep, deep fucking love. No one asked me to hold the baby, obviously thinking of what happened the last time I tried that. I am damaged. I am volatile. I am not to be trusted. Even in my safe little web of people closest to me, I never feel whole, I never feel ready, I never feel good enough.

"Mira," Ava asks me, "do you feel at home inside yourself?"

"No, not really," I say.

"Do you feel at home," she asks, "inside your body?"

"No, Ava," I say. "These borrowed lungs literally tried to kill me. How can I feel at home in this body when I don't even know who it belongs to?"

And this is why you come to these kinds of sessions, y'all, and tear your heart out your chest and parade its ripped, trailing vessels for strangers to see: the hope that you'll come outta it with an inky black gem you didn't even know you had, like that one for me right now.

Ava asks if she can guide me into a visualization, for coming home to myself, for rejoining my self to my self. I say sure. She explains that it's an interactive visualization; she asks if my awareness can remain awake during the journey, so that I can respond to some questions she'll ask me that will help direct my experience. I say okay.

So we begin. We take deep breaths together, expanding the belly and the chest. Ava asks me to imagine that I am diving into my own body as into a body of water. I have never properly dived into any body of water in the real world, so I have to imagine what it might be like: the almost painful crash into the surface, the silence of holding your breath against the loud rush of the water, the enveloping of your limbs. She asks me to swim in the lake of my own body, to meet my internal organs as I flow past. She tells me to approach my lungs. She asks me to describe them. I know a hell of a lot about lungs, at least medically. I describe them as two pink sponges, taking in air with their tubular branches. She asks me to encircle them with my own essence, the way you might move through a room with burning sage held aloft, the smoke blessing the space. She asks me if I will take them, if I will claim them as my own.

I tell her this reminds me of my marriage vows almost two years ago now, being asked if I would take my man to be mine. And I said yes, as I say yes now. She laughs and says, "Yes, exactly." She tells me I can claim something that exists all on its own as well to be mine, like how my man is mine, and also his own person. I nod, hard, and say, "Okay."

She tells me we are going to leave the lake of my body for now. We burst free of the surface of me, taking in the world's air once again. Ava asks me to emerge in my mind's eye on the beach, leaving the lake shores of my body behind. She asks me to tell her what it's like on the beach on the outside of my body. I say it's twilight, just past sunset. I've never been on a beach at sunset or dark before; I have to imagine. The night is indigo and velvet. The stars are starting to come out, one by one; they're so pretty the night goddesses are stingy with them, giving them out hard-won, only to the most intrepid of seekers. The air smells faintly of the fading smoke of a dead bonfire. Someone has just completed a ritual.

Ava says we're here to meet someone: my wise inner self. She says that wise Mira has only my highest good at heart. She says wise Mira represents the me who has utterly come home to herself.

I ask what that means; how am I to imagine that?

She says that wise Mira behaves the way that I do when I feel most like myself, when I am most fully in my power. "When do you feel most like yourself?" she asks me. "The most powerful?"

I say that I feel most like myself when I am playing my guitar and singing. I feel like myself when I am writing. I feel powerful when people look at me; your Mira is a shy girl who likes performing, who likes being looked at, admired, gets off on it.

I say I felt so powerful this past year, before all of the shit that happened to me. I say I felt like that wise future self, I already felt her, when I lay on the table and got a tattoo, taking all of the bodily pain and making of it art, tangible, indelible. I say that when they bury my body, or burn it to ashes, my ink will go with me. I say that I want to make money from my art. I am not Paloma, okay, dancing onstage in front of audiences. I am not Araceli, my creations hanging in galleries. But I want to feel a little bit of what they feel, trading my art and its emotional impact for the energetic power of money. I want to create the kind of change in the world that you can when you have money, like Hassan is doing for me by helping me pay for school, like Andre does when he pays ninety-five percent of our rent, like when I told Celi I wanted us to have a night together away from home, and she said she could make it happen, just like that. Wise future Mira wants to make things happen.

I tell her I feel most like myself, most in my power, when I have sex. Then, during sex, my body is a site of pleasure, pleasure that I have chosen, instead of pain that I have not. Sex brings me home to my self. I say I have felt it with Andre from the very first time we were together, when we knew nothing. I say I used the good pleasure of our sex as a guiding light, a north star leading me to that moment when we stood under the arch in the park in the springtime and promised ourselves to each other. I say I feel it when I make love to Paloma. I felt it even the night Celi and I kissed, though that night I was physically at one of my lowest points ever. But that good sex magic was enough to bring me back.

I say I feel it, that coming home to myself, when I wear my strap-on and fuck my lovers at their request. I say, though, that my strap-on and I have a long way to go, growing into one another. If I am still learning to inhabit my new lungs, my dick and I have just barely begun. But if I have learned to live with cystic fibrosis, and I have learned to live with new lungs, and I have learned to live with, and around, and through everything that has happened to me, incorporating it instead of trying to fix it, walking beside it rather than bypassing it, then a prosthetic penis does not intimidate me. I will grow with, and around, and through it too. I am a woman meeting her moment.

Ava asks me to ask wise Mira what next right step I can take to come home to my true self, my most powerful self. I see her on the beach at twilight, a me who is delightfully just out of reach, her hair, grayer than mine is now, tossed by the wind. There's a faraway look in her eyes; she's looking to the horizon, 'cause she's going somewhere: maybe inside, or maybe even out there in the external world. Imagine me, Mira, leaving this place where I have spent all my life, recasting me in the new landscape of someplace else. Imagine that, y'all.

I ask wise future Mira this question. And do you know what this girl says? She says that I have to get out there and do shit. She says that I am as a flower; I ain't made to stay inside. She says that I am made not only to take up space in this world, but to make space in this world: to leave a space for the ones who are gonna come after me too, for whom I will serve one day as beloved ancestor. (Imagine me, *mi gente,* as someday not a sad little tragic girl, but majestic as a beloved dead.)

Wise future Mira tells me to make another list, to dream even bigger than I did before. She tells me to get off the fucking bench and onto the field. (That's an intrusion from my brother, a baseball metaphor.) She tells me it's time to wake up. I'm awake, I tell her, and I'm ready.

Andre also has his last session with Ava. It was supposed to be on a Saturday, but she called at the last minute, said she had a family emergency, something with her son (I had no clue our girl Ava had a kid!), asked if they could move their session to the following day, Sunday. Andre said okay.

We had plans for Sunday afternoon: Paloma was supposed to come over, cook and have dinner with us. So on Sunday morning I ask Andre if he'd like me to cancel with her; will it be too much to have her over, and play kitchen-table polyamory, while also coming down from the emotional high of whatever will happen with Ava? But he says no; maybe it'll be good to have P's positive energy in our space while he's coming down from that.

"All right, boy," I say. "Sounds good to me. She does always vibrate at the frequency of love, doesn't she?"

He smiles and smooths my hair back. "Maybe I'm still adjusting to the whole poly thing, a little bit," he says. "But I love that you have a girlfriend, Mira. That you love her."

"Aww, ain't you sweet," I say.

Andre comes home from his session with Ava visibly shaky. I have been cleaning our apartment, listening to *bachata* on full blast. I ask him how it went, and he just shakes his head. I feel a little hurt, a little pissed, that he won't talk to me, but then it fades and I just feel concerned, because he goes into the bedroom and sleeps for hours straight. I turn off the music and write at the kitchen table altar in silence. I stop every few minutes to pick up and play with my phone, worrying if I should cancel with Paloma after all. Fuck, this polyamory shit is hard. When do you draw the boundaries; where the fuck are they? How much do we let Paloma see of our marriage: its lifelong secret languages, its messiness, its silly things that don't make sense to anybody else?

Fuck if I know any of that. But eventually it gets too late to cancel; Paloma texts me, with about fifty celebratory emojis, that she's on her way in an Uber, with gifts and dinner ingredients. I take a shower and put on a long white dress, loose and casual, with a pattern of little yellow flowers. I tie the silk scarf Paloma gave me as a headband around my head, tied in a bow at the nape of my neck. I put on perfume and eyeliner and the necklace she gave me.

Andre comes out of the bedroom in only a pair of boxers. He looks at me, bleary-eyed, and blinks. "Wow," he says. "You look really beautiful, Mira."

"Thanks," I say.

He gives me a long hug. He's warm and smells like our bed. After we came home from my twin's place last weekend, Andre gave me penetrative sex for the first time since all the shit happened. We did it on the couch. He sat with his very hard, very erect penis so fucking lovely in its thicket of hair, and I straddled his lap and filled myself with cock. How was it? I felt a little rusty, a little creaky. My muscles ached. It wasn't at the forefront of my awareness, but I did feel some nagging and pulling from my scars. But mostly it felt delicious: the heat and ache of him in me.

He held my arms, kept begging me, with a hoarse halfhearted whine that made me so fucking hot, to please slow down, please, please slow down, 'cause he was gonna come and didn't want to yet. I tried to, I did, but he felt so good, lighting a path of fire all the way up my belly, that I don't know how good of a job I really did, slowing down. I also couldn't stop squeezing him with my inner muscles, making him cry out and say, "Mira! I can't hold back." He came, shooting up into me. I kissed him messily and told him how much I missed having his cum in me, how much I liked him begging me. "Anytime you want," he said, still panting. I didn't shower till the next afternoon, relishing smelling like him, like our sex.

He doesn't say anything, neither do I, but the physical simplicity of our hug makes me feel much, much better.

"Maybe you wanna put on some clothes, *papi chulo*," I tell him. "Paloma will be here really soon."

"Okay," he says.

"It still okay that she's coming?"

He shrugs. "It's fine," he says.

Paloma arrives in her usual flurry. She's gorgeous in a luscious pink silk shirt and a stretchy white miniskirt. She smells like flowers and I low-key want to skip dinner and kitchen-tabling and whatever the fuck else and just lead her by the hand into the bedroom and make her scream. Her energy's buzzing and she's making me feel more Taurus than ever, all grounded and calm against her Gemini airiness. I want to tie her to the bed and restrain her, make her burn off some of that excess energy saying my name. Her dark eyes flash when I look at her, 'cause my girl knows what I want.

Instead, though, the three of us cook dinner together. We make tacos, a favorite of all of us. Paloma chops bright vegetables and Andre browns the meat. I blend spices and put taco shells into the oven. We listen to old music from Enrique Iglesias, romantic songs in Spanish, from before he got famous in the US around the time Marco and I were born.

We eat together. Andre is very subdued. Paloma is, in contrast, as gregarious as ever. She talks a lot about a trip she wants to take this summer, to the Bahamas for some kinda archaeology thing. I let myself imagine it: hot lazy sun and juicy pineapples on the beach and violet sunsets, like the one I imagined during my visualization.

After tea and dessert—lemon bars that I made yesterday, a springtime dessert—Paloma goes to the bathroom. Andre gets up and starts washing dishes. I stand next to him, beside the sink.

"Andre? Are you okay, *nene*?"

He shuts off the water and turns to face me. "I don't know," he admits. "I feel... weird?"

I reach out, biting my lip as I press my palm to his forehead. "What's wrong, baby? You okay?"

He squeezes my wrist. I lower my arm. "I'm fine, I'm not sick. I just..."

I look at my man more closely. I finally clock that he's... nervous, which doesn't make any sense.

"Andre? *Háblame*. What's happened?"

"Mira." He stands up straighter. "Something happened during my session today with Ava."

My heart jolts with fear. "What happened?"

"No… no." He touches my shoulder. "It's nothing bad. It's just that… something shifted. And I… I think I need to talk about it." We hear the toilet flush. Andre glances in the direction of the bathroom. He begins to speak more quickly. "I was wondering. Would it be okay with you if I told you? And Paloma? I don't wanna, I don't know, disrespect any boundaries? I was just thinking I need to talk to someone about this. I have to tell you. And I was thinking it's the kind of thing P might understand too. I'd like, I don't know? To be heard? To have some space to process this?"

Unable to wait any more, I pummel him with a hug, squeezing him as hard as I can around his middle. He puts his arms around me too. I feel my tube pressing between us.

"Andre," I say. I look up at him. "Of course you can talk about this."

"I just—"

Paloma reenters the kitchen, finds us hugging. Andre lets me go slowly, keeping an arm around my shoulders. I ask if they'd like to hear a little music. They both say yes eagerly, which makes me feel warm inside.

We sit on pillows on the floor in the living room. My guitar in my lap, I play "*Cosas Del Amor*" by Enrique, a love song *bien romántica y dramática*. I play "Purple Rain" by Paloma's namesake, which I practiced over and over again last night. It's a long, meandering song; it trails off into the background as I play more softly, just picking the notes like a quiet meditation.

"Andre?" Paloma says, touching him on the shoulder. "You okay, bro? Sorry if I'm being, like, weird. You just seem, I don't know…" She tilts her hand back and forth, the universal symbol for *así-así*. "I'm sorry. But you okay, my friend?"

"Paloma." He says her name with a deep sigh. "That is quite a question."

"With quite an answer?"

He laughs. "*Exacto*." He starts to get up from the floor. "I want to answer that. I do. But first I think I need a glass of that wine you brought. You want one too, P?"

"Oh, fuck yes," she says, stretching in a really sexy way, like a cat. He looks at her. I know I shouldn't, I know it ain't gonna happen, but I can't help allowing a momentary fantasy of the two of them together. I gotta say, I wish he were into it. They would be so hot. I'd die.

"Mira?" he asks me, pulling down the hem of his T-shirt as he stands. "You want a glass of wine, baby?"

"No, thank you, baby," I say, playing another soft riff from "Purple Rain." "You two just enjoy your wine and talk and pretend like I ain't even here."

"We could never forget you're here," my lovers say, at legit the exact same time. We all look at each other and laugh. I keep laughing, softly to myself, while my husband goes to the kitchen to get wine.

Andre comes back with glasses of red wine for Paloma and himself. He sits with his back against the couch and takes a long, deep swallow of his wine. He examines the glass like he's looking for answers. I'd look into my crystal ball for him if he asked, consult the tarot, read his tea leaves like an ancient tasseomancer.

Then he says to Paloma, "Mira and I have been seeing this, like, mystical grief counselor. Well, we just finished up a package of sessions with her."

Paloma nods, her face open like an empty vessel. She's listening.

"I really felt like I needed to talk to someone, even though it was fucking hard. And not fun," he says. "Because I felt so fucked up over us losing our pregnancy." He looks at me. He hasn't said it before, not quite so plainly, not like this, and you can fucking believe that I am listening. "And I felt like it got all mixed up in my brain. I mean, us losing the pregnancy. And me being scared. Of losing Mira." He looks at Paloma. "When she was sick in February, yeah. But also just, like, always. I mean." He takes a deep breath, a sip of wine. "It's a fear I just live with. All the time. Every day."

Oh, fuck, that one hurts, rips my heart right down the middle.

"I beat myself up sometimes. 'Cause I think I should be further along with that. Accepting that, or dealing with it. Or seeing my way to what that's gonna feel like. Being the person she will need me to be at that time. Being someone who could, I don't know, get up the next day after that and still want to keep being a person. Like, I wish I were." He drains the wineglass. "I am not all the way there. Not yet. But I'm trying. I guess."

He looks at us again, first me and then her. "Paloma? You okay hearing this? I mean, I don't wanna, like..."

She shakes her head, quickly. "Andre. No. Please keep talking. If you want to. I am listening."

He looks at me. "I'm sorry, Mira," he says. "You always say you wish we could talk about it. I mean, about you… dying. So I am. I'm trying to. You cool with this?"

I nod. I keep playing chords softly, keeping myself grounded in this world of sound and vibration and material and texture.

"I had a dream about you," he continues. "A nightmare. It fucked me up really bad. I told Ava—that's the grief lady—about it. In the dream, you were yelling at me, Mira. You were telling me you wished I never even gave you the lung." He starts tearing up. We do too, seeing it. "You said why, since you're still just gonna die anyways. So Ava led me in a visualization."

I imagine it: him sitting on the meditation cushion on the floor of Ava's room in the yoga studio, the room smelling like patchouli oil. He's sitting open and vulnerable, palms upturned on his knees, ready to be led.

"She asked me to re-enter the dream, but as my aware, waking self. She said I was going to talk to you this time, to answer. So I did. We went into the dream and you yelled at me again, saying you wished I had never given you the lung. Because it didn't matter. It hadn't made any difference." He closes his eyes a moment, opens them and looks at me. "And you know what I said?"

I shake my head.

"I didn't know what I was going to say. I hadn't planned it. But I said, 'Mira. Even if, the night before the surgery, they had told me that you were only gonna get one more day. That this was only gonna give you one extra day.' And, yes, I know it's not like that. I know it's not a trade-off. It's not a numbers game. There is no bargaining: you donate a lung lobe, you trade for *x* number of days more with the love of your life. But it was a dream. It didn't have that kinda logic. So I said, 'If they had told me, for sure, that this was only gonna give you one more extra day. Than you would have had otherwise. I would have said, sign me up. I would have done it still. In a heartbeat. And I would have taken that one extra day. And enjoyed the shit out of it.' *Eso es lo que dije.*"

I mean, what do I even say to that, y'all? I let the tears trickling down my face do the talking for me. I tuck my guitar pick between my fingers and wipe my eyes with the side of my thumb. Then I keep playing.

"Ava continued with the visualization after I said that. She asked me to imagine, what if not only that, but everything were a dream? What if this were all a dream; what if we were living our entire lives in the dream of a goddess? And part of me was, like, what… But I decided to trust. To go with it. What if this goddess had dreamed up our entire lives? And she had only our highest good at heart. Ava asked me to imagine that I was swimming, that we were all swimming, in an ocean inside of this goddess. Life, then, isn't about fighting. There is nothing to fight. Life is about flowing with the current." He makes an expressive gesture with his hand and arm. "She asked me to imagine that it's an ocean of clay, like a mud bath if you went to a spa. That it's warm and heavy and you're entirely held. If you move, you're cradled. When you move, when you go past who you've been before, you rub up against the little exfoliating beads in this bath. You know what I'm talking about?" We nod. "You move and grow and it purifies you. Sheds old skin off of you so you can move forward renewed."

He looks at both of us. "It was wild. I started to feel like I really was in this giant mud bath of life. That I was taken care of. That nothing truly bad could ever happen to me, because it was all to my good, like refining me in a fire. Like I really felt it, you two, in my body."

Paloma is nodding. "Sounds like she took you on a shamanic journey, Dre," she says.

"Yeah," he says, "I think she did. I've never been on a shamanic journey before."

"How did it feel?" I ask.

"Awesome," he says. "Like, both senses. Super cool. And also terrifying."

"Yeah," we both say.

"She said I could imagine this goddess, if it felt good to me, kind of like a dominatrix."

I have to smile. "Did that feel good to you?"

He hesitates for a moment, then nods.

"She's the kind of dominatrix who gets off on making you feel good. She holds you in constraints, so you can find creative ways to move within those constraints. It's not about being in control. You're not in control. It's about finding ways to let go. Once you think you've let go all the way, no, find a way to let go more. It's about being vulnerable so you can let life move you. Ava said she thinks I need to work on my surrender. That I can find power and guidance in surrender."

"Huh," I say. "And what you think, baby?"

"I think she's right," he says, right away. "I am not in control. I think that's what life's been trying to tell me lately. I'm hurting myself, trying to find ways to control things that I can't control. I need to let go. I have to find ways to surrender. I want to surrender. More." He looks at Paloma. "I want to work on my openness. My vulnerability. So I'm here. Telling you all of this." He tilts his head. "I hope it's okay?"

In answer, she crawls closer to him along the floor so she can hug him. She holds him tightly. He closes his eyes in the hug, one arm around her waist, the other hand touching her hair.

"Andre," she says, pulling back. "Of course it's okay. Thank you. Thank you for telling me all that. I'm really proud of you, dude. I think it takes so much strength to be able to be vulnerable like that."

"You think?"

"Yeah." She smiles, lets him go gently. "I definitely think so." She glances over at me. "And I think I should go."

"Shit," Andre says. He touches her waist. "Am I running you off, P? Scaring you away?"

She laughs, puts her hand to his chest. "Not at all, baby. I've had the most wonderful time with you two. I don't know, I just feel like you and Mira have a lot to talk about. Plus it's getting late, and I have to teach in the morning. I should go home, get some sleep."

Paloma gets ready to leave. While we wait for her Uber, we stand by the front door of my apartment and hold each other, arms looped around each other's waists.

"How are you feeling, Paloma? Are you okay?" I give her a squeeze. "And be real with me, *nena*. Please."

She nods. I can see the slight trembling of her lips, the pinching in the corners of her eyes, their faint sheen. "I'm okay, Mira," she says. "I definitely do need to go home and get some rest, though. I'm going to take a hot bath and, honestly, just let myself cry." She bites her lower lip.

"Are you okay, Paloma? Is there anything I can do?"

She shakes her head. "Not tonight, *sirena*. For now I just need to be by myself and cry and feel my feelings. Okay?" She reaches up, touches my face gently. "I'm feeling really sad tonight. Drinking wine and talking to your husband about… losing you, about you… dying. I mean." She cups my face in both hands. "That's a lot, you know?" she whispers.

"Fuck, Paloma. Is it too much? Should we not have—?"

"No, no." She leans forward, bends her head, quiets me with a kiss. "It was not too much. Not at all. I think it was good for us. For me." She kisses me again, a little deeper. "I want to be here. It's like what Andre said. I want to be the kind of person who can be here. I'll have to grow into her."

"Let me be there for you too, Paloma." I'm almost begging.

"You are." She touches the center of my lips with her thumb. "So there's also a lot going on for me right now. Stuff with my mom. With my family. I'd love to talk to you about it all. Sometime. When we have the space."

I hug her tightly. I feel the breath squeeze out of her. "Yes, I want that," I whisper against her. "And I'm so sorry, Paloma. Do I really always make everything about me?"

She laughs. It feels so good, her laughing against me, this close, nothing between us. "Mira, stop. You're wonderful. You're wonderful and I love you. So much." She gives me a last kiss, letting our tongues feel each other. "I'm not going anywhere. We have time."

"We have time," I agree. I hear the voice of my inner self again, telling me it's time to emerge from my cave and start doing shit again. She's right. I'm ready. "I love you too, *mi nena*. Text me later, if you feel like it? I'll be thinking about you, girl."

"I'll text you," she promises. "I'm gonna go outside. Get some air. My car's almost here anyway." She glances past me, into the apartment. "And I think your man is waiting for you in the bedroom."

I laugh, though just these words make my breasts feel heavy. I say goodbye to my girlfriend, close the door behind her, and open the bedroom door to find my husband.

Andre is waiting for me, naked in our bed. Maybe it should give me a little whiplash, huh, moving so quickly between my girl and my man. It doesn't, though. It feels good, and right. I feel like a woman who could meet her moment.

I take my clothes off too, trying to work out if I feel sexual right now, or if our nakedness tonight means something else. I gotta tell y'all, when Andre was telling me about his visualization, about swimming through his life on the current of a goddess who has his best at heart, about giving up control and submitting to a divine dominatrix who will take care of him, well, it made me wet. My clit throbbed and pulsed, hearing him say that he wants to learn to surrender more. I know just who can help him with that.

I get into bed with him. "Hi," he says.

"Hi, beautiful," I say.

He pulls me close. "Mira, I have something to ask you," he says.

I feel so alive, reanimated, feeling his bare skin against mine, whole body to whole body.

"*Dime, papi*," I say.

I feel his chest expand with a breath. "I don't even know how to ask for this," he says.

"Baby, it's me," I tell him. "I'm your girl. You can tell me anything. Ask me for anything."

He nods. I look at his eyelashes, curling over his big dark eyes. "Mira," he says. "I was wondering if you would fuck me more. Like, regularly? Like I would love it if you could give it to me in the ass like once a week. Or a couple times a month at least?"

I put my two fingers over his lips. I feel his breath against my skin. I can feel both our hearts beating.

"My man needs to be fucked regularly, huh?" I ask. I find the part of me inside that is able to say this. I find her easily.

"Yes," he says, in almost a whimper, a sound of longing, and of relief. "I need to be fucked regularly. God." He lets out a deep breath. "That is really hard to say."

"But you said it."

"But I said it," he agrees. "I just think it would be really good for me. It would feel good. Obviously. But I also think it would help me with… everything."

"With your surrender," I say.

"With my surrender, yes," he says. "And with the way I want to feel. How I want us to feel. Mira, we've talked a little bit before about how I want you to take control with us more. And I do. I want that. In the bedroom and outside of the bedroom."

"All right," I say. "What do you mean? What does that look like?"

"I don't know," he confesses. "I mean, I've always known that you're my queen. I want to take care of you. To… to serve you. I always have. So, I don't know. I guess I just want to… live into that more. I want you to own that. I'm yours, Mira. Take me. Top me."

"Wow," I say. It ain't every day that you get an offer like that, now, is it? "Okay, *nene*. I think I can do that. No, I can do that. We can do that." I hold his face in one hand, kiss his mouth. "Let's figure it out together?"

"Yes, *mi reina*," he says.

Last night, I asked Mira to spank me. So she did.

I didn't question the desire, at least not in the moment. I'm in a space right now safe enough to treat my desires this way: like something I can follow, unquestioningly. I just heeded, I surrendered, I obeyed.

I asked her if she would spank me, and she said yes, if that was what her man needed, then she would be glad to do it. I pulled down my pants and got on our bed and she smacked my ass with the palm of her hand. She laughed a little and said, "Hard enough?" And I said, "Harder," so she spanked me harder. It hurt and felt good and reminded me of something—I'm not sure what—and shook a lot of things loose in me. I didn't identify them. I let them float by. I gave myself only one job, which was to feel the thunder crack of the palm of her hand against the muscle of my ass. I just listened to the sound, let it reverberate inside me.

Now, today, I'm getting back into the dance studio with Paloma again.

I'm coming to the studio directly from our first in-person team meeting at work since March 2020, so it's a total mindfuck, trying to switch gears, to switch personas, from the me I am at work to the me I'm trying to rediscover in the dance studio mirror. I don't know how I'm going to do it. But, starting tomorrow, I will be taking the whole summer off from work. This will be the longest I've been off from work at a stretch since I got my first job at fifteen. Who the fuck will I even be, if I'm not working? I don't know. But I will be forced to find out.

"Treat me like I'm one of your students," I said to Paloma on the phone the other day. (Paloma isn't that much older than me, but she's just older enough that sometimes she prefers talking on the phone to texting. I really don't get that, but whatever makes her happy.) If I'm going to dance again, then there's no way I can do this half-assed. If I am going to dance again, then I need to make my body stronger. I need to restart, from foundations, from the ground up.

"Give me, like, an advanced beginner ballet class," I said.

"You got it, Dre," she said. I could hear the smile in her voice.

"Can I pay you for class?" I asked her.

"No, you absolutely cannot," she said, and then I could hear her rolling her eyes.

At the studio (I insisted on paying for our two-hour studio rental), I bow slightly to Paloma, just like my mom had all the male ballet students do in front of their teachers at every single class at her studio. (The female students have to curtsey. Once, when we were teenagers, taking a class with my mom, Araceli asked, with a completely straight face, "What archaic submissive ritual would you have a nonbinary dancer do, Miss Lisette?" And my mom said, "I'd ask the dancer which ritual they feel comfortable with. And stop being fresh, Miss Henriquez. Now, everyone, take your places at the barre, please.")

"Good afternoon, Miss Paloma," I say.

"Wow. Okay." Paloma blinks. "So we're really doing this, huh?"

"Yes," I say. "We are really doing this."

As for me, I always secretly loved this archaic submissive ritual.

"All right," she says, with a nod that says, *challenge accepted*. "Good afternoon, Andre. Please set up your barre."

At the start of every class at my mom's studio, we set up the ballet barres from where they're tucked away at the back of the room, arranging them in the center. Caring for the room and for the one piece of equipment that ballet requires shows your commitment to the art. I lift a ballet barre from the back of the studio and carry it to the center.

Paloma hooks up her phone to the studio's speaker via Bluetooth. "We don't have to go full traditional on the music, though, do we?" she asks. "I just taught two baby ballet classes online this morning. I have had enough of classical for one day."

"Not at all," I say. I reach out and place my hand on the smooth wood of the barre. "Whatever you want, Miss Paloma."

She laughs and starts the music. It's some smooth and sexy dancehall, played at low volume just to add some atmosphere, and as Mira would say, I ain't mad at it.

Paloma takes her place next to me at the barre. "Do you mind if I do the barre with you?" she asks. "I miss standing at the barre next to you like this."

"Go for it. You're leading, though. I haven't given myself a barre in, like, years."

So Paloma gives us a barre. I see her transforming in the mirror in front of us before my very eyes. I mean, Paloma is confident and elegant and even regal a hundred percent of the time, but watching her become Paloma the ballet dancer is something else. The carriage of her upper body becomes expressive and upright, her neck lengthening and her head reaching up towards the sky as though on a string. She leads us through a barre that's both flowing and precise, beautiful and exact.

I've always loved barre work: the simplicity and also the surprising difficulty of it, the comforting sameness and tradition of it—ballet dancers have done the same barre exercises in classes of all levels all over the world for many centuries—combined with the kinesthetic fact that no two sessions at the barre are ever the same, the rigidity and rigor of it tempered by the lightness of the arms floating into and out of the positions with seamless transitions.

Paloma leads us through our exercises. We do tendu and degage and grande battement, demi plies and plies and grand plies, and lift up and stand in relevé, from all five positions. My ear missed hearing all of the French ballet terms, a specialized language that was once as familiar to me as breathing. (Unlike most American ballet dancers, Paloma says everything with perfect French pronunciation; apparently her rich parents got her French lessons from the age of four, and she did one year of high school in France.) With the most basic movements, my body sinks back into them like I haven't been away from dance for years now. My hips remember what it's like to be in turnout; the inside seams of my legs, from heels to thighs, reacquaint themselves with each other as I turn my legs out. There is a degree to which turnout, the rotation of the legs originating at the hips, is a physical attribute that you are born with, or not. Like my mom, I have near perfect turnout, at least one thing in ballet that I didn't really have to work at.

When it comes to the more difficult movements, though, it's obvious to me, both from my experience in my own body and in the mirror, that I am out of shape and out of practice. My leg is not able to rise as high in grand battement; I used to be able to toss it up into the air well past ninety degrees, and now I can feel my hip protest when I try to achieve that kind of height.

"Andre," Paloma says. "Don't muscle your way into it. Let it come from your center."

I remember what it's like to engage the core, feeling like the middle line of my body is one integrated, unbreakable part, balanced over my center of gravity, enabling me to do things with my body that you just don't normally do in regular life. I remember the impeccable carriage of my upper body, the good ache of practicing port de bras. I remember how it feels to articulate through the whole foot—another thing you just don't do in regular life—peeling up the heel, and the midfoot, and the toes, from the floor, pointing through.

"Can I give you a piece of advice that I give my baby ballerinas?" Paloma asks me at another point.

I nod. I'm feeling a mix of frustrated and exhilarated that makes me feel like I cannot speak.

"Andre. Baby. Can you focus on what it feels like inside your body?" She makes a gesture like pulling something up and out from the center of her self. "Can you let go of looking in the mirror? Just a little bit?"

I feel my eyes hot.

"Let go of what it looks like," she says softly. "Focus on what it feels like. Dance from inside." She draws a finger down my chest. "Yeah?"

Maybe this sounds like bullshit, but I can tell you, it is not. Dancing from inside is harder than any of the near-impossible feats that ballet asks, especially when ballet is an art form so based on achieving a specific line aesthetically visible to the eye. And every time I look in the mirror, I am inundated by a wave of not so much clear, distinct memories, but rather the feeling I used to get, for so many years dancing at my mom's school, the sick feeling of knowing that I had to maintain my body as it was, or I would not be good enough. I'm heavier now than I've ever been, after giving up dance and the pandemic and working from home. Honestly, there's been so much else going on in my life, in our lives, that I've barely even given a thought to this. I've just been feeling grateful to even have a body, to wake up every morning with Mira and keep doing life. But an hour at the ballet barre in the mirror and all the old insecurities come tumbling back. The sick feeling of worry, of shame, taints the joy I'm also feeling, being back in the studio again. Where am I going from here?

Paloma and I move the barre to the back of the room again and she creates some combinations for us in the center and across the floor. Center and across-the-floor work are more freeing, more creative, they let you express your individuality as a dancer a bit more, but there's still the comfort of traditional choreography, transitions, and extensions— arabesque, ronde de jambe, pirouette. Paloma starts me slow, following my original request that she treat me like one of her beginning students, but soon there is no ignoring it, not for either of us: I started studying ballet around the time I learned to walk, I practiced pretty much every single day until I was twenty years old, and three years away has not erased my body's muscle memory. It is more than muscle memory, though. It's more, even, than the automatic lengthening of my posture and my limbs, the feeling of having pure, sparkling energy where my blood and nerves should be. My whole heart remembers ballet, and my soul.

So before long Paloma is calling out longer, more complex sequences of steps, and faster, clapping sharply to keep time. She's stopped dancing herself, to watch me, in front of her and in the mirror, to give me feedback and suggestions, to (after asking if it's okay with me) offer me hands-on, physical corrections. I've missed having someone's hands on me as a dancer.

She surprises me suddenly with a hug, a hard one, two bodies colliding. I catch her.

"Sorry," she says, pulling back, still holding me. Her cheeks are a little flushed, stray wisps of black hair have escaped her braid, there's sweat on her forehead. "Is this okay?"

I give her waist a squeeze. "Course it is." I smile down at her. "What's it for?"

She hugs me again, pressing her face hard against my shoulder. She squeals; I feel her practically vibrating with controlled excitement. "I'm just so glad you're dancing again, Andre. You're the most gorgeous dancer. The most beautiful man." She holds my face, gives me a peck on the lips. "I love you."

"I love you too."

Her eyes sparkle. "*Eres mi favorito.* Are you gonna let me choreograph a ballet on you someday? Someday soon?"

"I don't know, Paloma. Let me get my feet under me again first?"

"I don't know, Dre. They look pretty under you to me." She shrugs, lets me go. "But I get it. We'll take it slow. *Lo que tú quieras.*"

I've gotta smile at that one. It's something my wife always says.

Paloma turns off the music, hands me her phone. "My payment. I don't want your money, baby, I just want that big, perfect body in my arms for a few minutes." We both laugh. "Pick any music you want, Dre baby, and just dance with me? No pressure. Let's just play."

"Okay," I say. I open her Spotify app and find what I'm looking for.

She laughs as I hand the phone back to her and she puts it on the floor, propped up against the bottom of the wall. "The waltz? Okay, baby."

I take Paloma in my arms and we start to waltz. The delicate, lighthearted classical music lifts my spirits like a breeze. It's impossible for me to listen to a waltz and keep feeling shitty. Paloma is just perfect as a waltz partner. We float like two feathers, one-two-three, one-two-three, one-two-three, spinning around the entire studio. Our feet are in sync, our bodies perfectly arranged in the classical waltz hold. We dance till I feel gloriously dizzy.

As always when I listen to music, the notes transport me in my mind. Dancing the waltz brings me back to when I was sixteen, and I danced the waltz with Mira at her *quinceañera*. Dancing with her felt nothing like this. We practiced for weeks. Mira was so nervous, even when it was just the two of us dancing in my bedroom, that she trembled in my arms. She stepped on my toes, every time, including in her high heels at the party itself. She cried, a lot, when she couldn't "get it right," and many practice sessions ended with me rubbing her back, telling her it was okay, she was my perfect girl. And she was perfect. I felt like a king dancing with his queen when we danced. I was hyperaware of her body in my arms, every point of contact between our bodies feeling like a little fire, and I felt sweetly drunk, smelling her coconut shampoo and her flowery body spray, the one from CVS that made the skin at her throat sparkle. I remember dancing with her at her sweet fifteen: her plump lips bigger than ever in bright red lipstick; her long eyelashes; the scratchy, voluminous layers of her enormous dress brushing against me as we moved. Her dress was a creamy white, almost pink, tiered like a cake, with little red flowers. It was cut deep in the front, and whenever her breasts breathed against me, my penis throbbed.

It didn't feel shameful, like I sometimes used to worry my sexual desire for her was when we were younger; it felt like the sweetest ache and I welcomed it. We wanted to from the moment we realized what sex was and that we could do it together, but Mira and I decided to wait to have penetrative sex for the first time till she was sixteen.

I loved waiting to have sex. Does that make me weird? I don't care. I loved waiting. I loved sexting, I loved whispered phone sex in our childhood apartments, her whimpering as I told her the things I wanted to do to her body. I loved dreaming about her—her breasts, her nipples, her wet bush, her wet mouth on me—waking up in my bed sticky with cum. I loved getting hard while out with her someplace, knowing there was nothing I could really do about it, just ache for her and feel my feelings. I was seventeen when we made love for the first time. We were breathless for each other but still tried to be gentle with each other. I came so hard, so much, I was almost embarrassed by it. I loved waiting. I would have waited longer. I feel like it gave me time—time to build something real for her, time to make it good for her, time to know what desire was.

At the end of the party, the night of her *quinceañera,* Mira texted me to meet her in the bathroom. So I did. She was in purple sweatpants and a bra, her hair still piled all fancy on the top of her head, makeup still on. She was looking in the mirror when I came in, about to take off her red lipstick with a makeup wipe.

"Hey," I said, "leave it on?" My heart was pounding so hard it hurt.

"Yeah?" she said, brow furrowed. Her hand lowered. "Why?"

All the blood in my body rushed south. "I want it all over my face," I whispered.

Mira put in the cannulae for her oxygen tank. We kissed around it, like we did so many times back then. She smeared her red lipstick all over my face, kissing me, while I reached into her damp panties and stroked her greedy pussy. "I'm so wet for you, Andre," she said. "You feel so good." I held her while she came and listened to her tired, labored breathing. It was late and I knew she was exhausted. I felt sad and angry and so sick in love with her I was sure it would kill me. Her mom called her then, so we cleaned up and left the bathroom. She called me even later that night when we were both back home, asked if I could touch myself and let her hear. So I did. I came so hard, down into her ear, that I saw stars.

I remember all this while dancing in the studio today, Paloma and her lovely posture dancing the perfect, elegant waltz in my arms. I feel good and nostalgic and sweet, remembering. I also know that all of that is past, that we cannot go back. You can dance the most traditional dances you want, pieces that dancers have been dancing for centuries. And yet, every single day, with each new dancer that takes the floor, it's completely new. We can only go forward, never back.

The waltz music ends, changes to something else. It's a love song, something gentle and slow. Paloma and I step closer to each other, just naturally, a response to the music by two dancers familiar with each other's bodies.

"Dance with me?" I whisper to her. I pull her a little tighter against me.

She nods. "Absolutely. I'd love to." She swallows. "Let me just drink some water first." She nudges me. "You should too. Stay hydrated."

"You're right."

We release each other, pause the music, head to our dance bags in the back of the studio to get our water bottles. We lean against the wall and drink water. Now that I'm still, and hydrating, I feel how out of breath I am, how thirsty. I look at the heaving of my chest and stomach in the mirror, very apparent in the tight white leotard I'm wearing with black track pants. When I told my mother I was going to be a lung donor for Mira, she said (among many other things; Mom had a hell of a lot to say about my decision), "How will that affect you if you ever decide to go back to dancing?" I said, "I'll be fine." And I am fine. Do I feel exactly the way I used to when I was sixteen? No, I don't. But I'm not sixteen anymore. And I've also been through a global pandemic and all the losses of the past couple years and I survived finding Mira bleeding on our bathroom floor and scrubbing the blood off the floor later on my hands and knees. Living bodies change. I'm alive, I have a body. Our lost pregnancy, it had a heartbeat, but not a viable body. So, do I feel like I could join New York City Ballet as a principal dancer? No, I don't. But I definitely feel like I can dance with a friend in the studio for only the second time in the past three years. And, for today, that is all I need.

Paloma and I step closer to each other again, but this time, after a pause, after restarting the music and approaching each other with more intention, I feel different. I feel almost nervous. I take her in my arms and feel our hearts beating together. She wraps her arms around my shoulders. I touch her, feel the smooth material of her stretchy pink leotard under my palms, the deep curves of her waist, the delicious rolls of fat at her hips. I feel the chiffon of her flouncy little practice skirt. Her breasts settle against my chest as we get even closer.

I've asked myself many times, holding different people's bodies in my arms as we danced, if this feels sexual for me. I have always worried that I am not sexual enough, that I am not indiscriminately obsessed with sex like some other men, or other people, seem to be. And the answer is no. I can't lie and say I've never gotten hard before, someone rubbing their body all over mine, but even that's felt incidental, a physical reaction and not something emotional or even sexual, something in which I was invested. Paloma feels damn good in my arms. My heartbeat gets slow and thick, dripping like honey, enjoying how sweet it feels to be close to her, to dance with her, to smell her hair and her body, to sway and turn together. I don't know the word for it, for how I'm feeling. But it isn't sexual.

A lot's been going on for me sexually, though. I've been rolling with it, trying to just stay present to it, but I can't lie and say I haven't also felt a little unmoored. So I went to the place we often go when we have questions about something and don't know whom to ask: the internet. And, yes, I get it: there is a lot of bullshit on the internet. But something I've learned from Mira over the years is that the internet can be a powerful place for connection among communities that might find it hard, or impossible (like the cystic fibrosis community; since CF-ers cannot come within six feet of one another to protect their health, the digital world has become their meeting space), to be together in physical space.

I've loved taking anal penetration from my wife. I told her one night during anal sex that I wanted to feel helpless, like she was dominating me and there was nothing I could do about it. She smiled and said, "Okay, baby. Let's try it." There was some laughing, from both of us, some awkwardness, because we'd never tried anything quite like it before, but there were also some moments, my girl holding me down and making me take her penis, that I felt a blinding sense of absolute rightness. I felt something I have rarely felt in my life: as though I could fully let go. I loved being spanked last night. I've also loved Mira taking control in other ways, big and small, in our life, and I want her to continue.

One day, Colleen, the woman we had a threesome with before all the shit went down, what feels like a lifetime ago, texted us. She said it's been a while, would we be open to another hookup? I asked Mira what she thought. She said she is focusing her sexual energy on me and on her two girl lovers, Paloma and Araceli. She said, "How would you feel about hooking up with her just you? Like, alone?"

I said, "I don't know, baby. Could I think about it?"

And she said, "Sure."

So I thought about it. I talked to Mira about it. I said, "How would you feel if I did this? Had sex with another woman, just me?"

She said, "I'd be into that, baby. I love more sex and new connections for you. What you think?"

"If it is all right with you," I said, "and if it would please you, then I'd be into it."

She laughed. "Yeah. It would please me," she said.

"Okay," I said.

"If y'all start to catch feelings," she said, "talk to me about it?"

I don't see this happening, but I'm only twenty-three and there's been so much shit in my life that I never saw coming. We don't live like any shit is guaranteed. So I said, "Okay."

She said, "Good boy." She picked up my phone and handed it to me.

"Text her. Set something up, baby. At her place if you can, or a hotel? Maybe someday, but I ain't ready yet to have her over here."

So I did. Honestly, what's sexiest to me about this arrangement is knowing that my wife encouraged it, that she's into it, that the next day when I got home she was all over me, telling me how hot it is that I have a lover, that we're creating this unconventional life that works for us. She wanted to fuck, asked me to give her my dick. I said yes, of course.

I have also started exploring the submissive community online. There is… a lot of material. There seem to be infinite ways that partners explore their dominance and submission, from people who like to play one or both roles occasionally at sex parties to committed couples who have lived in a twenty-four-seven dominant-submissive dynamic for decades. With my wife's permission, I've been chatting with two guys who are their wives' submissives. It's just been nice to talk to someone who automatically gets it, where I don't have to worry about being judged or ridiculed or psychologized. And while I'm not ready quite yet for Mira to collar me and take me around as her little pet, I can see my way to a time where, maybe, if that felt right for both of us, I could be.

That's felt pretty vulnerable, of course. But, honestly, what's felt even more vulnerable is the other sex-related stuff I've been searching. I didn't even know what I was looking for at first. I just know I've always been worried, since I became aware of sex, that I wasn't as into it, as wild for it, as the stereotypes told me I should be. And did that mean there was something wrong with me? But as I got older, the picture got clearer. I can be super into sex, and wild for it, if it's with the only person I have ever had a romantic and emotional connection with, and that is Mira. When I first started reading about demisexuality online, I felt worried, because I felt like it didn't fully describe me. I can and do sometimes feel sexual attraction to people I'm not emotionally close to. I have had sex with people other than Mira, and everything worked, and I performed. I've had sex a couple of times now with Colleen, and it's been pretty good. That's the thing, though. Sex without an emotional connection for me feels okay. I can make it happen. But it feels like scratching an itch, like eating a snack. Sex with Mira, though, can feel like an explosion and a supernova and the deep, frightening joy of two souls touching.

But then I chatted with a sex coach on one of the forums, who reminded me that sexual labels are created and adapted to describe people and their unique sexual experiences, not the other way around. People and their sex lives are dynamic and ever-changing, with a speed and immediacy that words don't always have. So, he said, it's completely normal for a word to describe you only partially, or only sometimes, or for multiple words to fit different sides of who you are sexually or romantically, or not to have, or to want or need, any single word to describe your sexuality at all. I did feel better then, and allowed the resonances I felt with at least some parts of the demisexuality spectrum to settle into me and comfort me.

The song Paloma and I have been dancing to comes to an end, and another one begins. She pulls back just a little, rubs my back gently. She doesn't say a word, but with the way she's looking up at me, I know she can read, if not my exact thoughts, then the quality of my feelings. There just isn't any way to hide, not when you're dancing and the dance asks you to bring your emotions to your performance, and not when you're this close to someone who knows your body intimately. Both because I don't really have a choice, and because I trust her, I let her see me.

"Do you want to dance to another one?" she asks softly.

I nod, holding her a little tighter.

She rests her head against me again, relaxes into my hold. Another slow song begins; we melt into its sway. I release my thoughts and my memories and my worries and my fears, and absolutely everything else, and give myself over to the dance with her, and the beat and swell of the love song.

We dance until our studio time comes to an end. We turn off the music and the Bluetooth and the lights and the air-conditioning. We gather up our stuff and meet at the door to say goodbye, before separating to change back into street clothes in the bathrooms and go home.

Paloma stands on her toes, holds my face in her hands and kisses me, both cheeks and then my lips.

"Andre," she says. "Tell me to fuck off if I'm overstepping, okay? But I'm feeling like… I don't know… something's up with you?"

I shrug. "Yeah. A lot's been up lately."

"Okay." She gives my shoulders one last squeeze, then lets me go. "Just know that I'm here, all right? If you ever want to talk. Or drink wine and watch *Star Wars*. Or get back into the studio and dance. Or whatever. Okay?"

"Okay," I say. I bend down and kiss her forehead, and hope it's enough to tell her how grateful I am, to have friends in my life who can just listen and be present and hold space, figuratively, and hold me, literally. I don't know where I'd be without them.

In early May, I develop an infection around the site of my G-tube. It's mild, and easily cleared up, and only puts me in the hospital for a couple of nights. It's still fucking horrible, though. There's pain there, a dull constant ache, a tenderness, that radiates out towards my entire lower body, and which will take a while to fully heal.

Much worse than the pain, though, is the rusty feeling of resignation that has settled over me ever since the evening we checked my stoma and found it all yucky and red and swollen. There was a time in my life, before the lung transplant, where lengthy and traumatic hospital stays, though always fucking horrible, were a part of my life. I hated them. But I also accepted them as part of being me, and I found ways to live my life around them. Then the lung transplant happened. And I thought maybe that chapter of my life was over. That made me feel elated. Now I fear that era has returned, like the bad guy in one of them horror movies that's always coming back. I don't feel like screaming and running into the woods, though. Nah, I ain't got that kinda energy. If this is the terror that's in store for me again, I'm gonna have to sit back and ride it out.

I will also have to head into the dusty cupboards at the back of my mind, toss away the drop cloths, shake out and unearth all my old methods for finding joy in my life around chronic illness. I let all those parts of the anatomy of my soul see the sunlight again.

While I'm still recovering from the infection, Andre catches a cold. He says, "It's like my body knows we're off work for a while now, like it's safe for us to get sick." He's worried about me getting sick too, though. Just before the infection, Paloma and I had been planning to spend a few days together. So the three of us decide that now would be a good time for me to go away with her. She asks me if it would be okay for her to take me on a little road trip.

"A tiny, tiny one," she says.

I know Andre isn't thrilled about this. We had always planned that my first real trip away from New York would be with him. I ask him, "Do you not want me to go? 'Cause I won't go if you don't want me to."

"I don't not want you to go," he says with a sigh. "Mira, I want you to be happy. And safe. Go on this trip with Paloma. You and I will go away somewhere this summer."

"Are you sure you're okay with this?"

He looks at me for a long moment. Then he says, "I think this is one of those things I can't hold too tightly to, Mira. Things change, and it's okay.

It's not a race. I'm off from work until September. This summer we will go on a trip. For now, go on this trip with Paloma."

So on a warm, sun-drenched Wednesday in May, Paloma picks me up outside of my apartment building in a car. The car itself reminds me of her: it's red and low-slung, sexy and sleek, with a smooth sand-colored leather interior. It has all these futuristic-looking controls and seems to hum and glide along the roads. The air-conditioning is perfectly cool, the sound system playing flamenco music at a low volume but in an all-around, encompassing way, like the music is holding us in the palm of its hand.

"You are so sexy driving," I tell her, looking over to see her gold-edged sunglasses, her concentration on the street in front of us, her hands on the wheel, the little muscles moving in her forearms. She's wearing an emerald and diamond bracelet, on her middle finger a ring with a big blue *mal ojo* for its stone. I swallow. "Thank you so much for taking me on this trip."

"My pleasure," she says.

As the minutes pass by, the crowding of New York City thins and strings itself out into a bridge, carrying the two of us over the river and away from this place. My body, the site of so many sensations both visible and invisible to the eye, floats with a curious sense of lightness as we cross the border. I still feel the dull throb of my lower belly, and a persistent nausea like what I imagine seasickness must be like: integral, inescapable, part of the very ground you walk on. I wouldn't know for sure, as I've never been on a boat before. But I also feel like I have left some measure of what happened to me behind, even if temporarily. Maybe it ain't the epic border-crossings of our ancestors. But, for me, it is the first time my body has ever left the state where I was born.

We cross the bridge and enter New Jersey, New York's neighboring state that I have never been to before. I am not sure exactly where we are going, only that Paloma said, "I have something I really want to show you. I think you're gonna like it." Highways with exits to tall buildings and chain stores and strip malls dissipate like noise into silence, giving way to long expanses of nothingness, walls of thick green trees on either side of us, little rivers snaking their way through, rocky hills with ancient veins, the material from which, you can imagine, these roads were carved many years ago. Paloma tells me that dinosaur fossils were found decades ago in great quantities in New Jersey; she says that, millions of years ago, southern New Jersey, where Atlantic City and the Jersey shore are, was underwater, while the northern half of the state, where we are right now, was home to dinosaurs and prehistoric crocodiles and giant mastodons and woolly mammoths. I'm not sure what a mastodon is, but I believe woolly mammoths are the ones with the shaggy brown fur and enormous curving tusks, bigger than elephants.

Along with this paleontology lesson, as we drive, Paloma asks gently how I am feeling. This hospital stay was much different from my last one, and not only 'cause of its much shorter duration. This time, I texted Paloma about my suspected infection on my way to the hospital, and received video calls and funny memes and cute photos from her the entire time. When I got home, a bouquet of gigantic pink, purple, and white lilies, exuberant with their wide-open faces, was waiting for me from her, along with several bags of groceries. (My girl Araceli, who has sent me a gift after every hospital stay over the past several years, sent yellow roses. I am so spoiled.)

It ain't easy, but I tell her, in painful, halting words, gazing forward at the endlessly unrolling blue ribbon of sky and not over at her, about my hospital stay. I tell her that they decided to replace my tube, that there's a brand-new gastrostomy tube under my shirt right now. I am still testing negative for CF-related diabetes; she says how wonderful that is, and it makes me smile. I'm to wait a little while before trying to go back to work at Anthropologie, and then only to work short shifts and take it easy until I've done a little more healing. I tell her I'm still in some pain, feeling tender and a little sick but not broken.

"I just want you to know," I add, sliding my eyes over to her briefly as my heart pounds, "that I am okay to have sex. As long as we keep it gentle. I've actually been touching myself a lot the past couple of days."

"Have you?" The heat and the delight in her voice make me flush.

"Yeah. I have." I close my eyes and relish my heartbeat whooshing in my ears, the thick, salty pulse of my blood behind my ribcage. "I've been feeling kind of sexy. Plus, orgasms help with my pain management." I pause. "Along with, you know, actual pain medication."

I laugh, and Paloma laughs too, and though her laughter is kind of shaky, damn, have we come far, the two of us.

The warmth of the sun in the early afternoon, through the glass of the windshield, begins slowly to make me drowsy. I feel myself starting to drift, blissfully letting go of the thready pain beating through the blood vessels in my lower stomach. I lean my head against the door hot from the sunshine and close my eyes.

I awaken to the car easing to a stop. I don't open my eyes right away, my body clinging to the pain-free peace of sleep, my mind clinging stubbornly to a dream, an empty caterpillar shell rattling against the bark of a tree. Paloma turns off the air-conditioning; my skin registers the sudden steamy hot of the leather inside of the car. Quiet reigns when the rumbling of the engine is switched off. Without the white noise of the car, the music is louder; I look at the warm orange sun-glow on my inner eyelids and catalog the individual sounds that make up the sonic magic of the flamenco: the romantic twang of the guitar, the mournful wail of the song about love lost, claps and snaps and the percussion of flamenco high heels beating a wooden stage.

Paloma turns off the music. There's nothing for a moment, then another sound reaches my ears: a low buzz that seems to be coming from far away. It makes warm tears gather under my eyes, pooling at the seams of my lashes. I don't know why, I don't even know what the sound is; it just makes me nostalgic, for a summer I've never had, for I don't know what. I tuck myself smaller, a fruitless attempt to burrow back down into sleep. I don't want to wake up.

I feel Paloma's hand gentle on my shoulder. She unclips my seatbelt with a soft click. I inhale her scent, which is different than usual, lighter: something both salty and sweet, like vanilla melting over an ice cream cone, and a faint sheen of sweat, and her hair smells like roses. "Mira?" she says. Her fingertips press my shoulder. "Honey, we're here."

"Mmm," I say.

"Miranda? Sweetheart, are you okay?"

I open my eyes. "I'm okay. Are we here?"

"Yes, baby, we're here. Shall we go inside?"

I stir myself into an upright sitting position. "Yes. I'm sorry. Let's go inside."

"Don't be sorry," she says. She smiles at me, pushing her sunglasses onto the top of her head, her eyes crinkling a little bit at the corners. "I'm glad you got some sleep."

"Where are we?" I ask Paloma as we get our stuff out of the trunk. She carries most of my things, including my guitar, which I brought so I could play for her. I squint at the house we've parked next to, in a driveway up a slight hill. It's a cute farmhouse-style place, a light yellow like butter, with a pointed roof, a porch, two windows on the second floor like eyes. There's a walkway leading from the sidewalk that cuts through the neighborhood up to the front door of the house, curvy and lined with flowerpots of violets.

"What is this place?" I ask. Paloma has tapped something on her phone that makes the garage door open, unfolding from the ground with a slow, lumbering creak. "Is this an Airbnb?"

"No," Paloma says, leading the way into the garage. She tosses a smile back at me. "I own it."

"You… what?" I follow her into the garage. It's musty and hot, crowded with stacks of boxes, and smells of dust and paint. She flicks on a light and closes the garage door, which closes the way it opened, rolling towards the ground with a labored mechanical whirr. "You own here?"

"Yep." She leads us up a set of rickety wooden stairs to a door, which she unlocks. "Not even my parents, baby. It's my name on the deed and on the mortgage." We enter through the door, which opens into the kitchen. "I just closed on it two weeks ago. You are the first person to come here with me. My parents haven't even seen it yet."

"Wow. That's incredible, Paloma. Congrats. And thank you."

"My pleasure. How about I take our stuff up to the bedroom, and you just chill and make yourself comfortable? Anything you see you want, you can have."

The house is in a state of partial unpacking. There are boxes of dishes on the countertops, a set of glasses in jewel tones in the deep sink, brand-new, stickers still affixed to their bottoms. But the glass-fronted cabinets are full of boxes of cereal and bags of chips, the fridge is full of food, there are three tubs of ice cream in the freezer. I go into the bathroom to pee after our long drive, there's a basket of rolls of toilet paper, still wrapped, on the floor, a box of fancy round soaps on the back of the toilet, with delicate flavors like lavender, linen, and honey, enticing as wrapped pieces of candy. The sink is a big round white marble bowl, the faucet long and polished silver. The bathtub is pink, wide and deep. There's one window in the bathroom, high and small, with thick, bubbly glass, and a pot of perfect pink hydrangeas on the sill, the tiny prolific flowers growing towards the sun. In the living room, there's nothing but three empty bookshelves and a couch, light purple and extremely soft. I slip off my *chancletas* by the door and sit down on the couch. I pull my phone out of my back jeans pocket and start taking photos.

I hear Paloma coming back down the stairs. "Mira, you want anything?" she calls through to me. "Something to eat? Some water?"

"I'd love some water, thank you."

Paloma comes into the living room with a bottle of water for each of us. She kicks off her sandals and sits with me, pulling a fuzzy pink blanket, shot through with crinkly gold threads, off the back of the couch and draping it over her lap. She offers me a corner of it, and I snuggle under it with her.

"I shouldn't sit here and lie, though," she says. "I obviously was only able to buy this place because of my parents' money. And they're super on board with the idea. I sold a bunch of jewelry and took a little cash out of my trust fund for the down payment. I'm responsible for the mortgage, though. I've started teaching some more private dance classes. I have this couple who want to learn ballroom. And I'm working with this twelve-year-old girl who's extremely talented. I'm really excited about her."

"Paloma, come on, don't minimize it," I say, nudging her knee with mine under the blanket. "You've just bought your own place and that's freaking amazing." I take a private moment to wonder which would feel more foreign and unbelievable for me: to have parents who support me and my dreams, or to have diamond jewelry and a trust fund just lying around for whenever I want to use them. Then I get over myself and let that thought go. "Congratulations. I am so proud of you, *nena*."

"Thank you." She beams at me. "Will you come outside with me? I want to show you something, Mira."

Paloma takes me through the back door in the kitchen and into the yard. I gasp when I see it, I can't help it. The small space is lush with trees, casting their enchanted, green-dappled shade over a tiny garden. There's a profusion of rosebushes, a tangle of tomato vines, grapevines growing along a wooden wall, clusters of begonias. She shows me where she's growing romaine lettuce and kale. I ask her about the trees: she has two cherry trees that have already lost their blush-pink blossoms in April, a peach tree, a tulip tree, and three magnificent oaks. "I can't wait to see them in the fall," she says, putting her hand on the tree's bark. "They're gonna be so gorgeous when they get their fall foliage." She meets my eyes. Her eyes glow like amber in the sunlight, flecks and threads of gold. "Will you come back with me here in the fall and see, Mira?"

"Of course I will," I say.

As a witch, a kitchen witch, I'm a wild girl who loves the natural world. As a sick girl, I am someone who's spent her life regrettably divorced from nature, often tucked away inside. Somehow, I am both. So, finding myself for the first time in Paloma's garden feels both like entering a new world I have never once visited before, and like coming home. But I don't have to speak or to explain myself. She sits under one of the oak trees and lets me explore. It's small but dense and lush, perfect for a garden newbie like me.

It's springtime, everything is tender and new. The rosebushes are just beginning to bud, tightly held, velvety red and pink baby flowers like curled newborns. I touch them tenderly. They'll be large, luscious blooms come summertime, their perfume heavy on hot air. The grapes and tomatoes are tiny and hard; they'll soften and grow juicy and plump. The growing peaches are so sweet they make me feel dizzy. The fruits grow in green clusters, as fuzzy as every myth about springtime has said they should be. I imagine them, too, just a handful of weeks into the future, after the summer solstice. The sun will turn them to a lush, golden-red color, cleft and bursting, tiny green leaves still clinging to their tops. I can come and pick them and we can eat them raw in sunlight in the garden, juice dripping down our wrists and chins. We can bring them indoors in her little farmhouse kitchen and peel and wash them, immerse and drench them in syrup. We can blend them with butter and cake mix and sprinkle them with nutmeg and cinnamon, smell them releasing their substantial sweetness as they cook down in a peach cobbler. If we don't pick all of them in time, they'll grow too heavy for their branches and plop heavily down into the garden. Their soft skin will break and bruise, exposing hard pits. Insects will crawl over them and eat them. They'll decompose with a sour-sweet smell, fertilizing the garden soil for the next season.

I sit down next to Paloma under the tree. I brush off the bottoms of my feet. I'm not sure I've ever been outside barefoot in a garden before. "Will you live here in the summer and garden?" I ask her.

"I'll probably be back and forth," she says. "I've hired some gardeners and landscapers who'll help me too." She squeezes the bun on the top of my head. "Will you come and stay with me for a while in the summer and garden with me?"

"You kidding? Girl, I'd love to."

She smiles, takes my hand and kisses the inside of my wrist, where my hummingbird is. "I knew you'd love it here, *nena*. I looked at a lot of houses. I loved this one as soon as I walked in. Then I came out back and saw the garden and I just knew for sure. It made me think of you."

"I'm so happy for you, Paloma, owning your own place."

"Come here," she says, opening her arms, and I slide closer to her, feeling tree bark sticking to the back of my T-shirt. She folds me in her arms and kisses me in the garden in the shade, and my heart swells, it's every fantasy rolled into one.

When we come up for air, she says, "I thought we could maybe take a walk into the town. It's so cute. So many adorable stores. I think you'll really like it. You know, if you feel like it. It's about a mile away, a good walk. Or we could drive if you don't feel like the walk right now."

"Nah," I say, "a walk would be good for me. And I'm feeling okay."

She nods. "Then maybe we could have something to eat. If you're hungry."

"Yeah. I should eat." I touch her breasts gently, one under each hand. "Then maybe you could show me your bedroom."

She smiles. "I'd love to."

We go back inside and put on our shoes and leave for our walk to the town. I'm not feeling especially well, but I really want to be out with my girl, not at home, recovering, so I go anyway. It's an act of pure will and desire. We walk slowly up the steep neighborhood towards the downtown. The houses along the way are all charming, some large and some small like Paloma's, with front-yard gardens or porches with adorable swings or flowers flanking the paths up to the front doors or bits of sparkly art clinging to their front windows. I can just imagine this neighborhood in the fall, wrapped in harvest colors. They probably put carved pumpkins on their porches, and hang lights from every available surface at Christmas. I wonder if I could ever live in a place like this.

The town is as cute as she promised, though we don't see a single other dark-skinned person the entire time. There's a bookstore with a fat, fluffy black cat stalking amongst the aisles. Paloma squeals with delight at the sight of the cat, sits down on the floor to stroke and cuddle it. "I had no idea you were a cat person, *mi nena*," I say.

She smiles up at me, rubbing the cat's scruffy neck with vigor. "I travel too much to really take good care of a pet," she says. "But yeah, I love animals."

Paloma insists on buying me a copy of bell hooks' *All About Love*, which she's appalled I've never read. "You're gonna love it," she promises.

We look in a witchy store, selling crystals and tarot cards and sage and amulets and tea blends. There's a little park at the end of the main street with a romantic white gazebo, an ice cream shop, a Starbucks and another café, tiny fancy restaurants with an astonishing array of global cuisines

(Thai, Indian, Ethiopian, Peruvian, Japanese, and New Jersey diner), a massage place, a boutique fitness studio, and, at the other end of town, a small sex shop. It's high-end and minimalist, with just a few items, a woman with long, lustrous red hair behind the counter. Paloma and I choose a couple bottles of lube—it's become an essential part of my sex life lately, I just don't get as wet as I used to—and a set of candles that melt down into massage oil.

We stop at a Turkish bakery that's playing breathy, airy flute music, with evil eyes and hands of Fatima on the walls. Paloma gets baklava and a cup of extraordinarily strong, dark Turkish coffee. I just get Turkish tea in a little glass, no food, because I'd like to be able to eat lunch with her when we get home like a normal person. I watch her eat the pastry, licking honey and bits of crushed nuts from the corners of her lips, and listen to her talk about some of her many trips to Turkey to do research and archaeology. She talks about the country's layers of strata—Hittite, the supposed Trojan War, medieval Ottoman, tombs of Sufi saints—and about a friend of hers, who has been banned from the country for participating in pro-Kurdish protests. As always when she gets going like this, I understand maybe forty percent of what my girl is saying. Like, I'm not totally sure what Sufis or Kurds are. Maybe when I start school in the fall I can take some history classes, learn to keep up with her. My heart floats on the surface of my blood like a lily pad in a swamp.

We walk back to the house. Paloma slides her hand in my back jeans pocket like a high-school girlfriend. This is so cute. Back at the house, she asks if I'd like to eat lunch, and I say okay, and she smiles and says, "How about you sit out in the garden and I serve you?" And I laugh and say sure.

So I sit at the elaborate wrought iron table in her garden and she brings us food. She brings a fresh, colorful salad in a wooden bowl: bright, glossy green lettuce; crisp red and yellow peppers; thin, pale slices of cheese; wrinkled, gray-black olives, plump and savory; and large crunchy croutons a light toasted color. She says she made the croutons herself; I say, "Wow. Fuck." She serves the salad with a pair of actual salad tongs, which make me feel like a fine and elegant lady, not a little girl who grew up eating chicken and peas when Mom or *Abuela* was around to cook, homemade Rice Krispie treats with M&M's when they weren't and my brother and I were home alone. We'd stand over the pot on the stove and melt butter and big puffed marshmallows until they formed a sticky goo, then fold in the delicate crisps of the cereal. We'd toss in M&M's and layer the whole concoction in a casserole pan. Once it cooled, we'd cut the dessert into squares and eat it in front of episodes of *Hannah Montana.*

I think about this as Paloma and I place little piles of salad onto cream-colored plates. Instead of salad dressing she has olive oil, imported from Greece, she says. It has a rich, intense flavor. "Can I tell you a myth?" she says, and I say sure. So she says that once, long ago, the Greek gods got into a competition about who would become the patron god of the greatest of the Greek cities, Athens. It came down to Poseidon and Athena, who each gave the citizens of Athens gifts to seduce the people into choosing them. Poseidon gave them horses, best companions of humankind. But Athena gave them the olive tree: sacred to philosophers and scholars, able to live for five hundred years or more, abundant with their incomparable fruits that can be pressed into the oil that would anoint champions and come to symbolize an entire region. "And so they chose her," she concludes.

Paloma also brings out a wooden tray arranged with cold ingredients to make sandwiches: slices of cured meats in juicy pinkish colors, yellow cheese separated with translucent squares of paper, little pots of spicy mayo, miniature pickles with bumpy skins, bread rolls studded with seeds. I like this method of eating, where you just take as much or as little as you want. It makes me feel less pressure to eat the way I think everybody else is eating.

As we sit in the sunny afternoon in the garden and eat, Paloma says, "Can I tell you some stuff about my family? Some stuff that's been bothering me?"

"Of course, *mi nena*," I say, and sit back and listen.

"I'm worried about my mom," she says.

Both of Paloma's parents are doctors. They are also getting older; they're both around seventy years old. Paloma's parents had her when they were older, after many years of fertility issues; they were about forty, like my mom and Magdalena. Her dad is an anesthesiologist, and he's still able to continue working, especially as he's moved into more of a supervisory role as he's gotten older. "But it's different," she says, "for my mom."

Paloma's mother, Dr. Mariana Rodriguez, is—yeah, you gotta wait for this one, y'all—a pediatric cardiologist, specializing in operating on the hearts of infants. In fact, she is one of the top specialists in the world in her field, having performed surgeries once thought impossible, authoring innovative research, even inventing some kind of device to help repair arterial valves about a decade ago. Her hands are insured. But she's getting older now and the once-famous steadiness of her surgeon's hands is beginning to deteriorate.

"She's gonna have to retire from surgery," Paloma says, "and it's really messing her up."

She says her mom has changed, become withdrawn, uncommunicative, frequently ill, when she used to be one of them people who never get sick. "I'm scared she's depressed," she says, "and I really want her to get help, talk to someone, but I don't know how to bring it up with her. My mom's one of those people who's all like, oh, no one can understand me, my life really isn't like anyone else's." Paloma tempers her voice as she imitates her mother, performing a dramatic gesture with her wrist.

I smile sadly. "Can I ask you this? What was it like, baby, growing up with her?"

She shrugs, retreating a little into her body, the way you do when someone asks you a question you've never quite been asked before. "I mean, like, it was cool. My parents are really wealthy. They both came from rich families. Then they were both able to build really successful careers of their own. I had access to all kinds of stuff. I was able to have incredible experiences."

"*Bien de bien,* baby," I say. "Your girl gets it. You have rich-person guilt. I hear you. Now please give me some more real talk."

She smiles wryly. "Okay, girl. My parents always supported whatever I wanted to do. Even when I made some… nontraditional choices with my life. And that always made me kinda wonder, you know? I mean, my mother has the biggest savior complex on planet earth. She's spent my entire life flying around the world, doing research and saving these tiny sick babies. Which is, like, so… heroic. Or whatever. And she tried her best with me, for sure. We're very close. She always did her best to be as involved with me and my education, and my choices, and my pursuits, as she could be. But I always grew up feeling like… well, like her career, all those sick babies she was put here on earth to save, are more important to her than her only daughter." She puts one of the small pickles into her mouth and sucks on it, self-consciously. "I am being ridiculous, aren't I? You can tell me, Mira, if I'm being ridiculous. I truly have nothing to complain about here, and I know it. And I—"

"Baby girl, c'mon, stop." I reach out and squeeze her wrist. "You ain't being ridiculous. At all. You're my girl. You can tell me anything. You can share any feeling with me." I lean close and kiss her, tasting the pickle she's eating. "We've all got hurts and traumas from our childhood. Ain't none of them harder or easier than any others."

Her eyes are big and shiny. "Thanks," she says. "So do you think I should try to talk to her?"

I feel a moment of self-doubt. Many times during our childhood we tried to convince Mom to get help, real help. Marco was usually the one who handled conversations like that. They typically ended with Mom screaming in his face, asking him who the fuck he thought he was, telling her how to live her life. "I have a problem?" she'd say. "Boy, you don't know the first thing about having problems." This treatment center she's at now is the first time, I think ever in her life, that Mom's sought real help. And she certainly didn't go 'cause Marco and I succeeded in convincing her. She went because her new baby is her do-over, her second chance. So what the fuck do I know about talking to your parent about seeking help?

It still happens, this nasty-ass self-doubt, yeah. But I can say that I catch it quicker. That ain't truth. That ain't my wise inner self. That ain't my highest guidance. That's a voice of maternal trauma inside me, telling me for the millionth time that I ain't good enough.

So I take a deep breath and say to my girl, who's waiting to hear what wisdom I got, "Yeah, I do, Paloma. You and your mom are close. Y'all love each other. When there's love there, I think you can say stuff like that. I mean, it's possible she won't be that happy about it at first. But you can tell her you ain't trying to make her decisions for her. It's just that you love her and you're worried about her, and you want her to have all the resources. 'Cause, like, I'm sure that retiring, especially from a career like that where it's such a big part of who she is... *eso es muy duro.* She should have support, yeah?"

Paloma nods.

"And, hey, maybe you can talk to your dad too?"

"Yeah." She leans closer. "I mean, I want to. We haven't really talked about it yet, Dad and me. But you don't think my mom will be pissed? If Dad and I are talking about her behind her back?"

"It ain't behind her back. Y'all are family. They're married, and they're your parents. You should be a team, yeah? And, like, mental health is complex. Just as complex as physical health. I know your mom knows that, being a big-shot doctor and all. I know she swoop in there and fix babies' hearts, but she's got a whole team in there with her, believe me. People get better in community. Or not at all. This isn't something you, or your dad, or even your mom, can handle on your own."

She nods slowly, taking this in. She swipes away a few tears with her knuckles. "Thanks, baby," she says. "Thanks for listening to me."

"Girl. Come on. You don't gotta thank me."

"Okay," she says. "It's just. I don't really think it's that easy. For me. To, like, open up about shit."

I nod. "I know."

"Come here?" she says. "I want to hold you."

So I get up and go sit in her lap. She winds her arms around me. My stomach is starting to hurt, but it feels good to be held. I watch a bee, gold in sunlight, dip its heavy body, fuzzy with its curled legs, into the centers of the begonias, sampling flower after flower. Pollen will be clinging to those little bee legs, helping flowers have their distant, assisted sex with one another. This is how nature regrows the world.

"Thanks for talking to me about this stuff," Paloma whispers again, her breath against my body. My intuition tells me that this is not the only thing, maybe not even the real thing, that's been bothering her. I also know that, sometimes, it takes a while to reach the inner layers. But your girl can be patient. I lean close and try to tell her this with a kiss.

She smiles against my lips. "Mira? Can I ask you a question?"

"Yeah, sure."

"Do you believe in fairies?"

I have to smile back. "Do I? Of course I do. You kidding me?"

"Well, is there a way I can see them? And connect with them?"

"Of course there is," I say. "You can write the fae a letter. Do it on special paper; fairies love beautiful things. You can burn it at your altar at the full moon. Or, even better, you can bury it here, in your garden." I look around. "Did you get yourself this garden just so you could meet some fae?"

Paloma flutters her pretty lashes. "I mean, I didn't not get it so I could meet some fae."

I give her a playful nudge. "Thought you chose it 'cause it reminded you of me."

She nuzzles my nose with hers. "Both," she says.

"Well, it is the perfect place to attract and connect with fairies," I say. "They are gonna love it here. Get yourself some fairy art. Statues or pictures or signs. Then they'll know they're welcome here."

"Mira." She presses her lips to mine, gently, but with heat. "I want to take you upstairs and unbutton those jeans and open your lips and touch your pretty clit. I want to lick your nipples."

"Paloma," I whisper.

"Does that sound good?"

"That sounds incredible. Wanna show me your bedroom now?"

She squeezes me. "Can I carry you?"

"Okay."

Paloma picks me up easily and carries me inside. I hold onto her neck. "I better bring all that food inside first," she says, depositing me gently onto the couch. "*Quédate aquí*, okay? I wanna carry you the rest of the way upstairs."

"Okay, *mi nena*."

Paloma brings in the trays of food, taking them through to the kitchen. Then she returns for me, swinging me up into her arms again.

"Girl." I draw my tongue over her lips. "It is so fucking hot that you can carry me."

"Well, you're the perfect size for me to carry." She begins to climb the staircase. "Can I ask how tall you are, Miranda?"

"Sure, baby. I'm four-foot-nine."

She nods. "That's about what I thought. I am exactly one foot taller than you."

"That is so cool."

"I'm gonna put you down here, *mi sirena*. I wanna show you something."

Paloma has set me down in front of the open door to a literal, actual dance studio, right here in her house. There is a wall of mirrors and a barre set along the perimeter of the room and long windows that allow sunlight to spill all over the floor. "Can I go inside?" I ask her.

"Of course you can."

I go into the studio; she follows me. I realize the floor is some kinda special material, a pale gray color and springy. I reach out and put my hand on the barre.

"Paloma. This is amazing."

She looks around. "It is pretty cool, huh? I can teach my online classes for Auntie Lisette's studio here. And I already had a class here with my private client, the twelve-year-old girl I was telling you about, yesterday. She lives in Westfield. That's another one of these little New Jersey towns."

"Andre should come here and dance with you too," I say.

She smiles. "I would love that."

"He'd love it here. Can I take some pictures for him?"

She spreads her arms open. "Be my guest."

I take photos of the dance studio for Andre and send them to him. Then I put my phone in my pocket and slip my hands under Paloma's hair, holding her head in my hands. "I seem to remember an invitation to your bedroom."

She closes her eyes, smiles. "Come with me."

Paloma's bedroom is the most lived-in of the rooms of her new house so far, a little messy, like her bedroom at her apartment, with the door to the walk-in closet open and clothes scattered on the floor. It's cozy and pink. My bag is on the desk next to her MacBook, my guitar propped against the pink wall. Our new bottles of lube are arranged perfectly on the bedside table. Paloma sits down on the fuzzy pink blanket on the bed and draws me to her by my belt loops. She undoes the button on my jeans.

I hold her wrists. "Give me a second, *nena*? I should go to the bathroom."

"Okay," she says.

I go to the bathroom—leaving the door open; I hope that's okay with her, but y'all know me, I like that kind of intimacy—and come back to the bedroom to find her lying on her bed in nothing but her lace bra and underwear, her belly spilling prettily over the red waistband. I practically lose my breath.

"God," I say. "You are fucking gorgeous, Paloma."

She gets up too. "I'll be right back. Don't go anywhere, baby."

I don't go anywhere. I stand and look out her bedroom window, which faces out onto the garden. I keep my eyes peeled for little random sparks or flashes of light on the air, a sure sign of the presence of the fae. I don't see any, but the fairy realm cannot be rushed, and fairies can sometimes be shy. There's plenty of time yet.

She returns and stretches out on the bed. I come to the edge again, and she pulls me to her, with force this time, and unbuttons and unzips me. She sits up, belly on her thighs, hair flowing onto her face, her breathing going fast and deep. She pushes my jeans and panties down my legs. I pull them down the rest of the way and step out of them.

"You're so hot," she tells me. "I love this tattoo. I love your bush."

She curls her fingers in it. I hear myself gasp.

I pull off my shirt and toss it on the floor. I am not wearing a bra. She gasps too.

"Do you still find me sexy?" I whisper.

"Mira," she says.

"I mean, with the G-tube."

"Miranda," she says. She cups my boobs gently. "You're so hot it's, like, volcanic."

Laughing, I climb over her onto the bed. She surrenders under me, looking up at me with a sigh. She works the elastic out of my hair and runs her hands through it. Her hands feel so good on my scalp, I purr. I press my lower body gently into hers, feeling the warm, bare skin of her mound against my curls. I know she's wet in there, between her puffy lips, and I tremble all over, anticipating the moment I'll get my fingers in there to feel her.

"Mira," she says. She clutches my biceps. "God. I know I probably shouldn't be asking you this right now. Tell me to fuck off and ask you later, like when we're not naked, if you need me to. But." She nibbles my lips. "Would you like to meet my mom and dad? I mean." She lowers her lashes. She shifts on the bed, and I can smell her, that sweet musk of her arousal; it makes my mouth water. "I know you already know my parents. You've known them for years. They were even at your wedding. But I'd love for you to meet them as my partner. As my girlfriend."

"Paloma." I allow myself exactly one second of feeling bad—imagine what it would be like to have parents you could introduce your married polyamorous girlfriend to, and know that it would be okay—before I smile at her. "I would love to meet your parents. As your girlfriend."

She kisses me, a real kiss this time, parted lips and the curl of her tongue sweetly around mine and the hint of her teeth sinking gently into my lower lip. I squirm impatiently, my tongue reminded by the feel of the inside of her mouth of the taste and inner texture of her cunt. "Oh, Miranda," she says, slipping one of her thighs in between mine. "Thank you. I love you so much."

"I love you too, *mi nena.*"

I wrestle her down onto her back. She looks up at me starry-eyed, enchanted with the side of me that is dominant and takes charge and is aggressive. I hold her wrists above her head, pressing her like I could keep her there, like I could keep her from getting away. That she does not want to get away, that she would submit willingly to an illusion in which I have the power to affect the tide of the future that is coming, this is all part of the fantasy. Magic ain't any less magic when you're the magician herself, when you are in on the secret.

I press my hands to her hands and run my palms down the fleshy, exposed insides of her arms and skim the sides of her breasts, trace the shape of her curves and bring myself soft as a whisper to the seam of her thighs. She opens to me seamless as water, with a moan. And I wonder, as I part her, if she and I could be with each other as water is: taking the shape of the vessel that contains our love, gives it boundaries; and flowing with the current towards the river-mouth; and undulating our way into each other's lives in sinuous but insistent rhythm, water carving bed into rock. I part her open like an oyster shell, with much more give but no less treasure. This girl is my divinatory rune, my conch shell; the salty fragrance of her and the wet squelch when I put my fingers in her reminding me of the sea.

I make her come until she asks me to stop. I sit back and feel satisfied and rather smug, a cavewoman licking her bones clean. My anxiety ain't something that ever turns off, not even during sex. My erotic anxiety always is, and more so when I make love to women, whether I am making my partner feel good. I still feel so inexperienced when it comes to sex, so devoid of tricks, clueless and young, unsure if I'll be able to bring real pleasure. I'm still feeling too fragile right now, because of the infection and the small surgery to install a new tube, to wear my strap-on and fuck her with it. I know that ain't the only way to have sex. I know that there are so many ways to make love, to share pleasure. But I also know how much she likes it when I fuck her. So I've gotta say I feel a warm glow of joy, seeing her lying under me unraveled and undone, her chest heaving as she tries to catch her breath, her breasts dewy with sweat.

I like our slower, unhurried pace today, how we just switch places and then I lie still and get to enjoy her focusing on me, the simplicity of us touching each other, first one and then the other. I lie there naked and feel air on my body, the cool of her pink sheets under me. Paloma is exquisitely tender with my body today. She massages my hands and strokes the soft undersides of my forearms with her thumbs. She presses the wet, wide-open circle of her mouth to my shoulders and the hollow of my neck and my navel and just below, something between an imprint and a kiss, a sucking, a gentle devouring, sweet and almost vampiric. I bend one leg at the knee to open my legs and give her good access. She touches me with delicacy, hooking her finger inside me and touching my clit and my folds and my inner lips like taking something apart with patience and attention; something that feels messy, earthy, immediate, like defeathering and plucking a chicken clean, juicing a lemon, gently scraping tender insides from a shell. She drizzles me with thick strands of lube like syrup, and the warm, sticky wet awakens me, smooths the passage of pleasure from deep inside me, lets my breath deepen and my heartbeat rise heavy into my throat. Coming back into my body, I remember the itch and swell of the infection, the discomfort of the silicone tube, a dull, coppery headache throbbing at my forehead, lingering pain from the surgery. All of these hurts are obliterated, even if just for a minute, by my orgasm.

While she touches me, Paloma whispers sweet things to me. She tells me how pretty my clit is, how much she's missed pulling lightly on my lips and hearing their wet slurping sounds, how beautiful I am and how much she loves me. She tongues my nipples. I think about that one mystical book about water, you know, the one everybody has read, the one that says that water makes beautiful crystalline structures at its molecular level when loving, delicious words are spoken over it. The things she says to me while she gives me pleasure, they make me sparkle. And ain't the human body composed mostly of water? So imagine how our own molecules must rearrange inside when we are spoken to with nourishing words.

Briefly released from the pain coiling my body in its prickly embrace, I fall into a light sleep after I come. When I wake up again, it's dark in the garden outside of Paloma's window, and I'm alone in her bed. Damn, how many hours have I slept? In Paloma's empty place in bed next to me, instead of her warm body, there's a note on a little piece of paper printed faintly with butterflies. *Sweet Mira*, it says, *you're home here so please do anything you like. Sleep as much as you need to. If you need me, I'll be in the studio. I love you.*

I put on pajama pants and my T-shirt, go to the bathroom and brush my teeth and wash my face. Then I go find Paloma in the studio. She's standing by the sound system, which is large and impressive, in a corner of the room, looking down at her phone. She looks up, and soft instrumental music begins to play, swelling up in the empty space.

She looks over and sees me standing in the studio doorway. She rests her phone on top of a speaker and approaches me. "Mira, hi. How are you? How did you sleep?"

"Good." I smooth my hair back on the top of my head. "God. I'm sorry I fell asleep for hours like that."

"Oh, honey. Please don't apologize. You're home here, yeah? So whatever you need to do." Her arms flutter at her sides. "Can I give you a hug?"

"God. Please."

I didn't realize how much I needed a hug from her—how much I needed to be held in her arms, calling me back to the world of the living after my sleep—until I have one. She presses me close to her heart, and we draw circles across each other's backs with gentle but satisfying force. I feel the bony wings of her shoulder blades, though I have to press my way with my palms through the thick muscles of her back in order to find them. It almost makes me cry, being able to seek and find these shoulder blades of hers, feeling this physical evidence of all the structures and systems inside her that make her capable of standing here with me, holding me. Inside, she is a skeleton, stretched with muscle and fascia and tendon and flesh, like we all are. Thinking of her like that, the bleach-white of her bones, makes me feel impossibly tender.

We let each other go lingeringly. She smiles at me. "I was just practicing some combos for the class I'm teaching tomorrow. We have a few young dancers who were just going on pointe for the first time about when the pandemic started. It sucks to be doing this online, but we're just taking it slow, only a few exercises and combinations per class, plus a whole bunch of ankle-strengthening practices."

"That's really cool," I say, with just a taste of old envy.

"Now I need to prep a couple pairs of pointe shoes," she says. "If you don't mind me spending a bit more time in the studio."

"Not at all. Hey, maybe I could grab my guitar and play a little bit for you? While you do that?"

She rests the backs of her fingers against my cheek, a brief, sweet touch. "I would love that."

I go to the bedroom and get my guitar, and when I come back, Paloma is sitting on the floor with her legs spread and stretched out in front of her, while she holds a pair of pointe shoes. I sit down near her, against the wall, and look curiously at the shoes. They're thicker and more substantial than I would have imagined ballet shoes to be from afar, with heft and weight and breadth. Their pink color is glossy and bright, so smooth as to be almost reflective. Next to her are also a sewing kit, pink satin ribbons, and a few other items whose purpose I can only guess at.

She looks at me looking with a little smile. "Have you ever seen a dancer prepare a new pair of pointe shoes before?"

I shake my head.

"Well, you're welcome to watch," she says.

"Looking forward to it," I say.

I play around on my guitar, just picking notes with a slight melancholy air while I watch Paloma prepare her pointe shoes. The process is nothing like what I would have imagined. She holds and manipulates them with a firmness that seems at odds with the stereotype of ballet, all airy and delicate and light. I would have said, though, that while elegant and completely lovely, Paloma is also really fucking strong and muscular and powerful. I watch her deconstruct each shoe: ripping up the inner lining from the sole, bending and folding the body of the shoe, finally slipping the shoe on to, of all things, stand on top of a cheese grater on the floor and grind the wide, hard toe of the shoe into the grater.

"It's weird, I know," she says, twisting her leg back and forth to grind the toe of the shoe into the little metal holes. "But this is how I wear away a few layers of the toe box to make it interact with the floor a little bit better."

I nod, feeling fascinated and enchanted, like I'm being invited into a secret world I didn't even know existed.

Paloma then conducts a surgery to restore the shoes to internal togetherness again: she reinforces the toe boxes with a few layers of thread, sewing with brisk, expert efficiency; she glues the lining back onto the soles; she sews a transparent piece of elastic across the shoes, which will rest at the top of her foot, and sews the ribbons to the backs of the shoes.

As she puts on the shoes and laces her ankles into the ribbons, she looks over at me and says, "Mira? Are you seriously playing flamenco guitar right now?"

Feeling my face get hot, I drop my fingers from the strings. "Uh, yeah, I guess? I ain't no expert or nothing. I'm just playing around, you know?"

Paloma shakes her head. "If you call that just playing around, I can't even imagine what you'd call playing for real."

"Ah, girl. Stop."

"No, you stop, Miranda. You are seriously so fucking talented. I can't even."

I manage to mutter a thank-you before focusing back down on my guitar. I pick up where I left off, finger-picking an approximation of a flamenco melody, romantic and sad. Paloma closes her eyes, listening, like I am playing something really worth hearing, not like I'm just an untrained girl, messing around. I look at her face, quiet and placid as she listens, a smile tugging at her lips and wisps of hair escaping from her braid to curl around her forehead and temples. After a while she stands up suddenly, still wearing her pointe shoes.

"Is this okay?" she says, making eye contact with me in the mirror.

I nod.

Then, something that has never happened to me before, not quite like this, happens. Paloma begins to dance to the music that I am playing. Sure, friends have gotten up when I've played a *salsa* or a *bachata* and spun each other in circles around the living room, or nodded their heads and moved their shoulders in time to a guitar rendition of a pop song. Andre and Paloma even danced to my version of "When Doves Cry" that one time. But I have certainly never had a former professional ballerina and ballet teacher dance en pointe in a real dance studio while I played freestyle flamenco, creating a choreography out of thin air as I conjure notes out of the same fertile nothingness. Most of her steps and aesthetic are clearly ballet, but she's talented enough, and familiar enough with the style, to throw in some flamenco, the distinctive hand flourishes, the toss and carriage of her head.

I start out tentative, playing quietly, but I hear myself gaining strength and confidence in what I'm playing, even as she, in the flesh before me and doubled in the mirror across the way, enlarges her movements, making them more dramatic, which for the flamenco style is exactly right. I pluck the strings harder and with more intentional force. I make mistakes, lots of them, and maybe she does too, I don't know—but there are no mistakes here, not when we are making something, together, that has never been made before. Her pointe shoes are loud against the floor, louder than I ever realized they would be up close from having heard them on stage. I play louder too, responding to her, or maybe her body is responding to me, or maybe we are caught in an endless, beautiful loop, like the snake consuming its own tail. I even start to sing, just a little bit, or not singing exactly, just vocalizing. I remember the times, not so long ago and, also, a lifetime, when I wouldn't have had the breath to sustain singing like this at the end of a day.

I feel a part of me, a part of my soul, peeling away from my body. There is my body itself, bent over the hollow wood and steel strings of my instrument, completely in flow and the magic of creating with this woman that I've fallen in love with. But part of me steals away, an observer avatar of me. She floats above, seeing the whole studio, and the arcs that Paloma describes around it, and me, the physical me, powerful and intent in coaxing sound from my guitar. My spirit swells. I know it's a horrible thought. But I wonder if this could be what it's like to be dead, maybe you detach from your physical body and become the eternal observer, watching all the turns and dramas of life on earth, but peaceful, warm-hearted, removed.

Then Paloma, in the midst of a complicated series of turns, loses her balance and falls into a heap on the floor. I gasp and set my guitar aside to rush to her, but she's already sitting up and laughing her head off, clearly just fine. She crawls over to me and meets me halfway, wraps her arms around me and kisses me with breathless hunger. Between kisses I feel the heaving of her body from its exertion, the sweat under her clothes, the crackling of the excitement between us, and underneath the throb of my own body, pain coming alive under my skin again as with every hour the day gets later. Now, with her in my arms, I am back, I am so alive and present that I couldn't possibly be anything else.

"Mira," she says, also between kisses, "can we go back to bed?"

She nibbles me, as if I am something sweet she cannot get enough of: my jawline, my lower lip, my earlobe, my chin. It feels so good. It's so good between us, this magic thing that has blossomed between Paloma and me despite all of my fears. And, as good as it feels, I do not feel good. It makes me so frustrated I could cry. I know, though, that there's no fighting it. I feel the way that I feel, in the material reality of this body. I reach up and hold her breasts, one in each palm. I want to tell her no, that I can't. I should. But I find, holding her breasts and feeling them breathing, hearing her make needy little whimpers in my ear, and feeling my pussy start to get wet in response to her, I cannot tell her no. I can't say no to my body's desire, no to the passion boiling between us.

"Okay, *mi nena*," I say instead.

So we go back to bed, dropping articles of clothing along the way, like in a dirty movie. This makes me feel excitingly adult, a sexy woman to whom astonishing things can happen. Paloma struggles out of her sweaty dance clothing, sits down on the edge of her bed when we get there to undo her pointe shoes. She points and flexes her feet. I sit down next to her and kiss her.

"Mira," she says, "can I take a shower?"

I kiss her, harder.

"Yeah," I say, "you, like, really, really don't need to."

"I don't?" she says against my mouth.

"Nope." I tug on her braid. "You are perfect like this."

"I don't know," she says, "I'm really gross."

"*Lo que quieras,*" I say. "Take a shower."

"Okay," she says. "I really feel like I need to."

"*Bien de bien,*" I say.

So I lie on Paloma's bed, naked, and wait for her to get out of the shower. I rest my hands on my belly, below the tube, and breathe into my hands. I listen to the shower sounds, and cars going by on the road outside, and kids laughing somewhere, and, when I get really quiet, the same low buzz that I heard when we first arrived here. It's practically undetectable if you don't silence your inner noise and listen to it, so natural as to be part of the soul of the place itself, woven seamlessly into the fabric of its landscape.

I let my fingers trace, very gently, the scar where they removed my pregnancy from me. Am I any more of a woman now?

Paloma comes back from the shower naked. She crawls directly over my body in a way that makes it impossible for me to do anything except hold her, grab my arms full of her body, and fall in love with her again. Her eyes are tender and soft. Her hair is still braided but the braid is wet, wet hair sticking to her temples, the end of the braid, fat as a horse's mane, trailing a stream of water down the curved valley of her spine. I feel it as I hold her around her back.

"Hi," she says, and kisses me.

"Hey." I breathe her in. She smells fresh and sweet, like oranges and cream.

"Paloma," I say.

"Yeah?" she says.

"Baby." I take a last deep breath and decide to go for it: following an intuitive nudge from deep within that doesn't seem to make any logical sense. I only know that it feels dark and forbidden and like exactly what she and I need right now. "Can I see your butt? I mean. I want to look at it. Touch you back there a little bit."

"Uh," she says. "Okay."

Paloma rolls off of me, gets on her hands and knees on the bed next to me. Her long braid spills off one shoulder. "This good?" she asks, twisting her head back to see me.

"Perfect."

She slides her knees apart, opening her cheeks to me. I cup each of her parted cheeks gently.

She shivers, all over, sucks in a quick, deep breath.

"You okay?" I whisper.

"Yeah," she says. "I guess I'm really sensitive back there." I hear her swallowing. "I haven't been touched there that much."

"This okay?"

"Okay," she says.

"You've got goosebumps all over," I tell her, tracing the inner curves of her ass cheeks with my thumbs. She laughs a little, getting used to my touch. "It's really beautiful."

She's beautiful. Her ass is perfect, round and brown and firm. I want to bite it. I don't think we're ready for that yet, though; maybe next time.

"Thanks," she says, breathless.

I look at her asshole. I've never seen a shaved one, not in real life. (I mean, I've only ever seen two people's butts in any detail, but y'all get what I'm saying.) I imagine her lying on her back on the waxer's table, bringing her legs to her chest. (I'm not actually sure if this is how assholes get waxed; I'm just guessing.) She's hairless and smooth. I can see the beautiful arrangement of her parts, the symmetry of it all that makes it seem like there's order in this universe.

"Mira?" she says. "I'm not gross back there, am I?"

I bite my lower lip, glad she can't see me. I want to laugh, but I know I better not.

"Girl," I say. "No, you ain't gross. You are, like, the total opposite of gross. What is the opposite of gross?" I put my thumb on her anus. She contracts it and closes her knees and almost screams. Then her scream ends on a moan and she opens her knees again, wider this time. "You're exquisite," I tell her. I start to rub circles on her anus, gently, then harder when her breathing picks up and she starts to moan again. "You're delicious and I love you."

"Mira." Her whole body is into it now, flowing and breathing, her spine undulating, her big breasts like two heavy pendulums, hanging off her chest. "I love you too." She puts her forearms on the bed and rests her head on them. "This feels really good."

"I'm so glad. You want some lube?"

"I'd love some."

I sit up on my knees, remembering how tired my body is, and its many hurts. I select one of our bottles of lube and squeeze a generous amount onto my fingers. She gasps and flinches when I touch her again with wet fingers, but I watch her relax into it, her skin softening, legs widening, asking me with every part of her body for more. Best of all is how she starts, subtly at first and then with more purpose, to inch her ass closer to me. I don't think we're quite ready for it yet, but maybe sometime it'll feel right for us to put my finger inside her.

I lean close and press my lips to her gently. I feel the cling of lube on my lips and I taste her.

"Oh, Mira," she says. "Oh, my God, Mira." I kiss her again, let the tip of my tongue touch her. "Mira. I don't… smell gross back there, do I?"

This time, I do laugh. "Oh, Paloma. Honey. No." I close my eyes, breathe her in, deeply. "Oh, my God, no. You smell incredible. I want to smell you like this all the time."

"Mira," she says. I see her fingers thread through the hair at the top of her head, her braid now loosened and disheveled. "Can you touch me? Please? I really want to come."

So I slip my middle finger into her, from behind. She's so wet she draws me in easily, almost like her body is fucking my finger instead of the other way around. She is different, responds differently, as I take her from behind, louder, more uninhibited. I put my thumb on her clit and she says yes, yes, so I start to rub her little erection—so velvet soft on the outside, hard and ridged like a tiny mountain inside—and she screams and gushes wet all down my finger.

"Oh, Mira, I'm sore," she says, after she's come and the tight, greedy mouth of her cunt finally lets me go. "Gentle, please."

"Tell me if this is okay," I whisper, putting my other hand on her hip as I extract my finger from her gently.

"It's okay," she whispers, as I pull my finger free. "God." She collapses onto her belly. "I'm so sore."

I sit next to her, leaning against the pillows. I'm exhausted. I put my hand on the sweaty back of her neck, her braid tucked over one shoulder. "Are you all right, *mi nena*? Are you in any pain?"

Paloma rolls over, lets me see her face. "I'm not in any pain, no. I'm just really sore. Mira. That felt amazing. But it was a lot."

"What do you need? Is there anything I can do?"

"Can you just hold me?" she says, so I slip myself down on the bed beside her and gather her into my arms. I feel the way I often feel when my girl Paloma and I hold each other: like we are regathering each other, mending each other's torn places.

I hold her till I feel my neck and my breasts slick with her tears. I pull back to look at her.

"Paloma?" I stroke her hair back. Her nose is swollen and red; I have a sudden flash of her twenty-five years ago, when I wasn't even born yet, when she was a little girl. "Are you okay? Can you tell me what's going on?"

She nods. Her lips are trembly. "I'm okay, Mira," she says. "I mean, I'm physically okay. I am not hurt. And I love what we did. Love it. It's not that. It's just…" Her eyes flood with a fresh wave of tears. "What we did, I feel like it… opened this dam inside me. On my emotions. On all the shit that's been going on for me lately. And…" She takes a big, brave, shuddery breath. I hold her through it, feeling her ribs, her fluttering inside. "Can I tell you about it, Mira?"

I hold her tighter. "Of course you can."

Paloma pulls herself up to a sitting position. I sit beside her. I have moved far past exhaustion now, into a state where I don't even know what to call it. But I also know, somehow, that I am safe, that this is right, that this is one of those moments—not epic, but mundane—that I've been preserving myself for, that I've been saving my own life for. I promised my wise future self that I'd get off the bench and into the game. She didn't promise me that it would be easy, that it wouldn't hurt, that I wouldn't feel tired. Love never promised me that there'd be no risk, neither to my body nor to my heart. I promised to be present, to be alive. She promised to hold me through it, to meet me wherever I was.

"I had a really upsetting conversation with some people in my family," she says. "Okay to tell you about that?"

"*Mi nena.* Of course it is. Tell me."

"Okay. So you know I was telling you it was my mom's birthday recently. We all got together at my aunt's house on Long Island for dinner. My mom's sister. She and I, and my cousin Paola, we've always been super close. Paola is only two months younger than me. We were like sisters when we were growing up, and she's still one of my best friends. Or, like,

I thought she was." She shakes her head. "And Auntie Rosa was like a second mom to me, when I was a kid and we all used to live in Manhattan. I really thought they understood me. And supported me. But I guess not."

She sighs. "So we had a lovely dinner. And cake. My parents went home. I was going to spend the night with my aunt and my cousin, you know, like old-school, having a sleepover. Or I thought it was a sleepover. But, Mira, it was actually an ambush."

I reach out and put my hand on her bare thigh. "An ambush? What do you mean?"

"Yeah." She rubs both hands over her face. "My aunt was all like, 'Paloma, when are you gonna meet a nice guy and settle down?' And my cousin is like, 'Or a nice girl.' So my aunt is like, 'Yeah, or a nice girl. Whoever. Just find somebody who's good to you and settle down.' And I'm like, 'I've told you all. Plenty of times. I'm polyamorous. I don't believe that monogamy is the only relationship style that is permissible, or positive, or that works. I don't think our society should be solely arranged around, and solely privilege, monogamous, heterosexual relationships. I have no interest in ever practicing traditional monogamy. It doesn't work for who I am.'

"So I say this whole freaking speech and then my aunt is like, 'So you're never gonna settle down?'

"And I'm like, 'Auntie Rosa. I am very settled. I have my apartment, where I've been on my own since I was eighteen. I know that we're a really privileged family, but I've been working since I was sixteen. I danced in a professional ballet company. I'm turning thirty and finishing my PhD. I just bought my own home. Like, in what way am I not settled?'

"Then my cousin starts in. Paola's all like, 'So you're never getting married?'

"And I'm like, 'I don't know, okay? Traditional marriage does not appeal to me. At all. So if I did, people might not even recognize it as a marriage. I would continue to practice polyamory and communal relationships. Because that is how I love. And I do not like living with other people. To be honest, I didn't even like living with my parents when I was a kid. I need quiet and I need space. So, if I ever did get married, I would not want to be nesting partners. I would need to live separately. Because that is who I am.'

"And my aunt says, 'But that's the whole point of marriage, Paloma. To create a home with someone. To share your life with them.'

"And I'm like… 'Yeah. Exhibit A. This is what most people in our society think of when they think of marriage, and I have no interest in nesting with anyone or crafting my daily life around someone else's needs constantly and permanently. That does not work for who I am.'

"So then Paola says, 'But what about having kids? I mean, like you said, we're turning thirty soon. Don't you ever think about having a baby? I know I do, and I'm still on the apps, trying to find a guy who doesn't completely fucking suck. You're in relationships with multiple cool people. Don't you ever think about having a kid?'

"And I'm like, 'No!' I'm starting to get really upset with them by this point, Mira. 'No! No! I've told you. And everyone. Everyone who has ever asked me, since literally day one. Since I was a little girl. And that's fucked, by the way. That we're already conditioning little girls into thinking about having kids of their own. Fucked up. But anyway. I have known, and said, since day one, and I continue to say it now: I have no interest in, and no plans of, ever having a kid of my own. I don't want to be pregnant. I don't want to carry or birth a baby. I don't want to adopt a kid. I don't want to be a mother. Ever. I would be a horrible mother. I'm selfish and self-centered and I like quiet and space. I need my body to be my own, at all times, so things like pregnancy and childbirth and breastfeeding would not work for me. I love to travel and I need to be able to go wherever I want whenever I please, without getting anyone else's permission or consulting with anyone else's schedule. And, I like I said, I hate living with other people on a permanent basis. And I don't think living separately would work for, like, a newborn. So, no. And even if I wouldn't be a horrible mother, which I would, I still wouldn't want to have a kid. Because I just don't want to.'

"So I say all of that. By now I'm out of breath and angry and hurt and starting to cry. And you can just see the two of them getting ready to gang up on me and fucking ambush me. So then Paola says, 'But you date married people, don't you, Paloma? What if one of your couples has a baby? Where would you fit in? Like, if you hate babies so much, will you just be leaving any relationships you're in if the couple has a baby?'

"And I'm like, 'Wait! No! Wait, what? Hold up. When did I say I hate babies? Like, literally, when did I say that? I do not hate babies! I like kids! A lot! I teach ballet to two-year-olds, for fuck's sake. And I love it. I love kids. I don't want any kids of my own, but that doesn't mean I fucking hate babies or that I'm not open to having other people's kids in my life. If someone I was with had a baby, they'd know that I have no interest in being a parent, because literally everyone knows that about me. But, if they were open to it, I would certainly be open to being a part of the kid's life. Just like, Paola, if you have a kid someday, I'd love to be cool Auntie Paloma. To the children of other people in my life. And then, when me and the kid are done spending time together, I give the kid back to its parents and go back to my home. I don't hate kids. I just don't want to have any kids of my own.'

"And then they both started saying the fucking thing. The thing I hate maybe more than anything else. And that is: 'You'll feel differently when you meet the right person.' Which is a version of: 'This is just a phase.' Which everyone knows is the worst thing ever. And I'm like, 'There is no right person! There is no one right person! This is who I am and how I feel and what is right for me. It is not a fucking phase for me. And, if I ever do decide to change my mind about anything that I choose to do—because this is my life and my decisions, and I am allowed to change my mind whenever I please—it'll be because I've made that choice, not because I've been rescued by the mythical right person. Because I am not sitting around waiting for anyone or anything external to make me whole.'

"So I guess it sounds like I was talking a big game or whatever. But by this point I am really crying. I was really hurt, Mira. I was like… 'I thought you two understood me. Accepted me. Worst of all, though, I thought you were proud of me.' Because that hurts most of all, you know?" Recalling this, her eyes fill with tears again. "I wasn't sure if I even wanted to bother. I kinda just wanted to say fuck it and go home. But I decided to go for it. So I was like, 'You know, I thought you two were proud of me. I thought it mattered to you that I own my own home. That I have a career that I love. That I'll be finishing my PhD next year and getting the highest possible degree in my field. That I'm happy and healthy and living my life the way that I choose. But no. Apparently not. Apparently, what I'm hearing right now is that you don't really see me. Not in the way that's true for me. You want me to be what you want me to be. What the world wants me to be. And I am not going to be that. I need the people close to me to see me and accept me as I am. And if you can't do that right now, then I can't be here.'

"I mean, well… I probably wasn't as eloquent as all that at the time. So I said some crying, yelling, messed up version of all of that. They were starting to get upset too, I guess, but I just couldn't listen to them anymore. I couldn't be there anymore. So I got dressed and grabbed my stuff and just left. It was the middle of the night but I just left. I went and sat in my car and cried until I felt calm enough to drive. Then I drove, even though it was the middle of the night, to here. My stuff was still in the process of arriving and being set up so the house felt like chaos. Just like I was. My bed hadn't arrived yet, just the mattress, so I threw myself down on it and cried myself to sleep.

"Next morning, my aunt calls me. I'm like, okay, she's gonna apologize, we're gonna move past this and be a family again, everything's gonna be great. But no. This woman is still tryna call me out for not being what she fucking thinks I am supposed to be. She tries to guilt-trip me by saying, 'Oh, Paloma, your mother, she's getting older, you're her and your dad's only child, don't you think they want to see you settled? Happily married? And don't you think they want some grandkids?' I wish I could say I responded with, like, compassion and calmness. But I did not. I went off on her. I started yelling that I live my life for me, not my parents, and anyway, they support my choices and they always have. And she started yelling back that our parents do so much for us. That my parents do so much for me. That I do owe them my respect and time and consideration when making my choices. Eventually we… well, we just kept going back and forth. I felt like she wasn't hearing me at all anymore. I probably wasn't hearing her either. I felt so frustrated and hurt. I ended up hanging up on her. I have never done that before. I mean, you get it, Mira. I'm black and Dominican. I was not raised to do something like that. But I hung up on her. And maybe I feel a little sad about it. But I don't regret it.

"Later that day, Mira, my mom calls me. She tries to play diplomat. She's all like, 'I totally understand you, Paloma. She is being insensitive. She should be more supportive of your choices. She is proud of you. And she should express that more. But are you really never going to talk to her, or your cousin, again?' 'Cause, yeah, I guess I did say that. Multiple times. And I'm like, 'I'm not talking to either of them again until they apologize to me. And if they ever come at me with that kinda stuff again, I will cut off communication. Again. I was so hurt, okay?' And my mom, 'cause, like I said, she's a diplomat, she's like, 'Maybe you could call them? Apologize? Get the ball rolling?' And I am like, 'No. I don't have anything to apologize for. I am not the one who ambushed them, telling them their life and their love is wrong. So, no.'

"So… we just left things like that." Paloma sighs, letting out a deep breath. I know how that feels, how it feels to finally share something that hurts from the vault, the locked, sick inner sanctum, that often is family life. And, oh, damn, do I know how that feels: that feeling like you been running, that you are being pursued and you cannot stop; that panicked feeling of tears choked at the top of your throat; that scary, echoing thud of your heart against your breastbone, hard and reverberating like a rubber ball against a brick wall. Fuck, how well do I know leaving things as they are with your family, knowing it ain't getting any better, not tonight; that you are gonna have to get up tomorrow and keep being a person, no matter how messy or painful or imperfect you have left things tonight.

She meets my eyes, and seems to come back to herself, and to this room where we're together, this bed where we are both safe. "Yeah," she says, and her lips tremble. "So I kinda hate my family right now, Mira. I hate them all and I don't want to see them or talk to any of them. And I have no idea when I'm going to feel differently."

Fuck, y'all, you know that I know exactly what it feels like to hate your family, to hate them as much as you love them, to hate that you still love them even when they hurt you; I know how it feels not to have a clue where the boundaries lie or how to draw them in order to keep yourself safe.

And, y'all, now this don't happen often. It is not often that your girl Mira knows exactly what to do. I think I was sick the day they were giving out that instruction manual that tells you how to be a person in the world. But this, I know what to do with this. When you are in that space, that hurt, confused, broken space, there ain't nothing that nobody else can do. This ain't a hurt that can be fixed in a night or with a word or even with a single magic spell. As Araceli would say, there ain't no white-people life hack for this one. This is something that you've gotta feel all the way through.

"I hear you, girl," I say, finally, after having let her talk, get it all out. Her tears spill over when I say these words; I feel a shiver of recognition inside my self. "I'm so sorry all that happened. That sucks. And I am here. You're safe. I am right here."

She starts to cry then, the big, loud, messy tears. I ask if I can hold her, and instead of answering, she places herself in my arms. I slide us down on the bed and hold her while she presses her face into my neck and her breasts flatten against mine.

"Mira," she says, after a long while, I'm not sure how long, you can't rush this kinda crying on any sort of timeline, especially if you don't let yourself cry like you need to often enough. She pulls her wet face from my wet body and looks at me. I just about die of tenderness and love for her. This is because I can see in her, in this moment, again, the little girl she once was: swollen eyes and nose, puffy lips, lashes matted, looking for comfort.

"Am I being ridiculous?" she asks me. "I mean, I know that you… you just recently got out of the hospital, Mira. I know you're still recovering. Am I bothering you with my ridiculous crap? And, like, I know… you… and your mom… and, like…"

"Paloma." She falls silent the moment I say her name. For a moment I pause and just look at her. I've got a choice here, and I can feel it. I can spin her my usual crap, keeping the real truth to myself. Or I can be as honest with her as she has been with me.

"Baby, listen," I say. "Cystic fibrosis ain't a cold. I don't get over it. And there ain't no cure. Maybe one day there will be. I'd love that day. But until then, CF is a chronic illness that I live with. There are times when I am in the hospital a lot. Those times, I find ways to live my life around what I need to do for my health. So please don't say you're bothering me. Please don't call what you're going through *ridiculous crap*. I'm so sorry this is happening. But I am glad to be able to be here for you through it. Because I am here, with you, listening to you and being able to hold you, and not sick in the hospital by myself." I cup her chin. "You feel me?"

She nods and draws in a shuddery breath.

"And no matter what's happened with me and my mom, which, believe me, is a lot—" I roll my eyes. "None of that negates anything you've been through. Or how much it hurts." I touch her lips with my thumb. "*¿Me oyes?*"

"Yeah," she whispers. "I hear you."

It's so late at night now. "Turn over," I whisper to her, and she does, and I press the front of my body to the back of hers. I unwind her braid. I slip the piece of pink elastic from the end of it around my wrist. My wrist is so tiny I wrap it around two times. Her braid undone, I feel the immediate softening of the skin at her temples, loosening at her hairline. I feel her deep exhale. I rub my fingertips through her scalp and let her cry more. I entertain a long-held fantasy, which is that with tears we could water the world.

I hold her till she has cried herself out, for tonight, at least. I put my hand on her belly and feel it. As it quiets in the room around us, I become aware again of something that has been with us the entire time, humming under the sound of our words and our crying: the buzz of this entire place.

"Paloma?" I say.

"Yeah?" she says.

I hold my breath a second, listening. "You hear that?"

"Hear what?" she says.

"I dunno. It's like a buzzing sound. Constant. I been hearing it all day."

"Ah." I feel her body sharpen to awareness for a moment; I hear a smile in her voice. "Those are the cicadas."

"The what?"

"Cicadas. They're insects. That's their song. They are really ancient insects. They appear frequently in ancient art and myth." I feel myself smiling too; here is a girl who cannot stop telling myths. "Archaeologists have found amulets of cicadas in precious stone from various parts of the world. They were thought to symbolize immortality."

"Immortality," I say. "Love that for them."

I laugh, and she does too, and yeah, the sound is damn shaky, but here we still are, at the end of this day, laughing together.

We won't stay here forever; I know that. But we stay a little longer, immobile in bed, holding each other, the buzz of the cicadas flowing in, and under, and over, and around, our heartbeats.

On May twentieth, it's our twenty-second birthday. Last year, in 2020, our birthday fell during the lockdown and so, for the first time in our lives, my twin and I celebrated our birthday apart. We each ate cake in our separate apartments, him downtown and me uptown, while Zooming with each other. (I also, freshly home from the hospital following the transplant, had caught that fucking virus. If you somehow haven't gotten it yet, well, it sucked as much as advertised. I was weak and scared and pretty fucking ill. But you gotta understand: your girl Mira has had cystic fibrosis since I was five years old. I am a toothpick, but a toothpick made outta fucking titanium. I'm a hummingbird, but you don't fuck with a hummingbird. I fought that shit off like I've fought off any number of frightening respiratory diseases.)

This year, Marco and I are reunited. He and Hassan and Magda come over to our place for lunch and cake. Mom is, of course, still away at her treatment center, making this the second year ever that we've celebrated without her present. *Abuela* comes too, bringing lots of Dominican food with her. I haven't seen her, or eaten her food, in ages.

Now, I ain't said much about my grandmother, have I? I mean, we cool, I guess. I love her. She loves me, I think. I grew up with her from the time I was twelve. Mom's apartment only had one bedroom, so she, *Abuela,* and I all slept in the same room, three tiny beds crammed in together with only thin folding screens in between for a fucked-up Castillo family semblance of "privacy." But somehow, despite all that, I just don't feel as close to my *abuelita* as I want to, or maybe as I think I should. Maybe it's some type of misplaced generational anger: *Abuela* is Dad's mom, and he ain't alive for me to be mad at him—for what, you ask? I dunno, for dying, for being mega fucked up when he was alive?—so I'm mad at her by proxy. Maybe I actually am mad at her, for the same reason I know Marco kinda resents her: she had a front-row fucking seat to how bad our childhood was, and she didn't intervene in any meaningful way. (Would that have been her place? I ain't got any fucking clue.) Maybe it's just 'cause *Abuela* always had a very separate life of her own, with multiple jobs and friends and boyfriends and hobbies. She was always sweet to us, but she certainly wasn't the type to be home every night knitting and baking cookies.

Or maybe it's 'cause, deep down, I don't even really feel like my grandmother loves me. I know this because of how differently she's always treated Marco and me. And, I mean, your girl gets it, all right? Marco is super easy to love. He's the most perfect grandson any grandmother would want: smart and hardworking and protective of his family full of girls and religious and interested in his heritage. In about a week, he'll graduate from Columbia University with perfect grades. He'll be valedictorian and give a speech. I still don't know what the deal is with medical school, but he's only not going because he and his equally perfect husband are taking care of Magdalena like the saints that they are.

I on the other hand am much harder to love. *Abuela* came up here from the DR *sin papeles* to help my mom take care of Marco and me. I know I couldn't have been the granddaughter she dreamed of. I'm sick, like really sick—like she might outlive me, and what grandparent wants to bury a grandchild? My treatments are expensive, helping keep my family in poverty. I went to church when they took me, but my heart was never in it; I'm not even sure I believe in God. I'm not that smart, I only graduated high school by the skin of my teeth, I've never contributed to my family financially, and I am not at all successful in the way the world defines that word. I'm far from the stereotypical better life that our immigrant parents and grandparents wanted for us. I ain't no dream of my ancestors.

So anyway, *mi familia* comes over for our birthday. When *Abuela* arrives, everyone is in the living room playing with the baby, while I am in my kitchen, my witch's domain, brewing some tea. She comes through to the kitchen with all the food she brought, and within minutes she and I are back in an old familiar rhythm, transplanted from Mom's place and relocated here, warming up food, grabbing glasses and plates, *Abuela* asking me with a smile about what kind of tea I'm brewing today. I tell her it's a lemon ginger, and I'm serving it cold in honor of the season, with ice cubes also made out of the tea, which I made yesterday and froze overnight. She tells me that's beautiful. She puts on the latest Karol G album on her phone—my *abuela* is always in tune with the latest hits— and we sing along to "*200 Copas*" while we prep the food.

She wishes me a happy birthday and gives me a hundred-dollar bill. In another old familiar dance, I tell her it's *demasiado,* try to hand it back. But she won't let me. She tells me I'm her only girl and it's my special day, I must have it. So I put it in the pocket of my leggings and hug her. As I hug her, I imagine some really stupid things. Don't tell nobody, okay, that your girl is being *tan sentimental.* But I imagine, as she's hugging me, that my dad is hugging me, through her. What would he have been like? You know, I don't know. Maybe he was a total dick. Or would he have called me his only girl and brought me a gift on my special day?

I don't know. There's a whole lotta things that I do not know. But I do know that today's my birthday, and I'm sitting down to lunch and cake with my family in my and Andre's apartment, where I am safe and taken care of and loved.

Later in the day, Andre's parents come over for dinner. Now, I was not at all sure about this plan. Not everybody knows it, 'cause I try my best to hide it, but this much interaction and smiling and eating, and generally pretending to be well like everybody else when I am not, takes a whole lot outta me. Things are fraught both with my family and with my husband's. And this is my birthday, the last day I should be expected to perform for others. (My wonderful man reminded me of this when his parents called and asked if they could see me on my birthday, they haven't seen me in ages. He said, "It's completely your call, Mira. You get to say no here. You can say no whenever you want, but especially on your birthday, you should do whatever makes you happy." Bless him, ain't he a king among men?)

But I decided to say okay. Andre's parents haven't seen me since Thanksgiving of last year, before my latest giant health crisis, when I lost their not-grandchild. It's probably gonna bring up some shit, seeing them. I can't avoid it forever. So I said yes. They said I wasn't to do anything, I shouldn't lift a finger, I should just relax at home and they would bring dinner and dessert. "*Bien de bien*," I said. "Thank you."

So Andre's parents come over. Having them here feels strange. When Andre and I were both home from the hospital after the transplant, his mom and dad stayed with us, for several weeks, taking care of us both. As soon as Andre felt strong enough, they went back home, and he took care of me.

But now, whenever I hug his mom, whenever we stand in front of each other—her so elegant and tall, gray hair in the most perfect ballet bun, me all tiny and awkward and sticklike—I can't unsee in my mind's eye those dark first few days after I got home from the hospital. It was the very beginning of the pandemic, the whole city, the whole world, under a black cloud of fear and uncertainty. Were we all going to die? Andre's parents were worried about him; he was recovering okay, but there'd been a complication after his surgery and he'd needed a blood transfusion. I think they would've legit killed me if anything had happened to their son because I stole one of his perfect lungs.

I was so weak when I got home, I couldn't do anything for myself. Auntie Lisette helped me take a shower. She helped me put clothes on. She helped me slip on my underwear. I hate that she's seen me naked. I'm not even that self-conscious when my lovers see me naked. After all, when you're in bed with somebody, you've got the sex itself to distract from the fact that your ribs and vertebrae show beneath your skin, that you're actually not the kind of body that anyone would call sexy. But there were no distractions between her and me when she put me, naked, into the shower in my brightly lit bathroom. I was on a heavy dose of painkillers, loopy and not myself. I cried on her shoulder more than once during those days, hurting and scared, something I literally would not do for all the money in this world when I'm in my right mind. She had no choice but to hold me, judging me the entire time, I'm sure. I know she resents me, a motherless girl whose mother is still alive, worming my way into her family.

Even now, with everything between us, everything we shared those days, she still don't hug me like a normal person. She holds me at a distance, patting my back lightly, like anything stronger might kill me.

"Happy birthday, Mira, sweetheart," she says.

"Thank you, Auntie Lisette," I reply.

As promised, they've brought dinner, soul food. And I do love fried chicken and macaroni and cheese and Andre's dad's famous collard greens, his mom's recipe from Georgia, and banana bread pudding. But I'm tired and even the thought of chewing and eating food feels impossible. I only ate a few bites at lunch too. I'm weak and need nutrition. After just a couple sad minutes of nibbling at crispy golden-brown chicken skin and garlicky collard greens, I look over at Andre. He looks at me. I look at his parents, looking back at us, probably wondering what the fuck is going on. My heart pounds at the base of my throat, so hard I'm scared I won't get the words out. I hear my therapist Maya's voice in my head, saying that I deserve to take up space, that my health deserves whatever accommodations it requires. I don't owe anybody any idea of what health is supposed to look like. I remember standing there in the park with Andre two years ago, us promising our lives to each other, promising to be a family.

"Andre, baby," I say, "I'm sorry, but I can't really eat right now. Do you think you could help me with the tube?"

"Mira," he says. "Of course I can."

He gets up to get everything ready for a tube feeding. His parents watch him. I say, "I am so sorry I can't eat much of your beautiful food right now. Eating by mouth is really difficult for me." I swallow. I feel sick and shaky. I wish I didn't have to be fucking brave like this. "But I really want to have dinner with everyone. So I am going to feed myself through my G-tube. If that's, like, okay?"

"Mira," Andre says. "If it's okay with you, then it's okay. That is all that matters."

He looks at his parents. His mom says, "Yes, of course. Whatever you need, Mira."

His dad says, "Are you okay, sweetheart?"

I nod, too close to tears to say anything more.

I pull up my shirt and sit there and Andre feeds me. He eats meanwhile.

His parents just stare for a while. I mean, I get it, y'all. Most people will live their entire lives without seeing somebody getting liquid nutrition through a tube surgically inserted into their stomach. It's intimate and it makes people curious. So, I deal. After a while, they go back to eating and everybody tries to make conversation. But of course it's all awkward now. So this dinner is fucked. At least I'm feeling better, though, with a little nutrition in me.

After dinner we go sit in the living room. I escape to brew some more of my lemon ginger tea. Andre comes when he hears the whistle of the kettle and helps me carry it out. We drink tea and I hold my warm mug miserably, just waiting for this visit to be over.

Andre's parents give me an envelope. Inside is a really beautiful card, on thick, creamy paper, an image of a whimsical pastel butterfly dotted with multicolored crystals. For some reason, it brings tears to my eyes, imagining Auntie Lisette at some overpriced stationery boutique, choosing a card for me. Tucked into the card is a Best Buy gift card. It's for five hundred dollars.

"Andre told us you're going back to school in the fall," Auntie Lisette says. "We thought maybe you could use a new laptop. For class."

"Yes." My throat is thick. "I could. My laptop is really old." I try to laugh, but it is not a cute sound. I glance over at Andre next to me. We're squeezed together on the armchair, his parents on the couch. Just looking into his deep dark eyes makes me feel a little stronger. "Thank you. This is so generous of you."

"It's nothing," she says, with one of her elegant shrugs. "We are so proud of you, returning to your education, Mira."

"Thank you," I say again, and get up to hug each of them, give them a kiss on the cheek.

I sit with Andre again. "Mira," his mother says. "I got a text from your mother."

Fuck, can the floor swallow me up, please?

Andre puts his arm around me, tight.

"She shared that she's currently at a rehab facility in Pennsylvania," she continues.

I lick my lips. They're trembling, my tongue is dry.

"Yep," I say. What kind of response is that? I'm screaming at myself inside my head.

"She said she wants to do everything she can to get better for her kids."

I feel my palms flood with clammy sweat. I might have to go throw up soon, no lie.

"She told me about the baby, Magdalena." Lisette says her name tentatively, like moving over rocks. "That your brother and his husband have temporary custody of her while your mom focuses on her recovery."

"Yeah," I say. "I mean, I… I couldn't. With everything that's… going on, I just, like, couldn't."

"Oh, Mira," Lisette says. My ears are ringing with grief. Her voice sounds muffled, like I'm underwater. "We are so very sorry, my darling."

"I…" I say. "Um."

Andre pulls me into his lap. He winds his arms around me, tightly. It's definitely the most physically intimate we've ever been in front of his parents.

"Yes," his dad says. He flicks a look at his wife. "We don't mean to overstep. We just wanted you to know, Mira. How sorry we are. For… your loss. And…"

"For everything you've been through," says Auntie Lisette. I can't look at her face, I might cry or scream, so instead I focus my eyes on her hands in her lap. They're squeezing each other so hard it must hurt. I feel a tender, painful wave of empathy for her. "We are so sorry for you, Mira, honey." She closes her eyes briefly, takes a breath. When she opens them, they're a little wet. I look away again. I can't start crying for real, I'll never stop.

"I prayed for you every day," she says. "Every single day. When Andre told me everything that had happened, I was just heartsick for you, honey."

"We don't mean to overstep," his dad says again. "We just want you to know we're here, Mira. If there's anything you need. If there's anything we can do." He touches his wife's hand. "We love you very much, sweetheart."

I choke over the first words I try to get out. Andre kisses the side of my face. My eyes are swimming. I try again. "Thank you both," I say. "And no, you are not overstepping. It helps to know that you are here. And I love you too."

We sit a while longer. Auntie Lisette goes to the bathroom. Then I do too, as much because I need to be alone and regroup for a second as because I need to pee. When I come out, Auntie Lisette is in the kitchen, washing dishes.

"No, Auntie Lisette, please." I reach out an arm, as though to stop her. "Don't do that. Don't wash dishes. We'll do them later."

"Mira, really. I don't mind."

"Come on. Please. Don't."

"All right." She turns off the water.

In the living room, Andre's dad is showing him something from yesterday's Mets game on Andre's laptop, something about a home run. Auntie Lisette looks at me. "Mira, darling, are you feeling up for a walk?" she asks.

"Um," I say. "Sure."

"We're going for a walk," I tell Andre, slipping on a pair of sandals by the door. "Is it chilly out, does anyone know? Should I take a sweatshirt?"

"It may be a little chilly now that it's evening," his dad says. "I would take a sweatshirt."

"Okay, thank you," I say, grabbing Andre's Knicks hoodie from where it's draped over the little table by the door where we drop our keys.

"Do you want me to come, Mira?" Andre says.

"No," says his bossy mother. "She is fine. Watch your baseball."

He sighs. "Are you okay, Mira?" he asks me.

I pull the sweatshirt over my head. "*Estoy bien, nene,*" I say. "We're just gonna go to Fort Tryon. I haven't been out in two days. I should get some air."

"Okay," he says. "*Ten cuidado.* Text me if anything."

"Andre, really," his mother says, and she practically drags me out the door.

It's a lovely evening. About a month from the summer solstice, the days are long, but without the sense of urgency that'll come in June and July, and most especially in August, that deep longing necessity to squeeze every last drop of sunlight out of every day. People will feel guilty then, being inside, when the New York summer is so full of promise and also so fleeting. The summer will feel philosophic rather than tangible, a moral imperative.

But today, the last day of Taurus, the day that I was born, it ain't like that, not yet. In late springtime we get gratitude instead of guilt. I was born under a sign where every warm day still feels like an early, unexpected gift.

It's like that today, a soothing honey-drop of an evening, the sun like a lozenge glowing from inside with medicine, something you could suck, hold in the heat of your mouth, to feel better. Within minutes of our walk, I've pushed the sleeves of Andre's hoodie up to my elbows.

We walk to Fort Tryon Park in silence. The streets leading here from our apartment are a little steep. I'm breathing hard, but it feels good. The park looks formidable, so lush and overgrown with trees that they create a deep green darkness. I remember, one of those black first days after I got home from the hospital last year, at the chaotic beginning of the pandemic, I read an article by a green witch who lives somewhere here in New York City. She wrote about escaping her apartment and walking to Central Park, an act that felt illicit and dangerous. She saw the cherry blossoms, long-awaited springtime delight of every New Yorker, spreading their blanket of white and pink petals over a nearly empty park. She felt astonished, she wrote, that nature continued to put on the show of its splendor, even when there was no one around to enjoy it. And how anthropocentric, she chided herself, that she would imagine that the earth did anything for the pleasure of humans! She stood under the trees, in the terrestrial ocean-wave of their petals. Just weeks later, white tents would pop up all over Central Park—treatment stations for the infected, overflow from the hospitals, glutted with the dead and the dying.

We enter the park. The paths here are steep and narrow. I love the shadows of the trees' leaves cast on the ground by the lowering sun, the sharp arrangement and definition of their tips and blades. A couple run by, a young man and woman with miles of glowing skin on display in their shorts and tank tops, both with short ponytails bouncing behind them, glossy and brown as chestnuts. Squirrels leap and bound like kamikaze daredevils, so fast that, for long extended moments, their four feet with sharp nails don't touch the ground. As for me, I take a slower approach.

We reach the winding staircase, cut from the stone of the park, that leads up to the museum on the other side. We share a look of wordless communication, much more intuitive and comfortable than I would have thought I'd be capable of with my mother-in-law, and mount the steps. After just a few, we are both breathing hard.

"Damn," Auntie Lisette says, looking up. "This is a lot of stairs."

I snort a laugh. "Don't I know it, *mama.*"

She looks over at me with an almost smile. And I almost smile back.

"Give me your arm, Mira, darling."

I offer her my arm. She links her arm through it, tucks my body close to her side. Now I can feel her ribs breathing, her muscles moving as we trudge up the steps together, stair by stair. And I know it's awful, and it's stupid, but I feel just the tiniest bit better about how hard it is for me to climb these steps, seeing that it's challenging for her too, this ultra-fit ballet woman in her sixties. As we walk, I think about how once these stairs were solid stone, till somebody came along and carved out of them a path, where there had not been one before. Is this inventive, or is it anthropocentric? (I had to look up that word, of course, when I encountered it on that girl's blog. But just look at your girl now, using it like a damn boss.) I am not sure.

At length we reach the top. There, across the street and a driveway, there is the museum, the Met Cloisters. I unthread my arm gently from Auntie Lisette's and do a quick body scan, taking stock of how I feel. I don't feel great, I guess, I'm wildly out of breath and my calves ache, but I also don't feel as if I need to lie down on the ground and die. Two years ago, before the surgery, even with my oxygen tank, I would never have even contemplated climbing those stairs. Earlier this year, I remember, I came here with Araceli and Skye and we climbed the stairs, and I was so tired afterwards I had to sit down. And that was before my body tried to reject these new lungs, before the new scars I've got now. This seems to me incontestable proof that I am getting stronger.

I look down the staircase, its winding geography down into the park, from this vantage point. I watch as it seems to transform right before my eyes. It ain't a story about how I am not good enough. It's just a fucking staircase. More than that, *mi gente*: that is a fucking staircase that I have climbed.

"Shall we sit down?" Auntie Lisette asks me, and I say yeah, sure.

Once we're sitting on a bench, I turn my body towards her and take a deep breath. "Lisette," I say.

She gives me that almost-smile again. "Miranda," she says. She's almost playful right now, somehow, and I'm here for it. She's normally pretty humorless. Looking at her—my husband looks so much like her, it's like seeing an older version of him that I may not get to live to see—it strikes me, for the first time maybe, that she ain't just Andre's mother. And, yeah, I know, ain't I a grown woman, shouldn't I have come to this realization before. But, seriously, though: this right here is a woman with all her own hopes and hurts and humors and interests. She's a complete person, not some damn archetype, just like me. Will she and I ever get over our shit enough to meet each other, for real?

"Thank you for praying for me, when I was sick," I say finally.

She nods. "I pray for you every day, Mira."

"Thank you. I appreciate that." I dig my hands deep into the pocket of Andre's hoodie, where they meet in the middle, fingers curling tight around each other. "It was a time when I could really use prayer, I think. I mean, it sucked. Losing the pregnancy like that. When I didn't even know I was…" I look away, at the closed, imposing doors of the museum. It's evening now, after visiting hours. "It fucking sucked." I look back at her. "Oh, sorry, auntie. I know how much you hate cursing."

And now she gives me almost-laugh, can you believe it? What I can't believe is how my man, who's always so fucking down to laugh and joke and have fun and not take himself too seriously, came from this lady. Genetics is wild.

"You can curse, Mira," she says.

I study her face for a long, quiet moment. I realize, actually, that we're studying each other, that this woman is trying to understand me, puzzle me out, just as I'm contemplating her. And what a mirror it is.

"I am so sorry you had to go through that, sweetheart," she says.

I nod. I'm feeling hungry—but for what, though?

"I feel like I should tell you." I claw my opposite wrists with my nails. "I mean, this is something we all know. Something the doctors have told me before. But now we discussed it with more clarity, not, like, theoretically. And." I draw in a breath. "I can't get pregnant. I mean, I can get pregnant. Obviously. But I shouldn't. Because I can't carry a baby to term. It wouldn't be safe for me. Or the baby. The hypothetical baby. So. The doctors are saying I can't. And, I mean, you know me." I shrug. "Doctors have been telling me my entire life. The things I can and cannot do. And that's forced me to become super aware. Of my own body. My… inner landscape." I run my hand through my hair, which today is in a big Afro puff on the top of my head. Lisette is watching me closely, lights flickering on in her eyes.

"So doctors say all kinds of things. And, I mean, who cares? What do they know about me and my future? Except, this time, Lisette, I'm pretty sure they're right. I feel it. In my body. I can't safely have a baby. I can never go through what I went through earlier this year. I don't think Andre can, either." At the mention of her son's name, her eyes sharpen on me. "So. I guess. I just wanted to share that with you. That I can't have a baby. And, like, it sucks."

She nods. "I suppose it does," she says.

"It does. I've always wanted to. Have a baby. Andre's baby, I mean."

She allows herself a small smile this time. "I know you have, sweetheart," she says. "I heard you two on the phone once. You must have been what, I don't know, fifteen or sixteen? I think you were talking about baby names. How many kids you'd want to have, someday."

"Yeah," I say, as this homegirl goes and breaks my heart, clean and clear and straight down the middle.

"So," I say again. "Just wanted to tell you that. And say I'm sorry. I am really, really sorry."

She gives her head a quick shake. "Why on earth would you think you need to say sorry to me?"

"I… I don't know."

"Mira." Auntie Lisette takes my hand, pulls it right out of the pocket of my hoodie. I feel tears starting to form, angry and hurt, 'cause I know what this woman is gonna do now, she's gonna be patronizing to me. "Sweetheart." She pats my hand. "You and Andre. You two are so very young. You are just turning twenty-two today. Maybe it is too soon for you to be thinking about starting a family?"

Now, my mind cycles through about fifty trillion responses to this, y'all. Andre and I already are a family. We always have been. It didn't happen, and maybe we didn't plan it, but we did start a family, or we tried to. And, yeah, I know what I said. I know I said it wasn't a baby. And it wasn't. It was an ectopic growth in my right fallopian tube, and it almost killed me. But it had a heartbeat, and we made it, Andre and me, we made that little heartbeat, and it was ours, and it was our family. That heartbeat will always be a part of our family. And, yeah, I know what I said, which is that these doctors, they don't know jack shit. But they also been telling me that I might not live until thirty. And maybe that ain't true. I may be a kitchen witch, but I ain't got no crystal ball. Hearing that, though, that shit messes with your head. What, really, in the life I've led, am I too young for?

I don't say any of that, though.

What I do say is: "Auntie Lisette, I don't think you know that."

And she says, "Fair enough. It's your life."

And I say, "Yes. It is."

I tug my hand away from her.

And then I say, "I know you don't like me." And I can't believe I got these words past my lips, but I did. And facing down death in the form of infection in my lungs ain't nothing, let me tell you, compared to saying these hard words in my mother-in-law's face.

"Mira," she says.

"Or maybe you just don't like me for Andre. I don't know. But I know you don't like me."

"Mira," she says. "Don't say that."

"Why not? It's true, ain't it?"

She looks at me for a long moment without answering. And, I mean, it ain't that difficult of a question, is it? Then she says, "Mira, can I share a quote with you from bell hooks?"

I have two thoughts in response to this. The first is: no, you cannot. Can you please just talk to me for once, like a human being, instead of quoting all the wise black grandmothers at me? My second thought is a memory of the bell hooks book, *All About Love,* that's on the table next to my bed right now. Paloma bought it for me at that bookstore in New Jersey. Now, imagine if Andre and me told his parents that we've been exploring polyamory! They'd probably skin us alive.

I don't say any of this. I just shrug.

"bell hooks said that true love can save us, but only if we're ready for it," she says.

"Lisette, what the hell does that even mean?"

"Mira—"

"Nah. No. Why you gaslighting me, lady? Can't you ever just talk to me for real? I know you don't like me. But why don't you like me? Is it because I'm ghetto? Is it because I don't have a real college degree? Is it because I'm sick? Is it 'cause you don't like my family?"

"Mira," she says, totally calm. "Please stop."

"No, you stop. Please. Just talk to me. Why don't you like me? Like, what did I ever do to you?"

"Mira," she says again, for like the billionth time now. "Stop."

I take stock of my body again. My heart's beating like a hummingbird. I'm nearly hyperventilating, with the desperate effort not to sob. My eyes hurt. And when I get quiet, I realize something. I realize that Auntie Lisette ain't never gonna answer me, not in the way that I want. I am hungry for something, but it isn't something that she is capable of giving me. I'm beating my wings against a window that ain't ever gonna open. So, much as it hurts my little heart, I decide to take her advice. I stop.

"Okay, whatever," I say, 'cause I'm just real wise and elegant like that. I rub my face, roughly. "Let's just go back."

"Yes," she says. "Let's."

So Auntie Lisette and I descend the stairs back down into the park. The way down is so much easier, we don't have to link arms and support each other, but the winding of the staircase, the stops and starts as we reach the different landings in between, make me dizzy. Every step down feels like a jolt, a shock spreading from the sole of my foot up to the top of my fuzzy head. I have now said shit to Andre's mother that I can never take back. How do I come back from this one? Where do she and I go from here? Around us, the park is bathed in the orange-sherbet glow of a lowering sunset, the treetops dipped in citrus phosphorescence. Never have I felt less in tune with my surroundings.

We reach the bottom of the staircase and make our way to the exit of the park and the sidewalk. We walk home in silence, just like when we walked here. But if I thought that silence was a little bit awkward, well, I hadn't seen nothing yet.

When we reach the corner of my street, I put my hand up and say, gently, "Hey, auntie, stop." I'm still nervous, in this strange space where I've finally felt able to confront my mother-in-law, my heart racing painfully, but I've come this far. This ain't nothing.

She stops, looks at me expectantly.

I take a deep breath. "Look. I don't regret anything I said. I ain't taking back a word of it. But Andre. He's got a lot going on right now. And I do not want our shit, you and me, to be something he's got to worry about. So is there a chance we could put all this behind us? Like, at least for now?"

She takes a deep breath too. "Mira," she says. And this woman smiles at me. I don't know if I feel indignant, hurt, or loved—maybe it's a mix of all three. "It is already behind us. It is already forgiven and forgotten." She reaches out her hand, slowly—to give me time to tell her to get the fuck away from me if I want to, I think—then, when I don't push her away, she rests her warm palm against my cheek. She cradles my face in her hand. Now, I'd love to lie and say that I don't, that your girl has that kinda inner reserve of strength, but who do I think I be playing? I lean right into the simple sweetness and comfort of her touch. Your girl is damn hungry for love. And I guess I ain't ashamed of it neither.

Like her touch is a magic key unlocking chambers in my mind, a memory visits me. During the days when she stayed with us, helping take care of me, the backs of both my hands suddenly split and cracked into such scaly dry skin that bloody cuts broke open across the valleys of my knuckles. They itched and hurt constantly. I showed Auntie Lisette, asked her if she knew what was going on with me. I was in the space then when my body was not only my own, because it could not be. My other good peeps with chronic illness probably know what I'm talking about here. When you need help with things like bathing, feeding yourself, putting on a pair of undies, the grand adventure of your staying alive becomes a communal effort. Maybe you think you could survive all on your own. As for your girl Mira, I know that I cannot.

She smiled, a little sadly, taking my hand in hers, palm to palm. She said, "Looks like eczema. My mom developed it when she was dying." She did the thing then: looked up at me sharply, 'cause she'd forgotten who she was talking to.

I smiled back. "You can talk about people dying around me," I said. "I know people die. And I ain't dying, Auntie Lisette. Not anytime soon, I mean."

"God forbid, Mira," she said. She told me that her mom developed eczema at the end of her life, and every night she used to sit next to her mom's bed and rub Vaseline into her hands. "Do you have any Vaseline?" she asked me.

I didn't, so Auntie Lisette made Andre's dad go out and find some Vaseline for me, even though this was during the lockdown when literally everything was out of stock, and he had to visit three drugstores to find some, and even though I insisted I was fine, I had some lotion from Lot-Less that I could just use. He came back an hour and a half later with two tubs of Vaseline and a lotion made from Vaseline and aloe vera.

Auntie Lisette and I sat on the bed and she smoothed the light, sticky Vaseline jelly gently across my knuckles. I remember suddenly her tenderness with me that evening. Do I regret what I've said to her today, remembering that? No, I don't. But it does make my anger at her, my hurt, a little less clean.

We stand here a moment, on the corner of my street, my cheek cupped in her hand.

"Sweetheart," she says. "We're family, okay? We can talk. We are allowed to say things to each other. And then we forgive each other and move on. Because we're family." She pats my cheek. "Yeah?"

And even though I hate it when she moralizes and philosophizes at me—you see, this woman, she think she better than me—I reach up to touch her hand gently, resting on my cheek.

"Yeah," I say, and lead the way back to my apartment.

That night, after his parents leave, I'm kinda shocked by it honestly, I wouldn't have thought we'd be in the mood for it after the day we've had, but Andre and I go to bed together and have sex. We're so hot for each other, so unexpectedly ravenous for it, that we're panting over each other's bodies. I feel unleashed, something primal inside me released from its cage, a cage I didn't even realize it'd been living in. I ask Andre to be rough with me. I didn't fully realize this either, or maybe I just didn't name it, but he's been gentler with me lately in our sex, I guess since everything that happened in the winter. But I have reached a place now where I can shift that.

I direct our scene, tell him what to do: how I want him to throw me onto the bed, and pin me underneath him, and pull my hair, and bite my neck and leave his mark on me; I tell him when to take me, and how hard. He pounds me into the bed, corkscrewing me with cock. I love being his dominatrix, and I love being tiny enough that my man can throw me around. I love that I'm strong enough again to use my body in this way. And I love that our roots together are strong enough, his and mine, to get vulnerable like this with each other.

I fall asleep with his sweat still on my body, his cum still sticky and wet on the insides of my thighs. He kisses me on my face and then leaves me in bed to get something to eat. I bury my face in the rumpled, sweaty, sex-soaked sheets and smile to myself. I love that I've worn him out, depleted his reserves so completely, with the greedy demands of my sex. He leaves me alone in our bed with the memory of him: bodily, imprinted on my moldable skin. Within moments of his departure, I fall into a blissed-out, delicious sleep. And a dream visits me.

I dream of an amoeba. I dream that our whole life is not what we think it is. I dream that our grand experiment here, this performance we enact where we put on a fragile suit of skin and play out scenarios on a stage called earth, is being observed. We are the playthings of goddesses. Maybe they are the fates, like them ancient dudes used to say in myth, weaving our stories on a big loom in the sky. Maybe they're dommes who get off on love, like Andre was hypnotized to believe during his shamanic journey, gasping with pleasure every time they help us make our dreams come true. I dunno. All I can say is, tonight when I have this dream, the goddesses who direct the world are scientists. And they are watching all the tiny dramas of our monumental, infinitesimal lives on a slide focused underneath their microscopes.

So I dream of an amoeba. I dream that it and I are floating in a cosmic petri dish magnified thousands of times for the watching eyes of our goddesses. We feel safe, locked in fluid the same temperature, texture, and composition of our blood. Do you have blood? I ask my friend the amoeba.

No, I do not, says the amoeba. It says that it has a cytoplasm contained within a plasma membrane. That's cool, I say. And, I mean, the amoeba has to just sort of beam its thoughts into my mind; that's how we communicate. It can't talk, obviously. It's a literal amoeba, y'all; were you sitting here thinking it could talk?

Anyway, that's what I wanted to tell you, Mira, the amoeba says, in all its single-celled glory. Instead of speaking, the amoeba pushes out its thoughts by the force of its will, mysterious and determined as an egg hatching itself, past the cling of its plasma membrane on a limb like a finger. There is more than one way to communicate, to speak, it says. I eat the amoeba's thoughts; this is how I digest them. The amoeba says that, while we human beings know each other by face and by name, amoebas know each other by the shape of the limb that extends from them when they want to move or eat or touch the world outside themselves. That's rad, I say.

I've heard how amoebas eat, I tell it. I heard that they open their entire selves and encompass their food, internalizing it.

Yes, my friend the amoeba says, when we see something tasty that we want to eat, we extend arms of our selves, creating an empty space inside that was not there before. Then we engulf our food. The amoeba asks me if I wanna hear something cool, and I'm like, sure.

It says, that same process that amoebas use to eat, engulfing and ingesting organic matter, is used by cells in the human immune system to attack and protect the body from harmful pathogens.

Even mine? I ask the amoeba.

Yes, Mira, even yours, it answers.

I ask if it's true that human beings are related to the amoeba.

I mean, yes and no, it says. Sure, in that we are all eukaryotes. (This is a word I learned in the one biology class I've ever taken, and it refers to organisms whose cells have a nucleus. Nuclei are, if I'm remembering correctly, super important to the cell, holding all its genetic information.) But it's not all that simple, it reminds me. Evolution is a complex, multilayered process, millions of years in the making.

Right on, my friend, I say.

We float side by side in my dream, in prehistoric fluid, the churning primordial ocean where life first began. This is like the moment when you realize that earth, our imperfect but glowing turquoise planet, is the size of a pinhead when compared with the universe that contains it. Here on the great cosmic petri dish, I ain't no bigger or more significant than an amoeba. And the eyes of goddesses are on all of us, my amoeba and me.

Just a couple of days after my birthday, I receive a letter. And yes, I mean an actual letter, on paper, in an envelope with a stamp, that I get in my mailbox. It's from Andre's mother. It has her return address in the top left corner, like she's an ocean away instead of just a couple subway stops. When I first pull it out of the mailbox, along with the internet bill and a few pieces of junk mail, I feel a jolt along the center line of my body—of surprise, of anticipation, maybe even of delight. I mean, don't get me wrong. I actually love letters. I think they're a beautiful callback to a lovely, more romantic time in our history, a time of lush creamy paper and fountain pens with smooth ink and taking the time to write to your loved ones, the longing feeling of having to wait to hear from them, not texting dumb shit with them every five seconds. For example, my friend Carolina and I used to send each other letters all the time, with sparkly pens and fun stickers, though we've stopped for some reason since the pandemic. After I remind my body that this letter is from Auntie Lisette, and is probably super annoying and judgmental, my excitement cools, displaced by a faint sense of dread and foreboding anger. Like, why she always gotta be so pretentious and extra? She wants to tell me something, why don't she just call me or even come over? Instead she gotta invade my life with a letter.

I sit down at my kitchen table, rainbow electric candles lit for comfort and my crystals and one of my favorite tarot decks around me, to open and read her letter.

In some ways, the letter isn't what I was expecting at all. Auntie Lisette apologizes. She writes that there may have been some times, during the course of our long-standing relationship, that she was judgmental towards me. She says that represents her falling short of who she wants to be, who God calls her to be. She says that she admires me a lot. (Nah, I didn't see that one coming.) She says that it truly is my life, that I can and should live it however I see fit, and I'm such a smart woman, she knows I'll do great things. Can't lie, that is nice to hear. She writes that she's known me since I was a little girl waiting for Araceli to get out of baby ballet class (it's true, I'd stand in the hallway with my oxygen tank and wait for her to get out of class, straining my ears to hear the incomprehensible French ballet words), that it's been so special for her to watch me grow up, that I am extremely dear to her heart. Can't lie there either; that feels really good to read.

But in other ways, there is no mistaking the fact that Auntie Lisette was the author of this letter. She has to use big words. She has to throw in a few quotes from Octavia Butler, just to show how wise and cultured she is. And I freaking love Octavia Butler. *Kindred* is one of my favorite books; I reread it every couple years. I love all our black literary queens and sharers of wisdom, Audre Lorde and Angela Davis and Toni Morrison. I love reading them. I guess I just wish that my own mother-in-law, someone I've known most of my life, someone who helped take care of me when I was sick and my own mother was nowhere to be found, would speak to me in her own words. I wouldn't care if they were imperfect. I wouldn't care if her words weren't as badass as Octavia Butler's ('cause, let's be real, whose are?). I wouldn't care, if the words were honest and they were hers.

Also no surprise, but she stops just short of saying that she actually loves me. (If I were petty, I would show it to Andre as proof, exhibit A, that his mother really don't like me. But he lucky, 'cause your girl is not that petty.) She's kind in the letter, gracious and above reproach, but not warm or loving. She ain't outright offensive, but (as usual) borderline ableist. She signs the letter *with all my best, Lisette,* which—what the actual fuck, is this a work email or something?

I sit at my kitchen table for a long time with the letter, like it is made of flesh and bone, like it has a presence, like it has a heart and skin and muscles. I do the only magic I can right now, which is to let myself feel my emotions, feel all of them. I feel anger and hurt and gratitude and confusion and resentment and, finally, certainty that forgiveness is the only way to go. I may joke that I was sick the day God was handing out that manual on how to be a person. But truth is, I know there ain't no such manual. Auntie Lisette didn't get it neither. No one did.

I also think for a long time about how to write her back. Maybe I shouldn't write her back at all. I mean, why I gotta be all extra and dramatic just because she is? Maybe I should just text her a heart emoji and move on with my life. But then I laugh to myself and roll my eyes and pull out a sheet of my prettiest stationery, light pink and printed with a faint pattern of pink and purple fairies.

I just can't write her a letter back. I cannot be that basic. I can't be that fake, echoing her halfhearted sentiments and worrying if my grammar's perfect and debating if I should also sign off with *all best, Miranda.* So instead I get my dark purple pen and write the only thing I feel I can right now. I write about the memory that came to me when she held my cheek the other night. I write the whole story of the time she rubbed Vaseline into my cracked, broken hands, both of us sitting on my bed. I do my best to make it a narrative, but it's also a bit nonlinear, because I let myself include every detail I remember, as I remember them. I write about the red flannel PJs she wore, how it started to lightly rain against the windows while we sat there and it made me sleepy, about how I curled my body around the giant rainbow teddy bear in my lap, a gift from Araceli, while she took care of me. At the end I write, *you took care of me when nobody else could, and I'm really imperfect and not sure I deserved it, so, always, thank you.* I sign it *love, Mira,* with a silent echo of *fuck you and your impersonal corporate etiquette.*

Then, since I have all my letter-writing stuff out, and as an antidote to all the turmoil this woman causes, I shift my frequency and write a letter to Araceli. I make it a love letter, hot and tender and sweet. After I fold it to put it in its envelope, I smooth on some red lipstick and kiss the folded paper, leaving the imprint of my lips behind. I imagine her receiving it. It's the first love letter I've sent to her at her new place, where my girl is building her happily ever after.

Two other cool things happen around the time of my birthday. First, I go running with my friend Aaron again. It's been a minute since I seen him, which I tell him as we get started on our path in Central Park.

"I know," he says, turning to me. Our pace slows, I mean, from the super-slow pace we've been keeping in the first place. "And I'm sorry I haven't been keeping in touch, Mira. I've been reading all your posts on Instagram. Congrats on having your first story published, by the way. That is amazing."

I flutter my lashes. "I know. Thank you." He laughs. I give him a nudge. "But come on, bro. What's been going on with you?"

"Um," he says. He looks away, at a spray of tiny yellow flowers growing in the bushes next to us. Sometimes everything in the world fucking sucks, but then you see the sweetest, happiest rubber-ducky-yellow flowers in the park, and everything is okay, just for a moment.

"I tested positive for the virus, back in the winter, before I got vaccinated," Aaron tells me finally. "It was awful, Mira. I had to be intubated, put on oxygen. I was in the hospital for almost two months."

"Aaron." I grip his arm. I yank him off the running path and we practically fall into the flowers. "Boy. How could you not tell me that?" I search his face. This fucker won't look me in the eye. "I mean, ain't we friends?"

"Mira." Finally, he looks at me. His eyes look soft and sad, like melted chocolate. I know no one would take a look at the two of us—Aaron, middle-aged white dude who works in insurance and is obsessed with *Star Wars*, and me, Mira, Generation-Z aspiring writer and witch—and assume we're friends, but they'd be wrong. I know we only met 'cause we're both sick people—Aaron has terribly severe asthma—who wanted a running buddy. But I thought we'd grown a real friendship, he and I.

"Of course we're friends," he says.

I prod his skinny-ass shoulder. I did notice that he was looking even paler and thinner and bonier than usual. How could I, of all underweight people, have missed the signs of serious illness?

"Then why didn't you tell me?" I try to control my voice, but there ain't nothing for it—it shakes.

"Mira." He touches my shoulder too. "I knew you'd been in the hospital with everything that had happened to you. So I didn't want to worry you."

I open my mouth, but I find I can't talk without crying, so I just cry. "No," I say. "Don't give me that ableist shit, Aaron. If you are my friend, and you are sick, then you fucking tell me." I pull my phone out of my leggings pocket and flash it at him. "One of my CF friends went to the hospital the other night. I just ordered her flowers. Another guy I met online is thinking of having a feeding tube put in. We were just chatting about that. And my friend Madi, she has pulmonary fibrosis, she just went into hospice. I've been texting with her husband, making sure he is okay. Well, he's not okay, obviously, but we've just been letting him know that he isn't alone. So." I put my phone back and nudge him again. "Please. If we're friends, let me be there for you. We don't get any better all by ourselves." Aaron lost both of his parents in a car accident years ago, he has no siblings or other family close by, and no partner. I think about him, all alone in the hospital with a fucking oxygen tube, and want to scream.

He nods. "I'm really sorry, Mira. You're right. I should have told you."

"I hope you never get sick again," I say. "But if you do, you are not alone, okay? Text me. I have my phone next to me day and night."

"Thank you," he says.

I reach up and hug him. He's all shoulder blades underneath his skin. If I could make all my friends all better again, I would.

"You ready?" I ask him, pulling back. He nods. "Let's run."

So we resume our jog-walk. Aaron texted the other day and said that it was almost his fortieth birthday, and he wanted to see if he could run four miles, and would I be up for joining him? (I had no idea my good boy Aaron was a Gemini.) So, we out here trying. It's the longest either of us has ever run. It's hard, but it's a beautiful day.

"You want to talk about it?" I ask him.

"Don't know," he pants. "Maybe a little."

He tells me he lost his sense of smell, doesn't know if it'll ever come back. He has a lingering cough sometimes, a weird new heart issue that the doctors don't fully understand yet. He says he thought he would die, and he was so afraid. Your girl Mira has no fucking clue what comes for us after death. How would I? Being sick doesn't actually give you some kinda magic wisdom, you know. So I don't know for sure that it's in fact any worse than being alive. Like, maybe it really is angels and clouds and eternal fucking paradise. I don't know. All I know is today. And today, looking at the blue, blue sky, all that heaven shit would have a tough time competing with this day.

"But, I mean, I got better," he says. "Slowly. I'm still taking it easy. But I am here."

"You sure are, bro."

I'm here too. I ain't never gonna be that one chick you always see on the news who wins the New York City Marathon. You know her—all flat skin etched over abs, thin blonde ponytail, the American flag draped over her narrow shoulders, the most boss badass you ever seen. But your girl has come a long way since the first time I put on my sneakers after the lung transplant and tried to run my first half-mile in Fort Tryon Park. I can feel my G-tube moving with me as I run now, which kind of sucks, but also my whole body doesn't ache with every step. And that, my friends, is a win.

This shit takes forever, though. Are we really gonna make it four whole miles? I wonder, as we slow to a complete walk for like the tenth time, arms around each other's waists. I am really not sure. But we sure as fuck are gonna try. As soon as we are both ready, we start running again.

For my birthday, Paloma asks me if she can give me something big. When I ask what, she says, "An electric guitar." I think about it for a while. Then I say yes. I also say, "Can it be a pink Fender Stratocaster?" She laughs and says, "Obviously. What else would it be?"

I set up my new pink Stratocaster and amp and play it for the first time at Paloma's apartment. I tune up and put the distortion on the amplifier. I ask Paloma what song she'd like to hear for my guitar's maiden voyage, and she says, "Do you know any Tove Lo?" We listen to her song "Sweettalk My Heart" twice for me to get the feel for it, 'cause I've never played any Tove Lo, with her dirty electronic pop, before. It will also take me a while to adjust to my new guitar, to mold my body around its cool dips and curves and its jagged pink edges, to retune my ear to its gritty rockstar voice. But I play for her a rock version of the breathy, sexy song, its deceptively, poisonously sweet invitations. Paloma is as complimentary as ever after my song, clapping and cheering for me, shaking her head, as always, at the fact that I am not world famous, someone as talented as she believes I am.

After the song, we sit at Paloma's kitchen table, and she does a birthday oracle card pull and interpretation for me. When she asked me if there was anything I wanted for my birthday, I said I'd just love to have a reading. She said of course. She chooses an oracle deck based on abundance for my reading. The card she pulls for me is all about taking action. Its image is that of an angel, surrounded by golden light that seems to glow right off the surface of the card, her pale arms extended in blessing. The message of the card reminds me that I am in charge of my own life and my own abundance. It also says that, whenever I take even one step in the direction of making my dreams real, the ever-abundant universe takes ten steps towards me in vibrational reply. The power of the card shimmers through me in undeniable resonance. I listen to the whispers of the deck as Paloma shuffles expertly.

Paloma pulls another card for me, this time asking the oracle if my wise inner self has any guidance for me around the action that the universe wants me to take. I remember—not so much with my conscious mind but with my subtle body, the sparks of my intuition and the magical imprints we left on my body when we did my sacred mapping—visiting my wise inner self on the beach at sunset during my shamanic healing journey. I feel her awareness rising and tingling inside me, like a pair of invisible energetic antennae.

The card we get is the same exact one we just pulled: taking action.

"Wow," Paloma says, laughing and making a note in her notebook. "Seems like the universe really wants you to start taking action around your own abundance, Mira."

I feel the uncomfortable, needling sense you get when a message just hits too hard, telling you something you know you need to hear and heed, but don't fucking want to.

"The truth is." On the outside, now, it wouldn't look like I'm doing a damn thing. But on the inside, let me tell you, I am fighting with every single one of my demons. There's embarrassment with its petty insults. There's shame with its clingy black sludge, and fear squeezing its tentacles around my heart. There's apathy threatening to overtake me, to persuade me with its seductive lethargy to do nothing, to remain small. I am about to admit something that I have never said out loud before. I know that everything in my life won't change in a magic instant just by me saying these words. But I also know that speaking a thing gives it power. Naming a thing makes it much, much harder to keep ignoring it, to keep suppressing your desire for it. If I say this, I am taking the first step towards it, and I am scared.

"The truth is." I fold my hands on the table. "Paloma, I don't know how to take action around my own abundance. I want to." My heart flutters with terror. My whole being is shaking like the last leaf clinging to a branch of a tree in the wind. "I mean. I see you. Being a ballet dancer and teacher and a whole entire freaking scholar. I see Araceli creating a life for herself around her art. She always has, and now she's starting to find ways to make a real living out of doing what she loves. And I'm so proud of both of you. That I get to love two amazing women like you. And then it makes me look at myself. I want that for myself. What you two are doing. What this card keeps telling me I need to do. I want to create abundance for myself with my art. I feel ashamed admitting this. But I also know I need to admit it. I don't know how to make that happen."

Paloma looks at me for a long moment after I've finished speaking. I know that look: she is trying to decide what to say to me, and how much. Finally she asks, "Can I say some stuff, Mira?"

"Of course," I say. Fuck, if all the amazing people in my life had even a single clue how much I desire for them to just tell me what to do, how to be a person.

She hesitates another moment, eyes on mine, before saying, "Girl, you are already making that happen."

"Making what happen?"

"You are already making amazing art, Mira. You do it every day."

"I do?"

This fresh little girl rolls her eyes at me. She must be wanting a spanking. "Of course you do. That music you were just playing?"

"You really think so?"

"Mira. I am one hundred percent here for women building each other up. Calling out each other's gifts. I can do that for you all day if you want me to. But honey. Really? Is it actually possible that you do not realize how fucking talented you are?"

My skin prickles, like it's too tight for my body.

I realize she's actually waiting for an answer, looking at me expectantly. "Uh…" I say. My face goes hot. "I, uh, don't know?"

"Mira. No. Come on. I want to hear you say it. Tell me you know how talented you are."

"I mean, I… I guess I don't suck? Not, like, all the way?"

She sighs, like she's exasperated with me, but she'll force herself to be patient with me 'cause she love me. The uncomfortable heat in my cheeks spreads somehow, down to the region of my heart. It transforms itself into a warmth that feels like being loved, like being seen, like being accepted. I don't know if I've always made the best choices in everything in my life. But when it comes to the lovers I've chosen to have around me, I have done better than good.

"Fine. Good enough for now. Though our next reading is gonna be about how you can tap into more confidence and seeing your own gifts." She pauses. "If you'd be, like, cool with that."

I swallow tears. "You have no idea how cool I would be with that."

"Anyway, point is, Mira, listen." She taps the surface of the abundance card with one finger, her nail painted a perfect light petal pink. "If you wanted to start creating abundance for yourself with your art, you could start, like, tomorrow."

"Really? How?"

She hesitates again, though I have no clue why. "You want some ideas around that?"

"Uh, yeah. Of course I do."

So Paloma turns to a fresh page in her notebook. It's a beautiful journal, a piece of art: the cover is slashed with real streaks of paint in shades of apricot and shocking pink, the texture of the brushstrokes creamy and bubbly when you run your fingers over them; the paper inside is handmade, with tiny pressed flower petals and green leaves nestled somehow amongst its cream-colored fibers. Paloma opens to the page with a sense of a new beginning, her gesture like taking in and letting out a deep, cleansing breath. At the top of the page, she writes with her smooth pink felt-tip pen, *Ideas for Miranda's Abundance.*

"First of all," she says, "you're invited anytime to come to the studio where I record my podcast. It belongs to one of my best friends, this guy who does a podcast and YouTube channel on ancient history and mythology for a living. So I can use the studio anytime. And so can you. You'll go there and start recording yourself playing your amazing guitar covers." She writes this idea down as number one on the page. Paloma is left-handed, something I don't think I ever even knew, before today.

"You really think I could do that?"

"Girl. Come on. I know you've seen how huge cover artists and bands are on YouTube. Even on Spotify. And you are better than all of them. And if you needed any help with, like, marketing or advertising or whatever, on YouTube and Spotify, my friend could help you. He knows all about that stuff."

"And he wouldn't mind me using his studio?"

"Not at all. In fact, when he sees how amazingly talented you are, he's gonna be thrilled knowing you're using his studio."

I swallow, shaky. "Okay," I whisper. I have to whisper because my heart is firing off in a cloud of sparkles. I'm trying to be cautious, but just the idea of recording audio or even video of myself playing music is low-key making my life right now. There's always been a secret part of me that wants my music to be seen by more people. More than one person, hearing me play, has asked if I'm in a band, or if I'd like to be. I don't think that being in a band, especially with a bunch of regular, healthy people, especially a band that wants to do anything like play shows in dirty dive bars at eleven PM, or go on tour to play dirty dive bars around the country in a shitty van that we'd have to sleep in, or practice for hours standing up in a cold basement, would really be possible for me. (Honestly, as much as I love music, and sharing music with other people, I can't see how that life would appeal to anyone. But to each their own, and all that shit, I guess.) But if I had a YouTube channel, a Spotify, I could play as much or as little as I wanted to, and I wouldn't have to go anywhere.

"I… I actually really like that idea, Paloma."

"You do? Oh, I'm so glad." Paloma underlines the idea. "Next," she says, beginning to write again, "you're going to start an Etsy store."

"I am? For what?"

She gives me that look of fond exasperation again. "So many things, Mira. And I have this other friend, Delia, who also has a witchy Etsy store and loves helping new artists get off the ground. When you're ready, I can put you in touch with her. But anyway. What are you going to sell in your store? Literally everything. Your witchy tea blends. Those little bags you sew out of fabric remnants, with lavender or potpourri or crystals or whatever other delicious thing inside."

"Sachets," I say, automatically, in a kind of daze.

"Sachets," she repeats, adding the word to entry number two, *Mira's witchy Etsy store.* "You fucking kick ass at sewing in general, Mira, and you know you do. There's all kinds of beautiful little things you could sew and sell, from cheaply and easily sourced fabrics and other materials. Little pillows. Those small gift bags with drawstrings. Worry dolls and little clothes for them. Coin purses. I mean, anything. You could make your own clothes and sell those if you wanted to, if you got interested in larger, longer-term projects." She puts her pen down, meeting my wide eyes. "Mira. You could do all of this and more. You're the textile person and kitchen witch, not me; I'm sure you could come up with tons of other ideas. You're unbelievably talented. Resourceful. I see you make magic out of literally whatever's around you every single day." At this, my eyes well up with tears. "Yes, Mira. I know you see it too. Talent and capability and ideas aren't the issue." She swipes away a few fallen tears from my cheeks with her thumb. "The only issue is finding the space to let yourself dream."

What would it take, I wonder, to really let myself dream? Is there a way I could brush away all of the dirt that's accumulated to me, the accrued shit of a lifetime of other people's worries and judgments, and fears about my health, and the layers of hurt of my childhood, and the pain and weakness of my body, and the hollow ache of being sure that I am not good enough? Could I sift my way through all of that, and find my crystals, the raw gems I know would be left behind, gather them to me, polish them off with the gentle force of my dreams, string them together into something beautiful that I could offer the world?

For now, I only nod, a tender and tentative and wordless assent.

"A couple more ideas?" she says.

"Okay," I say, my voice wavery.

She starts to write again. "Next. You're a writer. And a witch and a journaling expert. You put all those things together and create some magical printables for your store. Like journal prompts for different moon phases or different points on the wheel of the year. Guides for rituals and spells, the things you already do for yourself. You could make them digital printables or even write them up really pretty and mail them to people. People love getting shit like that in the mail."

Caught up in the whirlwind of her ideas, Paloma begins to write and talk even faster. "Find an online course on doing tarot and oracle readings for other people. There are some cheap and probably free ones. Take that. Then offer audio or video recordings of readings for people on your Etsy store. Like what you already do for your friends on their birthdays and stuff. Mira, those videos are sheer magic. You here at the kitchen altar with all the candles and the crystals, and you all dressed in necklaces and leather and lace, your makeup all dark glam, flowers and fairy lights woven in your Afro. Looking like the literal embodiment of black girl magic. You're powerful, Mira. And you're irresistible when you're in your power like that. I know you love sharing that magic with the people you love. But if you're serious about creating abundance from your art and your magic, then that's one really meaningful way. I know people would be thrilled to just throw their money at you when they see what your presence can do."

I'm speechless. Paloma rips the pages she's just written, three of them, out of her journal. She folds them in half, then into quarters, then hands the little packet of paper to me. With tiny flecks of dark dried green leaves and pressed pink flower petals amongst the soft paper, it looks like a sachet of powerful magic all unto itself. I take it from her, the smooth feel of it against the skin of my forefinger and thumb helping ground me back into earth.

"I have tons more ideas," she says. "But I feel like that's enough for now. Enough to get you started. Like I said, you are the witch here, Mira. Take this as a jumping-off point to come up with even more ideas. The ideas that only you could come up with." She takes both my hands in both of hers, the written magic spell of all our ideas held safely within our four palms. "And I bet you already know what it looks like, baby. But when you can, and when you're ready, make some space to really let yourself dream."

So that night, I set myself to giving myself space to dream. I stay up until midnight, the witching hour. It's just a few days ahead of a powerful full moon, called a full supermoon, and on a night when there will also be a lunar eclipse. This means that any intentions we cast during this lunation will be amplified.

I arrange everything, as always, at my kitchen table altar. Andre bought me a bouquet of red and white roses today, so I set them in a red vase, its body wrapped in white fairy lights, in the center of the table, and place crystals—smooth tumbled rocks like marbles—in a diamond shape around it. I dab a few drops of frankincense essential oil onto my wrists. I give myself a short cacao ceremony—boiling milk, dropping in a few spoonsful of brown sugar, murmuring my favorite affirmations to myself as I stir in an ounce of cacao powder and inhale deeply of its rich, bittersweet, brown, earthy aroma—and sit down at the table with my journal. I open to a fresh page, remembering Paloma doing this earlier today, and write a few incantations for myself. I write that my intention is to be open to dreaming. I write that it is time for me to enlarge the size of my dreaming—I am ready. I write that the dreaming is not merely an indulgence but also a portal. We are going to dream me into a new, different self.

I take a few sips of the cacao. It is both comforting and fortifying. What if I were to hold a cacao ceremony, for just a few souls, seated around this table? I write this idea down.

I pick up one of the crystals on my table. It's tumbled amethyst, dark as grapes, with subtle striations of wavy white, absorbing light into itself. I press its cool, smooth surface into my forehead. There's a hollow dip in the crystal, like an angel pressed its thumb there, and I imagine my third eye, whirling and indigo, nestling right into the open invitation of this hollow. I send out the wish that this crystal, and this ceremony, and this moment, open me, awaken me, increase my capacity for dreaming.

When I set myself to the dreaming, what I keep coming back to is the moment when Paloma claimed that she sees me making magic out of whatever's around me every day. My intuition has responded to this because, more than anything else, I see myself in those words. The memories unspool. There have been so, so many times that I have woven magic out of whatever I found around me, whether it was a feast, or just scraps, or even nothing. This girl who can't go anywhere has built lifelong friends and found family around herself, sometimes even over the magic digital cyber-waves. This girl made of skin and bones, this girl who's worried since she knew what sex was that she wasn't sexy, that there was no way this world's sex could work for sick people, has cast for herself a trio of lovers, and what a trio of lovers they are; look how she twists them like a kaleidoscope, seeing fractals and versions and cubist reimaginings of herself in the reflection of every one. How many times did I think I was gonna flunk outta school? A whole lot, okay, that's how many. But here I am, a lotta scars behind me, going back to school to learn more about something I love more than almost anything else. Here I am, dreaming about ways to support myself doing these things that I love. Once, when I was about fourteen, I walked in on my mom preparing herself and setting up her webcam to do online sex work. Later she said, "Mira, I would do anything to take care of our family." So your girl comes from a long line of women who do whatever they gotta do to get it done. I myself have done what I gotta do, things I didn't particularly want to do, plenty of times. If there is here a way for me to create abundance doing all my good magic, being handed to me like a gift, then I need to take it. I need to take it for me. I also need to take it for my trainwreck mother and my grandmother and her grandmothers, all the women in my line who didn't get the luxury of their heads up in the clouds.

And how many times, how many times, y'all, has your girl Mira snatched her ragged-ass, stitched-together life straight out the jaws of death? Too many times to count, that's how many—and counting. This story ain't over yet.

I dream myself all the way through. I dream myself like I'm giving myself really good sex—this is how I feel when my dreaming is done. I feel raw, and tender, and undone, and like I want to take myself to the metaphorical balcony to smoke a moody, metaphorical cigarette. I dream myself to good exhaustion. I dream myself to sleep. I am dreaming myself into and through a portal. And when I emerge from that portal, wet and fresh from the dreaming, I will be able to let go and leave behind who I was, step into who I am going to be.

Maybe my character, Tina, had some trouble casting spells for her friends. I, your girl Mira, clearly do not.

Over the years, there've been so many times I've wished and hoped and cast spells for Araceli to find her success as a photographer. And now all of those spells are coming to their fruition. She's got her whole amazing boudoir photography business going on. I went on Google to write her a review the other day (hey, I may not have paid her, but I totally was a legit client, okay, y'all), and saw that she has twenty-four glowing reviews so far, and a flawless five stars. She landed her agent late last year. And now, there's this.

Tonight is the opening of Celi's very first solo photography show… or, I suppose I should say, almost solo. It's actually a collaboration with her girlfriend Skye. I have never made a real creative project with a lover before, so what do I know, maybe this feels even better than a solo show. Well, either way, it's fucking amazing, and I am so proud of my girl.

It all came about because a burlesque friend of Skye's (she's a set designer, y'all remember, right?) is putting on her first burlesque show since before the pandemic. It's at a tiny black box theater on the Lower East Side, which just happens to have a small gallery space in the lobby. The director was telling Skye that she wanted to show something in the gallery all the nights of her show, which is running through the summer, to increase traffic to her show, and help out another artist, and spread the wealth around, and whatnot. And did Skye happen to know any cool artists making racy art who'd be willing to offer some pieces to sell on consignment?

"Fuck yeah, I do," Skye answered. "My girlfriend Araceli is a photographer, and she and I have actually been working on a project together."

I had no idea Celi and Skye were working on something together, but apparently this has been in the works for a few months now. One night Skye was telling Celi how much she misses designing sets: collaborating with someone on a vision, bringing all of the pieces together, seeing the actors using her space and bringing the vision to life.

Araceli smiled and said, "Girl. I have an idea."

They decided to imagine that they were writing a play together. The script was scenes from their life at home together, during the strange, lingering days of a pandemic that feels like maybe it's ending but also definitely isn't over yet. They rented a black box theater together, much like this one. Skye set up several scenes on their empty stage, rooms from a New York City apartment, drawn together using pieces from their actual apartment plus some thrift-store finds, worked her magic with the lighting.

Skye set up each of these scenes on the empty stage at the theater. Then Araceli entered the scenes like an actress, animating them with her presence, and shooting photographs of herself in them, capturing herself with her camera on a tripod using a timer. All of the photos are black and white, in Celi's signature style. Sometimes, it's just her, tender and haunting alone in the rooms that are also not-rooms. In other photos, she and Skye pose together, like they are in the middle of acting out one of the scenes of this melancholy play. Celi is nude, or mostly nude, in all of the shots. The sight of her takes my breath away, as does the knowledge of how much bravery it must take to be seen this way, her bare body on these walls, in front of so many eyes, free to be bought and taken home to a place where she'll never see these shots of her own nakedness ever again.

In one photo, Araceli sits on the couch in the living room, completely naked, putting chips into her open mouth with one hand and moving her other hand on the trackpad of her laptop, about to choose something on Netflix. I love the honesty of her hunched-over posture, the way her eyes almost wander into the field of the camera's lens, but not quite. In another, she's in the bathroom, topless, in only a pair of panties, looking in the mirror. Her back is to the empty theater, so the camera has captured her twice: her back facing the viewer, her reflection in the mirror over her shoulder. In the shot, she's fully made up with a heavy smoky eye and bold lip, three hairpins stuck in between her pursed lips as she curls a lock of a long dark wig with a curling iron.

In perhaps my favorite shot of the whole show, Araceli nestles in bed, her naked body almost entirely shrouded in fuzzy blankets and pillows, just a peek of one dark breast visible. Her lipstick is smudged around her mouth. She's crying, black eye makeup smeared down her cheeks. She's wiping her face with the knuckles of one hand, and looking directly into the camera as she cries. The shot is so intimate it hurts to look at. It reminds me of the time during my shoot with her when I cried, and it was okay, it was more than okay, she made me feel like we could make art even out of a moment that the world would reject, and shun, and tell us to stop or throw away or hide.

Skye appears along with her in three photographs, a triptych. (Y'all like that word? I just recently learned it.) In the first, they stand at the kitchen counter, Celi in a bra and panties and Skye in a tank and boxer shorts, taking food out of containers. It's so domestic, so everyday, so casual and honest, I can imagine stepping into the room right along with them. In the second shot, they are caught clearly mid-argument, faces contorted and mouths open, arms frozen in wide, angry gestures. I feel a deep jolt, looking at this one. How often do we get to see what it looks like when a couple argues? In the third shot of the triptych, they've moved to the balcony, which is supposed to recreate the balcony in their apartment, but, in a nod to a play so famous even I recognize it, is designed to look like a Juliet balcony, all romantic railing jutting out from a pair of French doors. Skye and Araceli are embracing in this one, Skye holding her from behind, her muscular arm around Celi's bare torso. Their bodies are facing towards the camera, but their focus is on each other, Celi twisted around to gaze up at her lover. The heat between them makes my heart race. I wonder who is going to buy this photo of two women so clearly and obviously in love, this image made of sheer tenderness and romance.

In the last two images of the show, Araceli and Skye sit, alone, in the otherwise empty theater, gazing at both the camera and the stage before them. In Celi's shot, she's naked except for a pair of dark leather thigh-high boots, slouched in one of the theater seats in the first row, legs draped over the arm of the seat. Her long wig is a riot of wild curls, her eyes painted in perfect cat-eye style, lush and dramatic. She looks directly into the camera with boldness, and insouciance, and the sexiest, sultriest resting bitch face you have ever seen. In Skye's shot, she's wearing old paint-spattered clothes and tattered Converse—the clothes she wore to make the sets, maybe— leaning forward with a kind of weary intensity, forearms braced on her thighs as she gazes at the stage. I wonder how she felt, looking at the stage she created for a shadow play that nobody would come to see; did it make her miss her art less, or even more?

The show is called *Scenes from a Lockdown: A Shadow Play by Araceli*

Henriquez & Skye Washington, and its opening night is seriously packed, or as packed as an indoor event is allowed to get during these pandemic end times. The space has a bar, so folks are ordering drinks, and waiters are circulating with appetizers. People are pulling their face masks down to eat and drink, and it is nice to see people, to be amongst people, again, to immerse myself in the buzz of an event again. As for me, I keep my face mask on pretty much the entire time, in protection of my ever-fragile immune system. I'm wearing a big bracelet on my tiny right wrist, which tells anyone who looks at it that I have CF; this is so that, just in case there are any other CF-ers present here, they'll know to keep six feet away from me. I make sure that everyone I chat with tonight has a chance to see it.

Celi and Skye are utterly bathed in admiration the entire night, as they damn well should be. They're inseparable, a unit, a constant pair, arms threaded together, faces wreathed in smiles so big they're apparent from behind their masks. I can't get over how amazing they both look. Skye is in a red pantsuit and a black lace bowtie, her hair buzzed close to her head. Celi is in a high-waisted skintight red pencil skirt and black leather bra and the thigh-high boots she wore in her empty-theater shot. Her long red wig curls all the way down to her ass. Now, their outfits are giving me wedding vibes, obviously, but not as much as their energy together. The way my girl look up at her woman like she actually hung the moon, the way Skye holds Celi close to her body and gazes down at her like she's her whole entire world—well, damn, y'all, if getting to see that ain't worth staying alive till now for, then ain't nothing, okay. These two are gonna get married and promise each other forever—and soon, if my intuition don't fail me. I, along with everybody else at this event, long to get closer to them, to stand within their orbit, just to imbibe some of the dregs of their auras, which are radiating pure luscious love.

Now who is on your girl Mira's arm this fine evening? Now, this was a whole thing. I wanted to bring Andre. And he totally wanted to be here. But because, obviously, creating new works of art is in the air right now, Andre and his buddy Jordan and some of their other dance peeps are playing this game where they choreograph, rehearse, and put on an entire ballet show in three weeks. No one is allowed to miss any rehearsal for any reason other than grave illness, and of course they have a rehearsal tonight. I told Celi this, and she sucked her teeth and said, "Girl, don't be sorry. Tell Dre not to be sorry neither. Tell him to go kick ass out there with his fine ballet self." So Andre is out there kicking ass at rehearsal with his fine ballet self.

Then Celi sighed and said, "You probably wanna take Miss Paloma, don't you?"

I said, "I won't bring her if it'll make you uncomfortable, Celi."

"If you wanna bring somebody, you should, Mira. You shouldn't come alone if you don't wanna."

"I could bring, like, Marco?"

Araceli gagged. "No. Please, no. My girlfriend cannot take my ex-boyfriend, who is also her twin brother, to come see nude photos of me. I know I'm a freak, but that is icky even for me."

I laughed, because, point taken.

"Girl. Come on. It's all right. Just bring Miss Paloma. If she, like, free and stuff. Like, if she ain't got nothing better to do."

"You sure? I don't wanna make you uncomfortable. Especially not on your big night. This should be all about you, *mi nena.*"

"Like." She shrugged. "It's fine."

"Celi, baby, why don't you like her?"

She sucked her teeth. "Miranda. I like her just fine. I been knowing Miss Paloma since we were kids."

I rolled my eyes. "It is so fucking weird when you call her Miss Paloma. Can you stop?"

She cackled. "No. I cannot. Your girl will forever be Miss Paloma to me." She held a finger to her chin. "You think she still want me to curtsey to her when I see her?"

"Araceli! *No te atreves.*"

"*Ya. No te preocupes.* I will act like I got some home training. I will act like a lady." She fluttered her lashes. "Satisfied?"

"Not really," I said. I cupped her face in my hands. "Araceli. Why don't you like Paloma?"

"Mira." She lifted her arms to cover my hands with hers. "*Ya te dije.* It's not that I don't like her. I just don't have anything in common with her. She's…" Araceli's lifted eyebrows said it all.

I sighed. "Yeah. I know."

"*Pero no importa nada,* okay? P ain't my girl. She is yours. If she make you happy, and respect you, and take care of you how you want her to in bed, and if she good to you, then she good with me, Mira, all right? That is all that matters." She slipped her hands off mine, leaned in and kissed me, to soften the blow of what she was about to say next. "And. Honey girl. I love you. You know that. But we need to stop you caring so damn much what everybody else thinks. And yes, even me. It don't matter what I think of your thing, Mira. All that matters is that it sit good with you. Yeah?"

"Yeah," I said. I released her face. "Paloma is really good to me, Celi. She takes really good care of me."

"Good. You happy with her?"

"Yes," I said. "I'm very happy."

"Then I'm happy for ya, baby. Go ahead and bring her to the opening. Please."

So I asked Paloma if she'd like to attend the opening of Celi and Skye's gallery show with me. She accepted immediately, like it wasn't nothing, 'cause to her, it wasn't. This is how confident girls, girls who are nothing like me, operate.

And here I am, on the night itself, Paloma on my arm. She looks gorgeous, in a floor-length sleeveless vegan-leather dress the color of mustard, so striking against her dark skin, her jet-black hair in one smooth, shiny, silky column down her back. I don't look so bad myself neither, in a tiny beaded black dress (H&M, seven dollars), heeled sandals from Goodwill, and the velvet fringed black shawl Araceli bought for me from the thrift store in Brooklyn. When I kiss her hello, my masked cheek pressed to hers, she touches a corner of the shawl and gives me a secret look, just for me. In the midst of all these people, here to see her and celebrate her, our women on our arms, that look thrills me.

Earlier today, I went over to Paloma's place on the Upper West Side so we could get ready together. We ate lunch and tried to watch a movie, which got abandoned when I climbed into her lap and straddled her. It reminded me of the first time we ever made love, which started exactly like that, in her big elegant apartment by Central Park, me straddling her lap after we'd watched a movie. We have come a long way since then, though, she and I.

Paloma carried me to her bed. I went down on her, feasting on her warm sweetness, the way her flesh went all swollen under my tongue. Looking at me licking her off my lips, wiping my chin like a satisfied hunter, her eyes went dark and she said, "I want to go down on you too, Miranda." I told her I didn't know if I could come like that, like I say pretty much every time one of my girls wants to eat me, and she asked if I would still like it, and I said yes.

So she got between my legs and went down on me. I liked the way she slid her hands underneath my thighs to bring my pussy as close as possible to her face, like she couldn't bear to be away from my body. She licked me for a long time, till I was feeling tired. I asked her to stop.

Paloma lay next to me and held me. We were both tired, actually; she was panting. I could tell she was sad, so I touched her face and asked her what was wrong. Sometimes with Paloma I feel a way I've never felt with anybody before, which is motherly: like this older and sophisticated woman is younger than me, like she's somebody who needs my comfort and protection.

Her eyes got wet and she said, "I know it's dumb. And I'm sorry. But I guess I'm just a little bit sad."

"What you sad about, baby girl?"

"Like I said. It's dumb. But I guess I'm just sad that you don't like oral as much as I do."

I just looked at her for a moment, wondering how to respond to this foolishness.

"Uh," I said. "Am I, like, supposed to?"

"No," she said.

"Is it not okay that I don't like everything you like? That I have my own likes and dislikes?"

"Mira, no," she said. She wiped her face. "Of course it's okay. It's totally okay. I told you. I'm just being dumb. It just makes me a little sad. But I need to accept it and get over it."

This hurt, way more than I would have thought it would.

I said, "Do you still wanna have sex with me?"

"Mira," she said. She stroked my hair. "Of course I do. Are you kidding me? I'm obsessed with you, Mira. *Estoy loca por ti.* I always want you. Always."

We kissed then, and the moment passed; we found our way out of it. But things stayed weird between us, as we got ready side by side for the event, as she got us an Uber to the Lower East Side and we rode down here through the warm May sunset, and even now, though I do feel close to her, all her loveliness on my arm, her palpable excitement tonight for my friend and her girl.

I am trying to grow into somebody who is big enough to hold all of my feelings. I am trying to be somebody who can have a fight with her lover and not think her girl is going to leave her. I want to realize that I do not have to be, that I can't be, anybody's perfect match in order to have sex with them. I am me. I ain't moldable, conformable. I am trying to realize that it's okay, it's good, that Paloma and I have fought and moved through it. We are getting stronger. I am getting stronger. Or, well, I'm trying to. Do you think I'm doing a good job of it? Am I doing enough, do y'all think?

Paloma and I circulate throughout the space. We eat tiny tarts, some hot and savory with little bits of meat inside, some sweet with fruits and cream. Paloma looks impossibly elegant, drinking a glass of pink champagne with little bubbles like shards of crystal, a fantasy that's at once mine and still feels enticingly unattainable. I have a few sips of sparkling water. I eat and drink quickly, so I won't have to have my mask off for very long.

We say hi to them when we first arrive, but we don't get to speak with Celi and Skye properly till a good while into the event. They're surrounded by well-wishers and theater and photography people and art lovers who want to buy their pieces, or book Celi for a shoot, or learn more about their work. I want them to have their moment. This is why I'm here, why I put all my magic behind casting this spell: so Araceli could continue to take her place within her world. I'm her girl, always have been, always will be; I knew and loved her before all these folks knew her name, and I will be with her long after they post a cute selfie on Insta and shoulder their tiny purses and find the nearest subway stop on their phones and leave her alone in an empty gallery. So tonight, I wait my turn to speak to her.

We give them cheek kisses again when we all meet for the second time, standing together in a little circle of four in a corner of the space. We're clustered underneath the photo of Celi getting ready in front of the bathroom mirror on the stage. For a moment, we're quiet, just sharing an exhale, a brief island of calm in a chaotic sea, New Yorkers all a little manic at the breathless joy of getting to be together again, to see and be seen at an event, the feeling so unbearably good it almost hurts. Araceli looks at me with a smile quirking the corners of her eyes. She visibly relaxes her posture, her shoulders softening as she looks at me. I love getting to be a safe space for her. In our bubble of quiet swells the music playing faintly as background atmosphere to the event. It's heavy metal, one of Celi's secret loves. The unintelligible tortured screams and frantic distorted guitars send a thundering shiver zipping down my spine, a not unpleasant feeling.

"Congrats, you two," Paloma says, breaking our silence. "This is amazing."

"Thank you," they chorus.

"No, no," she says. "I feel like I should be thanking you. For making this beautiful art. For hosting this event. For having us."

"It's our pleasure," says Araceli with a warm smile, the perfect picture of graciousness.

"We're so glad you're enjoying yourself," says Skye.

"Oh, I am. You'll have to point out to me who to talk to so I can buy a few pieces. I've just recently closed on a house in New Jersey. I've been in the market for some pieces that really speak to me. I'd love to have some of your photographs hanging in my space."

"Thank you, we really appreciate your support," Skye says.

"Wow, a house," Celi says. "That is an amazing accomplishment. *Felicidades,* Paloma."

"Thank you," she says. Paloma snakes her arm around me lightly, touches my hip. "Maybe someday Mira and I can host you both there. I haven't really entertained there yet. But I want to."

I nod, low-key tryna swallow the plain fact that I am fucking a woman who casually uses the word "entertain," like it ain't nothing. "Paloma has a beautiful garden there," I say. "Flowers and greens and even fruit trees. It's, like, magical."

She smiles at me. "Mira is helping me decorate the garden so I can attract some fairies there."

Araceli smiles at both of us. "Mira's an expert at contacting the world of the fae."

"Araceli," Paloma says. Celi looks at her expectantly. "Can I ask about your use of black and white photography?"

"Of course," she says. "It's kinda my signature aesthetic style."

"I love that. Why did you make that choice? What does it mean for you?"

"Portraits are my photographic love," Araceli says. "People are my favorite thing to shoot and at the heart of what I do. I'm trying to capture people who might not have been thought of as traditional photographic subjects, not traditionally beautiful or 'photogenic,' and make art out of their portraits. Or make art out of people's moments and postures and expressions and emotions that have not traditionally been considered photogenic or even proper to be captured or looked at. I like to put the ugly, and the unfinished, the undone, the ungraceful, the awkward, the unpretty right front and center. And challenge us to find the art in it."

"Wow," Paloma says, saying what we are all thinking.

"Yeah," says Celi. "And as for the black and white, I like the way it makes the human subject just pop. When there ain't nothing else to look at, no colors to use as a crutch, you forced to look the person right in the eye. And confront them."

"It was such a great artistic challenge to light the scenes, knowing they were gonna be shot in black and white," Skye says. "I didn't know what they were going to look like, not like when you design a theater set and you know exactly what the audience is gonna be looking at. I had to just imagine."

Paloma nods. "Well, you did a fucking amazing job, Skye."

"You really did, baby," Celi says.

"Like in this one." Paloma points up at the photo hanging over us. "Skye, I love how most of her face is in shadow here, how it really makes her eyes pop."

"Skye encouraged me not to be afraid to make eye contact with the camera, with the viewer, in this series. I hope I rose to that challenge."

"You did," they both say.

"Skye, I just love your bowtie, by the way," Paloma says.

She touches it. "Thank you. I bought it in Athens, actually. I traveled to Europe in 2017."

"Athens!" Paloma says. "Are you kidding me? I love that city. I'm an archaeologist and historian, so it's a big part of my work too."

"That's cool. But nah. I was just running. My mom had just passed away."

"Oh, Skye. I'm so sorry."

"Yeah. Thank you. I was running from everything. My grief. My feelings. Myself. I had no money. I was living on a friend's couch in Brooklyn at the time. I got a credit card and flew to Athens 'cause somebody told me it was the cheapest city in Europe. I wandered around alone for two weeks in a total daze. I didn't speak to nobody. I didn't know nothing. I just cried and ate these little packets of cream crackers from the street vendors. 'Cause it was all I could afford."

"I love those cream crackers," Paloma says, though of course when she travels, she can eat and do and see whatever she likes, stay wherever she wants.

"Aren't they good? Well, I wanted to bring back something to remember the trip. And that time in my life. So I got this from a designer selling her stuff in this little stall in an alleyway. Really cute, butch, edgy stuff." She touches the bowtie again. "When I wear it, I remember that I can feel my feelings. I can run away. I can be alone. I can feel like complete shit. I can hold myself through it. And, somehow, I can come back from all that."

We all nod at this, like you do, like you do when you hear some deep shit that really hits, and there ain't words neither necessary nor appropriate to the occasion, so you just nod. Now this conversation, it fills me with longing, y'all. I'm feeling tender and permeable. I am feeling susceptible to dreams. Someday, one day, I want to run away, and cry for days, and survive however I can even when it feels like I might not be able to, and feel all the shitty feelings and hold myself through them. I wanna come back and make art. And it may not look like how Skye did it, or how Paloma would. But I wanna find my way. Tonight, though, my first step, it's feeling this longing. It's seeing this reflection of what's possible for me.

A little later, I head to the bathroom, and when I enter, I feel someone grabbing onto the door after me and entering too. I glance back and see that it's Skye, and in the brighter lights of the bathroom, she looks even cooler and more badass, her red suit and red sneakers and red silk face mask. We smile at each other and go into stalls side by side.

I lift up my dress and pull down my panties and squat over the seat. For a long, stupid moment, even though I really need to pee, I can't; I'm too nervous to go when Skye, this cool AF woman whom I like a lot and am also intimidated by, is right next to me and can hear everything.

But of course, she is here to pee too—she is human, just like me—and I hear her unzipping her pants and letting out a sigh, then beginning to pee. That little sigh she makes, that hits me hard, y'all. I feel a weird and sudden spike of joy, knowing that we're here, sharing this moment of privacy and relief together. Then I hear her start going, her pee hitting the water loudly, and this allows my bladder to release too, and then we're peeing together.

After, we wash our hands together at the sinks. I see that, under her red suit jacket, she's wearing a black lace cami, which matches her bowtie, the one she looks at to remind herself of her ability to hold herself through her feelings.

"Are you enjoying yourself, Mira?" Skye asks me. The way she looks at me, meeting my eyes in the mirror, a little furrow between her big brown eyes, lets me know that she ain't just asking to be polite or to bullshit. She wants to hear my actual answer.

"Yes, I am." Skye and I grab paper towels and dry our hands, throw the towels into the trash. Even then, though our business in this room is done, we stay, which reinforces my intuitive knowing that she wants some real talk from me. "I am so damn happy for you and Celi. I have wanted this for her for so long."

"I know you have." She smiles. "I'm so happy Araceli has you to love her. To love her too."

"You love her a lot, don't you, girl? Like really, really."

Skye puts a hand on her heart, on the black lace covering it under her suit jacket. "Yes. Like really, really."

I smile back. My heart lifts in my chest and soars.

Skye touches my arm. "How are you feeling, Mira? How are you, girl?"

I feel the smile dissolve from my face. I know it hasn't, but it feels like it's been a long-ass time since someone asked me how I'm doing, for real, and wanted to hear my answer, and waited for it, instead of assuming or anticipating what they thought I was going to say. And because she's giving me time, looking at me with gentle patience, I give myself time too. I take a quiet moment to probe inside my heart.

"Skye," I say, "can I ask you something, girl?"

"Course you can."

"Your trip to Europe. You said you were able to move through the feelings you were feeling. That you were able to feel the sadness and all of the shit. You were able to cry for days. And wander. And then you were able to come back. And..."

Skye puts a hand on my shoulder and squeezes it. It's wordless support, it's saying it's okay if I speak more, or if I stay silent, if I can do more, or if this is all I can do, it's okay and I have done enough. It helps me drag in a shaky breath—remembering all the days and years of my life when I simply couldn't take a deep breath like this—and keep going.

"And, so, like, how did you move through those feelings? Do you ever still feel that sadness? Were you able to leave it behind? Or do you ever feel like there's still a sadness?" My voice catches. This woman nods at me, like your girl is saying something really good. "Do you ever feel like, I don't know, like the sadness is insurmountable? That it's just lurking under the surface, always? That it's part of your being and you cannot actually outrun it?"

"Mira." Her brow creases again. "Baby girl, I hope I did not give you the impression that I'm, like, cured or some shit." She laughs, a big laugh that helps make me feel better. You can just see why my girl Celi loves this woman. "Because I am not cured. I did not go on some big spiritual journey and come back all healed from everything that had ever hurt me. If that's a thing, then girl, that is some white-people bullshit."

We both laugh, me through considerable tears.

"And I do not do white-people bullshit. Honestly, though, you even be seeing a lot lately about black and brown joy. To which I say, yes, girl, slow clap." We laugh again. "Give me some of that colored-people joy. Oh, yes. But…"

"Spiritual bypassing," I manage to get out.

"Right. And, like you said, the sadness. Yeah, Mira, you're right. There is so much sadness. I didn't cure that outta myself. I couldn't outrun it. I still feel sadness every day of my life. You don't believe me, you can ask Araceli." She smiles. "Stupid shit at my job makes me sad. Missing my mom makes me sad. That she doesn't get to see me and Celi together. Finishing a season on Netflix makes me sad. The prison industrial complex. Homelessness. My trans best friend getting harassed in the street. So much stuff, big and little shit, still makes me sad. Life can be sad. I don't think there's anything we can do about it."

"Maybe we don't need to do anything about it," I say. "Like, maybe it's okay there's sadness. Maybe it's okay to be sad. Not to judge our feelings as good or bad, allowed or not allowed."

"To feel all our feelings and all of that shit," she says.

"To feel all our feelings and all that shit," I echo. "Yes, right."

"Mira," she says, "can I hug you?"

"Yes, please," I say, and Skye pulls me into a lovely, tight hug. My best friend, my girl, is going to wear this woman's ring. She's gonna have this woman's baby. This is the first time they're gonna make art together and show it to the world, not the last. This woman is gonna take care of my girl, and listen to her, and support her, and hold her down, even after the days when I won't be in this world anymore. That's so many years from now. And that makes me happy—thinking about all the things I am still going to do. It also makes me sad, irreparably.

"I'm so glad Celi has you," I say, when we pull back.

"We have each other," Skye says. "We all do, baby girl. Let's all get together soon, huh, like your girl Paloma said. Let's sit in her garden and, like, contact some fairies."

I smile, big enough to make it past my tears. "I would love to contact some fairies with you."

We stay until the party begins to wind down. Waiters no longer circulate with food. The bar closes for the night. People say goodbye: some hug and kiss; others, who probably used to hug and kiss a year and a half ago, now bump fists or elbows. There are little red stickers now on many of the photographs, which means that someone has bought and paid for them and will be taking them home once the show closes after the summer. Paloma has bought *Front Row Center,* the shot of Araceli sitting alone naked in the first row of the theater in her thigh-high boots. She insisted on buying one for me too. I would've gone for *End of the Night,* the one of Celi crying in bed, but it was already spoken for, so I had to choose my second-favorite, *Girl's Night Out,* where she gets ready in front of the mirror with sharp hairpins held between her heavily painted lips. I think I'm gonna hang it in my bathroom.

We stay until there's almost no one left at the venue, just the event hosts and Celi's agent Naomi and the cleaning crew and Celi and Skye. After a long conversation ends—Araceli and Naomi and some, apparently, big-ass hotshot New York City art collector—and the collector sweeps on her literal red cape and heads out into the night, Celi grabs my arm.

"Come with me to the bathroom?" she says, voice low. I can hear it in her tone, the way only a best friend can: this night's amazing, to be totally fucking sure, but it's also damn overwhelming. She needs to shed the persona for a couple minutes, to be herself for a hot second with her best girl. I link my arm with hers and go with her.

In the bathroom, Araceli takes off her face mask. I take off mine too. She goes into a stall to pee, without closing the stall door, and I go into the stall next to her and pee too, even though I don't have to go very much, since I just recently went. We wash our hands. Celi is staring at her reflection, taking big deep breaths.

"Fuck," she says. She meets my eyes in the mirror. "Sometimes I wish I still did fucked-up shit. Like fucked three or four different randos in a night. Drank till I passed out in somebody's bathtub. Snorted coke off hot white girls' stomachs." She gives me a shaky smile. In fact, her whole body is shaking slightly. "Look at me now, Miranda. All domesticated and shit. Up in here making fucking art with all them bougie folks. I don't do nothing bad anymore."

"Celi, baby," I say.

"Look at me, Mira," she says again. She turns, leans back against the sink. I do too, looking at her. "Skye wants to marry me."

Celi makes an ugly face. She don't say it, she don't have to, I can hear it: how can someone, someone as boss as Skye, want to marry her? How can she, someone as fucked up and imperfect as her, be good enough for someone to make a lifetime commitment to her? I can hear it all not only 'cause I know Araceli so damn well, inside and out, but because I've had all those same thoughts myself. This is one of the many reasons why Araceli and I are soul mates: we know how to hold a believing mirror up to each other, when our trust in our selves wavers.

"Of course she does," I say. I nudge her shoulder with mine. "You're a fucking goddess."

She bares her teeth at me. "I don't even get drunk anymore, Mira," she says. "I just have half a glass of wine on the balcony like the fucking Duchess of Cambridge."

"Who?" I ask, unable to keep a laugh from bubbling up.

"Girl, I don't know," she says, breaking into laughter too. "But I don't really drink. I don't even smoke weed no more. I haven't gotten high in a literal year, Miranda. A year. Can you even believe that?"

"Do you miss it?" I ask her.

"Fuck yeah, I do," she says. She lets out a long deep breath. "I mean, it ain't that simple, right. I love being a good girl. I love waking up in the morning with a clear head like a chick from fucking Instagram. Like saying my fucking affirmations in front the mirror or some shit. I like getting to be, like, present and shit. I'm making the best art of my life. I think it's 'cause I have the space and time. I'm not partying and fucking around all night, waking up sick and lost, losing half the day. But, I mean, yeah. I do. Yeah." She looks at me, such an unguarded look, it's more intimate than being naked. "I do miss it. I miss numbing out, you know? I miss forgetting. 'Cause look at this shit." She turns around again, looks at her reflection in the mirror. "Y'all got me up in here feeling shit. I'm in love and I'm loved back and I'm scared. I'm getting noticed, 'cause I don't actually suck, I'm actually good. And good things are coming for me. But how do you turn the bad thoughts and memories off? How do you meet the good when there's so much bad shit behind you? Like, how are you supposed to feel your way through this fucking world? How are you supposed to live your life just feeling shit all the time?"

"Girl," I say. "I—"

Araceli's phone rings, from the pocket of her tight red pencil skirt. She pulls it out and looks at it. "Whoever the fuck that is," she says. "Naomi been saying I can't put my number on my card and then never answer my phone, though. So let me see who the fuck this is."

She swipes to answer the call and brings the phone up to her ear. "Hello?" she says. She furrows her brow as the person on the other end of the line speaks. She wraps her other arm around her middle, elbow supported against her wrist. "Uh, yeah, it is," she says, almost like a question, looking up to meet my eyes.

"Um, yeah, I do," she says. She squeezes herself tighter, arm banded over her belly, listening. "Oh, she did, huh?"

I wonder who she's talking about.

"Oh," Celi says. "Oh… fuck. God, she did?" Something in her voice makes my heartbeat spike. We meet eyes again. "Fuck. So do I need to, like… come there?" After the person answers, she says, "Okay. I'll come. I'm on my way soon. I just…"

Araceli pulls the phone away from her ear. She looks down at it. A woman's voice is saying something. She taps the red circle on the screen to end the call. I'm approaching her, coming into her space even before I've fully registered that she is shaking, harder now, and her eyes are watering.

"Araceli? Celi, baby, what happened?" I take her elbow in one hand and her phone in the other, I'm scared she's gonna drop it on the wet, grimy floor. "Celi, *bebecita. Dime que pasó. Por fa'.*"

I put the phone in my tiny purse so I can take her shoulders gently. I feel the vibration of her body down to my own bones.

"It's Rosita," she says. Rosita is the woman who "raised" Celi, a cousin of her mother's. Araceli's mother, fifteen when she had my sweet friend, undocumented, alone and afraid, gave birth to her alone in her bedroom. We don't know who Celi's father is. Her mother, Leona, left Araceli with a friend, and she ran away. (From what we know, she passed away a couple years later, we don't know where or from what.) Baby Araceli was passed around amongst a few friends and family members until Rosita agreed to take her. I wish my friend, my Aries springtime girl with the soul of a philosopher and the eye of an artist and dreams so big only New York City could hold them, had found her happy ending then. I won't say more, it ain't my place, but she didn't, not back then. That's where I come in, though, your girl Mira. Whatever this is, for the rest of our lives, I am here to be by this sweet girl's side.

"*Ella se murió*," she says. Her voice is surprisingly strong, even as she continues to shake. I hold her a little tighter.

I lean forward, putting my lips against her cheek. Her skin feels cold. "Oh, Celi. Do they know what happened?"

She shrugs. "Heart attack, they said." She shudders in my arms. "That means an overdose. With Rosita, you know that's gotta be what that means."

"Celi, honey. What do you need? What can I do? Is she at the hospital? Do we need to——"

A sound comes out of her, somewhere between a sob and a scream. She struggles back, so we can look at each other. "Mira," she says. Tears squeeze out of her eyes. "I don't know why the fuck I'm crying." She sobs again. "I'm not sad. *No estoy triste.* I'm angry." She works an arm between us to wipe her eyes viciously. "Why am I even angry, though? I mean, who cares? Rosita was… she did…"

She lets out another raw, angry sound. She gives her head a shake, as though to clear it, to reset. "But yeah, they said I have to——"

The bathroom door swings open. It's Paloma, wide eyes, a vision in yellow in the doorway. "Mira? Araceli? What's going on? Are you two okay?"

I shake my head. I grip Araceli by her biceps. "No, we're not okay," I say. I feel awful, my heart sinking down to my belly (which is starting to ache, as my many surgical scars sometimes do at night), but it also feels good to tell the truth—to be in a space, amongst a circle, where we can tell the damn truth. "Paloma, baby, can you please go get Skye?"

Against me, Araceli nods.

"Yes, Paloma, please. Can you go find her and bring her here? Celi needs her."

Within moments, Skye strides into the bathroom, Paloma, a little tentative, behind her. She hovers by the door while Skye approaches Celi and me, gently taking one of her girlfriend's arms. We stand in a circle of three while Araceli repeats the story, her voice more subdued this time, but still laced with the threat of angry tears. Skye nods and listens, her face gradually filling up with empathetic pain. It hurts to look at.

"What do you need, baby?" Skye asks her.

I nod. "*Lo que necesites.* We're here."

"They said I have to go to the hospital."

Skye nods. "Okay. Do you want to do that?"

Araceli pauses. For a moment, just a flash, I see the little girl in her, lost, confused, and afraid. My girl is so smart, so capable, so utterly able to take care of herself and see herself through anything, that I have only rarely seen this fragile whisper inside of her. I don't know if I'm glad to see it, or heartbroken. Then she nods.

"Okay," says Skye. "Let's go do that, then."

"Skye, will you come with me?" she whispers.

"Araceli. Honey," she says. And that is all she says. But in the silence after it, I hear it all: Skye is saying, girl, how could you even ask me that? She is saying, I got you forever and I will go with you anywhere, I'd follow you into the shadows underneath the earth if I had to.

"Okay," Celi says. She turns to me. "Mira, you can't go," she says. "There be way too many germs there. And I know you're still healing from that tube infection thing." She looks past Skye and me, outside of our circle, and says, "Paloma. It's late and this is a whole bunch of shit. *Oye.* Rosita, she was the woman who, like, raised me, or didn't raise me or whatever 'cause she was kind of a shitshow, but anyway, we just heard that she passed away. Skye and me, we're gonna go to the hospital and, like, claim her body or whatever shit. Can you please take Mira home? And whatever else she needs?" Araceli looks at me. "This woman was a real piece of work, but we knew her basically all our lives. Please take care of Mira. Make sure she's okay."

Fuck, this makes my heart hurt.

Paloma comes and puts her arm around me. Celi says, "Where's my phone? Let me see where this fucking hospital is." Skye gets Celi's phone from me and puts it in her pocket. She hugs her, for a long, silent moment. She rubs Celi's back while she washes her face at the sink. Someone pokes their head in the bathroom and asks if we're all okay. Skye tells them, firmly, that we are fine, and they leave. Skye hugs me, and then she hugs Paloma.

"Fam, we'll text you later," she says. "We're gonna go now."

They go, hand in hand, leaving Paloma and me alone in the bathroom of the venue where all their beautiful pictures still hang on the walls. Some of them have red stickers, waiting to go to their forever homes; others wait to be seen another night, when surely the one who is meant for them will see them and claim them.

Paloma hugs me to her. I go gratefully into her embrace, glad to be held in the circle of her strong body. "You okay, *sirena*?" she whispers into my hair.

I shake my head against her breasts. "Like, no, not really." My heart squeezes painfully, thinking about my girl Araceli and what she has to face now, in a place where I can't follow. Skye is with her, and I'm happy about that, but that doesn't mean I won't worry and think of her constantly.

"Do you want me to take you home?" she says. "To your place? Or mine? Or, well, wherever you want to go?" She squeezes me. "I'm here. For whatever you need."

"Let me text Andre," I say. I pull back and look at her. "I'd love for you to sleep over at our place tonight. I mean, if both you and Andre are cool with it."

She kisses my forehead. "Mira. Of course I am."

I text Andre. He doesn't answer, which means he's probably still in rehearsal. Their last rehearsal lasted until legit one o'clock in the morning, y'all. I can't even imagine. It's only, like, ten thirty right now, and all I've done all night is stand around, and I'm feeling so tired and achy I just wanna collapse. How can these people just dance for hours?

"Let's just get you home, hummingbird," Paloma says. "If Dre needs his space, I can always just grab an Uber home."

Just like when we came here, Paloma calls us an Uber. And when it comes, just like when we came here, Paloma and I ride in the back of the car in silence. But how different this ride is from the one we took here. My girl's arm snakes around me, holding me close, keeping me tied to the earth. I feel sick with grief, and with confusion, and with love, and gratitude, as she takes me home.

A week later, it's the night of Andre's show. I'm here in the audience at the theater by myself, sitting at the end of a row next to a stranger. I wanted it like this, just me, to see him dancing again for the first time in years. The house lights in the theater fade away, and the stage lights come on. The show is about to begin. I feel a lifting, swooping sensation in my stomach—part excitement, part anticipation, part nerves for my man. I know how much it means for him, and how nerve-racking it is, to be dancing again.

Last night, I recorded myself playing my new electric guitar for the first time. I had Andre take a video of me in our living room. I played this emo white-boy rock song from like twenty years ago, it's called "I Hate Everything About You." It felt cathartic to sing it, to scream its deceptively simple but skin-searing lyrics, and it floated all kinds of sick memories up to the surface. Araceli liked this song when we were kids. She played it for me and we listened to it over and over again, for hours, when we were two hurt, angry girls who hated our families and didn't understand why we also loved them. Back then, before my new lungs, I would not have had the lung capacity to sing a song like this.

But now, I was able to sing this song and play it on my new guitar and text the video to Araceli. For some people, when someone dies, you send them flowers or a card or maybe some food. But to my girl, I send this alt-metal song about also hating the people you love. What can I say, Celi and I just get each other. We are twin flames. In response to the video, Celi sent me a string of about thirty-seven emojis, a rainbow of hearts including multiple hearts on fire, the fireworks, the flaming meteor, the lightning strike, the rocket ship, and all the most emotive faces, like the one with its head blown off, the scream, the swirly-eyed one, and the one with thick streams of tears running down its face. She also sent me a selfie of her in bed in the dark, her own face wet with tears. Without a single word, my girl said everything.

And I guess I did too, y'all. With that music, I was saying, I know you, girl. I see your heart. I see and embrace even your darkness, and past the smoke in your mirror, I see the reflection of my own darkness. I was saying, girl, we got history. I share your memories and I know your secrets. And I was saying, you and me, girl, we got a future. In our lives, ain't nobody know what's coming next. But whatever it is, I will be with you through it.

I have a thought, as spotlights illuminate the stage and the dancers are revealed, which is that maybe what I do, what I have been doing, ain't all that different. You release your art out into the world, and it hits somebody. Maybe I've only been playing a song for one or two people, or writing a blog post that gets a few comments, but how, really, is it different? Maybe I am not on the stage, like the dancers here, but my art too, it has wings.

I had no clue what this dance performance would be like. Andre didn't tell me a thing about it in advance, which is just the way I wanted it. (If I had asked, he would have told me.) So as the dancers take the stage, I have no idea what to expect, and I am able to take it in with an open mind. Truth is, I seen Andre dance many, many times, since we were kids, but I have never seen him as a choreographer. I've seen him dance classic ballets and pieces choreographed by his mom or other teachers at the ballet school, he taught me how to waltz and we danced together at my *quinceañera,* I've seen him improvise and play around and even striptease, but this is the first time I get to see what he has done as a creator of dance himself, with time and space that belong only to him.

There are three dancers in the piece, Andre, his friend Jordan who owns the studio he's dancing at now, and Lana, a young woman also studying at the school. Lana is tiny and doll-like and blonde, eighteen years old, and, as I discover within minutes of starting to watch her, a remarkable dancer, both technically skilled and fearless. I wonder if I will ever become that good at anything.

I guess I can say I had no preconceived ideas, but still, the piece they made together is nothing like I would have expected. I wondered a lot about the music that they would choose. But there is no music. Instead, what begins to float in the dark, hushed space of the theater around us is the sonic landscape of a forest. I feel my ears perking up at every sound. There's the tinkling twittering of birds, faint, intermittent, sugar-sweet sounds that gain strength and volume over time, as the invisible birds pick up their call and response. There's the constant music of water. It drips rhythmically off leaves and onto the forest floor, a gentle rain. Somewhere blended into this soundscape there is a creek, or a stream, I can hear it bubbling and gurgling its way through the earth of this place. Sometimes there is a gust of wind and the symphony created by its disturbance in the world around it: a great rustling of all the trees in chorus, and a shower of water surprised from where it lay held in the cups of leaves, and a wet flapping of birds' wings, and a mysterious, unnamable sound like the goddess of the whole earth exhaling a breath.

Y'all know good and well that I ain't never been to no forest. But these sounds, and the darkness of the theater, and the possibilities of art, and the layering of the dancers' feet falling against the wood of the stage over the forest's music, well, it makes me feel like I am there. It all coalesces to allow me to imagine that I am there.

Projected onto the blank space of the backdrop behind the dancers, there is an image of a patchwork of leaves. It's transparent, and it casts a rippling, pale green translucence over the faces and bodies of the dancers as they move. I have never seen anything like it.

I don't know that much about ballet. I don't know nothing, though; I have been with a ballet dancer for most of my life, I've been surrounded by dancers. So I know enough to recognize that this is more ballet fusion than a pure form of ballet; its distinctive lines are broken, its perfect erect postures sometimes hunched or slumped or distorted. I even recognize that these looser, more fluid shapes originate in contemporary dance, a style Andre loved when we were teenagers.

Andre's mom didn't want him taking contemporary dance classes; she worried that it would "dilute his classical technique" (her words, obviously). But he paid for them with his own money and found a class that met at nine PM, after school and work and a couple of hours at his mom's studio. Hungry for time together, I'd sometimes go home after school, exhausted from my usual day of being a sick person carrying around an oxygen tank, try to sleep for a couple hours (if no one was yelling at each other at home), struggle with some homework, refill my oxygen tank, and then take the train with Andre to his contemporary class. We'd hold hands on the train, thighs pressed together as we sat as close as we possibly could, and talk about anything and everything. The class was on the Upper West Side, at a studio above a Fairway. Sometimes I'd wander the cold aisles of the store while he danced, looking at crates of produce and plastic containers of nuts and olives and cheese, which Fairway is famous for. The store was bright in the dark of the night, small and mazelike and cramped. Once I met there another girl who had cystic fibrosis; she saw my CF bracelet and tapped her own wrist and mouthed, "Me too," at me. So we waved at each other across the pasta aisle.

There was a tiny café in the lobby of the dance studio, up on the third floor in a rickety elevator. If one of us had an extra ten dollars, I'd sit there with a coffee and read teen paranormal romance novels and write and wait for him to get out of class. He'd come back exuberant from class, still sweaty even though he'd changed clothes. He'd frown and kiss me and say something like, "Mira, you don't have to wait for me like this." And I'd smile and say, "Baby, it's worth it." I'd say, "Tell me everything," and he would, on such a creative high that I could almost inhale it. If it was winter, we'd ride the train back uptown. If it was summer, we'd sit in the park outside of the 1 train station, talking and laughing and kissing and secretly working our hands into each other's pants. We'd stay an hour, so Andre could be home by his midnight curfew. Marco and I never had a curfew. Even when my mom was at her best, she didn't give a fuck what time we got home.

I'd pretty much forgotten about Andre's contemporary dance classes, those evenings at Fairway and in the park. But seeing him move his body in the ways he learned in those classes, it makes me remember. He'd show me in his bedroom sometimes, saying things like, "It gives you more freedom than the way you're supposed to move in ballet." I was so in love with that starry-eyed dancer boy with grit in his soul.

I'm still so in love with him now. My heart churns with every emotion as I watch him dancing. It rises to my throat and pulses there when I see him create a gesture with his body that communicates something to me, and to the whole audience, touching us in a place beyond words. My heart drops like a stone into my belly when he performs a jump or a series of dizzying turns or lifts Lana high over his head while she arches her body like a bow, or lifts Jordan too (I've never seen a man lift another man in ballet like that, and I've gotta say, it is damn hot). I had forgotten that I am married to a man who can move his body like that. We talked about how he feels now, dancing again post-transplant. He said he takes it easier now than he used to when he was seventeen, he won't be dancing for five and six and seven hours straight until the middle of the night anymore, he's a bit more careful with jumps and lifts, but, he said, his body is perfectly capable of doing everything that he wishes for it to do. "I didn't like that level of intensity for myself anyway," he told me, his face open, my serious and earnest and sweet and trusting boy. "I want to dance again, but I also want to take it easier. The way my body is now matches that."

Their piece is called "Wave." And it is indeed a dance like a wave; its overall arc of movement is that of a wave. The dancers leap and land on the ground. They fall intentionally. They fall artfully, 'cause it's ballet and the fantasy of the world of the dance and an illusion, and a performance, but there are moments when a real-world honesty shines through, and they fall to the floor of the stage in inelegant heaps. They let themselves fall. They get up, with visible difficulty, brushing and pulling and scraping invisible clinging things from their limbs. I wonder what they are. They help each other up, bare forearms stretched like ropes, muscles over bones. I wonder which parts of the dance, which gestures and movements, he came up with, and which ones belong to his dance partners. I wonder what it all means. I don't know, and I like not knowing. I'm glad, and grateful, to lose myself in a wordless mystery of movement tonight.

Also, I gotta say—'cause if I didn't, I wouldn't be me, now would I, y'all—that I forgot how seriously fucking hot my man is in ballet attire. The costuming for their piece is simple. Andre and Jordan are in black dance tights and white shirts; Lana is in a short, clingy white dress, bare legs, pale pink pointe shoes. It's good that at a performance you're expected to just sit there and look at the dancers, because I cannot take my eyes off of this man. The white shirt clings to his chest, showing in relief every single muscle and ridge and line of his upper body. His thighs and calves outlined in the dance tights are fucking obscene.

And, yes, well, what's at the front of those tights is fucking beautiful too, smoothed into a perfect bulge, held protectively close to his body by his dance belt underneath. (Are you someone who, like me, has just a little bit of a dance belt fetish? 'Cause I have watched him slide into one of those belts, tucking his penis up towards his tight belly. And I have slipped my fingers under its waistband and pulled his dance belt off, past his hips and his firm ass and down his legs. And, if that is something you, too, fantasize about, then your girl Mira can tell you: it is as good as you have dreamed.) Sometimes as he dances and I look at him, sheer awareness of his body shimmers over me, and every organ in me flutters. In those moments he has me gently panting, just on the polite edge of feral. When we get each other home I want to rip him open. I want to sink my teeth into every muscle on that body. I want to rub the scent of my desire all over him. He belongs to the world; this is how it should be. He also belongs to me. I want to find a way, with my body, for the world to know that.

This ain't all I want, though, no. I can feel myself swelling, shameless with wanting. I want to make my art like this too. I want my art to make me incandescent, I want it to make me magnetic, irresistible. I want bodies swollen with wanting me, too, made hungry by the lure of my art. I want clarity. I long for a bright vision. And I trust that they will come.

But tonight, tonight is for mysteries. Tonight is for taking a deep breath—I can do that now, you know—down, down into the farthest aching recesses of me. Tonight is for closing my eyes, seeing in the dark the ghosts of them still dancing. Tonight is for opening myself—opening myself up to the dreaming.

Acknowledgements

Like my character Mira says, we do good things in community. I'm glad to have so many people to thank for helping me see this book into the world.

Thank you to my writing circle and community, particularly the Writing Magic crew, all my Patreon supporters past, present, and future. Thank you to the writer and artist friends who read early drafts of this or other stories or lent their ear as I worked through the difficult process and themes of Mira's story—especially Narriman (for saying that my use of punctuation is erotic), Jenny (for our beautiful lunch date in NYC), Rubeena (for being my believing mirror every day through the magic of text messages), and Payal (for our phone chats that filled me up with light). Thank you for being with me on the journey.

A big and hearty and extra special thank you to my creative BFF Magnolia Fay—thank you for seeing Mira and seeing me, and for being the first other person on earth to read her story all the way through, and love it.

Thank you to the many writing courses, critique groups, and other creative resources I accessed during the very long process of writing and editing not only this book but other ones in the series. Special shoutouts to the NYC Writers' Critique Group, the erotica writing courses at Sarah Lawrence College, Creative Alchemy, the Kith community and mentoring, and the editors at Cleis Press. One of my dearest writing teachers and mentors, the poet Pat Schneider, passed away in August 2020. Pat, who was from the Ozark Mountains in Missouri, taught writers to write in and honor their own voices and where they come from. I could never have written in Mira's unique voice if not for her guidance and her creative permission slip. Thank you, Pat. I miss you.

Thank you to everyone who read one of the earlier books in this series or any of my other work. If I've touched even one reader, then my work here is done. Special thanks to Jobeth for the beautiful video you sent after reading *Book of the Flower Garlands*. I will never forget it.

Thank you to Ant for reading one of my early drafts and helping shape my thinking around the idea of happily ever after for queer folx.

I can't say thank you enough to my writing mentor and editor Jan

Fortune. This book would not exist, or be out here in the world, without you. You're a rockstar.

I also cannot leave this book behind without thanking the many writers, activists, and creators who have educated and inspired me around the themes of decolonizing health and wellness and our collective relationship with the body. Just a very few of these incredible activists are Shane and Hannah Burcaw; the HAES movement; Jessamyn Stanley; Claire Wineland; Christopher Ulmer (and every guest he's ever hosted on his show); Lupita and Carmen Andrade. Big shoutout to the activism and work of Sonya Renee Taylor and adrienne maree brown—*The Body Is Not An Apology*, *Pleasure Activism*, and the Institute for Radical Permission. This is a call to all of us to learn from and support more activists, artists, and creators who do the work of advocacy for disability, illness, and other forms of bodily justice.

I've been working with this story universe since the year 2011(!); it would be impossible for me to even name all of the people who've left their mark on it and on me over the past nearly 15 years. So I leave you here with a giant ray of gratitude beamed out into the world.

And finally, thank you to my family and the 5i crew: Jamal, Iris, and Bob cat. Thank you for being with me as I birthed a book and birthed a baby. You're my favorite people. I love you.

About the author

Your girl Nikki Ali is a writer, teacher, dancer, and activist originally from Brooklyn, New York, and now based in Newark, New Jersey, where she lives humbly on the original homeland of the Mohican and Lenape peoples. As her author persona, Nikki writes queer erotic romance, fiction, and poetry where love and fulfillment are for every body and sensuality is an integrated part of our lives. She also publishes books on writing craft and a yearly anthology of heartfelt writing with her creative circle.

By day, Nikki teaches on the university level at a small school in Jersey City, New Jersey, where she learns from and laughs with her students every day. She is privileged to travel the world, both solo and with her students, as an ancient historian and archaeologist.

By night, as her alter ego Mistress M, she mentors and guides writers in finding their own curated writing rhythm and deepest sensual expression. Books and stories saved Nikki's life, and she loves helping more beautiful books make their way out into the world.

Nikki is a belly dancer, slow but avid runner, devotee of Sufi poetry, and lifelong practitioner of yoga. She delights in art, symbol, mysticism, divination, and the esoteric. She is committed to the global rise, healing, and joy of the world's oppressed peoples, and to inner and outer liberation for all. At the time of this writing, she has recently given birth to a baby girl, one of the greatest creative endeavors of her life.

Nikki loves to connect with her peeps. Get in touch with your girl at mistressm.podia.com.